THE
CONGREGATION

THE
CONGREGATION

Rabbi Morton Levine
with Hal Kantor

G. P. PUTNAM'S SONS / NEW YORK

G. P. Putnam's Sons
Publishers Since 1838
200 Madison Avenue
New York, NY 10016

The Congregation is a work of fiction. Any resemblance
between the characters depicted here and persons living
or dead is purely coincidental.

Library of Congress Cataloging in Publication Data

Levine, Morton.
The congregation.

I. Kantor, Hal.   II. Title.
PS3562.E899C6   1985   813'.54   85-577
ISBN 0-399-13022-5

Printed in the United States of America
1   2   3   4   5   6   7   8   9   10

For my Children—Renan, Dalia, Ariella, and Uri.
"Our task is to act, not only to enjoy; to change, not only to accept;
to augment, not only to discover." —Abraham Heschel
— Rabbi Morton Levine

For my dear wife:
Who shares my dreams
—Hal Kantor

PROLOGUE

His face an anguished mask, Rabbi David Lee Benjamin sank slowly to his knees before the open golden doors of the Ark to begin his "good morning conversation" with his God, a ritual he had performed every day since entering the seminary in Cincinnati, Ohio, fourteen years ago. The monologues, usually internal, were most often self-deprecatory, lamenting in an almost bantering tone his incapacities, frustrations, his failure to achieve his goals. They were never delivered on his knees before the Ark. But Rabbi Benjamin's morning ritual had never before included a confession to his God.

"O Lord, I have broken Your commandments," he began in a barely audible voice. "Almost every one of them."

"I have taken Your name in vain."

THOU SHALT NOT TAKE THE NAME OF THE LORD THY GOD IN VAIN.

"I have dishonored my father and my mother."

HONOR THY FATHER AND THY MOTHER.

"I have been a thief."

THOU SHALT NOT STEAL.

Overcome by his emotions, David had to pause. Before continuing, he stared as if hypnotized at the twin scrolls of the Torah within the Ark. "I have betrayed my wife, Naomi. My father-in-law, Senator Mendes. My friends. My congregation."

THOU SHALT NOT BEAR FALSE WITNESS.

He hesitated. "Yes, I have even contributed to a man's murder."
THOU SHALT NOT KILL.
Afraid to say the words aloud, David paused before saying softly,
"I have committed adultery . . ."
THOU SHALT NOT COMMIT ADULTERY.
As if to shut out the vision of his crimes, David closed his eyes
tightly. "O Lord, though I am unworthy, I ask Your forgiveness. I
beg Your forgiveness." When he opened his eyes, they were misted
by tears of shame.

Motionless on his knees, David bowed his head as if waiting for
judgment. Then, wearily, he struggled to his feet. He closed the
doors of the Ark and walked with sagging shoulders out of the
sanctuary.

The only light in the corridor leading to his office was the soft
illumination coming from the display cases recessed into the walls.
The glass-fronted cases held exhibits of priceless Hebraic manu-
scripts on permanent loan from the British Museum, pieces of gold
and silver jewelry and rare coins unearthed during a recent archae-
ological dig, artwork and photographs depicting the horrors of the
Holocaust, a minutely modeled replica of ancient Jerusalem and a
miniature of the hilltop fortress of Masada during the siege by the
Roman Xth Legion. David stopped before each case and, as if for
the last time, studied each display.

Farther down the corridor, an elderly, fragile-looking black man
wearing gray coveralls was on his knees scrubbing the alternate
squares of black and white marble flooring. He stood up as David
approached and, touching soap-filmed, gnarled fingers to his forehead, said, "Morning, Rabbi. You're here bright and early. Can't
be much past four."

Although he had spent the night in the temple, after his arrival
from New Haven, Connecticut, on the midnight plane, David made
no explanation. He simply said, "Good morning," and strode past
the janitor, who shrugged and returned to his task. Suddenly David
stopped abruptly and turned. The black man was on his knees again,
scrubbing the floor. As he watched, David thought, I don't even
know his name. We've said good morning every day for over two
years and I never took the time to find out his name.

Continuing down the hall, David passed empty meeting rooms,
classrooms, the music room and the library before he entered the
hexagon-shaped rotunda in the lobby. To his right, the engraving

etched in the heavy glass doors of the entrance to Temple Beth Sinai, depicting a terrified Abraham, knife poised high, ready to sacrifice his only son, Isaac, caught his weary eye. He looked to the left, probing the darkened theater as he stood silently for a long contemplative moment before the suite of administrative offices. Though he had no desire to return to his office, where he had passed a sleepless night of self-confrontation, his feet began to move almost involuntarily and he found himself standing in front of a desk in the reception area that bore the nameplate: *Florence Stern—Executive Secretary*. The desk blocked the path to two doors. The door of the assistant rabbi, Morris Simon, was unmarked. The nameplate on the other door read: *Rabbi David Lee Benjamin*.

He suddenly had to know the black man's name: by doing so he would be making some kind of atonement. Going to the bank of green file cabinets against the wall, he yanked futilely at the bottom drawer of the middle cabinet. Exasperated now, he went to Florence's desk and rummaged through the top drawer, upsetting the neatly arranged contents before he found the locked cash box that held the keys. He pried the box open with a letter opener and dumped everything in the middle of the orderly desk top. He didn't know why, but the scattered debris on Florence's desk gave him a perverse sense of satisfaction.

He fished out a key ring and opened the file cabinet, where he found the manila folder marked *Personnel*. He ran his finger down the neatly typed list of names and titles until he found what he was looking for. "Custodian: Isaiah Norman," he said triumphantly. After repeating the name, David replaced the folder and moved to enter his chambers.

As he stood with uncertainty in the doorway, David's eyes swept the familiar room. Carpeted in a subdued sandalwood brown and divided into office and study areas by islands of burnished walnut furniture, it was a large, almost luxurious space. The paneled wall behind the glass-topped L-shaped desk was lined with neatly tiered rows of memorabilia accumulated during his two and a half years as Beth Sinai's head rabbi.

There were many photographs of David with some of the prestigious people he had met and dealt with, ranging from Henry Kissinger, Anwar Sadat and Billy Graham to Paul Newman, Coretta Scott King, Lee Iacocca, Senators Jake Javits, Mark Hatfield and David's father-in-law, the senior senator from Michigan, Walter

Paul Mendes. Many of the personal inscriptions included the phrase by which he had become known throughout the country: *To David Benjamin, the Rabbi's Rabbi. The Rabbi for All Reasons.*

At the far end of the large room, plush, chocolate-colored velvet draperies covered a huge picture window that looked out on a carefully terraced lawn that resembled the lush landscaping of the surrounding homes in Farmington Hills, near Detroit. David crossed the room, opened the draperies and stared out at the rainswept, predawn light.

Rotating his palm against the damp, moisture-covered glass, he cleared a space and studied his out-of-focus reflection. Fatigue gave his square, handsome face a pinched tautness. He hadn't shaved, and because he was a fastidious man, he grimaced with disgust as he cupped the prominent chin in his palm and ran his fingers over the dark stubble of beard. He tried to relax by drawing in several deep breaths and leaning over and touching his toes. But the backs of his knees grabbed with quick pain and he immediately straightened and stretched with his hands pressed firmly against his back.

Though he had given up cigarettes several years ago, his throat felt smoke-raspy and his lips were dry. He ran his tongue around his determined mouth. His deep-set eyes, usually bright and animated, were lusterless, and as he tugged at his nose out of nervous habit, he wondered if he would ever stop feeling so tired.

Loosening his tie, he attempted to smooth his modishly styled thick dark-brown hair as he walked over to the narrow panel of photographs of the Board of Trustees that faced him from between two floor-to-ceiling bookcases. Studying each face, David automatically counted votes. Florence had taught him to do that. "Don't let yourself think of them as people," she had explained. "Think of them as votes for or against you." He had taken her advice and had become expert at predicting what the final tally would be on any issue the board considered.

Looking at the stern face of the board president, Harold Fedder, David thought, When they know the truth, the vote to fire me will be 15 to 0.

Unless I resign first.

When he had begun his career, he had been fully committed to doing good, to being an exemplary rabbi. Through the years, though the commitment had never faltered, bitter experience had taught David that he could not accomplish noble and altruistic goals without the power to carry them out. To gain that power, he had justified some dubious actions by convincing himself that what his father-in-law, Senator Mendes, had told him was true: "There are times when you're going to have to hurt a few people. Times when, to do good for the many, you'll have to do things you don't want to do. David, your problem as a rabbi is that you inhabit two worlds—God's and man's."

David had listened carefully to his mentor and had consulted him constantly during his first year and a half at Temple Beth Sinai as he gingerly walked the fine line between those two worlds. But somewhere along the way David had gone too far. Alone and in torment, he now realized that he had used his position, his role as a rabbi, to get what *he* wanted. He was as accountable for the crimes committed in his name as he was for the good he had achieved.

He picked the photograph of Naomi, his wife, off the desk and studied the elfin-thin, attractive face framed by the short, wavy black hair. He couldn't help doing what he always did when he studied Naomi's picture or thought about her; he evaluated the quality and character of their marriage. More bad than good. More sorrows and disappointments than joys and satisfactions.

He took out his wallet and looked at another snapshot. Not even the flat dimension of an amateurish black-and-white photograph could diminish the voluptuousness of the body, the rich fullness of the shoulder-length titian hair, the classic beauty of the Irish face with its sprinkling of freckles dancing across the bridge of the small, upturned nose and over the high cheekbones. Remembering the joyous excitement of discovery and then fulfillment, David smiled back at the laughing face. With her there had always been more good than bad to remember. More joys than sorrows.

He slowly looked from one photograph to the other as if seeking an answer to the question that plagued him. How and why had he failed? Both as a rabbi and as a man.

In distress, he thought, O God, where did it start to go wrong? Where did it begin to fall apart? Was it back in North Carolina, where it all started . . . ?

BOOK
ONE

CHAPTER

1

The tinny voice coming from the cheap transistor radio slung around the neck of the marching picketer was talking about the unusual severity of the winter. David, toasting his hands over the wind-whipped flames of the fire in the fifty-gallon oil drum, nodded in agreement at the union organizer, Murray Kempter. He couldn't remember a winter as depressing or as severe as this winter of 1970. Suddenly he shivered. Not only because of the icy cold rain slashing all about them on this hillside overlooking the small North Carolina mill town but because for the first time in his sheltered life David was consciously aware of the stench of violence.

It was all about him. In the rock-smashed windshields of parked delivery trucks. In the stone faces of the rifle-carrying men who guarded the perimeter of the chain link fence around the textile plant. In the goading, jeering taunts of the sign-bearing strikers. In the silence of the idled mill. In the belligerent stride of B. J. Tremaine, the mill owner, who, flanked by two armed guards, was approaching the locked gate.

With a jerk of his head, Tremaine motioned at David and Murray Kempter. They left the warmth of the fire and went to the gate. The deputy sheriff got out of his car and sat on a fender, a shotgun across his thighs.

"Mr. Tremaine, I think we can settle this peacefully," David said through the chain link fence. "Can't we get out of this rain and talk?" He looked longingly at a small metal shed on Tremaine's side of the fence.

Tremaine, a craggy boulder of a man with a deep chest and thick arms, shook his head. His expression was as cold as the biting wind. Pushing a dented hard hat to the back of his head, he said in a voice tinged with a southern drawl, "Rabbi, just 'cause you're a man of the cloth don't mean diddly-shit to me. You and your commie, union-organizing, rabble-rousing, troublemaking friend have shut down my mill. I got nothing to talk about until those motherfucking strikers go back to work."

"But if we can just talk—" David's voice sounded helpless.

Furious now, Tremaine interrupted. "Rabbi, why don't you stay in your pulpit where you belong? I'm a God-fearing man, and like the Good Book says, I've turned my other cheek. But nowhere does Jesus say I gotta bend over and let you kick me in the ass. Are you going to tell my people to go back to work or aren't you?"

"First we talk, Mr. Tremaine," Murray Kempter said. "Then they go back to work."

Tremaine, working a foul-smelling plug of chewing tobacco with his tongue, contemptuously spat it out of the side of his mouth before pointing to a switchback road twisting down the hillside. "Both of you get off my property. You're trespassing. If you don't leave there's gonna be trouble."

The conversation was over. Tremaine, an angry look of disgust on his face, turned his back and went into the shed. Murray Kempter shrugged and then nodded at a parked Plymouth compact. He and David trudged through the mud, the throng of strikers opening to let them pass and calling words of encouragement after them as they got into the car. Patches of snow could be seen through the pine trees as the small car slithered down the mud-slick S-curve of the hillside.

A rail-thin man with an unruly shock of curly black hair, Murray Kempter hunched over the steering wheel and concentrated on the dangerous, potholed road. The thick lenses of his horn-rimmed glasses gave him an owlish expression. Out of the corner of his eye he saw David, shivering in his soaked mackinaw, shaking his head in disappointment. Impulsively, Kempter reached across and, in a gesture of encouragement, squeezed David's arm. "Patience, Rabbi," he said. "That's the one quality you've got to have in the union-organizing business. You have to be patient."

The men and women who worked in the smaller independent mills in North Carolina, such as the Tremaine Textile Company, had always rejected the promise of protection through union representation. The recession of the late sixties had changed their attitude. The millhands, who prided themselves on their rugged individualism, had to either swallow their pride or starve. A delegation went to the union headquarters in Washington, D.C., and requested representation because they wanted to make sure that when bad times happened again, they would at least be able to feed their kids.

Murray Kempter had appeared in the North Carolina mill town six months before, in September. A minor union official, he had personally taken charge of the campaign to organize the privately owned textile plants throughout the state. The purpose of the first meeting, held in a church, was to sign up members and to explain the demands he was going to present to B. J. Tremaine, owner of the mill Kempter had targeted to be unionized first. Tremaine, making an unexpected appearance, had torn up the list of demands and had contemptuously thrown the fragments into Kempter's face.

"There ain't gonna be a union in my mill," he announced to the sullen-faced audience. "I don't want one and you people don't need one." Turning to Murray Kempter, he added, "So get your union-organizing ass outa here before these poor ignorant bastards start believing the crap you've been trying to sell them."

After Tremaine had stomped out of the meeting, Kempter had asked the textile workers what they wanted to do. Give up or organize. The decision was theirs to make. Their answer was unanimous.

Strike.

The Tremaine Textile Company was shut down.

Neither side had budged in the five months that the strike had been going on. The first acts of violence, born mainly of impatience and frustration, had occurred three weeks ago. In a gesture of intimidation, Tremaine had brought in a gang of club-wielding strikebreakers to protect a shift of scab workers. The strikers had met force with force, and the bloodletting, club-swinging melee had made national television news. A few days later four of the strikers were killed, ambushed in their pickup truck on an isolated back road. The workers' response to the murders of their friends and neighbors was to torch and vandalize mill property. Kempter, powerless, had been expecting the violence. Impotent because of Tremaine's refusal to even talk, he could only hope for a settlement before there were more killings.

As he struggled with the steering wheel to avoid a skid, the union man said to David, "I know you don't understand why Tremaine won't sit down and talk. What would you do if you were a rednecked mill owner who's always had his own way and two Jewboys from New York marched in and told you they were going to shut down your plant unless you agreed to the demands of a union which they were trying to force down your throat? Admit it, Rabbi, you'd dig in your heels and you'd fight, too. So we'll give Mr. B. J. Tremaine a week or so to cool off. Maybe he'll talk to us then and maybe he won't. But we're going to keep on trying for as long as . . . oh shit, will you look at that!"

They had come out of the last curve and were heading toward the macadam straightaway that would take them to the paved state highway when they saw the fallen tree across the two-lane road. Kempter braked, fighting the wheel as the small Plymouth skidded to a perilous stop on the edge of the muddy shoulder. They got out of the car and stood in the freezing rain. Hands on their hips, they studied the barricade.

They never saw the six men coming out of the woods behind them, Winchester rifles held chest high.

A rifle butt slammed into the back of David's head and drove him to his knees. He tried to struggle to his feet, but a hobnailed boot between his shoulder blades shoved him facedown into the cold mud. His eyes filled with tears of rage, pain and fear.

"Stay put, Rabbi," a gravel-throated voice said. "Just do as you're told and nothing will happen to you."

Turning his head, David saw a red-faced fat man, the bulb of his nose swollen and veined, squatting on thick haunches beside him. The stub of an unlit cigar punctuated the heavy, protruding lips. The man cocked the rifle and placed the barrel against David's forehead. David whimpered with embarrassment as he began to urinate uncontrollably.

The fat redneck grinned and called over his shoulder. "Hey, the rabbi just peed in his pants!" Impotent rage flushed David's face. He wondered how he was going to explain his urine-soaked pants to his wife.

He could see Murray Kempter being held like a clothesline between the poles of two timber-thick men. A third man stood casually in front of them, waiting for the union organizer's ineffectual struggles to stop. David heard the man say in a slow drawl, "Mr. Tremaine, he don't take to being upset. Now he says, 'Teach the kike a lesson he won't forget.' "

Kempter's sudden scream was an explosion of pain when the rifle butt jackhammered into the bridge of his nose, shattering bone and smashing the thick lenses of his horn-rims, driving shards of glass into his eyes. Blood cascaded down his cheeks and stained his coat as he sagged limply between the two men holding him. With bored indifference they let him fall to the mud-clogged road.

"Don't move, Rabbi. Don't be a Jew hero," the crouching fat man warned David. He moved the rifle and David felt as if the small cold circle of steel were drilling into his forehead.

Through tears of pain and shame, David watched four of the men heft the fallen tree from the road. Everything seemed out of focus and unrelated to him. He hadn't noticed the dented, paint-faded blue pickup truck before. He now saw the men lounging around the truck, passing a chipped porcelain jug, and heard the sounds of their raucous, satisfied laughter. The fat man spat out his dead cigar and said, "Rabbi, it's all over. Tell your friend that there's no need in having a talk because Mr. Tremaine says there ain't nothing to talk about now."

David waited helplessly until the truck disappeared down the road before running to the still figure lying facedown in the frigid mud. Turning Kempter over, he gagged at the gore-covered face and fought the nausea heaving in his throat. He dragged the union man to the Plymouth, oblivious of the blood and slime covering his pants and jacket. After pushing and pulling his friend into the rear seat, David got behind the wheel. He cursed when in his haste to get away he flooded the engine. It wasn't until he felt the macadam under the wheels that he pressed down on the gas pedal.

The mud-streaked car swayed and fishtailed as it raced down the road to the state highway. David slowed when he saw the county sheriff's car parked across the intersection. A deputy, nonchalantly wiping his sunglasses, looked up and raised his hand. David skidded to a stop.

The deputy listened patiently to David's excited, almost incoherent relating of what had happened. With a bored shrug, he drawled, "Rabbi, I hate to disappoint you and I'm not calling you a liar, but no pickup ever came past me. I'd swear to that on a stack of Bibles."

His expression dared David to dispute the lie. When David didn't respond, the deputy smiled and after looking at Murray Kempter sprawled on the rear seat, said, "Your friend could use some help." Walking back to the police cruiser, he said over his shoulder, "I'll call for an ambulance. They'll take your friend to the clinic that Yid doctor runs on the other side of town."

After the ambulance had left, its rotating red lights and the rising and falling scream of its siren biting chunks out of his nerve endings, David made a wide U-turn to get back on the two-lane road. The deputy stepped in front of the car and spread his arms wide. He ordered David out of the Plymouth.

"I didn't say you could leave. Where are you going?" He made no effort to mask his belligerence.

"Back to the mill. Tremaine isn't going to get away with what he did to Murray Kempter."

The deputy shook his head. "Rabbi, you're not going back to that mill. I got orders to arrest you if you don't stay off Mr. Tremaine's property."

"On what charges?" David asked pugnaciously.

Ticking them off his fingers one by one, the deputy casually recited a litany of violations. "Inciting to riot. Trespassing. Threatening bodily harm. Unlawful assembly. Conspiracy." He smiled and added, "But if you promise to behave yourself from now on, Mr. Tremaine says he won't press charges. So why don't you be a good boy and go on home?"

David shook his head. "There's one charge you forgot. Resisting arrest." He turned and walked back toward the Plymouth.

The defiant act and words were impulsive, born of David's pent-up frustrations and feelings of impotency; of his fury over the cowardly ambush; of his self-disgust as he realized that he had no other alternative but to confront what passed for law and order in the Carolina hill country.

As he opened the car door, the deputy's gloved hand on his shoulder spun him around. The officer gripped a short, thick billy in his other hand. There was a look of hopeful anticipation on his face.

"You'd love to use that on me, wouldn't you?"

The deputy grinned and patted the weighted club in his palm, then shrugged and said, "You don't want to go to jail, do you, Rabbi? What'll that prove?"

David, his eyes hard with contempt, held out his arms with his wrists close together.

"No, I don't want to go to jail. But because you're going to stop me from going back to that mill, I don't have any choice."

"Sure you do. Rabbi, you can forget the whole thing. Tell yourself it never happened and go on home and behave yourself."

David shook his head. "That's no choice."

The deputy shrugged and pulled out his handcuffs.

David sat on the edge of the iron cot with his face cupped in his hands, calmer than he thought he would be, and stared at the cracked cement floor. He had been in jail once before, arrested in Biloxi, Mississippi, during a civil rights march. He had spent almost twenty-four hours in a stinking, overcrowded cell before ACLU attorneys had secured his release. His most vivid memory of the episode was that it had happened on his wedding anniversary and that Naomi had never forgiven him. Though he was pretty sure she wouldn't forgive him this time either, that didn't matter to him. He needed her understanding more than her forgiveness, and he was certain that she would never permit herself to comprehend his motive for the act.

She would blame his being in jail on Murray Kempter. One evening, shortly after his arrival in town, the union organizer had come to their house, and he and David had talked until six in the morning. The two men had liked each other instantly, developing a warm kinship through the commonality of their beliefs and their mutual enthusiasm for a cause. Kempter had asked him for help, and David, in spite of Naomi's objections, had agreed to use the prestige of his position to lend legitimacy to the drive to organize the textile workers.

"Somebody's got to care about these people, Rabbi," Kempter had said. "Somebody's got to care and try to do something for them."

The words were almost identical to those David had heard during an argument between his father, Morris, and his grandfather, Solomon Benjamin. Although David had been too young to comprehend the basis of the dispute (he was only eight years old), the sincerity and passion written on his grandfather's lined face and evident in his voice counterpointing his father's sarcasm and condescension had convinced David which man was to be believed. Besides, he knew his grandfather never lied. And he wasn't too sure about his father.

Solomon Benjamin, a lion of a man with a mane of white hair

and the physique of a longshoreman, had been involved in radical causes all his life. Retired, he lived with his only remaining son and his daughter-in-law, Thelma, and his two grandchildren, David and Martha. Stubborn, opinionated, self-centered, Solomon Benjamin was the patriarch of the family. Though his parents "raised" David, it was his grandfather who "taught" him.

The only real love in the old man's life was his grandson. Though an agnostic, Solomon was secretly pleased when thirteen-year-old David told him of his ambition to become a rabbi. It had happened on the day of his Bar Mitzvah, when David had been overwhelmed by his feelings of "Jewishness."

They argued constantly about David's decision, but the stormy debates were designed to cement his grandson's ambition, not to tear it apart.

"Question! Question!" he had roared at the intimidated boy. "Don't just accept! Question!"

Solomon Benjamin died shortly after seeing his favorite ordained. He was the only member of the family to attend the ceremony. David's older sister, Martha, was away at school. His father never even considered the idea of making the trip to the seminary in Ohio. To Morris Benjamin, business came first—and business was always terrible. His mother, Thelma, didn't argue with her husband's decision. If she privately disagreed with him, no one ever knew. And though she sent David a congratulatory card, she never once saw her son perform as a rabbi. It was as if she were intimidated by the grandeur of his role.

It was his grandfather's liberalism and social ideals that David carried into adulthood. As a student, he threw himself into every cause: civil rights marches, poverty protests, campus movements, voter registration drives, the plight of migrant farm workers, the Vietnam antiwar demonstrations. He believed that once he was ordained, his rabbinical cloak would add dimensions of authority and authenticity to his position as a dissenter.

Now, sitting in a damp jail cell, trying to ignore the hacking cough of a drunk nearby, he began to question the strength and validity of his social consciousness. He decided that he had failed. It wasn't that he doubted the causes that he supported, but he now had to admit to himself that he seemed to garner as much satisfaction from the prestige of his role as from his belief in the justice and ethical necessity of fighting for the causes. It was his first taste of power, and to his surprise, even though sitting in jail, he realized he liked it.

22

He heard a door open at the end of the corridor and the turnkey appeared with Dr. Milton Rosen, a tiny, thin-faced man wearing pince-nez. Rosen, who operated a three-man medical clinic, was the president of the Board of Trustees of the small Jewish congregation that David served. He seemed annoyed as he waited for the jailer to unlock the cell.

Stepping out into the corridor, David asked, "What about the charges against me?"

"They've been dropped. Dr. Rosen has taken care of everything."

"But what about—"

Rosen took David's elbow and moved him toward the door. "Rabbi, just don't ask any questions. You heard him. The charges have been dropped and you're free to go. Now let's get out of here."

It wasn't until they were out of the small cement-block building and under the night sky that Rosen released his grip. "Come, I'll drive you home," he said as he walked toward an old, wooden-sided station wagon. They got in. "Your wife's been worried sick about you," Rosen said as they drove away.

"What about Murray Kempter? Is he going to be all right?"

"Mr. Kempter has lost an eye," Rosen answered evenly. "But we saved the sight in his other one."

"Damn!" David sobbed, smacking his fist against the dashboard. He remembered Kempter's mentioning a wife and children in New York and wondered what he could say to Murray when he called him. His thoughts were interrupted when Rosen, reaching the edge of the single-street town, abruptly pulled the car to the side of the road and jammed on the brakes.

"We've got to talk," the doctor said. "Do you realize what you've done?" His voice rose. "Imagine—our own rabbi being thrown in jail! I should have fired you on the spot. But I can't. If I do, it will look like Jews don't support their rabbi when he's in trouble." Fingers shaking with anger, Rosen lit a cigarette before continuing. He glared at David, shook his head and said, "I blame myself as much as you. I knew this would happen when I hired you six years ago."

"So why did you hire me? I didn't hide what I was or what I believed in when you interviewed me. I told you then that I believed the role of a rabbi went beyond the needs of his congregation."

"You want the truth?"

"Of course."

"Let me give it to you straight, Rabbi. I hired you six years ago

23

because I didn't have any other choice. You were the only rabbi who wanted the job. I don't have to tell you that the pay is too low, the living conditions and the facilities are disgraceful. But none of those things seemed to matter to you. So I hired you."

"Are you saying that I'm not a good rabbi?"

The doctor's silent shrug was David's answer.

"Why? Because I'm involved with Murray Kempter? What's that got to do with my being a good rabbi?"

"Because even if what you're doing with Kempter is right, it's wrong because it threatens your congregation. Rabbi, even if you have to deny your social conscience, your congregation's interests must come first. Always."

"By telling me to deny what I believe in, you're asking me to cut off my balls. If I do what you want, I'd only be half a man. Half a rabbi."

Rosen smoked silently for a moment before saying, "Rabbi, you're a fighter. You're tough. Everyone admires those qualities in you. But we don't want our rabbi to be a fighter. To be tough."

"What do you want your rabbi to be, Doctor?"

"All we want of him is to stand up on that bema and lead our services. To Bar Mitzvah our kids. To marry our sons and daughters. To visit us when we're sick and to bury us when we die. That's all we want our rabbi to do for us. That's all we expect of him."

"That's not enough for me."

"I know that, Rabbi. But you can't see the forest for the trees. You fight the wrong battles in the wrong places and at the wrong times. I understand your dilemma. I want you to understand ours. I'm asking you to stay out of this union business."

"I can't stay out of it. I'm in it up to my eyeballs."

"Then, Rabbi, let me give you the bottom line. Your contract with this congregation is up for renewal in three months. Fighter or not, since you can't be the rabbi we want, we're not going to renew it. Period."

CHAPTER

2

Struggling to control his frustration and his anger, David got out of the car and began to walk. In spite of the cold, he took the longest route home by climbing the low hill behind the village and following a recently discovered, twisting deer trail. Pushing through thick brush, he was breathless when he reached the small clearing that overlooked the house that had been supplied rent-free by the congregation. He could see the light in the kitchen of the paint-peeled, weather-beaten, crackerbox-style cottage. Not even the bright moonlight could soften its ugliness.

On seeing it for the first time, Naomi had said, "I bet you haven't got a pithy or profound saying to cover this situation. Something that might make me feel better about what we're getting into."

She was referring to David's hobby of collecting the epigrams, folk sayings, proverbs and philosophical quotations that he used to dramatize or emphasize a point or to explain a situation. The collection, taken mainly from the Bible, the Torah and the Talmud, had been started as a hobby when David was a teenager, but through the years it had developed into a scholarly project. His office file cabinets were crammed with neatly printed notebooks and index cards filled with the efforts of years of study and research.

"How about, *In his own home, every man is a king?*" David jested as Naomi recoiled after inspecting the rust streak, caused by a leaking faucet, in the cracked porcelain sink.

Naomi had fought a continuous battle with the house. Though

she occasionally won a small skirmish by planting flowers or wallpapering a bedroom, after six years she had accepted the fact that she had lost the war. The house would always be tawdry and without charm. Tonight, as David looked down at the house from the clearing, he came to the same conclusion for the first time.

Because he wasn't ready to face either the house or his wife, David sat down on a fallen log and pondered why he had failed as the rabbi of his first congregation. Trying to determine what had gone wrong, he permitted a kaleidoscope of thoughts to cluster in his mind. He had come to the small rural North Carolina congregation bursting with enthusiasm and a sense of purpose and direction. He had truly believed he would lead his new congregants along a path of spiritual enlightenment and to a rededication of their Jewishness. After over six years of frustration, he had to accept the reality that it was never going to happen.

He wasn't surprised by Dr. Rosen's warning. This was not the first time Rosen had cautioned David that his obligation was solely to the congregation and that he was to avoid anything controversial. Previously, the resulting disillusionment and frustration had caused David to send out applications to congregations where he felt the emotional and intellectual environment would be more fertile. The responses were identical: he was too young and too inexperienced to head them. After several rejections, he stopped sending out résumés and began to feel he was merely treading water, waiting for something to happen.

"Maybe, because this was my first congregation, my expectations were too great," he mused aloud. "I came down here with my head in the clouds, thinking this was the opportunity of a lifetime for a young rabbi. But if nothing else, I've learned that a rabbi can't be effective unless he has some power and influence. And you can't get it by burying people and marrying them. By Bar Mitzvahing their children. By visiting the sick. So how do I get power and influence in a congregation that doesn't want a rabbi to stand up and fight for them?"

He began to realize that to be effective he had to function within the system, not on its radical fringes. But he regarded those constrictions as a denial of his individuality and as a dishonest compromise. Shivering and miserable, he wished with all his heart that his grandfather were still alive. Solomon Benjamin always had answers for him. But there were none now, no instant solutions to his dilemma.

Wearily, David rose and made his way to the brightly lighted house.

Coming into the shabby little kitchen, he found Naomi at her work counter, making strudel. He came up behind her, put his arms around her narrow waist and kissed her perfunctorily on the cheek. She stopped kneading the flake-thin dough and stood rigidly in his embrace. Finally breaking away, she went to the stove, saying, "I've already eaten. I'll reheat your dinner."

He sat down at the wobbly table and waited quietly until she served him. It wasn't until she had returned to the counter and was kneading the dough again that David realized she hadn't looked at his face. He watched her back for a moment and then said, "I'd like to explain about what happened today. I mean about my being in jail. I couldn't let them—" He fell silent when he realized that she wasn't listening to him. That she wasn't interested in what he had to say.

Absentmindedly, he began to eat, shoveling the food into his mouth. Frowning, he occasionally glanced at his wife and wondered how to interrupt her concentration. Naomi's face was a mask of intensity as she carefully lifted a sheet of pastry and laid it out on a damp towel. Then she brushed it with melted butter and sprinkled it with bread crumbs. She held her breath as she delicately placed a second sheet of the see-through-thin pastry over cinnamon-flavored apples. The aroma tickled his nose. Suddenly understanding, he relaxed and smiled.

When Naomi made strudel, nothing could interrupt her concentration. It was as if she were resolving an inner conflict or working out a problem. Some people go for walks to lock out the world, others take a long, lonely drive. Naomi made strudel. She had chosen this method because the challenge—to end up with a buttery-crisp confection rather than tasteless tissue paper and stewed apples—forced her to concentrate.

After carefully covering the baking dish with greaseproof paper, she inched the glass dish into the oven. Drying her hands on her apron, she turned and finally looked at David.

She guessed what he was thinking about from his expression. "I'm sorry about what happened to Murray Kempter. I'll never understand why people do the things they do to each other."

David looked at her and nodded. There wasn't anything he could say. His cheek muscles quivered and he kept eating in silence.

Naomi watched him mound his fork with mashed potatoes. She too realized there was nothing more she wanted to say on the subject. I want him to feel better, she thought. If I want him to listen to me, I have to change his mood. I have to make him forget what happened today.

She waited with forced patience until David had finished and stood up. Then she embraced him and kissed him lightly on the cheek. Guiding him into the gloomy living room, which was overcrowded with furniture bought at tag sales, she playfully pushed him into his favorite overstuffed chair and propped his feet on a vinyl-covered hassock. Handing him a newspaper, she said, "You relax while I do the dishes. You don't have to dry tonight. When I'm finished we'll talk."

She returned to the kitchen and began stacking dishes in the battered sink. She had never hated the sink as much as she did at that moment. Or the house. Or North Carolina.

Donning a pair of orange rubber gloves, she began to do the dishes, but quickly stopped because the task suddenly became too repulsive. She heard David rustling the newspaper pages and silently wondered, Do I still love him? She answered herself vehemently. As if to convince herself. "Of course I do!" Surprised by her own outburst, she hoped David hadn't overheard. She cocked her head and listened for a response from the living room and was relieved when there wasn't any.

If I didn't love him, I wouldn't be here, she thought. But I have to face the truth; things aren't right between us anymore, haven't been right for so long. He's not the same man I married—but I'm not the same woman either. If only I . . . oh, what's the use! Naomi sighed bitterly. It's all my fault that our marriage is falling apart.

Naomi knew she had turned away from David during the six years they had been in North Carolina. But she had been angry at him. He was wrapped up in his causes and his congregation and had left her behind. Her perception of what their marriage should be was so far removed from its reality that she thought of the two of them as intimate strangers.

She blamed David for taking her to a miserable, alien town where she had been unable to make any friends. She was a city girl from Detroit, the daughter of a prominent, liberal United States senator. She was accustomed to a different life, a different world, a different Judaism. She belonged neither with David's congregation nor with the conservative, straitlaced Protestants who dominated the tiny town.

Over the past years, she had sunk deeper and deeper into her self-imposed exile. She became withdrawn and distant and was usually so tired that even the simplest of tasks exhausted her. The pallor and gauntness of the face that looked back at her from the mirror frightened her. A single goal constantly occupied her thoughts: to save herself and her marriage, they had to get out of North Carolina. But because they had lost the ability to communicate meaningfully, she never discussed that need with David.

After she finished the dishes, Naomi walked back to the living room. She prayed David would listen to her and would understand. But if he didn't, there was no question in her mind about what she had to do. One way or the other, she was going to get out of North Carolina.

Even if she had to leave by herself.

CHAPTER

3

Naomi sat down on the hassock in front of David's chair and took both of his hands in hers. Afraid of his reaction to what she had to say and unsure of where to begin, she drew a deep breath and plunged right in. "It's important that we talk realistically. There's nothing more that you can do here—you must see that—and I can't take this place any longer."

Surprised by her unexpected candor and vehemence, David squeezed Naomi's hand in agreement and then looked into her face. She sensed he had something to tell her. He said, "I don't imagine we're going to be staying here much longer. My contract is up in three months and it's not going to be renewed."

Thinking, He can't refuse me now, Naomi forced herself not to show her elation. She took a yellowing newspaper clipping out of her apron pocket and handed it to David. He glanced at it, and his suspicions deepened. Sensing that she was hiding something from him, he read the clipping as if seeking a clue to her behavior.

The news story was from Naomi's hometown newspaper, the *Detroit Free Press,* and was dated nine months previously. She had shown it to him when the paper first arrived, but he hadn't reacted with any interest. Instinct had caused Naomi to save the clipping.

The small headline read: TEMPLE BETH SINAI RABBI DIES.

David read the first two paragraphs: "Rabbi Aaron Fedder, head rabbi of Temple Beth Sinai in Farmington Hills, suffered a heart attack while conducting the Yom Kippur Services yesterday morning. The 78-year-old rabbi never recovered consciousness and died late today in Mount Sinai Hospital. Trustee President Sam Bender said of the tragedy, 'Our grief is great because of the shocking loss of our beloved rabbi, but we must be concerned with the spiritual needs of our congregation. Therefore, though with heavy hearts, we will immediately begin the process of selecting a suitable replacement.' "

David looked up and asked, "Why are you showing this to me again?"

"They still haven't found a suitable replacement."

David looked at her suspiciously. "How do you know so much about what's going on at Beth Sinai?"

"I called my father and asked him. He's still a member of that congregation." She stopped his shocked interruption by placing her fingers over his mouth. "David, before you say anything, please listen to me. My father thinks he might be able to help you get that appointment. He knows he can get you an interview with the Selection Committee and that's the first step. But before he does anything, he wants to talk to you. He's waiting for your call, and I promised him you'd make it."

Angrily, David swung out of the chair and began to pace the small living room. Naomi watched him from the hassock; her expression was hopeful but uncertain. He stopped, pointed an accusing finger down at her and said, "How many times have I told you that I don't want any favors from your father!"

"But, David, after what you just told me about your contract not being renewed, I don't see where we have any other choice. Forget your pride. My father wants to help you. I'm not telling you to change your beliefs or your ethics. Or the kind of rabbi you are. All I'm asking you to do is to pick up the goddamned phone and call my father. Is that too much to ask?"

David put his hands on her shoulders and stared into her face. Her expression was both defiant and pleading. Ambivalent feelings pulled at him. But his paramount thought was, Any rabbi would give his eyeteeth for that pulpit with that congregation. And she's right—I don't have any choice.

Her eyes boring into his, Naomi waited tensely for David's answer. For some reason they didn't understand, the chasm between them narrowed slightly. "All right, I'll call your father," he said. "I don't think it will do any good, but I'll call him."

The tension went out of Naomi and she sagged against David.

He held her tightly, and at that moment they rediscovered an intimacy that had disappeared years ago. Impulsively, he kissed her deeply and she responded. Then, flustered by her reaction, she pushed away from him and said, "Call him right now, David. He's waiting."

Naomi adored her father. She couldn't remember a time when she didn't feel that way. He was her rock, and she had grown up wondering if she'd ever meet a man like him . . . hoping that she would.

She had mixed feelings about her mother. Adele Mendes was a plain, fragile woman who seemed unable to cope with even the simplest of life's demands. Her solution was either to retreat into herself or to flee in panic to her therapist. Naomi's memory of her early childhood was that her mother was never there.

Adele Mendes lived with the knowledge that her daughter's love was directed toward her father and that her own marriage was loveless. That Walter Mendes, except for the requirements of his public image, didn't need or want a wife. He had a mistress that consumed him: politics.

Because she didn't understand the relationship between her parents, Naomi had once asked her father why he had married her mother. He refused to discuss it, and she had interpreted his silence as meaning ". . . I made a mistake and I don't want to talk about it." Naomi's love for him deepened because she felt he was "enduring a tragedy." Her mother's responses to the same question were too vague and too incoherent to be an answer. Naomi, in youthful fantasy, believed that there was a deep dark secret (a secret lover somewhere?) between her parents that was too scandalous to talk about.

She was right. Adele Mendes did have a secret lover. Her therapist. He was dependable, reliable and he was always there for her. She disappeared with him when Naomi was sixteen. Finding the strength to end the loveless marriage was the most courageous act of Adele's life. Leaving also meant giving up her daughter, but Adele felt she had no choice and prayed Naomi would understand. Naomi never did. She never saw her mother again and felt no remorse when two years later, the telephone call came from the American legation in Majorca telling her that her mother and her lover had died in an automobile accident.

After her mother's death, Naomi became Walter Mendes's surrogate wife. She managed his needs at their home in Detroit when the Senate wasn't in session and in the townhouse in Georgetown when they were in Washington. His lifework became her obsession. She campaigned for him during his bid for reelection with an arrogant intensity that bordered on belligerence. After one landslide victory, a political pundit wrote that people were afraid not to vote for Walter Mendes because if his daughter ever found out, they'd have to answer to her for committing what she considered to be a cardinal sin.

Naomi was formidable as a young girl and overpowering as a young woman. Exotically attractive, she always had men in her life. But she rejected them as possible husbands because, when compared to her father, they were either too weak or without purpose and direction.

She finally chose a husband when she was twenty-five, and to everyone's surprise, it was David Benjamin. She married David because he appeared to be a younger version of her father. He had the same intensity, the same inner drive, the same commitment and the same hunger to achieve. That he was going to be a rabbi enhanced his desirability. It was not inconceivable to Naomi that someday David Benjamin would become one of the most influential and prestigious rabbis in America.

Senator Mendes not only liked and admired David but jokingly gave his blessing to their union by saying it would take someone with the patience of a rabbi to deal with the idiosyncrasies of "my headstrong, even pigheaded daughter." Because of her father's enthusiastic approval, Naomi was positive she had made the right choice.

They had married twelve years ago, when David was in his last year at the seminary in Cincinnati. Because she envisioned their marriage as an equal partnership, with her helping him in every way she could to achieve his goal, she went to work uncomplainingly to help support him and felt that was her contribution to their partnership. That was how she had seen herself vis-à-vis her father.

After his ordination in 1958, David had accepted the position of rabbinical adviser of the Hillel Foundation at CCNY in New York City, and Naomi had continued to work. Six years later David accepted the offer of the pulpit in North Carolina. Naomi was stunned and angered because he had made the decision without discussing it with her. Though she didn't realize it at the time, his act caused the first tiny crack in her perception of their marriage.

She complained to her father who, to her surprise, didn't seem to understand either her feeling of being left out or her anger. "When you marry a man like David Benjamin, you have to expect that there are times he will make decisions and choices without discussing them with his wife. David Benjamin is a strong, gutsy man and strong, gutsy men sometimes do things, if they think it's the right move, that their wives might not approve of. I ought to know, I've done it myself."

"But, Dad, why couldn't he have talked it over with me?"

"No 'buts,' young lady. You love him, don't you? You want to help him, don't you? You go down to North Carolina and do the best you can. David's a good man and he's going to need your help. You give it to him."

She had gone to the strange and alien environment of North Carolina and had tried. She had tried to be a good *rebbetzin,* but her heart wasn't in it. She didn't understand the basic attitudes of the people in their new congregation, didn't sympathize with their way of life and didn't get along too well with many of them.

On the other hand, because it was his first pulpit, David's congregation became his world, and he threw himself into every social cause that affected both the gentile and Jewish communities. He spent his days and nights fulfilling his commitments, and he and Naomi spent less and less time together. As he became increasingly involved, her sense of isolation grew, and she believed that because David didn't share that part of his life with her, he no longer needed her. She felt rejected and useless, and she began to withdraw. Her personality began to change. Once outgoing, aggressively enthusiastic and goal-oriented, she grew inhibited and without purpose. David's preoccupation with his own growing sense of failure limited his concern about what was happening to Naomi. He saw only that they had both changed and seemed to be heading down different paths.

The change in Naomi was accelerated and reinforced by the discovery that they couldn't have children. They had been trying to conceive for months without success when Naomi consulted a doctor. Then David did. And so began a year of seemingly endless tests and a schedule of lovemaking dictated by Naomi's thermometer and the calendar. For the first time, sex became an obligation and a challenge, not the warm pleasure it had been. Tense and distracted, Naomi became more and more desperate, consulting one specialist after another. During their third year in North Carolina she was diagnosed by an eminent specialist at Johns Hopkins as having blocked fallopian tubes. Microsurgery failed, and she was told she would probably never be able to have children. The realization that they were going to be childless devastated her.

What was a marriage, a family, without children? Before their marriage they had often talked about having children. "I love kids," David had responded to her question. "I want to have a kid in every bedroom and I want a house with at least five bedrooms." She had happily shared his dream and was as convinced as he that they would turn it into a reality. But she felt she had failed him, and she couldn't forgive herself. Or David.

The night after her operation, during visiting hours, while telling him of "her failure," Naomi tearfully apologized and told him he could, should, find himself another wife. That she was useless, no good. He had been stunned by the depth of her despair.

When he had suggested adoption, she had again surprised him. Pushing him away, her tear-stained face twisted in pain, she had screamed, "No, never! I wanted our children, yours and mine! I could never love a stranger's child. Never!"

She told him to leave the hospital room then, and they never discussed the issue again.

David kept his word to Naomi. He called the senator and had spoken to him for almost an hour over the phone. ". . . I'll get you an interview with the Selection Committee," Mendes had said to him, "but I can't put any pressure on Ben Adelson or the others because I owe them as many favors as they owe me. I'm not making any promises, but I might be able to come up with some leverage we can use to influence them. I'll have to think about it. . . ."

After David hung up with the senator, he went back to the kitchen and told Naomi the gist of the conversation. She was convinced the appointment would be his. He made no attempt to subdue her enthusiasm because he didn't want to suffocate her reborn excitement and optimism. He listened to her plans of how they would live in Farmington Hills and how she would work with old Detroit acquaintances in clubs and on committees and have Jewish friends again, and he allowed himself to be tugged along by her enthusiasm.

"I'll be going home, David! You can't imagine what that means to me. I'll be back where I belong. Seeing old friends and living like a normal human being again. Wearing decent clothes and going to parties and to the theater and eating out in good restaurants. I know it sounds ridiculous to you, but, my God, how much I've missed living like that!"

She talked of dinner parties with his older sister, Martha, and her husband, Brian McGraw, who had settled in Detroit, and of how close the two families would become. That appealed to David because he and his sister rarely saw each other after her marriage ten years ago to a gentile. It had been over three years since Naomi and David had seen David's nieces, Kathleen and Margaret, who by now were eight and six.

Naomi led him back into the living room and curled seductively in his lap in the deep chair. Talk of their new future had freed their sexual inhibitions and, as in the past, they kissed and touched and aroused each other. They hadn't made love in almost three months, and Naomi, suddenly embarrassed, scurried from David's lap. Her face was flushed as she hurried down the hall leading to their bedroom, saying over her shoulder, "I'm going to shower." Then she paused for a moment and, looking provocatively at David, giggled and said, "*You* I'll see in a little while."

David, in bed waiting for Naomi, stared up at the ceiling, his hands laced behind his neck. His sense of inertia was gone. Something was finally happening. He no longer felt trapped by a provincial, backwoods congregation. Whatever self-doubts he might have had about the future faded when Naomi returned from the bathroom. She purred and moved against him. He reached for her, and she came eagerly into his embrace.

The eagerness with which she came into his arms and let him strip her nightgown from her shoulders made them both feel that tonight would be different. Tonight was going to be like it used to be.

But it wasn't. Naomi wanted to respond and to feel. But all she could do was lie stiff and inept as he ran his fingertips across her breasts, her nipples, her thighs. Suddenly she clutched at him, dragging his face down to hers and desperately crushing her lips against his. Nothing happened. Not even when he entered her. She was aware of his penetration and the thrusting deep within her, but her only feeling was relief that it would be over quickly . . .

David sensed her distress, and as he climaxed, he felt as if he had been masturbating instead of making love.

They lay side by side in stony silence. They were afraid to communicate. To express what they were feeling at that moment. As if they knew the fragility of their marriage couldn't endure the effect of the words they wanted to say.

Naomi groped for a way to justify her frigidity, her thoughts racing haphazardly. She had wanted to give to him but couldn't. She had wanted to feel but couldn't. Accepting that she had no answers, she silently vowed, When we get to Detroit, I'll have to find out what I can do to overcome the nausea I feel every time he touches me.

CHAPTER

4

Ben Adelson, chairman of the Rabbinical Selection Committee, warmly greeted David, Naomi and Senator Mendes on the flagstone veranda of the Fair Hills Country Club, where the interview was to take place. Adelson, in his mid-fifties, a balding, heavyset man with a developing paunch and a double chin, had been both a friend and a political supporter of Senator Mendes for over twenty years.

Tall and solidly built, his silver-streaked hair fashionably styled, Walter Paul Mendes looked exactly what he was—a professional politician with a charisma that had made him a celebrity. His cultured, resonant, baritone voice added to the image. He was a handsome man whose brown eyes flashed with animation and alert awareness. His physique, though not athletic, was trim and solid, the result of working out at 5 A.M. every morning. There was a confidence and a sureness in his bearing, and it was rare when Walter Mendes didn't give the impression of being in control of himself and the situation.

The senator had learned the art of politics by studying the lives and careers of three experts: Franklin Roosevelt, Sam Rayburn and Lyndon Johnson. He learned never to ask a question unless he knew the answer and never to start a fight unless he was sure he could win. If he had to, he was not above a dirty, no-holds-barred, back-alley scrap, and had become so expert in compromising, in power politics and in twisting a reluctant arm or two when necessary that the losers never showed visible scars. Veteran reporters who had been covering the national political scene since the early days of television were the only ones who could recall the few times Walter Mendes ever lost a fight.

And he had no intention of losing to Ben Adelson. He hadn't come to Detroit to witness David's rejection but to help him get the appointment. However, he wouldn't show his hand until the timing was perfect. Impatiently he looked at his watch and waited for Adelson to start the interview.

As they waited, David thought of Murray Kempter. He couldn't forget his feelings of anger and guilt when, visiting in the hospital, he had looked at the bandages over the broken nose and the black patch covering Kempter's right eye. The union organizer, aware of David's discomfort, had laughed and said, "It might help if you try to think of me as a pirate. That's what my kids do. A Jewish pirate. They call me Captain 'Hook' Kempter, the kosher buccaneer."

He had admired Kempter's casualness and wished he felt more comfortable. "Murray, I feel like a traitor. Like I'm running out on you."

"Running out on me? David, you've helped me from the day I arrived in town. You've done everything you could for me. Besides, this mess is almost over. Tremaine's attorney came to see me to negotiate a settlement. We're going to get pretty much everything we've worked for, and we couldn't have done it without your help. So you go to Detroit and take your best shot at trying to be a hot-shot rabbi."

Ben Adelson began the interview and interrupted David's thoughts. "Rabbi Benjamin, I've studied your application, and your pedigree if fine. But I'm sorry to say that you don't have the experience or the maturity to lead a congregation the size of Beth Sinai's."

"The fifth-largest Reform congregation in the country," David said matter-of-factly. He had done his homework and could recite, if necessary, the size of the temple's budget, the amount of donations to the United Jewish Appeal, the yearly number of Bar Mitzvahs, brisses, weddings and funerals, and could give a financial and social profile of the congregation members.

Adelson looked at David with surprised respect. "That's right," he agreed. "Temple Beth Sinai is the fifth-largest Reform congregation, in terms of member families and money, in this country. That's why I'm hoping you'll understand why I have to turn you down, Rabbi Benjamin."

"I can understand your feelings, Mr. Adelson," David said. "What

I don't understand is what I'm doing here. You knew you were going to reject my application when you read it. So why did you agree to interview me?"

"Because your father-in-law can be very persuasive," Adelson said with a smile. He looked at the senator, who shrugged. "After talking with you, Walter, I guess I was hoping that your son-in-law had more experience or that I could find some valid reason to consider him."

It's obvious that I'm not going to get the job anyway, so what do I have to lose? David thought. Straightening in his chair, he said, "Mr. Adelson, I may be too young for your congregation, too inexperienced, but I am a rabbi and a good one. I'd like you to listen to why I believe I am the right rabbi for your congregation. Will you give me that courtesy?"

Thinking, I owe Walter at least that much, Adelson shrugged and with a casual wave of his hand indicated he would listen. David began to speak in a voice so low that the Selection Committee chairman had to lean forward to hear the words. He soon became entranced by the blossoming passion in David's voice as well as by what was being said.

"Mr. Adelson, I'm not *just* a rabbi. I'm also a human being. And though I may be a man of God, the transmitter of the Jewish tradition, because I am a human being I must be concerned with *more* than spiritual problems. Therefore, even though I know you will object, I *will* use my pulpit, wherever it will be, to speak out on issues that not only affect my congregation but also affect the world."

Naomi's nervous shifting in her chair caused David to look at her. He knew what she was thinking: David, don't screw it up! Tell him exactly what he wants to hear. Don't give him more ammunition for why he shouldn't hire you. But, at that moment, expressing his beliefs about the role of a rabbi, David didn't care what Naomi was thinking.

"What I'm saying, Mr. Adelson, is that I'm a man who is deeply concerned about the human condition. That's why I became a rabbi.

"I know what you're thinking," David continued. " 'How can a rabbi do that and still serve his congregation?' No, not by counting the number of weddings and funerals and Bar Mitzvahs I perform. But only by forcing you to face and examine the problems and conflicts that confront all of us just because we are Jews. Not ignoring or hiding from them behind the belief that we are the chosen people.

"For we are not just *Jews*, Mr. Adelson. We are *American Jews,* and as we become more and more assimilated into this society we face the loss of our Jewish identity. And *that* also is my concern as a rabbi. But we can keep that identity and still be a part of the American scene by building bridges between the Jewish and the non-Jewish communities; for only by walking across such bridges can we ever hope to create better understanding and eventually achieve total acceptance.

"I, as a rabbi, will be that bridge.

"I, as a rabbi, will force my congregation to face the questions that Jews *must* face and answer. Questions like intermarriage and the necessary reform of some of our ancient beliefs and traditions. The question is how can we do that without losing our identity and therefore our heritage?"

David paused for a sip of water and saw Adelson's thoughtful expression. He said softly, "Yes, Mr. Adelson, it is difficult being a Jew in these times. But hasn't it always been difficult? Only through confronting these issues can we ever hope to make it easier to be a Jew. To be a *good* Jew."

David leaned toward Adelson, his voice burning with passion. "It was Rabbi Israel, the Chafetz Chaim, who said it best: *It is no challenge to die like a Jew; the true challenge is to live like a Jew.*

Adelson stared intently at David, his face flushed by his sudden awareness. He had interviewed many rabbis. Sagacious scholars, flamboyant charismatic leaders, rabbis with national reputations and rabbis with great dignity and presence. He had interviewed rabbis who talked knowingly about fund-raising and administrative techniques. But he had never felt the passion of conviction and purpose as he had in Rabbi David Benjamin.

Adelson waited a moment to regain his composure. Then, making no attempt to mask his admiration of David, he said to Senator Mendes, "Walter, I owe you an apology. Now I understand why you insisted that I give your son-in-law a hearing. I can't remember when a rabbi has touched me as deeply as this young man." Sighing with disappointment, he then added, "But I'm sorry, I still can't—"

Mendes finally spoke, holding up his hand to interrupt Adelson. "Ben, I know what you're going to say. That you can't hire him." He paused for a moment and then asked dramatically, "But did I ever *ask* you to hire David Benjamin? Think about it, Ben. How many times have we talked about this meeting? Three? Maybe four times? During those conversations did I ever once suggest to you to hire David as the *head* rabbi of this congregation?"

"Well, you didn't come right out and say so, but—"

"No 'buts,' Ben. I never did. I only asked you to meet with him. Now that you have, I'm sure you'll agree that he's pretty hot stuff. And not just because he's my son-in-law. C'mon, admit it, Ben, he'd make a damn good rabbi for Temple Beth Sinai, wouldn't he?"

Nodding slowly, Adelson said, "Yes, he would. I'm not denying that. If he can touch me the way he did, I can imagine how the congregation would react to him. It's too bad he isn't ten years older. But there's no way I can hire him, Walter. You know that."

"Ben, suppose I showed you a way that would solve all your problems? That wouldn't make you look like a damn fool for hiring someone as young and as inexperienced as David?"

"You show me a way and I'll think seriously about it, Walter."

"Fair enough. Here's my proposal. *Don't* hire David as our head rabbi—" He answered Adelson's surprised expression by continuing. "*Hire* him as our *interim* rabbi. And if there are objections, you can say that we've been without a spiritual leader for too long. That you're taking David on for a year for the good of the congregation. That during that year you'll continue looking for another qualified rabbi."

There was a long pause before Adelson said thoughtfully, "Not a bad idea, Walter." An admiring smile played at the corner of his mouth. "Clever, Walter. Damn clever." He thought of the reaction and the concern of other members of the committee at being so long without a rabbi. "It just might work. Of course I'd want to clear it with the rest of the Selection Committee and present it for a vote to the Board of Trustees. But if the committee agrees, the board will approve it."

He turned to David and asked, "You'd be willing to come in for a year as our interim rabbi?"

Naomi held her breath until David slowly nodded.

Senator Mendes stood up and, smiling broadly, held out his hand. "Then we've got a deal, Ben?"

"No. Not yet. Don't go pushing me too far too fast, Walter. I'll let you know in a few days."

Two hours later, in a small meeting room in the temple, Adelson met with the other members of the Selection Committee, Stan Danziger and Sam Bender. Bender was also the president of the Board of Trustees. Also present were Meyer Loeb, the patriarch of the congregation, and the newest trustee member, Harold Fedder. Loeb, in his late sixties, had been deeply involved in temple affairs all his life and was regarded as an elder statesman whose advice and opinions were often sought by the Board of Trustees. Harold Fedder, the thirty-seven-year-old grandson of Rabbi Aaron Fedder, had been appointed to the board as a sympathetic gesture after his grandfather's death.

Adelson, after going over David's background and reviewing the interview, concluded by saying, ". . . I agree with Senator Mendes. His son-in-law *is* an excellent rabbi. I'm suggesting, in spite of his youth and inexperience, that we offer David Benjamin a year's contract as our interim rabbi. That will take the pressure off us while we continue our search for a suitable head rabbi."

"Ben, if you vouch for him then I think that's the way to go," Sam Bender agreed. "This congregation has been without a spiritual leader for almost a year. Several families have joined new temples because of that. We need someone up there in that pulpit."

"Even though some people are going to object, I think it's a good decision," Stan Danziger raised his voice in approval. "If we're all agreed, I say let's go before the board tomorrow night and get their okay."

"I don't agree," Harold Fedder interrupted. "After hearing about Benjamin's background and experience, I don't feel he's qualified to even be our interim rabbi," he said vehemently.

Harold Fedder's objection didn't surprise any of the other men. No rabbi could have gained his acceptance and support, for that rabbi would replace Fedder's grandfather, who had been the spiritual leader of Temple Beth Sinai for over nineteen years. Aaron Fedder, an aloof, bearded, autocratic spiritual leader in his late seventies when he died, had raised Harold after his parents' accidental death when the boy was only ten. A conservative, traditional rabbi who demanded and received respect, albeit tinged with fear, Aaron Fedder was idolized and revered by his grandson, and his influence on Harold's attitudes and beliefs about the role of a rabbi and his relationship to his congregation persisted even after his death. As a board member, Fedder became the devil's advocate to every suggested change, every proposed program. Surprisingly, more often than not he was right in his opposition.

In the months following Rabbi Fedder's death, eighteen would-be replacements had been interviewed. Fedder had rejected every candidate, and it was the board's opinion that his reason was because in his eyes his grandfather was irreplaceable.

"Be reasonable, Harold," Adelson said. "We're only hiring David Benjamin as our interim rabbi. How can you object to that?"

"Because you wouldn't be hiring him if he wasn't the son-in-law of Walter Mendes," Fedder said arrogantly. "Nepotism has its place, but not inside a temple."

Meyer Loeb finally spoke, his deep authoritative voice silencing the argument. "Maybe this young David Benjamin is wrong for us. But we'll never know until we see and hear him. And more important than you, Harold, or me, or even David Benjamin, this congregation has been without a rabbi for too long."

The following night, the Board of Trustees voted 14 to 1 to hire David Benjamin as Temple Beth Sinai's interim rabbi.

CHAPTER
5

As the Board of Trustees was meeting, David and Senator Mendes were nursing brandies in the den of the Senator's house. Naomi, after making dinner and cleaning up, had gone to bed, leaving the two men in animated conversation. The shared experience of the interview with Ben Adelson had brought them closer than they had ever been before. A new dimension had been added to their relationship. They were no longer father-in-law and son-in-law, but were becoming teacher and student. Mentor and disciple. Senator Mendes had once been in the same situation as David, when he had been the disciple and his father-in-law the mentor.

Mendes was in high school when the Japanese bombed Pearl Harbor in December 1941, and he had enlisted in the army the following day. As an infantryman in the First Division, he had fought in North Africa, Sicily, Italy, Normandy and Germany, and when he was discharged four years later, he was a well-decorated war hero of sorts.

He attended law school at Northwestern University, and after his graduation, he married Adele Frankel. He went to work in his father-in-law's law firm, not because he wanted a law career, but because Irving Frankel was a power broker: a behind-the-scenes wheeler and dealer in both state and national politics who was as at home in the smoke-filled back rooms where the political decisions were made as he was in a courtroom. Walter knew what he wanted from his father-in-law and waited patiently for the right moment to ask for it.

That moment came a few years after Naomi was born, when Irving Frankel said to him, "Walter, as a son-in-law and as a man I like and respect you. You've been a good husband to my daughter and you've made me a grandfather. But let's face the truth. You're a lousy attorney and you're never going to be much better because you don't want a legal career. So tell me what you do want to do with your life and I'll try to help you achieve it."

Walter didn't hesitate for a moment in his response. "In a month, you and your friends are going to pick a candidate for Michigan's next United States senator. I want to be that candidate."

"But you've no experience in politics or in government. No background. You've got nothing going for you."

"I've got more going for me than anyone you are considering. I'm electable and they aren't."

The bluntness of his son-in-law's response surprised Frankel. But as he thought about it, he sensed that Walter was right. He was the highly decorated war hero with the voice and the looks of a man who could be trusted. Walter Mendes might not have the experience but he had the image. He could win an election. That was the only criterion that mattered to Frankel and his friends.

Walter won his first campaign and had been reelected ever since by ever-increasing pluralities. And though inexperienced and innocent when he first went to Washington, when he had to, he could draw on the knowledge and guidance of a professional. He learned well, and during his years in office he not only became a respected, powerful and eminent senator, he also became an astute and influential politician. The combination was unbeatable. Though Irving Frankel had died several years ago, Walter Mendes never forgot who had put him on the path to power.

Just as he was going to do for his son-in-law, David Benjamin.

"I'm willing to bet that if we play our cards right, Ben Adelson will beg you to stay on at Temple Beth Sinai as the head rabbi after your year is up," Mendes said with certainty.

"Senator, they haven't even offered me the job of interim rabbi. And frankly, I didn't do so well down in North Carolina," David said solemnly.

"If you had only concerned yourself with the spiritual affairs of your congregation, no one would have opposed you. To argue with a rabbi or a priest or a minister, when they stay in God's world, is to argue with God."

"But as I said to Ben Adelson, the spiritual needs of my congregation aren't my only concern," David objected. "I must become involved in the world outside my temple. That's why I tried to help Murray Kempter. And look what happened."

"David, try to understand. When you took on B. J. Tremaine, you moved into his world. And, in man's world the rules are different. Even though I know it sounds distasteful to a man of principle, you're going to have to compromise and manipulate and maneuver. And, yes, there will be times you're even going to hurt people. To sacrifice them, if you have to, to achieve."

"I don't think I can do that," David said with a vehement shake of his head. "That would go against everything I've ever believed."

"Of course it would. But that's one choice men like you and I have to make. To violate temporarily our sense of morality and code of ethics to accomplish something we believe is worthwhile. David, nobody ever said it was going to be easy. But with the power and the prestige also goes the responsibility of trying to do the most good for the most people. Of making that choice even if you have to hurt and sacrifice others to achieve that good. Having power doesn't mean a damn thing, David. It's what you do with that power that matters. And it takes courage to put your neck out on the line and sacrifice others so that you can achieve. Especially for a rabbi. But I wouldn't be talking to you like this if I thought you didn't have what it takes."

After digesting what Mendes had said, David thoughtfully responded. "I don't know if I have that kind of courage, Senator."

The phone rang. The senator talked for a few moments and then motioned to David. Handing him the phone, he said, "You'd better have that kind of courage. It's Ben Adelson. The Board of Trustees has approved your appointment."

David was visibly pleased as he talked to Ben Adelson. When he hung up, the senator poured him another brandy and said, "Now that you've got your foot in the door, we've got to work on making you look like a winner. That will give you even more clout. When I get back to Washington, I'll call in a few IOUs and get you appointed to a couple of appropriate national panels and commissions. If I can swing it, and I think I can, I'll get you on the President's new international committee on civil liberties and human rights. The more recognition you have, the greater your image. But once you're in the limelight, you'll be on your own. And the best way a rabbi stays in the spotlight is to get involved in fund-raising for Israel. That keeps his image public and gives him legitimate ties to the power structures of the community and the congregation."

"I plan to do that, Senator, but I'm not sure how to go about it."

"You've got an in, David. Your brother-in-law, Brian McGraw. I've heard talk about him, mostly good, some bad. Through that insurance company of his, he's got all kinds of the right contacts. And because of his reputation, the three-time All-American at the University of Michigan, he's always involved with fund-raising for some charity or benefit. He's an expert at it. Ask him to show you the ropes. I'm sure he'd go out of his way to help you."

"I had forgotten about Brian's connections. I'll give him a call first thing in the morning."

CHAPTER

6

"Congratulations, Rabbi!" Brian McGraw said enthusiastically to his brother-in-law over the phone. "What's the Jewish word? Oh yeah, *mazel tov*. Now, what can I do for you?"

Leaning back in his chair behind his desk, he listened to David's request for his help. The ex-football player, broad-chested and wide-shouldered, nervously ran his well-manicured fingers through thick curly brown hair as his interest increased. David told him of his inexperience and how he wanted to use his expertise in running fund-raising benefits and banquets, and McGraw began to doodle dollar signs on a pad.

"Of course, I'll help you, David," he responded quickly. "I'm honored that you should come to me. Fund-raising, benefits, charity affairs, they're up my alley. Why don't we get together for lunch as soon as you're organized and we'll talk?" After listening to David's vociferous thanks, he added, "David, I want to help you in every way I can. The first thing I'm going to do is to have a party to officially introduce you and Naomi to the movers and shakers in the gentile community. They're people you should know, David. How about six weeks from this Saturday night? That ought to give you time to move up here and get settled."

After hanging up, making some notes under the dollar signs on the pad, McGraw thoughtfully digested the conversation. Then, unlocking the bottom desk drawer, he took out a telephone and dialed a number.

"Hello, Frank? This is Brian. Something's come up that we should talk about. If it works out, some of the problems we discussed can be solved. Okay, the usual place, in an hour."

After replacing the phone, he locked his office and told his secretary Barbara to cancel his appointments for the rest of the day. As he went out of the bank, he wished David hadn't come to him for help. Leaving the parking lot, he realized how complete was the hold that Frank Terhanti had on him. He wondered if he would ever have the courage to get out from under the Mafia boss's control.

A three-time All-American running back at the University of Michigan twelve years previously, there were no limits to Brian McGraw's horizons in those halcyon days. A guaranteed pro contract waited for him after graduation, and he was anticipating the well-paid career of a superathlete with a megabuck contract. But the anticipation ended, along with his dreams, when his knee was shattered in the next-to-last game of the season. No megabuck contract. No career.

Because of his reputation, Brian was signed by a major television network to do background color commentary during the upcoming collegiate football season. He liked the job; the money was good and because he was still a celebrity, the public acknowledgment satisfied him. But the following season his option was dropped and he was out of work. Though he had been told that falling ratings was the reason, the truth was that he wasn't good enough.

Through the influence of friends, he was hired by WJR, a leading Detroit radio station, to work with Paul Carey and Ernie Harwell as a weekend sports analyst. A year later, they dropped his option for the same reason. A smaller Detroit station, trying to milk the last drop of publicity out of his name, took him on. He still wasn't good enough, and they fired him.

On the night he got so drunk that he was arrested, he had been out of work for almost two years. In jail, he faced the truth about himself. He had only one talent, the ability to run with a football. An athlete all his life, he had no other training, no other skills. Outside of his personality and good looks, he had nothing else to offer. His string of failures and his bleak future were proof of that. He had one other quality, but it was hardly salable: the way he loved his wife, Martha, and their two children. With total commitment. They were his life.

They had met at college. Martha, shy and introverted, had never heard of Brian McGraw, the three-time All-American halfback. She knew him only as a fellow student in one of her classes who had come to her for tutoring because he was in danger of being declared academically ineligible for football. She was the smartest student in his class.

No man had ever sought her out before. Gregarious, loving, warm Brian McGraw gave emotionally starved Martha Benjamin all of the positive expressions of feeling she had never experienced but knew existed. She fell in love with him.

At first, Brian was merely intrigued by Martha. He fell in love with her after realizing that her feelings for him had nothing to do with his celebrity status. She didn't even know he was a football star, a big man on campus. She loved him for himself. Even then, during those glory days, although she sensed his limitations and knew him to be weak and indecisive, because of the way he loved her, her belief in him was unshakable. She had no doubts he would reach his horizons.

He had proof of her feelings for him when, with no future, she had married him after the loss of his career. During his down days, when he had been rejected by everyone else, Martha had never doubted him and was always there for him. She struggled with him through his financial and emotional hard times, worked uncomplainingly and without bitterness as a waitress and a cashier to help support them.

Sitting in the drunk tank, ashamed and disgraced, Brian realized that all he had was Martha's love. When she bailed him out, he silently vowed he would do whatever he had to do to give her the life that he had promised her before they were married. He owed it to her because he knew that without Martha's strength and her love for him, he could never begin the long, hard climb back.

Done with living in past glories and finally motivated, McGraw seemed to have a change of luck. Because the story about his drunken escapade had made the papers, he got a call from a stranger, Johnny Lessio. Lessio's office on the second floor of the Bennet Building was lettered: T&L UNDERWRITERS. Lessio, a small man with a sharp, angular face, sat behind a too-large desk. He offered Brian a job as an insurance agent.

"McGraw, you're a natural for the job. You got the looks, the charm and the image. Though most of our business is with the National Bank of Detroit, we've got a lot of clients involved with sports in one way or another. They're either jocks or they own professional franchises or stadiums. With your reputation, you'll fit right in. I know the spot you're in now, but I'm willing to take a chance. If you work hard and keep your nose clean, you'll be making more money in the insurance business than you ever made as a jock or a sports announcer."

Lessio had been right. Brian worked hard and he kept his nose clean and he earned big money. Not enough at first to warrant buying the mansion he now owned in West Bloomfield, but more than he was capable of making as a mediocre sportscaster. Brian had found something he was good at besides running with a football.

He was also aware that his success had come too quickly and too easily. That Lessio kept throwing business his way that he wasn't entitled to. At first he couldn't help but uneasily wonder why. One day he asked for an explanation.

"What are you, a dumb jockstrap or a smart operator?" Lessio answered. "Didn't I tell what would happen if you worked hard and kept your nose clean? All you gotta worry about is that your commission checks don't bounce and how much of a bonus you're going to get this Christmas." Seeing the skepticism on Brian's face, Lessio added mysteriously, "You'll know when it's time to know."

Because his increasing success translated into the life-style he had vowed he would give to Martha, Brian forced himself to ignore the obvious: that T&L Underwriters was a front for some kind of nefarious activity that involved the savings and loan company on the sixteenth and seventeenth floors of the Bennet Building. Because of his innocence about marginal business dealings, he wasn't quite sure of the connection. Because of his success, it was too easy to look the other way. Because of his greed, he never made more than a half-hearted effort to find out.

Brian finally discovered what was going on the day he walked into his office and found Frank Terhanti casually seated behind his desk, finishing a cigar. He had seen the Mafia boss's picture often enough to know who he was.

"McGraw, you've been dying to know what's going on and now it's time to tell you. I won't go into all the details, but we wash dirty money here. My connections all over the country, in Vegas, Atlantic City, New Orleans, Miami, and in the Bahamas, send in their dirty cash to the insurance company and the bank and it comes out all fresh and clean."

"I suspected it was something like that," Brian said, a vague tinge of fear tightening in his chest. "But why did you hire me? You didn't need me. And why are you telling me now?"

"I hired you because you're the perfect front. An ex-jock with a big name. You worked out just the way I figured you would. And now that you've proven yourself, I'm ready to make you a real offer. With big money. Not the penny-ante stuff you've been making up to now. You interested?"

"What do I have to do?" Brian heard himself ask.

"Be our man in Detroit," Terhanti said matter-of-factly.

"Your man in Detroit! I can't be associated with you. If anyone ever found out I'd be ruined. I'd lose everything. Maybe even my wife and family."

"Jock, you've been seeing too many movies about the old Moustache Petes. Times have changed. It's not like in the old days. We have men all over who front for us. Legitimate men, just like you. We want it that way. On the surface, you run the show. We stay in the background, but we call the shots."

"But suppose someone finds out I'm connected?"

Terhanti shrugged. "I'm telling you it can't happen. Not the way we've got things covered. We have more people in three-piece suits with their computers and their MBAs and their law degrees working for us than we do muscle. We're covered by so many interlocking corporations and Swiss bank accounts and syndicates within syndicates and conglomerates within conglomerates that even I'm not sure of how it all works. The only way anybody can find out that you're connected is if you tell them."

"But if someone does?" Brian insisted.

"Jock, I'm not worried about it, and I got a hell of a lot more to lose than you do. You don't even have to think about it. If the FBI and the IRS can't figure it out, neither can your neighbors. But if it happens, we'll take care of it then. That'll be so far down the road that there's no sense in worrying about it now."

Brian, testing the waters, asked cautiously, "And all I have to do is front for you?"

"That's all. And to give you even more legitimacy, we'll move this office right down into the bank. Which, in case you didn't guess, we own. But if you say yes, remember, you're in for the rest of your life. I'll set you up and take care of you. I don't want you to come back five years from now and tell me you didn't know what you were getting into. If you say no, you can walk out of here right now and we'll both forget that you ever worked for T&L. I'll even give you a great letter of recommendation. So what do you say?"

He wanted to turn down Terhanti's offer but he couldn't. If he did, he'd lose everything. The mansion in West Bloomfield, the life-style and the image of success and wealth. Maybe even Martha and the kids. How could he humiliate Martha again by asking her to return to an uncertain life with dubious prospects for the future? Because he had accepted his weakness and his limitations, he knew he had no other choice but to accept Terhanti's offer.

He tried to save face by pretending that he needed time to make his decision. "I just front an insurance company?" he asked hesitantly.

"Yeah, that's all we want from you, jock. Nothing else. Just do your job like we tell you to. If you do, at the right time we'll move you into an office in the bank on the main floor. Nothing's changed except you're going to make a hell of a lot more money."

Brian's skeptical look brought a shrug and a hard laugh from Terhanti. "Okay, so maybe now and then you'll get a phone call and you'll be told to take care of something. Or someone. But it won't be anything you can't handle and there won't be any risks."

The interview was over. Terhanti rose and held out his hand. Brian, reluctantly, shook it.

A week later, the gilt lettering on the door of the T&L Underwriters' office said, BRIAN McGRAW, PRESIDENT. Below his name, in small, neat printing, were listed several companies. Within the year, he moved into a luxurious suite of offices in the bank. There wasn't a person in Detroit who didn't think of Brian McGraw as the ex-All-American football player who had been down on his luck and had turned his life around.

Three or four times a year, the private telephone locked in his bottom desk drawer rang. He followed the instructions without question and without apprehension. There was always a large bonus delivered in a brown envelope the following day. He never felt personally involved.

That was six years ago. Each year he became more and more enmeshed but always managed to justify his position by telling himself he was making more and more money and didn't have to deny Martha or the kids in any way. That was true. His largesse toward his family often embarrassed Martha. He also justified what he was doing by believing his newfound stature and prestige had restored his confidence and his reputation. That wasn't true. He just didn't want to give them up.

But now he wanted out. Fear stopped him. He didn't have the nerve to face Frank Terhanti down. To do so might cause him to lose everything. He told himself that when he ever had enough money salted away in a numbered Swiss bank account, he would have the courage to walk away. He set a goal of a half a million dollars.

Two bodyguards carefully ran their hands over Brian's body before allowing him to approach the long black limousine with the dark windows. Satisfied, they nodded, and Frank Terhanti in the rear seat opened the door. The two men took their places in the front, and the car slowly moved out from under the copse of concealing trees into traffic. The Mafia boss didn't speak until a nod from the driver indicated they weren't being followed.

Terhanti, an older man who through the years had survived many gangland wars, ran his Detroit family with an iron fist. Though of slight build, his physical strength was legendary. He had "made his bones" in his youth by strangling his victim. Sitting next to him on the rear seat, Brian was, as always, intimidated by his presence.

Terhanti's high-pitched voice belied his power as he ordered, "Go ahead, jock. You've got fifteen minutes of my time."

Brian nervously talked about his brother-in-law David Benjamin's appointment as interim rabbi to the wealthy congregation of Temple Beth Sinai, and of his request for help in future fund-raising affairs. He was telling Terhanti about this new avenue to wash money because he was afraid not to. Once Brian got involved with David, Terhanti was sure to find out. Terhanti knew everything that was going on in Detroit. Especially when it came to money. If Brian didn't tell him about his connection with David, Terhanti would consider it a disloyal act. The Mafia boss had an immediate solution for people whose loyalty he doubted. He put them in the hospital, where they had time, while recuperating, to think about the error of their ways.

"It just might work," Terhanti said thoughtfully after Brian had finished. "Because the IRS has been snooping around the bank, we're stuck with a lot of dirty cash sitting in safe-deposit boxes that I'm afraid to launder. But the government people aren't going to ask questions about a front like a benefit or a charity affair for a wealthy Jewish temple like Beth Sinai. Will it work the same way as when I set you up with those Catholic charities and benefits?"

"That's right, Frank. Like I always do, I'll be handling all the details, the nuts and bolts of running the affairs for my brother-in-law and his temple. I'll lay out all the expenses, the caterers, the florists, the waiters, the entertainment, the unions. But they'll be paid in dirty money. When the temple reimburses me, it'll be with a clean check. So we move some dirty cash that way. But that won't compare to the amount that we move through the funds that are raised. Donations are always in checks, Frank, and I'll replace them with the dirty money that we've been stashing in the safe-deposit boxes in the bank. When I make the accounting, my brother-in-law will have a bankbook or a cashier's check showing the amount raised less the expenses. That's the way you set it up for me, Frank, and it's always worked before."

While Brian sat stiffly beside the Mafia boss, waiting for his reaction, he struggled with his conscience. Previously, though he knew he was being used, he had always been able to look the other way because he had never felt personally involved. Though he had to tell Terhanti of the coming fund-raising events and the opportunity to launder money, he couldn't escape the guilt he felt for involving David Benjamin.

"Frank," he began nervously, "I feel funny about using my brother-in-law to launder our money. After all, he's my wife's brother. A member of the family. How about if I just help him out a few times so he can get his feet wet, and we forget about washing our money?"

"No way!" Terhanti exploded. "This is too good to pass up. We ought to be able to launder a couple a million a year through your brother-in-law."

"But, Frank—"

"Hey, jock, listen to me. Listen good. Laundering money is part of my business. You work for me, but don't tell me how to run my business. Let me spell it out for you. Dealing with the Jews from that temple is more important to you than dealing with the Catholics in this town, because the senior senator from this state is Mendes, a Jew, the father-in-law of that rabbi and a member of that congregation. So you got a great connection there. Somewhere down the line I'm gonna use it."

"But I don't want to put my brother-in-law in any jeopardy," Brian said weakly.

"What kind of jeopardy? You do this right and your brother-in-law's got no problems. You screw it up, jock, and you both got problems. And if it happens, you're the one who got your brother-in-law involved, not me . . . "

CHAPTER

7

David, uncomfortable and self-conscious in a rented tuxedo, turned the station wagon into the oak-lined private road that led to the manor-sized home of his sister and brother-in-law, where he and Naomi were to be the guests of honor at the party that would introduce them to the movers and shakers of the gentile community. He wondered if that was the reason for his almost unbearable nervousness.

Naomi, her cheeks flushed with excitement, was dressed in a black cocktail dress, a dangling strand of pearls accentuating the cleavage showing above the low-cut neckline. It had been over a month since David's appointment, and he was aware that he and Naomi were already drifting back into the same unhappy relationship that had triggered her periods of depression in North Carolina. He had hoped that in Detroit and its environs, where they frequently socialized with members of his congregation, Naomi would feel less isolated and less alienated from her surroundings. He realized, however, that her only concern was projecting an image of the close, happily married couple. He sensed that her vicarious sharing in his rise in the world often enabled her to forget their inability to communicate on any level.

Through a break in the line of handsome oak trees, they suddenly saw the three-chimneyed Tudor mansion that sat solidly on a rise overlooking the rolling countryside. David, driving slowly, wondered if his mother and father, were they alive, would have finally accepted his sister's marriage to the obviously successful Brian McGraw. Over ten years ago, when Martha had announced in her senior year at college that she was going to marry McGraw after graduation, her parents had tried to dissuade her because of McGraw's position. "You want to marry a football player! It's bad enough that he's a goy, but a football player!"

In front of the house, a uniformed attendant opened the car door for Naomi, and David's thoughts, while watching him then maneuver the station wagon into a parking area filled with Lincolns and Cadillacs, went back to the vitriolic family arguments. He wondered again if there was anything he could have said or done that would have made, if not peace, at least a truce in the family. He remembered the stormy evening that was the last time Martha ever set foot in their parents' home. Desperate, close to hysteria, and wanting an ally, she had turned to David for support. He was in his last year as a rabbinical student, and his dual role as Martha's brother and as a cleric had tugged him in opposite directions. As her brother, he had wanted only her happiness and so sided with her against their parents. But as a rabbi, he couldn't condone her breach of faith.

Martha's defense of her break with tradition and with her parents' wishes was but a single simple statement: "I'm going to marry Brian McGraw because I love him very much." David, recently married, had no rebuttal because he understood. He did the only thing he felt he could do. In the end, he reluctantly gave Martha his blessings.

He was brought back to the present as the hand-carved oak doors opened and his sister and brother-in-law, in evening clothes, waved to them, their arms around each other's waists. David couldn't remember a time when he hadn't seen them touching. Martha turned at something Brian said to her and laughed. The look on their faces was of adoration for each other. They were always together and, as David walked across the black-topped parking area with Naomi, he wondered what it would be like to feel for someone the way his sister and brother-in-law felt for each other.

Martha ran to David and hugged him tightly. Brian kissed Naomi's cheek before shaking David's hand. Arms around each other's waists, Martha and David went into the house. A gracious and attentive Brian followed with Naomi. In his lovely, luxurious home, away from the bank and his role in Frank Terhanti's crime family, Brian projected the image of the successful, prosperous man who is comfortable within himself and fits in his environment. The forty-foot sunken living room was filled with guests, whose attitude toward Brian was of warmth, admiration and acceptance.

Uniformed maids were unobtrusively passing trays of iced champagne and canapés. Brian stopped one and passed out four champagne glasses. He called for attention, and the guests turned and raised their glasses as he toasted David.

"To our guests of honor, my brother-in-law, David Benjamin, the new rabbi of Temple Beth Sinai, and his lovely wife, Naomi." Turning to face David, Brian added, "Welcome to our city. Welcome to our homes. Welcome to our hearts."

The guests applauded warmly as David awkwardly and self-consciously acknowledged the toast.

After asking Martha to take care of Naomi, Brian led David down into the living room and began making introductions. This was the purpose of the party. The opportunity for the new rabbi of Beth Sinai to meet Detroit's gentile power structure.

David recognized many of the men and a few of the women, as he and Brian toured the room. He had seen their photographs in influential business and news magazines and on television. As Brian made the introductions, David began to feel as if he were on display. After a while, the names and faces began to blur and his interest began to wane until Brian steered him to a strikingly lovely young woman.

"Now here's one automobile executive you've got to watch out for, David," Brian warned jokingly. "Not only can she be very persuasive, but from the stories I've heard, don't ever get into a poker game with her. Sheila Harrington, Rabbi David Benjamin."

They shook hands, and, from the firmness of her grip, David became aware of her self-assurance. "You two get to know each other," Brian said as someone called to him. "I'll be right back."

Sheila Harrington, whose titian hair, parted in the middle, fell smoothly to her shoulders, would have stood out in any room, In her early thirties, she wore an off-one-shoulder evening gown made of varying shades of green panels that contrasted with the green of her eyes. Tall and leggy, she reminded David of a roan colt.

"Do I call you David or Rabbi?" she asked smiling.

"I'd prefer David."

"Good. I've always pictured rabbis as having long beards and being old and looking very sagacious and very solemn. You hardly fit my image."

"And you don't fit my image of an automobile executive."

They suddenly realized they were still holding hands and stepped apart. An impish smile dimpled her cheeks as she quipped, "Maybe that's because you don't know the right ones."

"And maybe you never met the right rabbi," David responded a bit too quickly.

They began to talk, and David found it easy to converse with her. He began telling her about what he hoped to do in the temple in Farmington Hills and also in Detroit. Of his plan to reach out into the non-Jewish community and of his awareness of the difficulties he faced.

Sheila, caught up in his enthusiasm and sense of purpose, listened intently. "Maybe I can help you," she said thoughtfully. "Will you come as my guest to next Monday's luncheon meeting of the Detroit Economic Club? You can meet many of the city's most influential citizens there." After the words were out, she wondered why she had invited him.

"I'd love to come. Thank you," he answered promptly, wondering, in the same breath, why his acceptance had been so automatic. He had no idea what was on his calendar that day.

He was relieved to hear his brother-in-law, who had overheard Sheila's invitation as he rejoined them, say, "That's a great idea, Sheila. Economic Club members are the people David needs to know."

They said their polite glad-to-have-met-yous, and as he walked away from her, David forced himself not to ask Brian questions. But throughout the rest of the evening, he was troubled by his reaction to Sheila Harrington. He didn't deny that he had been attracted to her. So attracted that he found himself nervously looking around the crowd for her and wondering what kind of an excuse he could make to talk to her again. Though he chided himself for what he felt was sophomoric behavior, he was secretly pleased that he was capable of such a response. For the rest of the evening he forced himself to be more attentive to Naomi.

As he was returning through the crowded living room with a glass of champagne for Naomi, Sheila Harrington stopped him. She had a wrap around her shoulders and was preparing to leave.

"I was serious about next Monday." His perplexed expression brought a tingling laugh from deep in her throat. "The Detroit Economic Club? Don't you remember?" Then, in a voice that sounded as if she were challenging him, she asked, "Have you forgotten about me so soon?"

"No-o-o," he said carefully. "I haven't forgotten about you."
Her face brightened. "Good. I'll see you on Monday."

Sheila, her elbows anchored into the tablecloth, sat at the table
directly in front of the dais. David, her guest, sat to her left. With
her chin resting on the bridges of her hand, she listened to her boss,
Anson Harley Phillips, the president of United Motors, address the
members of the Detroit Economic Club. There were several hundred
men, including Henry Ford II, Walker Cisler, chairman of the board
of Detroit Edison and president of the Economic Board, Max Fisher,
a prominent industrialist, and Edward N. Cole, vice-president of
General Motors, as well as a sprinkling of women, all there to pay
homage to Phillips. Sheila, looking around Cobo Hall, thought,
Damn it, Anson's hooked them again. I don't know how he does
it with that warmed-over speech of his, but he gets their attention
every time.

As Phillips droned on, occasionally interrupted by bursts of laughter and applause, Sheila grew bored. She took a memo pad and a
small gold pencil from her alligator bag and began to doodle. She
became aware of David looking over her shoulder. Glancing up at
him, she saw a slow, understanding grin spread across his face.

He had thought of Sheila Harrington often after meeting her.
When she had called him to confirm her invitation to the Economic
Club's Monday luncheon, he had wondered if he would have ac-
cepted so quickly if he hadn't felt so lonely.

His relationship with Naomi, though normal on the surface, continued to deteriorate. The distance between them was once again
increasing. More and more frequently, Naomi was falling into periods of deep depression, and David's ineffectual attempts to raise
her mood were usually met with stony silence and even further
withdrawal.

He finally gave up trying to breach her periods of sullen hostility,
but when alone in his study, reading his sermon for the Shabbat
service or digesting a report in preparation for a meeting, his thoughts
often wandered and he was acutely aware of the empty chasm in
his life. In the past he had sometimes fantasized about the woman
who might fill that void and what he would do if he ever met her.
But because the woman had always been faceless, the product of
his imagination, he knew he was merely playing an innocent and
harmless mental game, one that in some incomprehensible way safely
satisfied his needs.

But the reality of Sheila Harrington and his attraction to her were tangible. And because of who and what he was—a husband and a rabbi—the thoughts caused an inner turmoil and feelings of deep guilt that he had never had to contend with before. The alacrity with which he had responded to Sheila's telephone call confirming the luncheon caused him to question the path he was about to take. Seated beside her at the luncheon, deliberately limiting the conversation to surface responses and reactions, he could control his guilt by telling himself, I may be feeling like a teenager, but I've got to act like a rabbi. And because I am a rabbi, even if I wanted something to happen between us, nothing can or will . . .

It wasn't until the luncheon was almost over and Phillips was getting ready to address the audience that David had realized Sheila was reacting less and less to his being a rabbi and more and more to his masculinity. The awareness both pleased and frightened him, but he did not step back from the brink of their developing intimacy.

He had no way of knowing that most men were intimidated by Sheila Harrington and that the fact that he wasn't pleased her. She had immediately recognized his isolation and could relate to it because she, too, felt the same way. Studying him over coffee, she was surprised and pleased by the many similarities she sensed they shared. It was at that instant that she momentarily forgot about his being a rabbi.

Even his obvious boredom with Anson Phillips's speech from the dais pleased her. He leaned closer and stage-whispered, "You've heard all this before, haven't you?"

The man to Sheila's right, a board member of a utility company, shushed at them with annoyance.

Sheila, grinning conspiratorially, scribbled a note on the small pad and slid it to David: *I should know it by heart. I wrote it.*

David smothered a laugh and took the pad and pencil: *I'm very impressed. I bet you're very good at whatever it is you do.*

Sheila quickly scribbled her answer: *Mister, I'm damn good at what I do!*

She laughed when she saw him flush at the implication of the message as he wrote: *I believe you!*

While David waited for her next message, he studied Sheila's profile. Her bottom lip was thrust outward in concentration. He wondered what it would be like to kiss its moist lushness. The image caused a surge of guilt feelings and he thought, I've got to stop this. Right now. But I don't want to stop this. Not yet, anyway.

After reading her next memo, *That's not the usual reaction I get from men,* he looked at her quizzically.

He wrote: *And what is?*

There was a look of near defiance in Sheila's face when she handed him her answer: *Most men believe I have my job because I sleep with my boss.*

He was aware of the pressure of her fingers on his arms as she tried to read his response over his shoulder: *That's a normal reaction.*

She couldn't wait to write her reply and said, with loud indignation, "The hell it is!"

Her voice interrupted Anson Phillips. Scowling, he looked directly at her. She mouthed, "I'm sorry," and he waited a beat before readdressing his captive audience. Sheila sat quietly until she was certain he had regained their attention before quickly scribbling her response to David: *How dare you make such a chauvinistic statement to me!*

He answered: *It's not chauvinistic. It's a fact of life.*

She studied David carefully and thought, When you're introduced to a cleric, you tend to forget he's also a man. You put him in a neatly labeled compartment called "Man of God" so you don't have to deal with him. But not this man. There's no way I can ever put him in a compartment. Or do I believe that because I want to deal with him as a man and not as a rabbi . . . ?

She rubbed the edge of the gold pencil against her cheek and continued to scrutinize him. Their eyes met and challenged, and her provocative look prodded David's conscience. He found himself guiltily thinking of Naomi. Sheila wondered what had caused his sudden pained expression. She attributed it to her belligerence, and her demeanor softened.

David tried to push Naomi out of his thoughts. Sheila's presence made him realize that he was approaching a dangerous precipice and he wanted to back away. I'm flirting with a woman who's responding and I'm enjoying it, he told himself. But I've got to stop this. Even if I don't want to. But he couldn't do it.

I'm losing control, Sheila told herself. What started out as fun and games is getting out of hand. She was intrigued and angered by the realization. She was sure David was thinking about her relationship with Anson Phillips. If you're like most men, she told herself, you're hoping that if it happened with him, why can't it happen with you? But it didn't happen with Anson Phillips, and if you and I ever get more intimate than this, I just might tell you the real story. I don't know why, but it's important to me that you know. Yes, Anson and I came close, but close doesn't count, does it? Maybe with a rabbi close does count . . .

She and Anson Phillips had been working late, going over the presentation he was to make before a House Energy Subcommittee. When he had finished reading the document, he had put his hand on hers and said, "A great job, Sheila. One of the best presentations I've ever read." Moments passed and he didn't remove his hand.

Sheila didn't respond to the compliment because she had sensed his mood shift and knew what was going to happen. And she wished it wouldn't. Not from Anson Phillips.

Then he had edged closer and said, "Boardroom gossip has it that you got your promotion because you're sleeping with me."

"Anson, you're not going to proposition me, are you?"

"I could make things a lot easier for you at United Motors."

"Anson, that's beneath you. I've never asked or expected you to make things easier for me. All I've ever wanted from you is to be judged on my ability. I know there isn't an executive on the ninth floor who doesn't think my brains are between my legs. Who doesn't believe I've gotten where I have because I'm fucking you. But if I go to bed with you, Anson, that will only reinforce the problem, not solve it."

"A little fucking for fun never hurt anyone."

"I've done my share, Anson. But that's not what I'm talking about and you know it."

"What are you talking about? Something more permanent than a quick roll in the hay? What if I asked you to be my mistress?"

"Anson, I don't want to be your mistress. Or anyone else's."

"What do you want, Sheila?"

"Just that you believe I'm good at what I do. That right now my job is the most important priority in my life. And that you understand that I need your help to do it."

She had waited tensely while he pondered her vehement response. Finally, smiling, he stood up, took both her hands in his and said, "I do understand. And it's as important to me as it is to you that you succeed. So let's go back to work and forget this ever happened."

After that, he had treated her as if the incident had never happened. But while Sheila watched Phillips addressing the Economic Club members, very much aware of David Benjamin seated next to her, a new thought entered her consciousness. That maybe there were men who did regard her as more than a woman to go to bed with.

She wrote a single word on the memo pad and handed the note to David: *Truce?*

He nodded and smiled warmly.

She listened to the speech for a moment and then whispered, "He's almost finished." Impulsively, she rested her hand on David's arm while she waited for his response. She wasn't aware of what she had done. Just of the urge for physical contact with him. "Will you have time for a drink later?"

He looked down at the graceful, long fingers resting on his arm and wanted to cover her hand with his. The simple desire caused him to whisper back, "I'm sorry but no, I don't have time for a drink." His ability to resist made him feel righteous.

The speech ended in a burst of applause, and Sheila watched a throng gather around Phillips. She took a deep breath. "Why not, David? Rabbis drink, don't they? It's not against your religion. And I know you want to make a pass. I've been encouraging you to make one. I still am."

David felt his face turn crimson. "Of course rabbis drink." Their eyes locked in another challenge. "But not alone with an attractive woman who's as seductive as hell. My congregation wouldn't understand, much less approve."

"Rabbi, that's a cop-out and you know it." Her tone was playful.

"Maybe it is. But it's the safest thing I can think of to say at the moment. Besides, I don't have any other choice."

Sheila absentmindedly pushed the cascade of titian hair off her face, thinking about what he had said. He found her gesture highly erotic. "Is it important to you that your congregation approve of your actions?" she asked evenly.

"Of course it is. As important to you that I don't think you're successful because you might have slept with your boss. Which, by the way, I'm sure you haven't."

She couldn't hide the surprised expression that blossomed on her face. He grinned and then said, "I have to go now." He stood up and hesitated before adding in a low voice, "I have a confession to make. You were right."

"About what?"

He touched her shoulder briefly before turning toward the exit. "I did want to make a pass. But I didn't have the courage."

CHAPTER
8

"David, this is Senator Mendes. Can you make it to Washington next Wednesday? There's someone coming from Israel who wants to meet you."

"Who?"

"The next prime minister. Menachem Begin. He can spare some time for you between his meeting with Kissinger and his address to the Senate Foreign Relations Committee."

"Menachem Begin wants to meet me! Why me?"

"He's not coming just to meet you, David. You're not that important. Not yet. But he did mention hearing about you because of your fund-raising successes and I figured I could squeeze you into his schedule. David, it can't hurt knowing the next prime minister of Israel, so do whatever you can to get here."

David whistled quietly and then, after checking his schedule, said, "Wednesday's a bad day, Senator. I've got a heavy schedule. But I'll get Morris Simon to take my place at a couple of meetings. He won't like it, but he'll do it."

They talked for a few more moments before the senator hung up. Stretching wearily at his desk, David noticed the clock on his study wall. It was a little before ten. His day had started at seven-thirty in the morning as a member of the minyon at early morning prayers. That was over twelve hours ago, and a stack of newspapers, journals and two recently published theological books he had wanted to scan remained unopened on his desk.

He studied the filled-in squares of his datebook and muttered, "I don't live by the Bible, I live by the calendar." He relived the day by running his fingers down the long list of scheduled activities:

8–9 A.M.: MORNING PRAYER MEETING

9:30–10:30 A.M.: MEETING WITH SAC/DIRECTOR, TED WOHLING

The director of Detroit's Social Action Committee (SAC) had asked David to become a member of the commission. Thinking, How can I insist that my congregants become involved in social action if I don't, David had accepted the appointment.

11 A.M.–1 P.M.: SEMINAR/UNIVERSITY OF DETROIT

The seminar at the university was an annual three-day symposium titled "Current Thoughts." David was a member of a panel that answered random topical questions from the student audience. Previous rabbis of Temple Beth Sinai, afraid to face the penetrating and often emotionally charged interrogations, had always declined the invitation. David felt he had no choice but to accept.

1–2 P.M.: LUNCH/FATHER HANRAHAN, DR. SEARLES

He had reluctantly left the seminar. He would have preferred to continue the dialogue with the young students than to meet over lunch with the priest and the minister. During the hurried meal, the three clerics attempted to coordinate their positions on abortion and to determine how they might influence upcoming legislation. David felt comfortable stating his position because to him the subject was not a political but a moral issue. The time was spent in determining the fairest way each of the three could present their different positions.

2:30–4:30 P.M.: BOARD MEETING

After hurrying back to the temple, David had attended the two-hour Board of Trustees meeting, at which the operating nuts and bolts of Temple Beth Sinai had been discussed. Though he had no vote, David's opinion was often sought on various issues. David always opened the meeting with a Bible lesson supposedly apropos to the issues under discussion. It was a tactic by which he let the congregation's leadership know where he stood on an issue before they began their deliberations. A tactic that enabled him to be political without being obvious about it.

5–6 P.M.: STAFF MEETING

A weekly staff meeting was held with the group that dealt with the everyday operation of the temple. The group consisted of Board of Trustees President Sam Bender, Assistant Rabbi Morris Simon,

Cantor Jay Sachs, Executive Secretary Florence Stern and Educational Director Arnold Rosten. David, as acting head rabbi, was the titular head of the group.

During his first month at Temple Beth Sinai David had realized that he would have to battle with the assistant rabbi for a place in the hearts and minds of his congregation. The rivalry had come out in the open at the last meeting of the Executive Committee, when Simon had openly disagreed with several of David's positions. The relationship of a rabbi and his assistant is that of a working partnership, and disagreement should occur only in private. David, realizing he was being undermined, knew that sooner or later he would have to put Simon in his place. Or fire him.

6:30–7:30 P.M.: PERSONAL MEETINGS/CONGREGANTS

After dinner, consisting of a gobbled turkey sandwich and a cup of coffee, David had spent an hour establishing a Bible study session for senior citizens; he set up a program for a young Philippine woman who wanted to convert to Judaism; he met with individuals and couples who brought him a wide range of interpersonal problems. They came to him because they felt that as their rabbi, he would give them an impartial hearing. It was also a way to air their grievances. David was their "voice of authority." In a sense, he was their parent.

7:30–8:30 P.M.: PRE-BAR MITZVAH MEETINGS

David had held hurried meetings with five families regarding the coming Bar Mitzvah ceremonies of their thirteen-year-old sons. Making notes, he discussed the special requirements to be included in the ceremony that would make the ritual unique to each particular family and the role of each family member. He reassured them that this would be a day their young sons would long remember.

8:30–9:30 P.M.: JEWISH FEDERATION MEETING

At the meeting, David participated in discussing methods by which the organization could improve their techniques of communicating their goals and programs to the Jewish community. Remembering a promise he had made, he left early to participate in a meeting of the "Jewish Parents Without Partners."

Meetings of various special-interest groups were held every night in the temple, and at first, David had attended every meeting of every group. It wasn't until he questioned whether it was his ego or his interest that required his attendance that he had cut back on the number of meetings he went to.

10 P.M.–midnight: STUDY

By definition, David was a teacher, a scholar, and the congregation's interpreter of Jewish law and custom. Attempting to keep abreast of changing philosophical and theological points of view, he read a minimum of two books a week and four periodicals a day.

He was often asked to act as the arbitrator between congregational members embroiled in personal or business disputes. They came to him because he was the qualified interpreter of Jewish law and custom. His decision, though not legally binding, was usually accepted. Unknown to the conflicting parties, the pressures of arbitration often left David mentally exhausted and physically drained. He hoped he had the wisdom to make decisions that were reflections of his knowledge and interpretation of Jewish law, rather than of his personal views.

David's calendar was booked so solidly that social invitations to the Benjamins had to be extended months in advance. He had become more selective in those invitations he accepted after discovering that an evening at the Adelsons or the Benders meant hours of discussing "business." The most enjoyable and relaxing evenings were spent with congregants who were not active in temple affairs.

He checked the next day's calendar, thinking, If there are no outside interruptions, I can get it all in. But there were always unscheduled interruptions. His phone rang constantly. Many of the calls were from lonely people who merely wanted someone to talk with who would listen to them. His mail was heavy, nearly fifty pieces a day. The bulk of the letters had nothing to do with the temple's business but were requests for help ranging from financial aid to job placement.

The clock on the wall chimed the midnight hour, and David wouldn't have been surprised if someone had appeared at this late hour. It was happening more and more frequently as his congregants turned to him for help and guidance. The constant emotional tugs and pulls strained him. It was a lonely battle and he fought it every day. He had discovered that there was no one but himself he could turn to for help. He was learning what it meant to be a rabbi.

But he was grateful that the demands on him rarely left him the time to think of Sheila Harrington.

CHAPTER
9

Because Sheila was regarded as Anson Phillips's protégée, she was tolerated but not accepted by the hierarchy of senior vice-presidents. Having spent over twenty years working their way up the United Motors corporate ladder, they didn't believe that a young woman belonged on the otherwise all-male ninth floor. Their attitude toward her was an old-school gentlemanly one of tolerant indifference. Even though Sheila understood that this behavior had been forged and entrenched by years of corporate custom, she still resented it because their chauvinism effectively blocked her credibility. The only executive on the ninth floor who treated her as a professional equal was Anson Phillips.

Sheila had worked for over seven years at midlevel executive positions in finance, public service and manufacturing. She knew she was good at what she did, and when she felt she was ready, she had applied for a coveted executive internship at United Motors. Because whoever was hired would work directly with the company president on Executive Row, Phillips had done the interviewing. Sheila had been the only woman candidate selected from the hundreds of applicants, and, given Phillips's attitude as she sat in front of his desk, she had wondered if the decision to include her as a contender had been made to silence feminist activist groups. Throw them a token female and they'd shut up.

Midway through the interview she had sensed that Phillips was not going to hire her. He was going through the motions but seemed far more interested in her legs than in her background and experience. She had tried to think of something she could say or do that would pique his interest so that he would seriously consider her, but nothing had worked and the interview had sputtered along with embarrassing pauses between her responses and his next question. Phillips was obviously relieved by the interruption of the operations manager, Lawton Collins, who had burst into his office waving a telex.

"Can't it wait, Lawton? We're almost finished here."

"Bill Thompson is dead." Collins waved the telex as if verifying the calamity. "And, Anson, the shit is about to hit the fan. The board has called an emergency meeting for two o'clock. That's only an hour from now. They're going to want answers to some hard questions. We don't have any."

A jungle air crash had taken the lives of a United Motors task force that was supervising the construction of a new facility in São Paulo, and the answers to the questions the Board of Directors was going to ask Anson Phillips had died along with Thompson and his top lieutenants. Sheila, feeling like an interloper, listened to what she was sure was privileged information. She sat quietly, hands demurely folded in her lap, hoping neither man would notice her.

"We can't continue the project as if nothing's happened in São Paulo, Anson," Collins was saying. "Unless we come up with a satisfactory solution, we're looking at a ten-million-dollar disaster. That's United's investment up to date. Without answers, we're faced with two tough choices: We either write that ten million off or start all over again. That's the sixty-four-thousand-dollar question the board is going to ask. Anson, what do we recommend to them and why? Whatever way we suggest we go would just be a guess."

"And you can't run a business this size on hunches," a worried Phillips had agreed. He folded his hands under his chin and closed his eyes as if to shut out the disruptive anxiety caused by the disaster in South America. When he opened them, he saw Sheila still sitting in the room and said politely, "Would you mind waiting outside, Miss Harrington? My secretary will take care of you." He ushered her out of his office and introduced her to a matronly secretary in the reception area. "We'll wind up our interview when I finish." From his expression as he quickly went back into his office and closed the door, she realized the interview was over.

"Would you like some coffee?" the secretary asked, pointing to a pot on a hot plate. When Sheila shook her head, she returned to her typing.

Damn it, I want that job! Sheila had said to herself. And I'd be good at it. But how am I going to prove that to Mr. Phillips?

The secretary picked up some folders and left the reception area. Sheila, alone, debated with herself for a moment, then quickly went to the secretary's desk and flicked on the intercom. She listened to the two executives discussing the disaster. Her eyes suddenly widened with memory, and she searched her briefcase for a specific document, praying she had remembered to bring it along. She sagged with relief when she found the blue-covered portfolio. Returning to the secretary's desk, she again listened intently to the voices through the intercom.

"Miss Halsted, bring in some coffee, please," Phillips said. "The usual for me. Mr. Collins takes his with sugar."

Startled, Sheila hesitated. Taking a deep breath, she shrugged and went to the coffee station and poured two cups. She put them on a small tray and, holding the blue-covered document neatly beneath it, hipped her way through the door and back into Anson Phillips's office.

He had looked at her with surprise and suspicion as she said matter-of-factly, "Your secretary had to leave for a moment."

He watched her place the cups on the desk before he said, "Thank you, Miss Harrington. Although I admire both qualities, I'm not sure if you're being considerate or just opportunistic." The other executive shuffled impatiently, waiting for her to leave. She ignored Lawton Collins and directed her attention at Anson Phillips. She hoped he didn't notice her trembling fingers when she handed him the blue-covered report and said, "I think you ought to look at this, Mr. Phillips."

He didn't mask his annoyance. "I'm very busy, Miss Harrington. If what you want me to look at is so important, why don't you leave it with my secretary and I'll get to it later."

"Mr. Phillips, I hate to sound like I'm interfering, but I think it's important that you read this document now. It details how the Delvy Corporation retrieved a situation in Chile when faced with the same problem you now face in São Paulo. Terrorists blew up a plant under construction and murdered the top executives in charge. This document will at least suggest what the questions are that you have to answer before you can make a decision on which way to go."

As if against his better judgment, Phillips thumbed through the report, stopping to read a page here and a paragraph there. When he had finished reading and looked at Sheila, it was with both interest and curiosity. "Tell me some of the questions you think we're going to need answered, Miss Harrington."

Speaking authoritatively, she continued. "Who were your key executives working with within the Brazilian government? Did they make any payoffs? *Mordita?* To whom? Did they have to make any concessions or deals with local labor unions? What was the construction timetable?" She took a breath and then asked, "Do you want me to continue, Mr. Phillips?"

Before he responded, he read the report again. Slowly and carefully. Noting that her name was listed as its author, he said, "It states here that you headed up the task force that retrieved the situation for Delvy. Why you? What qualifications do you have for a job with those responsibilities?"

Her response was firm and positive. "I speak both Spanish and Portuguese. I'm an attorney who's versed in international law. I'm a labor specialist who's also knowledgeable in crisis management. And, in addition to those qualifications, I have one more. I can open doors that men can't get through."

"How come?"

"Because, Mr. Phillips, I've got a great ass."

He burst out laughing and then said to the operations manager, "Lawton, I get the feeling Miss Harrington might be able to help us out. But I think she'd be more comfortable dealing just with me. Why don't you leave the two of us alone and I'll get back to you."

Phillips waited until they were alone before motioning her to the empty seat in front of his desk. "Would you like some coffee, Miss Harrington?" he asked politely. "Something to drink?" When she shook her head, he turned back to the document. He read it more carefully than he had the first time, and when he was finished, he began to question her. She rattled off facts as if she had just been waiting for his cue to recite.

"Miss Harrington, you're very convincing," he said when she finished. "But we have a problem. I'm not the one you have to convince. Can you convince my Board of Directors?"

She leaned forward. "You have one other problem, Mr. Phillips. Because you don't have any other option but me, you're going to have to gamble that I can."

"Just so we understand each other, if I had any other choice, I'd take it. But we both know that I don't. Miss Harrington, you'd better be as good as you think you are."

Sheila remembered how her expertise had convinced the board and they'd named her director of the task force.

That was about four years ago. She spent the first three months in Brazil, and when she returned to Detroit, the crisis was over and the situation in São Paulo resolved. Her greatest difficulty had not been the problems the group had encountered but having to head the otherwise all-male team.

A year ago Phillips had reorganized the executive structure of United Motors and had created a group with the catchall title of Special Projects. On his recommendation, the Board of Directors had voted to put his executive assistant in charge of the newly created division. Though pleased, Sheila hadn't been surprised. Her entire life had been one of achievement. Growing up, she had been more competitive, brighter and more self-confident than her peers. Her role model was her father, Dwight Harrington, who had parlayed those same qualities into a small fortune. He had had the most influence on the direction of Sheila's life.

Her friends thought of her as compulsively driven to succeed because once she established priorities, nothing could stop her. She had wanted a college degree. It took her a little over two years to get it. She had wanted a law degree, not because she had any intention of practicing law, but because she knew having one gave her a competitive edge. She graduated third in her class from Yale Law School. Sensing she belonged in "big business" because of the challenges it offered, and because even its ruthlessness appealed to her, she got an MBA from Wharton.

The standards she set for herself were always high, and she applied them in every area of her life. They were so high she had difficulty finding men who could measure up. She was attracted to dynamic, ambitious men, but most males thought of her as a threat. What they didn't realize about Sheila Harrington, something she had yet to face, was that in many ways she was a paradox: a modern, achieving, capable woman who also desired marriage and children but only in a context in which she would be able to fully express everything she was.

Those beliefs had been tested when she was still in college. She had met Spencer Tolliver, her history professor, in one of the few liberal arts courses she had allowed herself to take. Over ten years older than Sheila, he had appealed to her because he was far more mature in outlook than the young men who sat in the classroom with her. They become lovers, but they didn't live together because exposure would have meant her expulsion as a student and his dismissal from the faculty. Their liaisons, therefore, were limited to occasional weekends well away from campus.

Tolliver fell deeply in love, and a year after their relationship began, he asked Sheila to marry him. She gave the proposal serious thought. The age difference didn't bother her: Sheila handled it better than he did. It was Tolliver's image of her role in the proposed marriage that disturbed her. Home and children, wife and mother. She didn't blame him for wanting that at his age, but at her age, marriage and children were not among her priorities. "Settling down" was for later. Now was for proving, achieving, conquering. She did not want to be a wife and mother. Not yet. And when she was ready, it would not be in the context she knew Spencer Tolliver envisioned.

They parted as friends, and four years later Tolliver married.

Sometimes, especially when lonely, Sheila wondered if she hadn't made a mistake in rejecting the professor. Meeting David Benjamin had sparked her memories, and they were reinforced when a month after the Economic Club luncheon, she saw David's smiling photo in the *Free Press*. He had been appointed to the Citizens Committee on City Planning and Programming. Sheila, representing the automotive industry, had recently replaced Anson Phillips on the same committee.

She now studied the picture again, convinced that their attraction had been mutual. She had thought about him often after the luncheon, wondering if religious leaders had affairs. After chastising herself for being so naive, she faced the reality of her troubled imagination.

Am I that vulnerable, that susceptible, that I'm thinking about having an affair with a rabbi? she asked herself. Or am I so lonely and frustrated that I just want a man in my life? Or do I feel this way because I sense that this man is something special? That even though he is a rabbi, I've never met a man like him before.

Impulsively, she told her secretary to get Temple Beth Sinai on the phone. That she wanted to speak to Rabbi Benjamin.

"Is Rabbi Benjamin available?" she asked. She wondered about her choice of words. *Available.* "This is Sheila Harrington. From United Motors."

David answered immediately, from the tone of his voice obviously glad to hear from her. They glided easily past an initial awkwardness, testing each other's interest as they became less hesitant and more relaxed.

She thought of a valid excuse to meet with him.

"I've got a proposition for you," Sheila said. She winced, wondering why she had chosen *that* particular word. "United maintains a fleet of cars that we loan out to public figures. I think it's time we included a rabbi. It would be good for our image. David, how would you like the use of one of our cars for a year?"

Her offer had little to do with United's public relations: it was only a legitimate excuse to see him again.

"No strings?" he asked suspiciously.

"No strings," she quickly reassured him. "Your only obligation is to see that United gets a credit line every time a picture is taken of you with our car."

"That sounds fair. What do I have to do?"

"Come down to my office. I'll take you over to our garage and personally pick out the model I think best suits your image. Why don't you come over now and I'll let you buy me lunch?"

He was tempted not only because he wanted to see her again, but because he was flattered by her obvious interest in him. In the early years of his marriage, very much in love, he had been unresponsive when two women of his congregation had made suggestive overtures. The first was a pathetic young widow and the second a divorcée. But now, because of the continuing dissolution of his relationship with Naomi, he felt the temptation he had never permitted himself to feel before. Besides, he justified, Sheila Harrington is neither a lonely, empty widow nor a recent divorcée desperately seeking a man to brighten her life. Sheila Harrington was a vibrant, lovely, sensuous young woman who undoubtedly could have picked and chosen any man she wanted. That she was interested in him, whatever her reasons, was not only flattering to his ego but also stimulating to his masculinity.

He thumbed through his desk calendar and saw that he had a tentative lunch date with his brother-in-law to discuss a coming fundraiser. We can do that anytime, he told himself. I'll call Brian and make it for tomorrow.

"Where do you want to meet?" he said into the phone. He noticed his hand holding the mouthpiece was shaking.

Sheila was surprised and pleased by his acceptance. "I'll leave that up to you," she said almost inaudibly. David didn't respond, and his silence made her sense his hesitancy, so she added, "You're the one who has to worry about a congregation's understanding and approval, Rabbi. I understand."

"Sheila . . ."

His voice was suddenly muffled as he folded his hand over the mouthpiece, and Sheila knew immediately that someone had come into his office.

"Naomi—what are you doing here?" David demanded nervously. He removed his hand from the receiver, mumbled into it, "Please hold on a minute," then replaced his hand.

"I've got a Sisterhood meeting a little later," Naomi answered from the doorway. "Thought I'd kill a little time." Noticing that he was on the phone, she said, "I didn't mean to interrupt . . . I'll come back." She started to leave.

"No!"

His peremptory tone stopped her. Bewildered, she froze against the doorframe.

Naomi's unexpected appearance had shattered the game of pretense David had been playing. He looked at her and couldn't help comparing her with Sheila Harrington. She's so thin, so plain. So frightened. But she exists. She's my wife. I am a rabbi. His fingers tightened around the phone and he asked himself, What am I doing? This isn't only wrong, it's stupid!

"Let me take you to lunch," he said to Naomi. "Someplace special." He hesitated, then added, "I need to take you to lunch."

If Naomi was aware of the anguish in David's voice, she didn't react. She looked at him suspiciously—he had never invited her to lunch before. He must be feeling guilty because of the way he usually ignores me, was her immediate thought. But she didn't have the courage to confront him, so she said, "But you're very busy . . ."

"I'm never too busy to take my wife to lunch." His tone was gentle, with a forced note of gallantry.

I'm glad he feels guilty, she said to herself. It's about time I make him pay for what he's put me through. Still afraid of the confrontation, she said, "But I have that Sisterhood meeting. And then I'm supposed to get together with Florence to make plans for redecorating the preschool classrooms."

"Cancel the meeting," David insisted. "They can get along without you this once. And tell Florence you have something more important to do."

Pleased by her sense of triumph, Naomi shook her head. Before she left, she said, "I appreciate the offer, David, but you're not the only one with a busy schedule. Maybe we can make it tomorrow when I have more time."

His face was rigid as he sank back into his chair and stared at the empty doorway. David believed that if Naomi had only understood how badly he had wanted her to agree to the luncheon date, the game he had been playing would have ended; the fantasy he had permitted himself to indulge in would not have stood a chance of becoming a reality.

He lifted his cramped fingers from the phone and said quietly to Sheila, "Something's come up. I can't make it for lunch today. Some other time."

"When?"

"Soon."

"Is that a promise?"

"Would a rabbi lie?"

CHAPTER

10

David's image as a rabbi of importance began to grow as he involved himself in social programs that reached beyond the Jewish community. From his appearances on various committees and panels, he also began to emerge as a figure of local importance, further enhancing his growing power and prestige.

The demands on his time continued to isolate him from Naomi. Because she was usually asleep when he returned home, his desire to discuss the events of his day went unfulfilled. Though they occasionally socialized with congregants, he spent most of the evening discussing temple "business." For much of the weekend, he locked himself in his study, either preparing next week's sermon, catching up on the paperwork or preparing an article he had been requested to write for a theological journal.

As David became more deeply involved in his work, Naomi personalized their growing separation. She convinced herself that David was deliberately isolating her from his life. Because of her loneliness, especially in the evenings, she resented the demands on his time. She was angry that he was so fulfilled and she was so empty.

Now comfortable within his role, David took a more active part in the workings of the temple, presenting new programs he wanted to inaugurate and directions he wanted to pursue. Harold Fedder more often than not opposed his positions. There were times when David wondered if Fedder's resistance was a personal vendetta, since his disapproval was usually expressed in private rather than at a public hearing . . .

It was nine-thirty in the morning when Fedder stormed into David's office and pounded his desk, shouting, "What's this about your approving four homosexuals as members of this congregation!"

"Harold," David said calmly, "there are homosexuals in this world. There are Jews in this world. There are Jewish homosexuals in this world. We can no longer pretend they don't exist. My concern is not with their sexual preferences, but with their spiritual needs. And because of their sexual preferences, I wouldn't be a bit surprised if their spiritual needs weren't greater than yours or mine."

"But to accept them as members of this congregation! To sit in the same sanctuary with them!"

"What's the matter, Harold, are you afraid you'll become contaminated? That their sexuality will rub off on you?"

Fedder raged out of the office and David realized he had mishandled the situation. Disturbed, he needed to talk with someone about his difficulties. He felt that if he could get them out in the open, he could objectively examine his own motives. Reluctantly, he called Naomi, who listened without comment to his account of the situation and the remarks he had made.

Deliberately, she remained mute after he had finished, and he had to break her stubborn silence by asking, "Naomi, don't you have anything to say?"

"What do you want me to say, David? I'll say whatever you want me to say." He couldn't miss the heavy sarcasm in her voice. "If you want me to tell you that you said the wrong things to Harold Fedder, then that's what I'll tell you. If you want me to agree with you, then I'll agree with you."

He hung up, vowing that was the last time he would include Naomi in that part of his life. He felt a stab of guilt as he asked himself, But what part of my life *do* I include her in?

He paced back and forth in front of the picture window, muttering, "I've got to get away from here for a few hours and try to forget that I'm a rabbi. I need a break, a respite of some kind."

He scribbled a memo to Florence, asking her, without explanation, to cancel the day's appointments and reschedule them as best she could. Then he wondered where he would go and what he would do. He glanced at his watch before looking up a phone number. He smiled as he dialed it.

"This is Rabbi David Benjamin," he told the secretary who answered. "May I please speak to Miss Harrington?"

When she answered, he said lightly, "See, a rabbi doesn't lie. I told you I would call to take you to lunch. We can talk about that car you promised me."

"Why don't you meet me at my office at twelve-fifteen?" she answered immediately.

He was smiling nervously when he hung up. Though he had kept his promise, he knew it was only a convenient excuse to see her. He didn't know that she too hung up with a nervous smile because she would have to cancel two meetings to be with him. She had never done that for any other man.

In the underground garage, Sheila checked a list on her clipboard and then pointed at a black Escadrille, United Motors' midpriced luxury car. She and David walked toward it, deliberately staying far enough apart to not touch. When they reached the car, she asked, "What do you think? Isn't that a good-looking automobile?"

"And you think it fits my image?"

Not sure of how to respond, she said, "Wait here. I'll go get the keys."

He watched her walk to a small glassed-in booth at the far end of the garage and talk to an attendant. What am I doing here? he thought. Why am I lying to her? I'm here because I want to see her, not because of a car. Because I want to be with her.

She came back with the keys and held them out to him. Looking at the car and then at Sheila, he said, "Do you have time for a short drive?"

They drove north out of Detroit on Highway 75. She sat as far away from him as she could, her hands folded tightly in her lap. Their conversation was deliberately impersonal, as if they knew that to talk about anything but cows and trees and isn't-that-an-interesting-looking-barn might take them into unsafe areas. Then, afraid of appearing dull and uninteresting to the other, they attempted to liven things up. But their jokes and their laughter were too brittle, too forced, and the inane chatter gradually petered out until they sat in silence. The thunder of their private thoughts added to the tension.

He's not only a rabbi, he's a married rabbi, she told herself. Her attitudes, forged when she was young and still a member of the Church, came alive. She had always thought of herself in an inferior role to her priest. He was the shepherd and she was a member of his flock. She confessed to Father and he absolved her and therefore the equality she needed in a relationship with a man didn't exist with a man of the cloth. Her thoughts confused her because the conflict raised by the dichotomy of what David was appeared unresolvable. And though she knew he was as attracted to her as she to him, she wondered if the restrictions caused by his role would inhibit any real communication.

She shrugged away the fact that he was married. He's a sensitive, charming and intelligent man, the man I've been looking for, she told herself. But nothing can happen between us, so what difference does it make if he's married or not? At best, maybe we'll have some kind of friendship. That thought caused her to grimace. She didn't want friendship with David Benjamin. She wanted much more, and because she sensed she couldn't have it, there was no longer any need to pretend or fantasize.

David turned to look at her profile. He wanted to reach across and carefully push off her forehead a stray strand of hair that glinted in the sunlight. The depths of his reaction to the projected intimacy of the unfulfilled act surprised him. He smelled her perfume, and though he knew he was violating some unspoken ground rule, asked softly, "What's the name of the perfume you wear? It's a lovely fragrance."

Her head turned slowly and she looked at him, her large green eyes wide with pleasure and surprise. "Replique," she said quietly. "Do you like it?"

"Very much. It suits you."

Embarrassed, she quickly strove to rebuild the wall between them. "Do you like the way the car handles?" she asked briskly, sounding like a new-car dealer romancing a reluctant buyer.

Imitating her mood he responded, "Not bad, not bad." It was the safest thing he could think of to say.

The awkward silence reappeared and stayed with them as the miles swept by. Noticing a small restaurant on the outskirts of Clarkston, he U-turned on the highway, and, tires squealing, pulled into the empty parking lot. She looked at him in surprise.

"I promised to take you to lunch," he said. "Remember?" She nodded and he added, "Besides a lunch is a small price to pay for the free use of a brand-new car."

She read the sign: *Clarkston Cafe.* Though she had never been there, she had heard of the place. An out-of-the-way restaurant with atmosphere. A place for lovers to rendezvous. She wondered if his choice had been deliberate or accidental.

The restaurant looked and felt as if it had been lifted out of a French province. Small and intimate. Checkered tablecloths, freshly cut flowers on every table, bare wooden walls, and a well-scrubbed buxom young waitress who greeted them as if she knew they were lovers having a secret tryst.

Though the restaurant was empty, she seated them in a secluded area and then took their drink orders. (Martini up, no olive but with a twist for Sheila; Black Label, water, no ice for David.) They both filed away the other's preference for the future. Just in case.

They began to talk, awkwardly at first and then reaching a level of intimacy where the reluctance and the hesitancy disappeared. They told each other of their backgrounds and marveled at the wide contrasts. They talked of their childhoods and their pet peeves and their likes and dislikes. They laughed a lot and eventually, having gotten comfortable with each other, even harmlessly teased.

David listened intently as Sheila talked about her life as part of the upper strata of Washington/Virginia/Palm Beach society and how she had never fit into the expected role so easily accepted by her friends, that of a pampered young woman who dabbled at life. Watching her, he thought, No, Sheila Harrington, you're anything but a dabbler.

He asked her about her work at United Motors and then marveled at how much she had achieved. Eyeing her over the rim of his glass, he asked casually, "I'm curious—where do you go from here? What are you after?"

"Power," she said instantly, then laughed at his perplexed expression. "Whenever I say that to a man, it scares the hell out of him. Why? Power isn't a dirty word. It's neither masculine nor feminine. It's not evil. So why do men think it's not quite nice for a woman to want it? Don't you think I can be assertive in a boardroom and still be sexy in a bedroom? Don't you think I can be feminine and still be powerful and rich? Don't you think—" She suddenly stopped talking and stared intently at David.

"What's wrong?"

"David Benjamin, you scare the hell out of me. I've never revealed all of myself to a man before. You make me feel vulnerable, and I'm not sure I like that."

He sat quietly, waiting for her to regain her composure. She laughed nervously and changed the subject by asking, "You've told me a lot about yourself, but you haven't told me why you became a rabbi."

"To help people."

She thought about his answer and then shook her head in confusion. "Why do you have to be a rabbi to help people? Can't you just be a man? Are you sure there isn't something even more basic than wanting to help people that made you become a rabbi?"

"Like what?"

"Oh, I don't know. Maybe the prestige and the power and the ability to influence that go with the role?"

Her question put him off balance. He focused on making small concentric circles in the tablecloth with the bottom of his glass. When he looked up at her, he said, "Sheila Harrington, you scare the hell out of me, too. I never thought of that possibility before, and if it's true, my being a rabbi makes me the biggest hypocrite in the world."

They sat silently for a while, thinking about each other. Finally David said, "You're nothing like the image I've had of someone like you. It must have come from romantic novels. The rich spoiled society girl from Virginia riding to hounds. Sheltered and protected and made of porcelain. I always wondered if you ever dirtied your hands." As if to prove his curiosity, he picked up her hand and pretended to scrutinize her palm and fingers.

"And the image I've had of someone like you also came from novels," Sheila teased. "I always saw rabbis as being so heavy and so intense and so determined. So driven. So weighted down by all your guilt and so one-dimensional that I wondered if you knew how to romance a woman."

They fell silent when they became aware that their fingers were entwined. David looked down at her graceful and delicate fingers curving into his palm and awkwardly said, "My image was wrong. You're not made of porcelain."

"So was mine. You do know how to romance a woman."

"I had the feeling the first time we met that good things could happen between us. Now that I know you, I'm sure."

"I had the feeling, too. And I agree with what you're saying." She paused before adding, "If we want good things to happen." Her voice was a conspiratorial whisper.

David continued to play with her fingers until, reluctantly, he let conscience and guilt smother his desire. He said sadly, "But I can't let those good things happen."

"I know that. I understand." Sheila drew her hand away and David made no effort to stop her.

The waitress, who thought they looked so cute and perfect together, was surprised when David motioned for the check and they left abruptly without finishing their lunch.

CHAPTER

11

Though David thought of Sheila frequently during the next two months, he accepted the impossibility of a relationship with her. They met occasionally at social functions and treated each other with rigid formality. Every time he saw her, the struggle to suppress his feelings became more difficult. He deliberately increased his workload, accepting more invitations for public appearances, so as not to have to contend with his feelings. The effect was to enhance his growing public image. He became a minor celebrity, adding to his stature within his congregation.

Because of his blossoming local public image and his growing prestige, a stream of individuals began to either telephone or come to the temple seeking David's endorsement, his support or his opinion. State and city politicians, Detroit's journalists, a congressman, a union executive. The rabbis prior to David, without the ability to influence outside their congregations, had never given them a reason to visit Temple Beth Sinai. Florence, David's secretary, though impressed at first by the continuing flow of prestigious visitors, gradually accepted their visits and calls as commonplace. Therefore, though curious, she wasn't surprised by the unannounced appearance of a federal marshal.

The marshal handed David a subpoena and left. He read it, picked up the phone and placed a call to Murray Kempter, who was now employed by his union in New York. The strike against the Tremaine Textile Company had continued after David had left North Carolina, and there had been more bloodshed, violence and vandalism before it was settled. David sensed that the subpoena had something to do with his involvement in the labor dispute. It commanded him to appear in Washington before a Senate labor subcommittee in five days.

Kempter got on the line. "Hello, Mr. Head Rabbi! How's it going?"

"Murray, you got the wrong man if you're looking for the head rabbi. Around here I'm only the interim rabbi. And when my year is up in three months, I might not even be that."

"Interim-shminterim. Haven't you unpacked your bags? Aren't you planning to stay?"

"What I'm planning and what my congregation is planning may be very different."

"Trouble in River City, huh? Patience, my good man, patience. Didn't I teach you about patience? Wait till they get to know you. To know Rabbi David Lee Benjamin is to love him."

"Murray, how'd you like to come to Farmington Hills and give next Friday night's sermon? You'd make me a star."

"Davey, my boy, from what I hear and read about you, you're already a star."

"Maybe that's why I was just served with a subpoena to appear before a Senate subcommittee investigating unions."

"I figured that's why you were calling. The good senator from North Carolina, Bob Murchison, is supposedly investigating violence during strikes and organizing campaigns. What he's doing is making a career out of union-busting, and he's using what happened at the Tremaine mill to prove his case. He claims he has evidence that I used the threat of violence to organize that mill."

"But there isn't any truth to that."

"Of course not, David, but this son of a bitch isn't looking for the truth. He's looking for headlines. How better to get them than by having a well-known rabbi he can make look like a former radical union activist in the witness chair? David, I'm sorry you're being dragged into this mess, but there was nothing I could do to stop it. I tried."

"It's not your fault, Murray. I was a part of what happened down there. We both tried to prevent the violence. Everyone who was involved knows that. I'll just tell Murchison the truth."

"I wish it were that simple. But, as I said, with Senator Bob Murchison, the truth doesn't matter. David, a word of caution:

Murchison is not a very nice man, so be discreet when you testify. Choose your words carefully. He's made a career out of destroying people and he's the expert. Because you're a rabbi, he'll be gunning for you."

Less than an hour later, Senator Mendes gave David the same warning.

"I wouldn't go so far as to say that Murchison is anti-Semitic. He's too clever for that. But based on his voting record and some of his speeches, he obviously isn't a friend of the Jews or of Israel. And to make his case in this union business, he's going to discredit you any way he can. Those are his tactics, and up to now they've always worked."

"Senator, I don't understand. This is a hearing on union activities. On who caused the violence at the Tremaine mill. What has my position on Israel or that I'm a rabbi got to do with what happened in North Carolina?"

"David, David, there are times I can't believe you're so naive. In the public's mind, troubles in unions are caused either by communist infiltration or by racketeers. In certain minds, Jews are commonly linked with Red plots. It doesn't matter if it isn't true, that's the propaganda that many people believe. Bob Murchison isn't stupid. He caters to those people by ferreting out communist and racketeering interference and influence in unions, whether they're there or not. That makes him come across like a superpatriot. It's been done before. Joe McCarthy did it in the fifties. Murchison has taken a page out of history and has gotten God, flag and country on his side, so anyone who stands up to him comes off looking like a traitor. Just like during the McCarthy era, nobody has the courage to stand up to Murchison because if you do you're labeled as being un-American. Don't underestimate the man, David. Give him the ammunition and he can make you look like a Red subversive who's out to undermine this country."

"But, Senator, this is just a minor subcommittee hearing," David protested. "The chances are that nothing important is going to be said."

"I'd agree with you, David, except for one thing. You're going to be the star witness. Not only are you a rabbi, but you're a well-known liberal rabbi who got himself involved with a union. Murchison is going to try to make you look as if you take orders directly from Moscow and Jerusalem. He's going to turn that hearing into an inquisition."

Remembering Murray Kempter's warning, David muttered, "And he's going to destroy me in the process."

"Only if you let him. But you can turn it around, David. I've shown you how. You've become more than an altruistic, idealistic young man with a social conscience. I've seen you on TV. Heard some of your sermons. Now you're a hard-nosed realist, too. So fight Murchison with the same tactics he's going to use to distort and discredit you. You are a rabbi, a man of truth and faith and justice. Because you are a rabbi, you have credibility and authority on your side. Use it. You have charisma and reputation. Pull out all the stops. For the first time, though he doesn't know it yet, Bob Murchison is going to be taking on a heavyweight. If you have as much faith in yourself as I have in you, you can come out of that hearing with a bigger and better reputation than you had when you went in. You can look good and make him look bad. You can beat him, David."

"And if I don't?" David asked skeptically.

"Then I'll have to be conveniently out of town until the fuss he creates about you dies down. Remember, I can only afford to back a winner."

"You mean you'd abandon me?" David let the words slip out in half jest. "After all, Senator, you are my mentor, my father-in-law."

The senator laughed. "True, but first I am a politician, and loyalty is a quality to be balanced against other practical considerations. I've given you all the help I can. You fight this one the rest of the way by yourself. If you do this right, I'll be on your side loud and clear right out in the open. But if you blow it and come off as some crazy, radical, hotheaded agitator, then I can't afford to know you."

"I don't like what you're saying, Senator, but I understand it. I've still got a lot to learn, haven't I?" David said with a deep sigh.

"David, learning goes with the territory. Whether you're a United States senator or a rabbi."

Because it was one of the rare nights David was home for dinner, Naomi made his favorite dessert, cheesecake. He leaned against the counter, watching her deftly blending the ingredients in a large bowl. She began to beat the mixture, occasionally stopping because she was too fatigued to continue.

Naomi had been aware for some time that her troubles were

physical as well as emotional. There were mornings when she woke up so enervated that she had to force herself to get out of bed. She had lost weight and was constantly run-down, but blamed her lethargy on a low-grade fever she'd had off and on for months. Though aware that something might be terribly wrong with her body, she refused to do anything about it. That's what her hypochondriac mother did. Run to her doctor with every imagined illness. Besides, Naomi attributed her poor health to her persistent depression, and blamed the aching within on the void of childlessness. In spite of her relief at being back home in Detroit, she knew that her misery would not go away on its own—she knew she had to do something. She promised herself that someday she would think about it.

She was breathing so heavily from the exertion of baking that David asked with concern, "Naomi, are you all right? You always seem so tired. Why don't you go see a doctor?"

She gave David the same answers she gave others who had commented on how run-down she looked. "It's only a virus. It's nothing that important to see a doctor about. Besides, a *rebbetzin* isn't allowed to get sick. I don't have the time to see a doctor."

Naomi's days and nights were filled with charity work, the woman's club, Hadassah meetings. Keeping busy buried her constant depression, so she drove herself with an intensity that was also a form of self-punishment.

"Naomi, that's ridiculous." David put his hands on her shoulders. "You have to make time. I'm worried about you. You've got to take better care of yourself. Not only are you run-down, you always seem so depressed. So worried."

"I worry about you, too," she said. That's a lie, she told herself. I worry about myself because I know, in spite of what you're saying, that you don't. "Like you having to go to Washington. If it weren't for Murray Kempter, you wouldn't be in this situation. See, didn't I tell you that nothing good could come from knowing him?"

From his silent disgusted reaction, she knew that she had once again said the wrong thing. She had pushed David away again. She could feel the wall of his isolation separating them. She groped for words that would in some way bring them back together and, after wiping her hands on her apron, she said, "You're always going out of town and you never take me. David, please take me to Washington with you. Maybe I can help in some way. Maybe by just being there, I can make it easier for you. We can make this a small vacation. We haven't taken a vacation together in years."

He shook his head sadly. She didn't understand the treacherous situation he was going to face in Washington. That even if he won, his reputation and career might be ruined. "This isn't a vacation, Naomi. I'm not going to Washington on a pleasure trip. I'm going because I've been subpoenaed to appear before a Senate subcommittee. I would give anything in the world not to have to go, but I have no choice. Besides, I'll be there for less than forty-eight hours and I won't have any time for you."

"You mean you don't *want* to make the time for me," Naomi snapped. She was so upset by his rejection of her proposal that she didn't even consider the validity of his reasons.

"Why can't you understand?" he asked wearily.

"Oh, but I do understand," she shot back triumphantly. "Only too well do I understand. You don't need me anymore. You probably don't even want me anymore. You've cut me out of your life. If it weren't for me and my father, you wouldn't be the rabbi of Temple Beth Sinai. And this is the thanks I get? This is how you repay me? You won't even take me to Washington on a short vacation. Is that so much to ask?"

He tried to reason with her, to make her comprehend, but, realizing that she was incapable of doing so, he answered, "Maybe you're right. Maybe we don't spend enough time together."

"So take me to Washington with you," she insisted defiantly.

He shook his head. "I can't. Not this time. It's impossible. But I promise to take you with me on my next trip out of town. Will that satisfy you?"

"It's a start," she said with a shrug.

Later that night, David went to the temple. Unable to shake off the effects of his disturbing conversation with Naomi, he spent almost two hours writing a memo to Florence with detailed instructions for Assistant Rabbi Morris Simon, who was to cover him while he was in Washington.

He itemized each scheduled meeting, listing the agendas and stating the positions he wanted Simon to express. He made a list of the congregants who were to be visited either in hospitals or in convalescent homes and suggested ways to cheer them up. He noted the families who were to meet with him to make arrangements for upcoming weddings and Bar Mitzvahs and offered ideas on how to individualize the ceremonies to suit each participant. He enumerated every appointment that had to be canceled, directing Florence to reschedule them as quickly as possible. Though Murray Kempter had told him he would be in Washington for two or three days at the most, the meticulously written memo covered an entire week.

He knew what he was doing. The forced concentration was a way to forget the unresolvable rupture with Naomi. But when he had finished and left the temple, he remembered.

It was raining and, not wanting to go home, David slowly drove around the quiet, rain-swept suburban streets of Farmington Hills that surrounded the temple. Needing to talk to someone, about a half hour later he found himself parked at the curb before the entrance to Sheila's condominium.

He wished he had the nerve to go into the lobby and ring her buzzer. Would she believe that all he wanted to do was talk? The ugly, futile scene with Naomi had stressed that need. Parked in the rain, the engine still running, he realized that his feelings about Sheila had to do with more than the need for physical warmth. But though he sensed that she could give him the answers and the reassurance he needed, he slowly pulled away from the curb.

Sheila paced her living room, suddenly stopped, slammed one small fist into her palm and said excitedly, "I'm going to Washington! Damn, Anson is sending me to Washington!"

She fell back into a chair and finally allowed the fatigue to seep into her bones. Then a wide, self-satisfied grin broke across her lips as she deliberately forced the memory of the day back into focus.

Anson Phillips had come into her office, dropped a report she had given him a month previously on her desk and said, "That document makes you our resident expert on air bags. So you're going to Washington to testify before a congressional subcommittee to convince them they've got to delay passing their proposed legislation until all the facts are in."

"Just me?" Sheila asked apprehensively.

"No, you'll be a part of a team. There'll be a design engineer and a safety engineer who will testify about the technical data. But you're my cleanup hitter. You've got to be so convincing that the pending legislation about air bags is shelved until we've done more research and development. I'm sending you because not only am I too busy to go, but I've heard you at other hearings and you can do the job. You're damn good."

After Phillips left, Sheila stayed at her desk and absorbed the personal importance of the assignment. She had arrived. Anson

Phillips was trusting her with an important assignment because he had no doubts about her ability to pull it off.

Now, in her apartment, emotionally drained, she realized she no longer wanted to be alone. She wanted to talk to someone. Sighing wearily, she pushed her way out of the chair, went to the window and faced the truth as she looked out into the darkness and watched a black Escadrille pull away from the curb and drive slowly down the deserted street. There was only one person she wanted to talk with.

David Benjamin.

With a sad shake of her head, she turned away from the window. It had been over two months since the romantic luncheon at the Clarkston Cafe. She had thought of him often, always with warm feelings. And though she understood and accepted his position, she had waited with hope for him to call . . .

CHAPTER

12

After dropping David off at the airport, Naomi drove toward downtown Detroit. David had been so engrossed in thinking about tomorrow's hearing, that their conversation had consisted only of grunted good-byes and the assurance that he would call when he had the time. Anger added to Naomi's dejection and melancholy and she began to cry.

"I can't go on like this," she told herself. "I can't deal with this by myself any longer. I need someone to talk to."

A month previously, the unbearable persistency of her depression had caused her to discreetly ask a friend whom she knew was in therapy for the name of her psychiatrist. After looking up the address, she had parked down the street from the small clinic on East Grand Boulevard. Entering, she found the office at the end of the corridor.

But she couldn't force herself to bare her soul to a stranger.

"There's nothing wrong with me," she whispered aloud. "It's David who should be here, not me. He's the one who needs help, not me." Her anger at David began to boil, and she silently recited a litany of real and imagined hurts and slights.

In a shocked voice, she said to herself, "This is what my mother used to do whenever she had a problem she couldn't face. Run to her therapist. Oh, my God, I can't be like my mother. I won't let myself be like her."

Defiantly, she straightened her shoulders and left the clinic. As she drove away, she forced herself to think, There's nothing wrong with me. Nothing, nothing, nothing . . .

David couldn't sleep. His mind churned with apprehension and anticipation about the next day's hearing. Though he had read the documents and notes he had brought with him several times, he got out of bed and restudied them. They didn't relieve his anxiety, but it was better than the futile tossing and turning in the queen-sized bed.

Arriving late in the day, he had been met at the Washington airport by Murray Kempter, who had driven him to the Mayflower Hotel. They had had dinner in the hotel coffee shop and had made arrangements to meet the following day for lunch with the union attorney, Daniel Fowler, who would brief David on what to expect and how to conduct himself during the hearing that was scheduled to begin at three in the afternoon. Fowler would act as his counsel and be at his side at the witness table.

Though it was now only six in the morning, David was too nervous to remain in the hotel room. As he dressed, he recalled Kempter's advice: "While you're waiting to meet us for lunch, why don't you sit in on another hearing to get an idea of what it's like. The first time I ever appeared as a witness, I was scared shitless, so I know what you're feeling."

After a tasteless breakfast, he took a cab to the Rayburn Office Building. Harsh, biting wind hurried him up the wide marble steps. He turned before entering and saw the domed Capitol Building across Independence Avenue and he blinked in surprise. Now acutely aware of where he was and what he was there for, his apprehension increased.

Inside, a guard at an information desk, looking up the schedule, said, "Sir, there's a hearing just starting in Room 2451. The same room you'll be in this afternoon. Go up the stairs to the left and follow the yellow quadrant."

He went past a bust of Sam Rayburn and stopped to read the dedication to the Texas congressman before going up the flight of stairs. He walked down a wide, yellow-painted hall, passing the offices of several congressmen whose names he recognized before coming to Room 2451.

He slipped into the room and took a seat at the end of the last row. Around the horseshoe-shaped, double-level dais, eleven congressmen filled the high chairs. The Republican members were to the left and the Democrats to the right. The chairman, a portly Southerner, sat in the middle of the lower row. A large rectangular table faced the interrogating congressmen, and at the witness table David could see the backs of a man and a woman. A stenographer at the end of the table was busily transcribing the hearing. He could hear the murmur of voices and an occasional burst of laughter, and as the warmth of the room penetrated his overcoat, he began to relax.

The witness, whom he couldn't see, said, "The reason I'm here, Mr. Chairman, is to try to get you and your colleagues to listen to our point of view."

"I can't think of a more charming witness to listen to," the chairman said and smiled warmly. There was a touch of southern gallantry in his voice.

"Sir, I'm grateful for the opportunity."

The witness's voice sounded familiar and David became suddenly alert. Sitting upright, he strained to look around the head of the person in front of him. He could barely believe his eyes.

Sheila Harrington rose from the witness table and with the help of a congressional page placed a series of charts and graphs on easels at the side of the room so they were in view of the audience and the congressmen. Ignoring the bored looks and the indifferent shrugs, she returned to the witness table and sat down beside the United Motors attorney, Lyndon Masterson.

She was dressed in a soft-gray knit suit, the neckline and jacket front trimmed with delicate seed pearls. Her hands were clasped on the table in front of her, and there was a faint, confident smile on her face while she waited for the questioning to begin.

"Miss Harrington, we've listened patiently to your experts talk about air-bag technicalities and specifications," the chairman said. "But the purpose of this hearing isn't to evaluate technical data. What we're trying to determine is if the carnage on our nation's roads would be lowered if every car were required to be fitted with an air bag. Surely, you as the representative of United Motors aren't against an effort to save lives, are you?"

"Sir, that's like asking me if I'm against Mom's apple pie."

"Well, are you?" the representative from New York asked sourly, obviously spoiling for a fight.

"Sir, my mother makes a lousy apple pie." She waited for the laughter to subside before continuing. "Of course United Motors is in favor of any legitimate effort to reduce highway fatalities. We're more concerned about consumer safety than you are. We build safe cars, and our budget reflects our concern over safety. We've spent almost half a million dollars in research and development on air bags alone to determine if that is the way to go."

A pudgy, badly dressed congressman from Oregon held up a document and said, "This report from the Department of Transportation's National Highway Traffic Safety Administration thinks it is. To quote: 'It is estimated that air bags will save 9000 lives a year because drivers cannot avoid using them.' That's a pretty tough statement to refute, Miss Harrington."

She quickly leafed through a pile of documents and found the one she was looking for. Holding it up, she said, "I agree. It is a powerful statement to refute, Congressman. However, this report, from the same agency, claims that air bags are no safer than the present combined safety belt and shoulder strap. I'm not here to dispute the relative merits of reports. I'm here to tell you that we *are* working on air-bag development. Before you propose legislation that we'll be forced to live with, you have to give us more time. Considering the present state of the art, air bags work only forty percent of the time. And only when there is a head-on collision. We know, if given the time, we can come up with a much better reliability factor than that. No matter what kind of a collision occurs. There's one more factor that must be considered before you make your decision. Cost. If we were to install air bags on cars coming off the line today, a cost of $179.67 would have to be passed on to the consumer. We're trying to keep car prices down, not raise them. If we get the time to fully develop this device, we estimate we can cut that cost in half."

The man from New York tried to rattle her by coldly stating, "I'm still not convinced that air bags aren't the way to go right now. Even with their shortcomings. Not when eighty percent of the driving public won't buckle up their seat belts. With air bags, they won't have that option."

"Mr. Congressman, that's only part of the issue. But would you answer two simple questions for me?"

"Of course."

"Didn't you buy a new Cadillac Eldorado last year?"

"Yes," he said hesitantly.

"And did you buy the air-bag option?"

"No, I'm afraid not," he slowly responded and then grinned sheepishly.

"You're not the only committee member in this room who didn't," Sheila said with a smile. "Four of your associates also chose not to buy that option with their new Cadillacs." She looked at the congressman and said sadly, "Sir, I guess you can still lead a horse to water but you can't make him drink. Any more than you can legislate that a motorist buy an air bag."

Now less belligerent, the New York representative asked, "So what are you recommending?"

"Mr. Congressman, I go around the country making speeches about how foolish it is not to wear belts and harnesses. But free people have the right to do foolish things. What I am recommending is that we remove that choice from the car-buying public. Give us the time to fully test and develop air bags, and chances are we can reach that point where they won't be an option but will be standard equipment on every American automobile."

Silent nods of agreement by many of the committee members brought Sheila to her feet. Her goal was simple: to change the mood of the committee. She went to the charts and graphs that had been placed at the side of the room and, using a pointer, traced the downward path of a bright red line on the first chart. "Gentlemen, every innovation in the automobile business, including air bags, is linked to car sales." She tapped the bottom of the red line for emphasis. "And as you can all see, we're not doing well."

She regaled them with facts and illustrated her point with a report about what was happening in the automotive industry. She talked about emission standards and harassing environmental regulations and the ever-increasing costs of steel and labor and rising, unpredictable interest rates. She discussed tariffs and foreign imports and quotas and market projections. She was authoritative without being aggressive or condescending and was confident without being overbearing. She never hesitated, never paused, and answered every question with directness, surety and poise. She knew when to interject humor but never let the committee members forget the seriousness of the subject.

David got up from his seat and stood against the rear swinging doors to have a better view of Sheila in action. He felt his nervousness diminishing when Sheila's quick responses took the bite out of the baiting interrogators. He could see the admiration for her spreading from the question-asking congressmen into the audience. She's good, he thought proudly. Damn good. I hope I'm half that good.

When she finished her presentation, Sheila graciously thanked the committee for their attention and returned to her seat, where she waited for their reactions.

"Do I hear any motion?" the chairman asked the committee members.

The congressman from New York responded. "Because Miss Harrington has so articulately given us so much to think about, I don't feel this committee is ready to make any decision at this time. Therefore, I make a motion that we send the measure back to committee for further study. Hopefully, United Motors will use that time to find the answers we need when this legislation is proposed again."

The motion passed unanimously.

Sheila sank back into her chair. They believed me! They listened to me and they believed me! Her hands were trembling. She sucked in a deep breath of relief and a satisfied smile stretched across her lips. People stopped at the table to congratulate her, and she nodded even though she barely comprehended what they were saying. It felt good just to sit and nod and know.

Suddenly, while replacing documents and reports in her attaché case, a wave of depression swept over her and the triumph began to fade. What good was a triumph unless there was someone to share it with?

Her mood changed slightly when a television newscaster and his cameraman pushed through the crowd and said to her, "Miss Harrington, you've just taken the wind out of an extremely unpopular position. I'd like to do the real story about air bags. You obviously know what you're talking about. Can we talk over lunch?"

Other reporters clustered around her as she rose from the table. She concentrated on their questions, carefully wording her answers while the small entourage worked its way up the crowded aisle toward the exit.

At the swinging doors, David watched. He waved when he thought Sheila was looking, but she didn't respond. He started toward her but was halted by Murray Kempter's grip on his arm.

"I see you took my advice and went to a hearing," the union organizer said. "Do you feel more relaxed now that you know what you'll be up against?" After David nodded, he added, "You'll feel even more comfortable after we have lunch with Dan Fowler. He'll brief you on exactly what you can expect from Murchison."

David thought of writing a quick note to Sheila, letting her know where he was staying, but Kempter's presence prevented it. Reluctantly, after one final glance, he allowed himself to be led out of the hearing room.

CHAPTER

13

A few minutes after three, Sheila returned to the hearing room and said in hushed tones to the guard at the door, "I was here this morning. I think I left my gloves."

The guard smiled at her and said, "I'm sorry, Miss, but nobody turned them in to me. Have you tried the Lost and Found?"

She listened to his directions, but her attention was diverted by the pounding of a gavel by the senator seated in the middle of the dais in front of her. Inadvertently, she looked at the witness table. She couldn't believe her eyes.

The witness was David Benjamin.

Hurriedly seating herself, she glanced around the familiar hearing room. The press table was filled, and the glare of television lights was blinding. The noise of chattering spectators subsided as Senator Murchison repeatedly pounded his gavel.

"I want everyone's attention. We're here to investigate communist infiltration into unions and their use of violence to get what they want. A serious threat to the security of our country. I'm not going to permit these hearings to be turned into a circus, so there will be no laughter or applause. We're here to get at the truth, not to have a good time."

One reporter laughed sarcastically, then mumbled something behind his hand to another, who nodded and grinned. Murchison silenced them with a glare, thinking, They might laugh at me in Washington but they'll fucking well vote for me in North Carolina.

He acknowledged David's presence at the witness table by asking, "Don't you agree, Rabbi, that this is serious business?"

David answered warily. "Yes, Senator, I agree completely."

"Then let's get right down to why you're here. Before we begin the questioning by asking you about your relationship with the communist union organizer Murray Kempter, will you please identify yourself for the record."

"Mr. Chairman, Murray Kempter is not a communist."

The touch of anger in David's voice made Murchison smile smugly. He's not going to be as tough as I thought, he told himself. An angry man is a man out of control. He can be manipulated and maneuvered. The rabbi will say exactly what I want him to say— and he'll hang himself . . .

"We'll get to Mr. Kempter's politics in a little while. And yours too, Rabbi." Changing tactics, Murchison leaned back in his chair and smiled and said, "But first would you please identify yourself?"

"My name is David Lee Benjamin and I'm the rabbi at—" Reluctant to involve Temple Beth Sinai, David hesitated and then weakly concluded, ". . . And I'm a rabbi. I live in Farmington Hills, near Detroit."

Murchison sucked on a pencil thoughtfully and belched slightly before saying, "That's a limited sketch of yourself, Rabbi. It's almost as if you have something to hide." He interrupted David's protest by holding up his hand and adding, "But we'll find out more about you at the proper time." Suddenly, shifting to his prosecuting attorney act, Murchison leaned forward, pointed a thick finger at David and asked, "Let's get right down to business: your relationship with Murray Kempter. How long have you known him?"

"I met Mr. Kempter about a year and a half ago, in the fall of 1969. In North Carolina."

"Would you tell us the circumstances under which you met? Describe, if you will, the closeness of your relationship and your activities together."

Selecting his words carefully and trying to make them as innocuous as possible, David talked about his friendship with Murray. When he finished, he sat back and waited quietly for Murchison's response.

Murchison scribbled some notes on a pad, which he handed to an aide. Turning his attention back to David, he said, "Rabbi, the reason we're here is to investigate the way unions use violence and the threat of violence to blackmail management into giving in to their demands. From what you've said, I think we have a perfect example of that technique. A technique, I might add, that communists have always effectively used. And, from your background, a technique with which you are very familiar."

A tense, expectant murmur rippled through the hearing room. Struggling for composure, David said, "Senator, I haven't the faintest idea of what you're talking about. By innuendo and suggestion, you're—"

Murchison interrupted. "Rabbi, maybe it's not clear to you, but I'm sure that everybody else in this room has a picture of what happened in North Carolina. After Murray Kempter's attempts to force recognition of his union by the Tremaine Textile Company failed, the effort escalated into violence. Isn't that right?" He paused and then added the word "*Rabbi*" in an unmistakably contemptuous voice.

"It may be true that violence did occur, but the union didn't instigate it. I should know. I was there," David said evenly.

"Someone started the violence, Rabbi."

"Violence occurred because emotions were running too high and reason lost out to impatience. If Mr. Tremaine had sat down and negotiated with Mr. Kempter in good faith, there wouldn't have been any violence."

"How can you be sure of that, Rabbi?"

"Because, Senator Murchison, reasonable men don't need, want or use violence to settle their differences."

"Do you consider yourself a reasonable man, Rabbi?"

"Of course I do."

Murchison made no effort to hide the triumphant tone in his voice as he read from a memo, "Rabbi, you were arrested on February 5, 1970. The charges against you include inciting to riot; threatening bodily harm; trespassing; conspiracy; resisting arrest. You went to jail on those charges." His expression when he looked at David had changed to sad resignation.

"I can explain—"

"Those were hardly the acts of a reasonable man who supposedly wanted to sit down and calmly negotiate in good faith."

David, realizing that any explanation would add fuel to the fire of Murchison's charges, sat stiffly without responding.

"Rabbi?" the senator asked after a long silence. "Don't you have any comment to make?"

"Those were the acts of a foolish man."

"A foolish man, Rabbi? Aren't you as a man of the cloth supposed to be a wise man?"

Struggling not to rise to the bait, David, with a faint smile, said, "Senator, even a fool sometimes says something clever."

Murchison nodded as if in agreement, and the two antagonists smiled at each other. At that moment there was a bond of begrudging admiration between them: David for the subtle cleverness of Murchison's trap, and the senator for the adroitness with which the trap had been avoided.

Murchison quickly returned to the role of prosecuting attorney as he said, "But you left the area, so you don't know for sure who instigated the violence, do you?"

"That's true, but—"

"*Rabbi,* let me tell you what happened. Six men were killed. Fires of supposedly unknown origin destroyed twenty-two company trucks. Property damage ran into the hundreds of thousands. Threats were made to Mr. and Mrs. Tremaine. Though I'm not suggesting that the union was the source of all that violence and destruction, I think any impartial jury would think so."

"I think that depends on whose side that 'impartial' jury sat, don't you, Senator?"

Murchison silenced the burst of laughter from the audience with one savage beat of his gavel. "*Rabbi,* no one can be positive who was behind it. You might be just as prejudiced to your point of view as anyone else."

"It's my belief, Mr. Chairman, that the union had nothing to do with it."

"Oh, I don't doubt that, *Rabbi.* Especially when we understand where your beliefs and philosophy come from." He paused and reached for a dossier, which his aide had readied. "According to this FBI report, your grandfather, Solomon Benjamin, was a communist." He waited for the gasp of surprised reaction from the audience before continuing. Looking up from the report, he casually said, "Your grandfather never denied it. And, quoting from a news story about you in *Time* magazine, you said, '. . . my grandfather was the man who had the greatest influence on my life.' A communist had the greatest influence on your life, *Rabbi?*" he asked sarcastically.

"Being a communist at that time doesn't mean what it means today. You know that as well as I do, Senator." David's voice shook with anger.

Murchison shook his head vehemently. "No, I don't know that. A communist is a communist, Rabbi. And your grandfather, Solomon Benjamin, was a member of the Wobblies, a Moscow-backed union organization that advocated the use of violence to achieve their aims. Sound familiar? Solomon Benjamin was also a member of—"

"Senator Murchison, my grandfather and his activities have nothing to do with this hearing!"

Aware of the focus of the audience on his words, David knew that Murchison was achieving his goal of guilt by association. He attempted to change the thrust of the questions and answers. "Senator, maybe, as you pointed out, all rabbis aren't wise men," he said in a brittle voice. "But in spite of your opinion, I *am* a rabbi. And my stock-in-trade isn't wisdom, but faith and patience. Especially faith. And I do have unlimited faith in my country and its people. And I'm patient enough to know, because of my faith, that this country, its institutions as well as its people, is strong enough to survive many kinds of attacks. Especially those of demagoguery."

For a moment there was a heavy, hushed silence in the hearing room. A reporter, after hurriedly making some notes, lifted a phone and spoke quickly into it. The other senators on the dais hunched forward with renewed interest in the proceedings.

Murchison's close-set eyes narrowed as he wiped a film of perspiration from his forehead. He filled a tumbler from the canister in front of him and downed the water in one long swallow while David sat quietly waiting.

"Your faith and your patience, *Rabbi*, aren't going to protect this country. Do you know what will?" Murchison didn't wait for David's response but answered his own question, directing the words at the attentive reporters at the press table. "It's men like me who are willing to get down in the mud and get dirty fighting for it."

David answered quickly. "Norman Thomas said it much better than I could ever hope to, Senator. He said, '*There has always been a saving common sense about our democracy . . . and the end has always been victory for reason and decency. The struggle against demagoguery scarcely fits the St. George-against-the-dragon myth . . . our democratic St. George goes out rather reluctantly with armor awry. The struggle is confused; our knight wins with no clean thrust of the lance or sword, but the dragon somehow poops out and decent democracy is the victor.*' I hope with all my heart what Mr.

Thomas said is true, Senator Murchison. That before long you poop out."

The audience waited in hushed silence for Murchison to strike back. He picked up the FBI dossier again and said tensely, "I imagine you learned that quotation sitting at the knee of your grandfather, Solomon Benjamin, an admitted communist. It's indicative of the influence he had on you. A known Red who—"

"Senator, I said this before and I'll say it again. My grandfather and his activities have nothing to do with this hearing."

Murchison continued reading from the FBI dossier as if David hadn't spoken. "Every union he was associated with was known to have been infiltrated by Reds and Red sympathizers. Solomon Benjamin was the leader of—"

David rose. The softness and firmness of his voice brought the room to complete silence. "Sir, I have only been told of your reputation. Of your disregard for the truth and of your headline-seeking distortions. I was informed of your demagoguery and of your anti-Semitism. But now that I have met you, those are insignificant traits. Sir, you are a cruel and vindictive man who would, without compunction, sully the reputation of a great man who obviously cannot defend himself. But I will not judge you. I will leave that to a higher authority than myself. I am not here to defend my grandfather or his life's work. I am here to answer questions about specific events at the Tremaine Textile Company's mill. Since that doesn't seem to be the purpose of this hearing, I will no longer attempt to deal with issues that are as defamatory as they are irrelevant. Issues raised only to put you in the headlines and on television. Good day, sir."

David picked up his briefcase and stepped down from the witness table, then forced his way through the throng of newsmen and cameramen who surged forward into the aisle.

"Come back here!" Murchison shouted. Standing up, he pounded the gavel repeatedly and roared, "Rabbi Benjamin, come back here! Damn it, you can't leave here until I'm finished with you!" He was still pounding his gavel as David left the hearing room.

David walked the rainy streets of Washington for hours. Stunned and outraged by the attack on his grandfather, he didn't know or care about the outcome of the hearing. Because of Senator Mendes's warning, he had expected a vituperative attack on himself, but he hadn't been prepared for the vulgar and premeditated assassination of Solomon Benjamin's character.

He found himself in front of the Mayflower Hotel and went into the dimly lit bar and ordered a double scotch. Downing it quickly, he nodded at the bartender to refill the glass. It was the first time in his rabbinical career he had ever done that. He stared at the glass, trying to sort out his feelings. He felt stripped naked and didn't understand why.

He thought of going to his room and calling Naomi, but decided against it because he was too physically and emotionally drained to contend with any justified or unjustified bitching. He didn't know what he needed. Not sympathy. He just wanted some comfort, because he had never felt so desolate before.

He sat slumped at the bar, nursing his second drink and listening mindlessly to the soft buzz of conversation around him. He wondered how these well-dressed men and women would react if they knew who he was and what he had just done. The bartender stared at him, and he lowered his face as if ashamed of something.

A light tap on his shoulder made him spin around nervously.

"Hello, David," said a smiling Sheila Harrington.

"I saw you today!" David exclaimed. "You were fantastic at that hearing!"

"You were there? I didn't know that!"

David pulled out the barstool next to him and ordered her drink ("Martini with a twist and no olive, bartender"). "You were good. Damn good. So believable. So convincing. You played those congressmen like an old pro. That's a side of you I've never seen before. I'm impressed."

Sheila reveled in his praise. This was what she had missed: someone with whom to share her triumph. Excitedly, she relived the event, relating incidents and impressions, asking rhetorically why-didn't-I-say-this? and berating herself for not-having-told-them-that. David listened to her intently, a deep, warm smile on his lips as he enjoyed her exuberance, her uninhibited excitement and pleasure. She rambled on, aware of his concentration as he listened to her, sensing that he was enjoying her victory over the politicians as much as she had.

Talked out, she concluded by saying, "I may have been good, and I may have been effective, but I sure didn't shake people up the way you did. Rabbi, you were something else. By the end of the hearing, I expected the wrath of God to come down and strike Senator Murchison."

"You saw me?"

Sheila nodded and explained the circumstances. As David listened to her recall the emotional ordeal he had been through, his somber mood returned. "How did you find me here?" he asked, almost suspiciously.

She shrugged and drew circles on the mahogany bar with the bottom of her wet glass before quipping, "Do you know how many hotels there are in Washington?"

"And you called every one of them until you found which one I was registered in?" She nodded and he said, "But I could have been anyplace. I might not have returned for hours."

"I'd have waited for you to return," she said matter-of-factly.

"Why?" He demanded an answer. "Why did you want to find me?"

Pondering her answer, she continued to toy with her glass. She couldn't tell him that the look of fury and anguish on his face as he left the hearing room had caused her to ache and to want to reach out and comfort him in some way. That she had returned to her hotel room and had debated whether to leave Washington on the next available flight but that the memory of his tortured expression had kept her from making the reservation.

"Because I thought you might need me," she said in an almost embarrassed voice.

Impulsively, in gratitude, he reached out and took her hand and squeezed it. He struggled with his conscience as they sat quietly for a long moment. The barriers between them were crumbling. They were alone together in a strange city. And she had said, "Because I thought you might need me." He remembered the nasty scene with Naomi the night before he had left for Washington. And he knew that Sheila would never say those words to him again if he failed her now. He sat silently, his conscience battling his desire.

She looked down at their entwined fingers and whispered, "David, you once told me that good things could happen between us if we let them happen. Do you remember saying that to me?"

"I can't make myself forget it. But I also said that I had to find the courage to let them happen."

There was a tremor in her voice as she asked, "David, do you feel as brave as I do?"

The last barrier came down.

He leaned over and kissed her moist lips for the first time.

She closed her eyes and moaned softly: reality had more than equaled anticipation. He could feel her arms trembling as he held them, and at that moment, his guilt buried, he didn't give a damn about anything but her. His inhibitions, his pangs of conscience, his standards of morality and the day's depression and anger were shattered by the thunderous explosion of his desire.

They broke apart and looked at each other. Their need, emotional as well as sexual, was written in their expressions. Sheila waited to hear the words that would bring them one step closer to satisfaction, then realized that his silent awkwardness was caused by inexperience, not lack of passion. She kissed him again and washed away his misgivings.

"Do you want another drink?" he asked.

She shook her head. "David, I don't need another drink."

Holding hands, they left the bar and walked toward the bank of elevators in the lobby.

CHAPTER
14

Their lovemaking was the way they had imagined it should be: skilled and free from tension.

Initially there was a near-frenzied ferocity to their movements. As if they were afraid of losing what they had discovered and were overwhelmed by the urgency to capture every nuance of it. Gradually they drifted into near-imperceptible motion, as if by lingering over every detail of every sensation, they could prolong them.

The only cries came from Sheila: the throaty repetition of "OhmyGod, ohmyGod, ohmyGod." As if the expression were her way of saying she couldn't believe or endure what was happening to her or what she was feeling. Tears filled her eyes. For the first time in her life she was terribly pleased about being a woman.

When it was over, they lay on their sides facing each other with their chins cupped in their hands, the rumpled sheet carelessly draped over their shoulders. He carefully pushed a damp tress off her forehead and said, "I've wanted to do that since the first time I ever saw you."

"And now that you've done it, how do you feel about it?"

Not replying, he leaned forward and kissed her lips. With a gasp of pleasure, she snuggled closer to him. Taking his hand, she guided it to cup her breast.

She lay quiet and fulfilled, acutely aware of her feelings and savoring the moment. She wanted to give even more of herself but she wasn't sure how.

She eased over onto her back and slowly pulled the sheet down her body, closing her eyes as she bared her nakedness to him. She wasn't trying to be seductive, she wasn't even trying to arouse him. She was offering herself to him, saying, *This is me. All of me. I belong to you. Pleasure yourself . . .*

He looked at her face framed within the spread of long, titian hair draped across the pillow. Her eyes were closed, and her soft, contented smile added to her expression of serenity. He delicately kissed her throat, and she murmured with satisfaction.

He feasted on her, devouring every nuance of every discovery. The erection of her nipples, the firm uplift of her full breasts, the small scar under her left breast, the nova-explosion of a beauty mark on her bare right shoulder, the gentle mounding of her rounded stomach, the still-moist glistening patch of her reddish-brown pubic hair, the five moles on her right calf, the feline petiteness of her ankles and toes.

He let his fingers roam delicately, and she whimpered a wind chime of pleasure. He kissed her softly, his lips drifting aimlessly down the length of her body. She sighed, arching her back as tension-tight springs of sensation coiled within her.

His touch on her thighs was feather-light and, as if in invitation, she immediately spread her legs. The promise aroused by the pressure of his mouth and the sweep of his tongue brought a sudden burst of unexpected delighted laughter from her throat.

"Oh my, oh my, that was nice . . ."

He lifted his head and, over the sweet rise and fall of her breasts, looked into her flushed face. Sensing that he was watching her, she opened her eyes and a smile was reborn on her lips. She raised the graceful swan-necks of her arms and held them out to him. She took him into her embrace and they fell asleep, face to face, with his hands cupping her buttocks, his erection thick and deep inside her.

The tickle of her breath in his ear awakened him in the middle of the night. Carefully, he disengaged himself from her embrace and eased out of bed. He sat down in a chair by the window and looked at her sheet-covered body illuminated by moonlight.

Reality contaminated his image of what they had shared.

Moments ticked by and his torments intensified, for he knew that if she were to awaken and look at him with that seductive expression that didn't mean to be seductive and hold her arms out to him, his resolve would vanish and they would make love again.

He chastised himself unmercifully. I have betrayed my wife and my temple. What kind of a rabbi am I? What kind of a man am I? I have committed adultery. I took advantage of opportunity and anonymity and shut out reality. I can make a million excuses and justifications, and none of them are valid. The truth caused his face to contort in self-inflicted pain.

He sat quietly watching her. He was glad of the darkness, for it gave him a feeling of being disconnected. Without light he was faceless and without identity. He wasn't the rabbi of Temple Beth Sinai who had an unhappy wife named Naomi. In the quiet blackness of the characterless hotel room he was a nameless man who had made love to a nameless woman.

Exhausted by the struggle with his thoughts, David fell asleep in the chair.

When he awoke, he discovered Sheila had covered him with a blanket. The bed was empty and he could hear the sound of the shower, then silence. He rubbed his eyes, and the movement caused a newspaper to fall from his lap. He picked it up and was fully awakened by the scream of the headline: DAVID TAKES GOLIATH.

As he read the story, he forgot the anguished thoughts of guilt and recrimination.

Toweling herself in the bathroom, Sheila hugged herself in response to her own delight. She studied her body in the full-length mirror and thought, I'm glad I'm a sexy-looking broad with great tits. She twisted, and looked over her shoulder and added, And with a fantastic ass.

When she stepped back into the bedroom naked, David drew the blanket up to his neck. He was fascinated by her femininity and watched with intense delight as she cupped her breasts into her bra, straightened the seams of her mauve pantyhose and, after tucking in her blouse, deftly slithered her skirt into place.

He enjoyed seeing a woman being a woman, and when she was aware of his pleasure, she deliberately prolonged every movement and gesture, grinning at his smug look of satisfaction and approval.

Fully dressed now, she knelt down between his spread thighs. "Now what?" she asked. Her hand rested lightly on his waist. It was the most natural gesture of belonging that she had ever made toward a man.

He wanted to take her in his arms but resisted the impulse. She saw his expression and realized what had happened to him. His

113

reality had returned. She felt no anger or disappointment, only understanding and compassion. She took his hand and pressed it against her cheek.

"Now we go back to the way it was," he said gently.

"I understand. You made no promises."

"No, you don't understand. I don't want to go back. But I have no choice."

"Yes, I do understand. I'm not asking you to make a choice."

"I'm a rabbi," he said. As if that explained everything.

"I know that." He wished she would at least argue with him.

"I have a wife."

"I know that too."

"And when I go back to Farmington Hills I go back to being a rabbi again. And a husband."

She looked at him sadly, thinking, Everything about us is so good. The way we met, the time we spent together, the way we made love, what we are. Everything. In another time, in another place . . . She didn't allow herself to finish the thought but kissed him softly on the cheek and then walked slowly to the door.

CHAPTER

15

David, packing slowly, let his mind fill with thoughts of Sheila Harrington. His memories were a mixture of guilt and pleasure. He couldn't escape from the hours they had shared and the feelings that had been generated. I can be very righteous now and tell myself I'm going to pretend last night never happened, he told himself, but how will I react if I see her again in Detroit? He shied away from the truth and was relieved when the phone on the nightstand rang.

It was Senator Mendes. "Hello? My big-shot son-in-law? Congratulations."

"What for? Oh, the hearing. Well, I guess I didn't embarrass you, did I?"

"Embarrass me! My phone hasn't stopped ringing since I got back in town. Everybody wants to meet you."

"But I'm going back to Detroit in a couple of hours."

"Oh no you're not. One of those calls was from the White House. The President's giving a reception tonight and you're invited. You're coming as my guest."

"The President wants to meet me?"

"He's not the only one. I can't tell you too much over the phone, but after the reception we're having an important meeting in my office with some people who are coming all the way from Israel to talk to you."

"Senator, I don't understand what's happening. Why all the excitement? Just because I didn't permit Senator Murchison to make a fool of me?"

"It's simple—you're the new hero on the block. The way you handled that demagogue made headlines. Your timing was perfect. Your performance was fresh news on a dull day. The Russians didn't invade Europe today and the Dow Jones remained high and steady, so every major newscast featured you as their lead story this morning. They made you a star, David. A hero. And in this town we're always looking for a new headliner. You're it. So let's cash in on the publicity while we can."

David laughed with embarrassment. "I still don't understand why. But you've never steered me wrong before, so whatever you say, Senator."

"First, you're going to that White House reception tonight. I'll pick you up at eight. Be ready."

"What'll I wear? I didn't pack my tie and tails. All I've got are the clothes I came in."

"You're a rabbi, aren't you? Wear a yarmulkah."

Trying to understand all the excitement, David reread the *Washington Post* story on the front page of the national news section. A subheading read: *Prominent Detroit Rabbi Walks Out of Subcommittee Hearing Investigating Union Violence.* A blurred photo in the second column of the story showed David surrounded by newsmen as he left the hearing. The story was carefully and cleverly worded. Murchison was made to look like an anti-Semitic rabble-rouser, and David, although not the hero of the senator's enthusiasm, emerged as a dignified, justifiably angry and credible witness who had successfully defended his honor.

He wondered if Naomi had seen the news and how she had reacted? The thought of his wife engulfed him with remorse. He reached for the phone. He had committed adultery the night before and he had betrayed her. The compulsion to talk to her increased as he listened to the phone ring.

Naomi answered on the sixth ring. Her voice was distant and muffled.

"Naomi—hello, are you all right?" David's concern was genuine.

"Yes, David, I'm fine. But the phone has been ringing off the wall all morning and I'm tired of answering it."

David winced at the sound of her resentment. "So you heard the news? Did you catch it on television?"

"No, but apparently everyone else did, and they've all called to fill me in about it. So I've heard what happened."

In spite of Naomi's obvious indifference to his success, David couldn't conceal his excitement. "Who called?"

"Everybody. Ben Adelson. Harold Fedder. Brian and Martha. The mayor. The governor. Everybody. I'll tell you about it when you get home tonight."

"I'm not coming home tonight, Naomi, because tonight"—he paused for dramatic effect—"I'm going to a reception at the White House at the President's invitation. With your father, of course."

He suddenly remembered her begging him to take her to Washington, and he wished he hadn't said the words. It was like rubbing salt in the wounds of her disappointment. Her response was even worse than he expected. Disinterested and unemotional. "That's nice. Say hello to my father for me. Have a good time."

David stared at the dead phone and thought, Damn it, why must you always rain on my parade? Naomi, why can't you ever share what I feel? Disappointment, then rage, replaced guilt. He slammed down the receiver and the phone rang almost immediately.

Sheila was crying. "I'm at the airport and I had to call you. I saw you again on the news, and I want you to know that I've never been so proud of knowing anyone as I am proud of knowing you."

David didn't know what to reply.

"You don't have to say anything. I understand. I tried not to call, but I couldn't help myself. I had to tell you how I feel about the kind of man you are."

"What kind of man do you think I am?"

The words poured out. "The kind of man that I could easily fall in love with." She hung up before he could answer.

David sat holding the receiver for a full minute before he put it down. With Sheila Harrington, not only had he betrayed his wife, he had betrayed himself and his God. He had besmirched his trust. As a rabbi, he knew what had to be done, but as a man he didn't know if he could do it.

He was grateful for the coming White House reception because, for the time being, he didn't have to face the inner conflict that was beginning to torment him.

Entering the East Room of the White House, where the reception for the Indian ambassador was being held, David felt ill at ease in the crowd of diplomats and dignitaries. Senator Mendes, aware of this, pointed to the curious faces turned in their direction and said, "Relax—you belong here. You wouldn't have been invited if you didn't."

A tall, distinguished, gray-haired man pushed his way through the throng. "See?" Mendes said encouragingly. "That's the new secretary of state, Leland Thompson. He obviously wants to meet you."

"You look familiar," Thompson said to David. "Have we met before?" He studied David and then his face brightened with recognition. "Of course. You're the rabbi that's been all over the news. You walked out of Murchison's hearing. About time somebody did. I'm surprised he let you get away with it."

David thanked Thompson for the compliment and added, "Maybe he let me get away with it because a fool thinks everybody else is a fool."

The secretary of state laughed loudly and before he moved on, warmly shook David's hand.

The Israeli chargé d'affaires came over, introduced himself and bussed David on both cheeks. "Thanks to you, Rabbi, a good day in the press for Israel. Watching you on television, I was reminded of Moses debating Pharaoh."

"Oh, come now, sir, that's carrying things a little too far. Besides, I'm not sure if that's a compliment or not."

The Israeli was surprised by David's response. "A compliment, of course. Don't you like being compared to Moses?"

"In the world to come, I shall not be asked: *Why were you not like Moses, but rather, Why were you not like David Benjamin?* Yesterday, I think I was like David Benjamin."

After cocking his head to one side and carefully studying David, the Israeli said, "Yes, I think so, too. Rabbi, do you mind if I call you in a few days? I'd like to have lunch with you soon. Get to know you better."

They shook hands and the official left. Senator Mendes took two glasses of champagne off the tray of a liveried waiter and handed one to David. Over the lip of the glass, he eyed David and said, "You really are a dedicated man, aren't you?"

David thought he heard an undertone of skepticism in Mendes's voice.

He sipped his champagne for a moment in order to collect his thoughts, then said, "Senator, everyone is dedicated to that which he desires and chooses. Your desire and choice was politics. I'd say you're very dedicated. My desire has always been the rabbinate. In my way, I'm just as dedicated as you are."

"But there is a difference. You have faith in your God to see you through. Me? Sometimes it's difficult to have faith in your fellow senators. Or even in yourself. My dedication doesn't cover my disillusionment. I realize that you, on the other hand, don't permit that to happen. Is it your faith that sees you through?"

David laughed and the senator looked at him quizzically. "Senator, you just reminded me of something an old rabbi said to me about faith: *I know the Lord will help—but help me, Lord, until you help.*"

Two business-suited men hovering nearby overheard the quotation and laughed along with Senator Mendes. The thinner of the two, who was drinking straight bourbon, introduced himself. "Tom Jenner of Associated Press, Rabbi. Can we get together and talk? An interview for the record."

David shrugged. "What would I have to talk about? Who would be interested in what I have to say?"

"How about something referring to God and truth and the hearing?" Jenner suggested. "Throw in another homily like I just heard you use and we can tie it all together."

A crowd had gathered, and David, looking from face to face, thought, This isn't real. This can't be happening to me. "You're embarrassing me, sir," he said to the newsman.

"I didn't mean to. But, Rabbi, you'd better get used to being in the public eye. At least for a while. A word of advice: learn to endure."

David's face brightened as he said, "Then I'll do what the Talmud cautions and *pray that I will never have to suffer all that I can endure.*"

More laughter coupled with a splattering of applause came from the bystanders. Someone pushed a heavily laden plate of hors d'oeuvres into David's hand and refilled his glass with cold champagne. A beaming Walter Mendes stood with his arm around his son-in-law's shoulders. After some small talk, the crowd suddenly fell silent and moved aside as two burly Secret Service agents cleared a path for the President of the United States.

Richard Nixon held out his hand, then chuckled at David's predicament—the plate of hors d'oeuvres in one hand and the brimming glass of champagne in the other were preventing the rabbi from shaking hands with the chief executive.

"I invited your friend"—the President laughed loudly—"but he didn't show up. Rabbi, you didn't have anything to do with that, did you now?"

"Mr. President, *a guilty man runs when no one is chasing him.*"

"But I'm thankful," Nixon said gravely, "that Senator Murchison didn't keep on interjecting your Jewishness into the hearings. That could have gotten messy."

"Mr. President, maybe he didn't because he realized and accepted that Jews are just like everybody else . . . only more so."

A wry smile crossed Richard Nixon's square jaw. "I wonder if the good senator hasn't learned how to repent. It's my understanding that he goes to church every chance he gets."

"Maybe he would be better off, sir, if he didn't repent so much and sinned less."

Nixon studied David thoughtfully for a moment. Then he took the plate of hors d'oeuvres out of David's hand and presented it to one of the Secret Service agents hovering nearby. David and the President were finally able to shake hands before Nixon disappeared into the crowd.

"Well, Mr. Celebrity who talks with presidents, there are a few more people who want to meet you before we have to go back to my office," Senator Mendes said. He glanced at his watch. "Circulate by yourself for another half hour or so, and after I make the arrangements, I'll come find you to drag you off."

"Who are we meeting in your office, Senator?"

Mendes drew David closer and in a low voice, said, "Two Israeli agents. From Mossad. They want to talk to you."

"What could they want from me, Senator? What could I possibly do for the Israeli Secret Service?"

"Rabbi, after the way you silenced one of Israel's enemies in Washington, plus the way you raise money, I can think of at least five reasons why Mossad would like you to go to work for them. And ten ways in which they could use you."

"Rabbi, we're here because we need your help. It was the senator's suggestion that we talk to you. He says you can do the job we need you to do."

David was unable to see his father-in-law's reaction to the agent's statement because Walter Mendes was seated behind his desk well beyond the ring of light cast by the desk lamp. The rest of the room was barely illuminated. David wondered what other precautions the men from Mossad, who had been introduced as Asher and Leiber, had taken in setting up the interview. Tape recorders? He also wondered if they were armed.

"But I'm just a rabbi. I don't know anything about espionage. I don't see how I can possibly help you."

Asher, the smaller of the two, smiled and said, "Rabbi, don't let your imagination run away with you. Who said anything about espionage? We're here because we need your help in raising money. And with your reputation, you're eminently qualified."

"Raising money?" David asked suspiciously.

"Disappointed, Rabbi?" Leiber, tall and thick-chested, laughed. "You were hoping we'd want you to become involved in something more glamorous than fund-raising?" Asher joined in his partner's joke.

David didn't respond, and Leiber continued. "Rabbi, let me lay it out for you. Israel's Trojan horse is our complete dependency on oil imports for all of our energy needs. The Western democracies supply one hundred percent of our requirements. If Moses had turned to the north instead of to the east when he left Egypt, we wouldn't be in this position. But he didn't, so we must get that oil from the free world. The Arabs know this and have been looking for a way to cut off our oil supply. They've found it. Mossad agents have discovered that sometime in the future the Arabs are planning to stop all oil sales to the West by establishing an embargo. They just need an excuse. Like another war. Rabbi, wars aren't fought just on the battlefield, they're also fought in the marketplace. Politically, they can then justify an oil boycott against every country that is friendly with Israel. Our intelligence suspects that war will happen within the next eighteen months."

His partner, Asher, his expression determined, finished the explanation. "But we haven't been sitting on our hands doing nothing, Rabbi. A nuclear power plant will free us from dependency and vulnerability. Three years ago we started construction. We ran into the same problems every country has in building a nuclear facility. Prohibitive, skyrocketing costs. When we broke ground in the Negeb, it was estimated that it would take a little under a billion dollars to bring the plant on line. We're still a year and a half away from completion, and the revised cost estimate is now over three billion dollars. Originally, the Israeli government underwrote the costs. But we're tapped out now. You know the state of the Israeli economy; we don't have that kind of money to put into a power plant, no matter how badly it's needed. Rabbi, that's where you come in. We need to raise around nine hundred million from private dona- tions in the next year to finish that plant. Will you help us?"

The senator spoke for the first time. "David, this isn't just for a good cause like the United Way. This is for the survival of Israel. You're a part of this, whether you contribute or not. We all are."

A sense of his newly discovered power and prestige flowed through David. Though he liked the feeling, the enormity of the secret Mos- sad plan caused him to say, "Of course I'd like to help you. But I don't see how I can. Nine hundred million dollars is out of my league. I've only been a fund-raiser for a little over seven months."

"Rabbi, we're not asking you to raise all of it," Leiber interrupted. "We've contacted many, many people all over the world, in France, England, West Germany, Canada, South America, Asia, who have agreed to help us. Each will raise a portion of that money. Men like Senator Mendes are helping us to find those people. You're one of several in this country we want to use. In seven months you've proven yourself a big fund-raiser. That's why we're asking you to help. Over the next eighteen months, we'd like you to try to raise around twenty-five million dollars for us."

Doubtfully, David said, "I want to help, but I still don't see how I can. There's a limit to how many fund-raising benefits I can hold in a year. Even the UJA or the United Way or the Red Cross has only one or two a year. How much do you think I can raise that way? Certainly not twenty-five million."

"You're right, Rabbi, you can't raise the money through benefits or charity affairs. We want you to use your contacts, the big phi- lanthropists in Detroit, in Cleveland, in New York, and tell them what we're up against. Tell them the truth. After you make them understand the urgency, they'll dig deep. In 1948 when Israel be- came a state, Ben Adelson and Meyer Loeb donated a quarter of a million dollars apiece. They've done it before to preserve the integrity of Israel and they'll do it again. It won't take too many Ben Adelsons and Meyer Loebs to raise that twenty-five million. Four or five such donations a month will do it."

Though he admired the simplicity of the intelligence agents' plan, David was still hesitant. "But I don't know that many people capable of donating two hundred and fifty thousand dollars."

"But I do," the senator interrupted, "and I'll introduce you to them. I can't get personally involved because I'm a United States senator who chairs a couple of subcommittees dealing with Israel.

But I know people in Los Angeles, Dallas, Atlanta, Pittsburgh, Denver, all over this country, who would make the donations we need. And if I don't know them, I'll find someone who does, and if I have to, I'll call in a few IOUs and twist a few arms to get you the introductions. With your reputation, David, it won't be as tough as you might think."

"Four a month is all you need, Rabbi," Asher chimed in. "That comes to a million dollars every thirty days. In a year and a half we'd have our money."

The senator came out of the shadows and sat down on the front edge of his desk between Asher and Leiber. The three of them intently watched David, waiting for his decision. Slowly, he nodded and said, "I make no promises, but I'll do my best."

"Thank you, Rabbi. We hoped that's what you would say. And your best is damned good," Leiber responded. Then, rubbing his hands as if in anticipation, he added, "Now, here's the way it'll work. The money you raise can't go through the normal channels of different banks all over the country and then the overseas transferring of those funds to an Israeli bank. We suggest using your brother-in-law's bank. He's helped you before, maybe he'll do it again. If he agrees, have him convert the donations into cash. We'll pick it up every four to five weeks and get it to Israel in diplomatic pouches."

"You'd use Brian McGraw?" David asked.

"We'll use anyone who can help us," Asher said. "We've checked McGraw out and he seems okay. He's worked with you in the past and you've had no troubles. So we have no objections to using him."

"How do I know he'll agree?"

"Ask him."

CHAPTER

16

Immediately upon his return from Washington, David called Brian.
Told by Martha that his brother-in-law would be out of town for a
week on business, his sense of urgency regarding the Mossad money-
raising plan abated. The postponement opened the gate to an avenue
of thought that he had been able to block only because of the priority
of meeting with Brian. Now back in Detroit, he couldn't forget what
had happened at the Mayflower Hotel in Washington with Sheila
Harrington. When he had returned home, if Naomi had responded
to his triumph at the hearing with anything but an indifferent shrug
and a casually sarcastic "This time you were lucky. But don't ever
put yourself, or me, in that position again." He might have been
able to pigeonhole the one-night affair. Instead, remembering
Sheila's emotionally charged phone call on the following day, he
allowed himself to romanticize their lovemaking and to magnify his
need for her.

He vacillated between wanting to see her and knowing he shouldn't
see her, and struggled with the constancy of his thoughts about her.
And though he had vowed that he would never see her again, he
found himself looking for a legitimate excuse to cause their paths
to cross. He knew what he was doing, but because he couldn't keep
her out of his mind, he continued to conjure up accidental meetings
and chance encounters. It was what he was, not what he wanted,
that prevented him from picking up the phone and calling her.

He was a rabbi, so committed that he didn't have a single doubt as to the parameters of his role.

David was grateful when Brian returned from out of town. After dinner, in the paneled library of Brian's home, he could hear Martha and Naomi laughing over the protestations of the two young McGraw children, his nieces, who for over an hour had been fighting being sent off to bed. The youngsters barged into the room, followed by the women, and clambered into David's lap as if hoping their uncle would override their mother's orders. Surrendering, they kissed him good night. David envied Brian as he watched them being herded out of the room.

After closing the door, his brother-in-law brought him out of his reverie. "You had something important to discuss with me?"

David sketched his role in the Mossad plan and explained the need for Brian's participation. Brian listened intently, and when David was finished, he said, "Let me go over it to make sure I understand what you expect me to do. You're going to raise money from private donations for the next year and a half. You'll turn those donations over to me and, through the bank, I'm to convert them into cash. The money is to be stored in a safe-deposit box in the bank's vault until it's picked up by those two Mossad agents. They plan to make their pickups every thirty days and to take the money out of the country in diplomatic pouches. Have I got it right?"

David nodded and said, "I know it's a lot to ask, to use your bank to convert those checks into cash and then to hold it until it's picked up, but will you help me?"

"When you were appointed as interim rabbi over eight months ago, I said I'd help you in any way I could. Have I lived up to my word?"

"Without your help, those fund-raisers and benefits I ran would have been a disaster, Brian. But this is different. This time there are no fund-raisers; the Mossad is involved, and when you come right down to it, I'll be using you because of your bank connection."

"Am I complaining?"

"No, Brian, of course not. It's not in you to complain. But I feel awkward asking for your help again."

"Don't. I'm not going to stop helping you now. Besides, thanks to you, David, I feel I'm contributing to something worthwhile.

What happens to Israel has become important to me. I want to do whatever is in my power to help."

"I'm glad you feel that way, Brian. Then I feel like we're a team and we're in this together."

"Partner, when do we start?"

"Immediately. I'll be going to Los Angeles next week to meet with two studio heads, and I expect to leave with half a million dollars. The following week I'll be going down to Miami."

Brian nodded and said, "You forget about everything except having a successful trip. Leave the rest up to me. I'll watch that money like it's my own until it's picked up by those Mossad agents."

The first pickup had been made thirty days ago, and Leiber and Asher had been given close to one million dollars by Brian. A month later, the agents appeared again in the bank to make the second collection.

"I'm Mr. Leiber," the Mossad agent said to Brian's secretary. "This is Mr. Asher. Mr. McGraw is expecting us."

She smiled with forced pleasantness at the two stone-faced men who didn't respond. "Oh yes, Mr. Leiber, I have a message for you from Mr. McGraw. He's going to be a little late. You're to wait until he returns."

The agents stiffened suspiciously. Professionals, the slightest deviation from routine caused them to react with caution. They had phoned Brian and made the appointment. Why was he late? They moved out of the secretary's earshot and talked quietly for a few moments, nodding in mutual agreement at a previously arranged fall-back plan.

The secretary watched them apprehensively and then stood up to object when Asher walked around her desk and pushed his way into Brian's office. The look on Leiber's face silenced her protest and she slowly sank back into her chair. She thought of picking up the phone and calling the bank security guard but her fear overcame her anxiety. But I'll tell Mr. McGraw about them, she said to herself. He'll take care of them.

"He's not there," Asher said as he came out of Brian's office. "Neither is the money."

"Where is Mr. McGraw?" Leiber asked the secretary. She shook her head quickly. "He's somewhere around the bank." If she had known she would have told them. Leiber knew she was telling the

126

truth and smiled reassuringly at her before adding, "When he comes in, tell him to wait. We'll be back."

She watched them walk through the savings and loan rotunda, fading into the crowds of customers like two shadows. The phone on her desk rang and her attention was momentarily diverted. They had disappeared when she looked for them again.

They had gone down the marble steps to the vault that housed the safe-deposit boxes. Outside the strongroom, Leiber said, "I don't think he'd pull anything. From what we've found out about him, he doesn't have the guts. But when there's that much loose money around, anybody can be tempted. I don't like the way this is going down."

"Maybe we shouldn't take any chances? Let's get the rabbi over here to get us the money. He's got a key to the vault. Besides, we can't wait, we've got a plane to catch."

Leiber looked at his watch. "We'll give McGraw another fifteen minutes. You go back to his office and I'll stay here. If he doesn't show, we'll get the rabbi. Let's keep him out of this as long as we can."

As Asher started for the stairs, the door to the safe-deposit box room opened. Brian came out and staggered in surprise as the Israeli agents pushed him back into the vault.

"What the hell are you doing!" he yelled, trying to smother his sudden surge of fear.

"Where have you been?" Asher demanded. "We made an appointment. Why didn't you keep it? You knew we were coming, so why weren't you waiting for us?"

"Personal business," Brian answered. He found the courage to add, "You're not the only people I deal with. And I resent your pushing me around. I'm not your flunky. I'm doing you a favor. I'm going to tell my brother-in-law about this."

Without waiting for a response, Brian went to the wall of safe-deposit boxes. Removing one from its compartment, he placed it with feigned indifference on the high table in the center of the room. The two agents watched him suspiciously as he unlocked the strongbox with a grandiose gesture. "There's your money," he said magnanimously. "Nine hundred and seventy-five thousand dollars."

He dumped neatly packaged bundles of bills onto the table, along with a list of the names of the contributors and the amounts of their donations. Leiber glanced at him and then with a curt nod of his head, said to his partner, "Count it."

"What's the matter, don't you trust me?" Brian asked indignantly. Leiber looked at him contemptuously.

Brian, realizing how they regarded him, leaned with pretended nonchalance against the wall. While he watched Asher slowly counting, he trembled as he thought, They're as bad as Frank Terhanti. They'd rough me up without giving it a second thought. Maybe even worse.

"It's all here," Asher finally said to Leiber.

"What did you expect?" Brian asked.

Leiber, his eyebrows furrowed in thought, looked at Brian and then at the bundles of money. He went to the table and took a bill from a packet and held it up to the light. "It's not counterfeit," he said to Asher. Turning to Brian, he said, "We get nervous when someone has control of our money for thirty days. So a word of advice. Don't ever be tempted, Mr. McGraw. Because if any of our money is ever missing—"

As if hypnotized, Brian asked, "What'll happen?"

Leiber smiled and with a sad shake of his head said, "Mr. McGraw, you don't ever want to find out."

Unknowingly, the Mossad agents had planted a seed. Back in his office, Brian nursed the growing idea. Though his first reaction when David had involved him had been to tell Frank Terhanti that he had a new source for laundering their dirty cash, for some reason he hadn't. Even though he had known it would have been worth a bonus. Now, prowling his office because he was too excited to sit still, he realized why he had kept his silence. For the first time large amounts of money was going through his hands and Frank Terhanti had no way of knowing about it.

The Mossad agents inadvertently had given Brian the key. Leiber had said it: "We get nervous when someone has control of our money for thirty days." Brian now realized he could use the money or any part of it for one month without anyone knowing about it. It was the situation he had been looking for since he had gone to work for Frank Terhanti. The opportunity to make a profit with someone else's money and to stash it away in a numbered Swiss bank account. He began to believe that at the end of the eighteen months, he could have the five hundred thousand dollars that would give him the courage to walk out on Frank Terhanti. He knew exactly how he was going to make it. The opportunity had been there for almost a year. He had never had the courage or the bankroll to take advantage of it before.

He went over the plan again and again until satisfied. Then he dialed a number in Los Angeles. "Sonny, this is Brian," he said. "That deal we talked about? Is it still open? Good. You'll have my money in a few weeks. I'll let you know when."

Sonny Thornton, a football buddy during Brian's college days and now a tight end for the Rams, had approached him with the deal the last time he had been in Detroit. Thornton had access to unlimited supplies of Mexican marijuana and cocaine. He needed financing and had come to Brian, offering to front the deal for fifty percent of the profits. Brian's only participation would be to bankroll part of the buy. After Thornton made the purchase, it would take about a week to cut and package the dope before reselling it. Brian would then receive his share of the profits and his investment would be returned. He had been tempted to use some of Frank Terhanti's dirty money to bankroll Sonny Thornton, but because he only had a week's leeway to use the unlaundered cash and get it back from Thornton before washing it and making the delivery to Terhanti, he had felt the risks were too great. Reluctantly, he had had to turn down the deal.

Now, with about a month to manipulate unlimited funds, Brian believed the risk had been eliminated. Satisfied, he returned to his desk and went over the scenario again. He would have the use of the Israeli money for eighteen months. Enough time to bankroll five or six deals and make a profit of about a half million dollars, which would be banked in the numbered Swiss account until he was ready to have it out with Frank Terhanti.

He went over the risks. That he would be dealing in drugs was dangerous, but he convinced himself that because he had nothing to do with the deal, Sonny Thornton would be taking all the risks. He thought of what would happen to him if Frank Terhanti ever found out and shivered. But remembering Leiber's threat, he believed he was safer if found out by the Mafia boss.

He spent the rest of the afternoon debating with himself. Then he flipped a few pages of the desk calendar and circled the date. It was the day that David was scheduled to return from Atlanta and turn over donations of a half million dollars to him.

Brian was in the drug business.

CHAPTER
17

Three months had passed, and David, after trips to Los Angeles, Miami and Atlanta, had raised a little over three million dollars. Leiber and Asher, appearing once a month as planned, picked up the donations, which Brian had converted into cash. Initially, because of the importance of the fund-raising to Israel, David had made the operation his highest priority. But gradually, as the scheme seemed to be working to perfection and because of the pressures caused by his role, his monthly fund-raising trips around the country became just another item on his busy agenda.

After his return from Washington and the confrontation with Senator Murchison, he began to emerge as a rabbi of national prominence. His performance before the subcommittee had triggered newspaper and news magazine features about him. His appearance on several national television panel shows further enhanced his image. As he developed an international reputation, invitations were extended to join civil liberties and human rights commissions. Sought out by political leaders, he began to make his own Washington connections without the support of his father-in-law, Senator Mendes. In his own right, Rabbi David Benjamin was becoming a man to be reckoned with.

Members of his own congregation regarded him somewhat differently: first, he was their rabbi, then a national figure. Most of the congregants were pleased by his notoriety because it reflected well on Temple Beth Sinai. Others were annoyed because the requirements of his public role meant that he had to travel a great deal and so spent less time on the affairs of the temple and their needs. In spite of the schism between the two factions, rumors began to spread throughout the congregation that because of his reputation and image, Rabbi David Benjamin was going to be offered a contract as head rabbi.

His relationship with Naomi, accelerated by the demands on his time, which caused him to be away from home more frequently, continued to deteriorate. Not comprehending that she was feeling more and more shut out and isolated from him, David instead sensed a hidden resentment of his growing prestige. He expected an outburst of elation, or warm compliments at the least, over the news that he might be offered the head rabbiship by the board and was appalled when Naomi remarked sarcastically, "If that's true, then Rabbi Fedder must be turning in his grave."

He couldn't help it: the hurt and indifference caused by her vicious, bitchy jab forced him to think of Sheila and how she would have reacted.

He couldn't escape Sheila's presence because circumstance forced them together at the monthly meeting of the Citizens Committee on City Planning. He had no way of knowing that because she had the same fantasies as he, Sheila had to force herself to attend the Tuesday night meetings.

The sessions were an ordeal for both of them. Seated across the conference table, and though awkwardly restrained by the forced formality of their acknowledgment of each other in public, they pretended an indifference neither of them felt. Occasionally, their eyes would meet surreptitiously and for that instant the masks would be replaced by their true feelings. At those moments, he knew that she wanted him as much as he wanted her. But he also knew that because of who and what he was, there was nothing he could do about it.

Sam Bender, the Board of Trustees president, turned the meeting over to Ben Adelson.

"As head of the Selection Committee, let me bring you up to date. For the past eleven months, while Rabbi Benjamin has been our interim rabbi, we have continued the search for a head rabbi. Though we have interviewed several applicants, we have yet to find a qualified spiritual leader. In less than thirty days, Rabbi Benjamin's contract as our interim rabbi will expire. The purpose of this meeting tonight is to discuss his future with Temple Beth Sinai."

"What future?" Harold Fedder asked. "You're not going to offer him another year's contract as interim rabbi, are you?"

Adelson shook his head. "No, Harold, I'm not. But not for the reasons you think. I'm not going to offer it because Rabbi Benjamin won't accept another year's contract as our interim rabbi. He's outgrown that role. I know for a fact that four other congregations want him to be their head rabbi and are waiting to hear our decision before making him an offer."

"He might be right for any other congregation," Fedder argued. "But he's still not the rabbi for us. Now that I've tried to work with him for almost a year, I'm more convinced of that than ever."

"Harold, you're entitled to your opinion," Adelson responded. "It's no secret how you feel about him. But leaving personal feelings aside, all I know is that because of the way he conducted himself at that congressional hearing, Rabbi Benjamin is now an important rabbi. Wherever I go, I hear good things about him. His reputation as a fund-raiser for Israel opens every door. He even has an open invitation to meet with Prime Minister Begin whenever he's in Israel. He's becoming as well known in Washington as he is in Detroit. And I've lost track of the number of committees and panels he serves on. All of which reflects on this congregation. Therefore, it is my recommendation, and the recommendation of the Selection Committee, that we offer Rabbi Benjamin the head rabbiship. If we don't, we're going to lose him."

"Head rabbiship!" Fedder interrupted angrily. "You can't be serious!"

Meyer Loeb, seated in the audience, rose wearily to his feet. "Gentlemen, may I say a few words?" he asked. The board members quieted because of their respect for the older man's judgment and influence. "Of course, Meyer," Sam Bender said. "The floor is yours."

"Harold, you're right," he said softly to Fedder. "Rabbi Benjamin is very young and very inexperienced for a position of such importance. And I once thought as you do. But how do you measure the worth of a man? By his age? By his experience? No, by the results he has achieved. Rabbi Benjamin's achievements impress me. I'm not impressed by his notoriety or his growing fame; I'm too old to be impressed by imagery. I care only about substance, not shadow. The rabbi has done good things here. He is constantly trying to bring the young back into the temple. People listen to him because they know he cares about them. He has become a part of our personal as well as our spiritual lives. Yes, Harold, admittedly he is becoming controversial. And why? Because he is not afraid to express an unpopular position on the issues that we face. With all due respect, Harold, not even your grandfather would do that. Rabbi Fedder, God bless his soul, chose the easy way out by straddling the fence and not taking a public stance on controversial issues. Rabbi Benjamin is a good man, a good rabbi. He is a strong man, a strong rabbi. This congregation needs such a man and such a rabbi. So it is my feeling that in spite of his age and limited experience, and in spite of your personal differences, Harold, we offer Rabbi Benjamin the post of head rabbi."

Meyer Loeb sat down and a contemplative silence spread throughout the room. It was broken by Harold Fedder. "Meyer, though I respect what you say, I still must object to Rabbi Benjamin's being considered as our head rabbi. To me, he is self-serving and ambitious, and I feel he is using this congregation as a stepping-stone to further his ambitions. Some of us have let his popularity blind us. And though there are many who are impressed by his growing fame because it reflects on Temple Beth Sinai, it is the congregation who must pay for it. The outside demands on his time cause him to spend less and less time with us. More and more frequently, he simply is not here when someone needs him. More and more frequently, he is forced to turn over his duties to Assistant Rabbi Simon. My grandfather, in spite of his shortcomings, was always here, Meyer. He was the rabbi for and of this temple. It is my belief that we will never be able to say that about Rabbi Benjamin."

The discussion continued for another hour before Ben Adelson said, "We've heard all the pros and cons so I'm making a motion that we offer a one-year contract to David Benjamin to be our head rabbi."

The motion was seconded and voted upon. David Benjamin was chosen to be the next head rabbi of Temple Beth Sinai by a 9 to 6 vote.

Elated, David hung up the phone. He burst into the living room looking for Naomi, who was sitting quietly in the overstuffed chair knitting a sweater for her father.

Triumphantly he announced, "That was Ben Adelson. I've just been offered the head rabbiship and I've accepted!"

She had but one thought: to hurt him as she imagined he had

hurt her. She knew that his excitement and happiness made him vulnerable, so she looked at him and said in a voice devoid of emotion, "That's nice."

Memories of her many put-downs flashed through David's mind. Shaking with rage, he stood over her and shouted, "That's all you can say? 'That's nice'?"

She knew he was right to be angry, but she couldn't force herself to say the laudatory words he so badly needed to hear. Her hands shook, and the ball of yellow yarn rolled to the floor. David picked it up and, with careful self-control, handed it to her. She thought of holding on to his hand but couldn't do that either.

He went over to the mantelpiece and toyed aimlessly with some porcelain animal figures. Because his focus was on Naomi, he dropped one and it broke on the brick hearth. Looking at her defiantly, he dared her to say something, but she shrugged as if it didn't matter. While he busied himself picking up the pieces, Naomi thought, Now you're beginning to know how it feels to be disappointed. To have your expectations shattered as you've shattered mine . . .

He carried the fragments into the kitchen cupped in his hands. When he returned, her head was lowered and she seemed to be concentrating on the knitting. Watching her, he forced himself to calm down. His exuberance began to blossom again and he thought, I don't want to fight with her tonight. I want to share this with her. To make her feel what I feel.

He began to pace, trying to think of something to say or do that would change her mood. He stopped in front of her and, gently taking the knitting needles out of her hands, tried to tug her out of the chair. "C'mon, Naomi, let's go out and celebrate. This is what we dreamed about before we were married. Being the head rabbi of a congregation like Beth Sinai. This is what you sacrificed so much of yourself for. And now it's happened for us. So let's go out and celebrate."

She brought him back to earth by saying, with a defiant shake of her head, "It didn't happen for us, it happened for you. I've nothing to celebrate. It was all your dream, not mine. What does your being the head rabbi of Beth Sinai mean to me? Not a thing—because it doesn't change anything. I'm still just the rebbetzin."

He dropped her hands as though singed by her anger. "I don't understand what's happened to you. Tell me what's wrong."

"If you don't know, I don't want to talk about it." She snatched the needles from his hand and began to knit again.

"Damn you to hell!" he snarled as he wheeled away from her. He stormed out of the living room, and she cringed when she heard the front door slam. Then a smug smile crossed her face and she casually began to count stitches . . .

David drove aimlessly until he came to a small shopping center in downtown Birmingham. He saw a phone booth, which seeemed to give him a sense of purpose, stopped his car next to it and hurried to make a call. The phone rang incessantly and he waited impatiently before someone answered.

"Sheila, this is David. I want to see you. It's important that I see you."

"Of course. Where shall I meet you?"

"I'll come to your place."

"Are you sure you want to do that, David? Someone might see you."

"I don't give a damn. I'll be there right away."

"I'll be waiting."

Sitting on the edge of the deep sofa, ankles crossed, Sheila watched David. She was dressed simply in a tan cashmere sweater and contrasting pleated skirt. He opened the large, sliding glass door that led out onto her balcony. Leaning on the parapet, he stared out at the night. Sheila came up quietly beside him. He could smell the sweet aroma of her perfume as he turned to face her.

"David, help me to understand," she said softly. "Nothing's changed. You're still married. You're still a rabbi. Now you're even the head rabbi. So why are you here and what do you want from me? Just to get laid, is that all?"

"That's part of the reason," he admitted sheepishly. "I can't forget that night in Washington."

"Neither can I," she agreed with a lecherous smile. Her expression changed. "But that's not enough of a reason. Are you here because you're having troubles with your wife and you think you can get from me what you don't get from her? That you can use me as a substitute?"

"I don't know," he said helplessly. "That could be the reason I'm here. I don't think so, but I'm not sure."

"Well, that isn't what I want to hear, but at least it's an honest answer." She paused and then added, "David, if things ever work out between us, you'll learn that I'm too much of a woman to settle for being a substitute."

They studied each other until he said, "Let me ask you a question. Maybe your answer will tell me what I need to know about myself."

"Shoot. I have nothing to hide."

"Why did you let me in tonight? You knew that nothing had changed. I told you that over the phone. To an outsider, we'd look like two horny sons of bitches who only want to screw. Is that how you think of me? Is that why you let me in here tonight?"

She burst out laughing and then said, "David, you told me the truth so I'm going to tell you the truth. I let you in here tonight because you're the most interesting, most fascinating and exciting man I've ever met. You turn me on like nobody ever has. I admire you and I respect you. There's something about you, I can't define it, that's so right for me that I'm not going to give you up without giving you every chance to work this out. And if I have to give you up, at least I'll be able to walk away knowing I gave it every opportunity."

"And you can live with that?"

"Damn right I can. Can you live with that?"

"I'll try," he said, "because I feel the same way about you. But I make no promises. I'm scared shitless, but I'll try."

There was nothing more to say. They had both made a single step toward some kind of a commitment. At that moment, neither one of them cared about where it might lead. She slowly unbuttoned the front of her sweater. She was unaware of the chill of the night air on her bare shoulders as she stood childlike in front of him and let him undress her.

CHAPTER
18

"So how much money are you going to ask the board to help you raise at this special meeting you're having?" Ben Adelson asked.

David, behind his desk, answered, "What makes you so sure that I'm even going to mention money to the boar, Ben?"

"Because I know rabbis. Especially you. And when a rabbi asks for a special meeting of the Board of Trustees, it's because he wants to raise money. So how much are we talking about? And what's it for? The how much is more important than the what's it for."

David laughed and said, "Come to the meeting and find out. And one more thing, Ben . . ."

"What's that?"

"Don't forget to bring your checkbook."

Adelson exploded with laughter and then shook an admonishing finger at David. "See, you don't fool me." He paused and after studying David for a moment, said, "It's for that senior citizen project of yours, isn't it?"

"It's a good cause, Ben. I need all the help I can get."

"But, Rabbi, it's more than just a cause to you. It's a compulsion."

David had become involved with the project of a home for the elderly shortly after his appointment as interim rabbi. Still new to the Detroit area and unsure of his position, he had given it little more than cursory participation. But as his power and prestige grew, he became more active. Soon recognized as an authority on the medical and social effects of aging, he often appeared as an expert witness at congressional and Senate hearings considering proposed legislation.

As his personal stature and importance blossomed, David became a champion of the aged. Using his prestige and his rabbinical role, he began to dominate the Detroit board charged with building a small home for the elderly. Appointed chairman by dint of his charisma, his knowledge, his experience and his energy, he forced approval of the program's expansion. What was once a small project had developed into a massive program to build a vast senior citizens' complex. The center became identified with him, and even after completion he continued to be the driving force behind its operation.

David began to wonder if Ben Adelson wasn't right. Had the cause become a compulsion because it had become a monument to his ego?

He was relieved when Florence's call over the intercom interrupted his thoughts. "It's Mr. Loeb, Rabbi," she said. "Shall I tell him you're too busy to see him? He doesn't have an appointment."

David smiled fondly. Meyer Loeb, who dropped by his office at least three times a week, never made an appointment. The old man, a patriarch of the congregation, loved to debate the finer points of recondite meaning in the sometimes vague and obtuse writing of the Torah and the Talmud. David usually looked forward to the give-and-take discussions, but at the moment he was too distraught to spend even fifteen minutes arguing abstractions with an old man who had nothing else to do.

It had been two months since he had established his relationship with Sheila, and though intellectually he had been able to accept the separation of self, especially when he was with her, emotionally he was being haunted by the specter of his dual role. Though he tried not to show it, Sheila was aware that he lived with the fear of exposure, and suspected that because of the masquerade, he was castigated by his conscience and felt he was walking a precarious tightrope. When he was alone, the constant battle between his passions and his conscience exhausted him.

He started to tell Florence to make some acceptable excuse but then thought, Why not? With Meyer I live in the comfortable past, not in the disturbing present. "Send Meyer in," he told Florence briskly. "And no interruptions until he leaves."

With genuine warmth, David greeted the old man, who smiled at him out of sad watery eyes set in a round, time-etched, creviced face. There was a mutual affection between the old man and the young rabbi, born of an awareness of the other's love of and pride in the cultural and religious heritage that united them. To Meyer Loeb, his Jewishness was not merely a way of life—it was his whole life. He believed that David's approach was the same.

Their frequent meetings were always informal, and Loeb eased himself carefully into a deep chair away from the desk. David waited patiently for the old man to make his usual provocative statement about some accepted point of theology that would set the tone of their friendly argument.

"Today I'm not here to discuss how many angels can dance on the head of a pin," the old man said. "Today I'm here to talk about my future daughter-in-law."

"Stephen's getting married!" David said with sincere pleasure. "Mazel tov!"

To Meyer Loeb, his son Stephen was the ultimate gift from his God. Childless until he was forty-one, Meyer was convinced that the birth of a son, twenty-eight years ago, had happened because God had been testing the surety of his beliefs and convictions and He had been pleased. The reward to the barren couple, who had given up hope of ever having children, was a son. Loeb treated the growing boy like a treasure. And now, at sixty-nine, he was to receive another blessing.

But David was aware of the sadness in the old man's face, which contradicted the expression he had expected to see. He waited patiently until, with obvious reluctance, Meyer Loeb said, "Rabbi, you're going to find out anyway, so I might as well tell you now. My future daughter-in-law is a shiksa."

Understanding Loeb's anguish, David forced himself not to react. Jewish law was what Meyer Loeb lived by. To Loeb, a Jewish family was the foundation of his Jewish heritage, and a new family began life together with a traditional wedding performed by a rabbi in a temple. Stephen Loeb's marrying a non-Jew was more than a violation of his Jewishness to his father. It was an insult to over five thousand years of time-honored continuity born of custom and culture.

David shared the old man's pain because it was also his pain. He understood the demands of his Jewishness more deeply than he ever had before. Demands which he realized were set in concrete and etched in stone. And which, in spite of the charade he was playing with Sheila, could never be denied.

Loeb felt compelled to make an explanation, as if by spelling it out, he too might understand. "They met when he was a resident at Mt. Carmel Hospital, where she's a nurse. At first we didn't pay much attention because all his life Stephen has been telling us about this girl or that girl that he was in love with. But when we realized how serious he was, we had to accept the truth. Oh, what we've been through with that boy. We've cried over him until we were out of tears, we've argued with him until we were blue in the face, we've begged him on our knees not to go through with it. But he wouldn't listen. Instead, he tells us that though he understands how we feel, he's sorry he has to hurt his mother and me, but that he loves the girl deeply and she loves him. That they're going to get married even if it means going to City Hall. Rabbi, what would you have done if that had been your son and he tells you he's in love with a shiksa and he wants to marry her?"

David shifted uneasily. How could he answer that question honestly? Instead, he sidestepped it. "Why didn't you send him to me, Meyer? I probably wouldn't have changed his mind, but at least I could have talked to him."

And what would you have said? David asked himself. What set of standards and rules and laws would you have held up to Stephen Loeb? Those that you apply to yourself?

"I tried to get him to come to you, but he wouldn't do it," Loeb continued. "And because I was so desperate, I did something I'm ashamed to admit. I went to Mt. Carmel to see the girl and I tried to bribe her to leave my Stephen alone. I'm telling you this because you're my rabbi and I want you to understand and to forgive me."

The need for absolution intensified the agony in the old man's face, and David looked away. A Talmudic expression seared into his conscience. *You can look into someone else's eyes, but not into someone else's heart.* He took both of Loeb's hands in his and, in a strained voice, said, "Of course I understand. Meyer, there is nothing to forgive you for."

Relieved, Loeb continued. "I went there wanting to hate her, but, Rabbi, I couldn't. She's everything my Stephen said she was. Do you know what that mensch did? Because she understood what I was going through and what Stephen's being married in the temple means to me and his mother, she took me in her arms and we had a good cry together. And she's the one who maybe figured out a way to make this come out all right."

"What did she suggest?" David asked guardedly.

"She wants to convert. Says she's a half-assed Catholic anyway, so why not? Now you know why I'm here. To ask you to accept her as a convert."

Shaking his head, David said, "Meyer, you know the answer to that as well as I do. I can't accept her as a proselyte if her reason for wanting to convert is so she can be married to Stephen in this temple to please you and because she claims to be a half-assed Catholic. The test is not one of desire but one of faith. I'm sorry, Meyer, but given the circumstances, I can't help you."

"David, my good friend, my good Rabbi, I'm glad you said that. I understand and I agree with you. All I'm asking is that you meet with her. Maybe then you'll change your mind about her. Like I did. Will you do that for me?"

"That's the least I can do for you, Meyer. Bring her to the Shabbat service tomorrow night and I'll talk with her. But please, don't get your hopes up too high. Though I wish I could, I can't promise you a miracle."

Years later David would remember the words and the event. For at that Friday night Shabbat service, though David was unaware of it at the time, a miracle did begin to unfold.

CHAPTER

19

It was the Sabbath and David was at peace. The one-hour service welcoming the Sabbath was the only time all week when he didn't feel as if he were leading a double life. From sundown Friday to sundown Saturday, he was unequivocally and solely a rabbi whose only purpose was to lead his congregation to reaffirm and renew the ancient covenant and to embrace their Jewishness. His ego was at rest and his spirit was satisfied. Nothing ever interfered or intruded on David's observance of the Sabbath ritual that made him feel so linked to his God.

Organ music played softly as he sat, with head bowed, alone on the bema. He was dressed in his black robe; a tallis, the prayer shawl given to him as a Bar Mitzvah present by his grandfather, was draped over his shoulders and an ornately brocaded yarmulkah from Israel capped the back of his head.

His concentration was interrupted by the murmurings of congregants slowly filling the sanctuary. Trying to recapture his reverent thoughts and mood, he fixed his eyes on the twelve twenty-six-foot-high stained-glass windows. Almost every synagogue, no matter what its design or architecture, contains either twelve windows, representing the twelve tribes of Israel, or fourteen, commemorating the fourteen major Jewish holidays. Looking at the windows generated a sense of unity and belonging in David. He knew that everywhere in the world Jews could participate in the Shabbat service and be welcomed and belong.

He looked at his watch. It was ten minutes to eight. Before the services began, he gently touched the Ark with his palm spread wide. By performing this personal and private ritual David honored the Torah inside the Ark and the multitude of Jews who had died for it. In this way, every Friday night, he consciously reaffirmed his belief in the profound, almost mystical meaning of the Torah.

Because David wanted his congregation to feel the same satisfying spiritual renewal that he did, he conducted a more traditional service than most Reform rabbis. As a result, his service drew many visitors from other congregations who preferred a more formal observance of Shabbat.

Looking up from his prayer book, David checked the items on the bema. The lectern had been moved from the far left to the center directly in front of the Ark. To the Ark's right, on a small mahogany table covered by a hand-embroidered lace cloth, an intricately designed silver candelabrum holding thick candles sat atop a silver tray. Only the middle taper had been lighted. From its flame the other candles would be ignited during the service. The Kiddush cups, three silver wine goblets covered by a lace napkin, and a wine bottle in a silver holder were placed behind the candelabrum to be used when David said a blessing over the wine to give thanks to God for His generosity. Flowers of many colors arranged with ferns banked the three carpeted steps leading from the floor of the sanctuary to the bema. The quiet organ music and the patiently waiting choir were concealed behind a decorative panel at the right.

A few talkative worshipers continued to file into the sanctuary, making their way down the aisles. David, alone on the bema, contemplative and pious, commanded their silence and respect while they waited for the service to begin.

David looked at Meyer Loeb seated in his usual place, directly in front of the lectern in the middle of the first row. Loeb was flanked by his plump wife, Muriel, his son, Stephen, and Stephen's fiancée, Kelly Prentis. David was to decide that night whether to accept her as a convert. Naomi sat at the end of the row.

Because David rarely accepted applicants for conversion, other rabbis regarded his attitude as harsh and narrow. His reason was not arbitrary: he was often unconvinced of the legitimacy of their motives. Meyer Loeb anxiously watched David, looking for some sign of approval of his prospective daughter-in-law.

It was eight o'clock.

Ushers closed the doors to the sanctuary and the services began.

From a small waiting room offstage, Assistant Rabbi Morris Simon and Cantor Jay Sachs, also dressed in black robes, led a small procession onto the bema. Board President Sam Bender; Sisterhood President Arlene Marks; and Henry Morse, a tall, thin man with sunken brown eyes, his wife, Janet, and their thirteen-year-old son Richard, who was to become Bar Mitzvah the following day, took their seats of honor in the high-backed, hand-carved oak chairs arranged at the rear of the bema on either side of the Ark.

David, after shaking hands with the men and kissing the women's cheeks, moved with Cantor Sachs down to the lectern. He looked out over the congregation, which was stirring with anticipation. Then he bowed his head and silently expressed his feelings about those in attendance: *A Shabbat Jew is a Jew by choice. A Jew who is concerned with the next generation of our people, and the next, and the next. A Jew who observes Shabbat identifies unmistakably with our people. A Jew who does not identify as a Jew is not a good Jew. The Shabbat Jew is a Jew by choice.*

Satisfied with the pledge he had made to his God about his congregation, David indicated the services could begin. A nervous Janet Morse lit the Shabbat candles, and afterward, Cantor Sachs and the choir led the congregation in singing a prayer blessing the lighting of the candles.

Following a period of responsive reading interspersed with prayers and songs, David, Richard Morse and Henry Morse approached the small mahogany table. David filled the three chalices with wine as he recited the Kiddush. After drinking from the cups, the father and son followed David to the Ark.

David, as always, genuflected a moment before opening the doors to reveal the Torah. His reaction was always the same when he stood before the ancient scrolls of parchment on which the first five books of the Bible had been laboriously copied by an unknown scribe so long ago. He was overwhelmed with reverence and awe, for he was about to touch the Words of God.

Temple Beth Sinai's Torah had been buried in a crypt in Florence, Italy, during World War II. After the war it had been retrieved and restored and presented to the Farmington Hills congregation because of the generosity of their contributions, which had helped to rebuild the sacked and razed synagogue in Florence. Except for the legends passed from generation to generation, its prior history was unknown. Tests had determined that the scroll had existed at the time of the Crusades: Jews had been reading Beth Sinai's Torah for over seven hundred years.

After the Shema, the most important prayer in the entire litany of Jewish prayers, David placed the hallowed relic in Henry Morse's arms. The proud father in turn handed it to his solemn-faced young son. After the boy returned the Torah to him, David put the scroll back in its place.

The Shema was repeated, and a hushed silence, born perhaps of a mixture of the pain and pride of the past, spread throughout the sanctuary. Even the children were quiet. David turned from the open Ark and nodded at Henry Morse who, along with his son, had been patiently waiting for this moment.

Morse held up a discolored, dented chalice that he reverently handed to the young boy. The congregation savored the moment as the father prepared to honor his son on the Shabbat Eve of his Bar Mitzvah.

"This is the Kiddush cup that belonged to my father, your grand-father," Morse said to his son. Tears of remembrance brimmed in his deep-set eyes. "The day before your grandfather died, may he rest in peace, he said to me that if God would grant him one wish, it would be to live long enough to see you, his grandson, become a Bar Mitzvah."

The tears began to course down his cheeks. Morse opened his mouth to continue but couldn't speak.

His son, tightly clutching the silver cup, watched his father with a mixture of pride and embarrassment. He looked at David for guidance. David smiled and patted his back consolingly.

The hushed congregation, many with tears in their eyes, sat quietly and watched. A child's cry broke the silence as David helped Morse back to his chair.

Not wanting to intrude on this private moment, David waited patiently for Henry Morse's sobbing to subside before nodding at Cantor Sachs to sing Aleinu, the prayer that accompanies the closing of the Ark. He then moved to the rostrum, where he stood thoughtfully staring out at the congregation who waited expectantly for his sermon.

In an emotion-filled voice, David finally spoke. "I am not going to use the sermon I prepared because there is only one sermon I can give you tonight. About why fathers cry when their sons become a Bar Mitzvah." The murmur of approval rippling through the congregation brought a wry smile to his face.

"I speak to you not only as your rabbi but also as a son who remembers the day his father cried when he became a Bar Mitzvah. Why were my father and Henry Morse so emotionally overcome by this seemingly simple ceremony? Partly, of course, because of pride. But I think my father cried because he realized that this simple ceremony, this acceptance of his son into manhood, was his first awareness that he was losing his son. I was growing up and he would have to let go of me. Is there not a father in this congregation, or in any congregation, who has not cried because of that loss?" David paused and waited while many of the men responded with quick abrupt nods of agreement.

"I suppose he cried that night because it was the first time he had ever stepped back and looked at me in my own right and not as a child. And I guess he cried because he was facing an unknown future with me and he knew that he could no longer shield and protect me."

After speaking with deep feeling for a few more minutes about his father and grandfather and their relationship, David went on. "Men cry at their son's Bar Mitzvah because it is one of those infrequent moments of truth in their lives when they can un-ashamedly express a multitude of feelings and emotions that they have either buried or never known. Men cry because of pride, be-cause of joy, because of regrets, because of disappointments and because of understanding and empathy. But most of all,"—he paused—"a man cries at his son's Bar Mitzvah because of love."

He turned away from the lectern, thinking, Will I ever have a son so I can cry at his Bar Mitzvah? Will I ever have a son to love?

Then he nodded at Sam Bender to take his place and make the announcements about the upcoming social, educational and business events of the temple. Only those whose names were mentioned or who were interested in the coming meetings paid any attention to the board president. The others talked quietly among themselves about David's sermon.

It was now time to recite the Mourners' Kaddish. The anniversary of a death on this particular date. Those affected rose from their seats. David searched his soul for something to say that would bring meaning and comfort to them. His feelings were reflected in his voice as he read the alphabetical list of names of those congregants who had died on that date in past years.

"Kenneth Altchuler . . . Bernice Barron . . . Dorothy Chasen . . . Edward Diamond . . . Franklin Engels . . .

Ys-ga-dal ve-yitt-ka-dash she-me ra-ba . . .

David left the bema as the closing hymn of joy, "Hinei Ma Tov," was being sung. He walked down a single aisle to the rear doors. When the song was over he stood behind the last row and with arms outstretched in supplication, he gave the benediction:

> May the Lord give strength unto his people.
> May He bless His people and all people with
>   peace.
> Shabbat Shalom.

"Shabbat Shalom," the congregation responded, and the services were over.

At the open rear doors, David waited in the receiving line with Naomi, Assistant Rabbi Morris Simon, Cantor Jay Sachs and Board President Sam Bender. As always, the first congregant to reach him was Meyer Loeb. Loeb's wife, his son and Kelly Prentis trailed respectfully behind the old man.

"Shabbat Shalom, Rabbi."

"Shabbat Shalom, Meyer."

Repeating a ritual that took place after every Shabbat service, they embraced and squeezed each other's shoulders. The familiar ritual continued as David, referring to his sermon, asked as he always did, "Well, Meyer, how did I do?"

Loeb responded as he had the first time David had ever asked the question of him after a Shabbat service. First with an indifferent shrug and then with a slowly widening grin before repeating the words he had said hundreds of times. "Not bad, Rabbi. Not bad. A pretty good beginning but a little too schmaltzy at the end."

The old man and the young rabbi beamed at each other.

"Shabbat Shalom, Rabbi," Mrs. Loeb said. After David responded, she kissed him on the cheek. Her gesture was also a ritual repeated after every Friday night service. David then turned and faced a nervous and apprehensive Kelly Prentis.

"Shabbat Shalom," he said warmly to her. "If Mr. Loeb hasn't explained, Shabbat Shalom is a greeting Jews say to each other to welcome the Sabbath."

She answered timidly, stumbling over the alien words. "Shabbat Shalom, Rabbi Benjamin."

147

Meyer Loeb laughed with pleasure and pride as he asked, "What do you think, Rabbi? Can we make a good Jew out of her?"

"Meyer, after I speak with her in my study, I'll let you know."

"I understand your nervousness, Miss Prentis, but there are some questions I must ask you," David said pleasantly from behind his desk.

"I'm nervous because I've never talked to a rabbi before."

David studied Kelly Prentis. Her constant fingering of the cameo brooch pinned beneath the shoulder of her off-white knit dress expressed her anxieties.

"I'm not an inquisitor," he said. "I'm only trying to determine whether to accept you as a convert. Your wanting to marry Stephen Loeb, to please his father isn't a good enough reason."

"I guess if I were a rabbi it wouldn't be a good enough reason for me either."

Her round pretty face was framed by a halo of dark auburn hair, and the freshness of her unblemished complexion accentuated her large brown eyes. A frequent smile brightened her guileless features. David doubted that she knew how to lie; he was sure that subterfuge of any kind was alien to her. Because she was delicate and petite, she gave an impression of fragility. But in the few minutes they had talked, he had sensed her determination and knew that Kelly Prentis was anything but fragile emotionally.

As he watched her, one word came to mind to describe her. Good, David told himself. She is good. She is open and receptive. She has no rough edges. She can be trusted.

"Kelly, are there any other reasons why you want me to accept you as a convert?"

Resting his chin on the bridge of his folded hands, David hoped he wouldn't hear the two shopworn replies that would-be proselytes often gave to him: "There's been something missing in my life and I believe Judaism can fill it," or "I've always been a searcher and I've tried every other religion. None of them satisfied me." More often than not, at that point, David ended the interview.

Kelly Prentis gave him an answer he had never heard before. "I want to convert because I see the closeness of the Loebs and other Jewish families. Because I see how Mr. Loeb feels about his religion. Because I see the serenity and peace in his face when he goes to temple. And when I marry Stephen I want that closeness and for us to share that serenity and peace."

David tugged his lip as he mulled over what she had said. That's one of the best definitions of Jewishness I've ever heard, he thought. Why does it take a non-Jew to articulate it? He couldn't help himself, and for the first time that night, he thought of Sheila. She'd understand why, he told himself. But he knew that her understanding would also increase his frustration. So close and yet so far apart, he thought.

"Tell me about your family. Don't you have that closeness?"

While Kelly framed her response, she studied the array of photographs and memorabilia on the wall behind David. Pointing to a picture of him shaking hands with the leader of the Detroit archdiocese, she asked, "Do you know Cardinal Dearden?"

"Yes," David said patiently.

"I met him once. He gave a sermon at our church." Continuing to study the photograph, she suddenly shuddered. "He terrified me."

"Do I terrify you, Kelly?"

Her face broke into a warm and open smile as she shook her head and said, "Oh no, Rabbi Benjamin. I feel very comfortable with you."

"I'm glad you feel that way. Because now you have no reason not to tell me about your family," David said with a mock-triumphant grin.

Realizing he had trapped her, Kelly broke into laughter that sounded like tinkling crystal. "All right," she said, "my father is a police officer and my mother is a teacher. They're both devout Catholics." He wondered if that was the reason she had been hesitant about discussing her family.

"You're aware, aren't you, that what you hope to do will hurt your parents very much? You'll be rejecting everything they believe in. Not only their faith, but also their heritage. And yours."

"I've thought of that, Rabbi, and the only answer I can give you is that I love my parents very much. My conversion won't stop me from loving them."

It was obvious to David that Kelly had thought about the consequences of her conversion on her family. That pleased him. It added another dimension to her character, increasing his understanding of why Meyer Loeb would accept her as a daughter-in-law.

"If you convert to Judaism, do you think they will reject you?"

"I don't know," she said in a tremulous voice.

"And if they do?"

She shook her head slowly from side to side and repeated, "I don't know. I wish I could give you a better answer than that, Rabbi, but I can't. I just don't know." Her eyes filled, and she dabbed at them with a small handkerchief she had taken out of her purse.

Waiting for Kelly to regain her composure, David thought, What a question! How could she possibly know? Even I can't answer that question. It was the only honest response she could give me.

To put her at ease, David changed the subject. "What made you decide to become a nurse?"

"Because I wanted to push a little harder," she answered in a faraway voice.

David looked at her quizzically, and she laughed at his confusion. "I was eight years old when I was taken to the hospital to see my Uncle Ed for the last time. He was dying. Everybody said so. The doctors. The nurses. My folks. Even the priest. But Uncle Ed didn't die, and they brought him home to my house to convalesce. Why hadn't he died when everybody said he was going to? I wondered. One day, when we were alone, I had the courage to ask him. 'Because I pushed a little harder,' he said to me. 'Because I love life and I wasn't ready to let go of it.' That's when I decided I wanted to be a nurse. So I could help people push a little harder."

David didn't hide his admiration as he studied her face for a long moment. Quietly, he said, "I guess that's the reason I became a rabbi. To help people push a little harder." He turned away to hide a smile because he knew what Sheila's response would be. *And who helps the rabbi push a little harder?*

"I understand," Kelly said.

"I know you do."

They smiled comfortably at each other, then David said, "Let's push a little harder and see about accepting you as a convert. Do you have any questions for me?'

"Yes, I do, Rabbi. When are you going to ask me how I feel about Jesus and Mary? About my Catholic beliefs? I have a friend who converted, and she said those were the first questions the rabbi asked her."

Those usually are the first questions a rabbi asks a would-be convert, David thought. Why didn't I feel the need to ask them of Kelly Prentis? An answer came to him, and he was positive he had guessed the truth.

"I'll ask you another question instead. Kelly, do you remember when you stopped being a believing Catholic? When you lost faith?"

She looked at him strangely. "I don't know exactly, but this is the first time I've had the courage to admit it. But how did you know?"

"Because I know the kind of a young woman you are. If you still believed, you wouldn't be here. Nothing could make someone like you give up her faith. You wouldn't do it even to please Meyer Loeb."

"But I still have doubts. I'm still not sure of what I'm doing and what it really means."

"Of course you have doubts. And you should be confused."

"I want to believe. I want to embrace Judaism. I want to have faith. Rabbi Benjamin, will you help me?"

David grinned. Even though he hadn't indicated his decision in any way, she had assumed he was accepting her as a convert. He realized that it had never occurred to Kelly Prentis that he wouldn't accept her. It was the process, not the goal, that had caused her apprehension.

He went to the bookcase and picked out several volumes. Handing them to her, he answered quietly, "Yes, I'll help you. I want you to read these carefully. They talk about Jewish history, Jewish background and Jewish culture and tradition. We'll meet once a week and discuss what you've read. I expect you to have many questions. My answers should clarify most of the confusions I know you'll have. When we've finished our studies, in about nine months to a year, you'll know what Judaism means."

"That's all I have to do? Study with you for nine months?"

"You'll also have to learn Hebrew. You can either attend classes here at the temple or get Meyer to teach you. I'm sure he'd love to do that. And, of course, you'll have to observe every holiday and understand its significance."

"And after nine months?"

"You'll appear before a board of rabbis, the Beth Din, who will question you about what you've learned and about your feelings and attitudes. Your answers, hopefully, will affirm your faith. That same night, during the Shabbat service, you will publicly embrace Judaism and I will present you to the congregation, which will formally accept you."

"But how will you know, after only nine months, that I still won't have doubts?"

"With you, I'll know."

The interview was over. Kelly went to the door, and, tilting her head, said with a faint trace of Irish cockiness, "In nine months I'll be Jewish. Come, let's tell Mr. Loeb. He'll be so pleased."

"No, you don't need me," David said. "This is a moment of joy, of pleasure, that just the two of you should share."

Before she left David's study, Kelly asked, "This isn't going to be as easy as it sounds, is it? I've learned that nothing worthwhile comes easily."

David agreed. "No, it won't be easy. But together we'll make it. We'll just have to push a little harder."

CHAPTER
20

The rage that had been festering within Naomi, expressed only rarely by a biting remark or merely a shrug of the shoulders, finally exploded when she walked into the bedroom and found David packing his suitcase.

"Where are you going?"

"To Washington." He didn't look up, but continued to fold the jacket of a new pin-striped suit. "That Interfaith Council meeting I told you about. Don't you remember?"

"I thought that was next week."

"There are some important symposiums that I want to attend before it begins."

The lie came easily. He had rearranged his schedule and was leaving a week earlier than planned to meet with Sheila. She would also be in Washington, attending a consortium of high-level industrial executives at a series of IBM-sponsored conferences. He closed the suitcase, swung it off the bed and turned to face Naomi. Her usual sullen, resentful expression was gone. He couldn't define the look on her face.

"What about me?"

"What about you?"

"You made me a promise that you've yet to keep. That you'd take me on your next trip out of town. That we would turn it into a short vacation. Don't *you* remember?"

His dismay was not caused by his having to lie again but because he could do it so easily. "I can't take you this time because I'll be tied up every minute of the day and night. What kind of a vacation would that be for you?"

"You never intended to take me, did you? You lied to me just to shut me up."

"That's not true." Realizing that whatever he said would only cause him to hurt her even more, would make him feel more guilty because of the truth about his leaving early, he looked at his watch and added, "My plane leaves in less than an hour. I've got to go. We'll talk about it when I get back. I'll make it up to you."

He couldn't make himself kiss her good-bye because he felt the act would in some way be a betrayal. After he left, she stayed frozen in the bedroom, putting away the clothes he had taken out and then for some reason decided not to pack. She dumped the drawer filled with his shirts onto the floor, stomped on them and defiantly marched out of the bedroom.

Throughout the rest of the day, she nursed her wounds by plotting elaborate and nefarious schemes of revenge: she would send letters from an anonymous congregant to the Board of Trustees in which she would recite a list of his imaginary crimes and filthy vices; she would end the letters by saying that unless he were removed as head rabbi, she would transfer her affiliation to another congregation along with many of her friends who felt exactly as she.

She would resign from the many committees she was on and refuse to fulfill her obligations as his rebbetzin. She would openly support those she knew were opposed to his programs. She would refuse to attend those functions where her presence, as his rebbtzin, was not only expected but required. She would brazenly and publicly embarrass him in any way she could.

Her nerve endings were so raw that first night he was away that she couldn't sleep. The phone rang once, but conjecturing it might be David calling to apologize, she didn't answer it. No apology or excuse he might make for the way he had mistreated her was acceptable. In some way he would have to pay dearly before she would even consider any peacemaking gesture she was sure he would make.

She spent the next day mindlessly roaming the silent little house, trying to figure out the price she would exact from him. She didn't wash, and her ebony hair hung in straggled, unkempt mats around her thin, tormented face. She wore an old bedraggled housecoat, not caring how she looked or felt. She ate tasteless food and threw the leftovers onto the sideboard. Dirty dishes and glasses were piled haphazardly in the sink. She smoked incessantly, dripping ashes on herself and wherever else they happened to fall.

With darkness, her anger turned inward. "I'll show him," she snarled as she went into the bedroom. "I'll make him pay for what he's done to me. For misleading me when we were married. For ruining my life. I'll get even with him. He's not going to get away with it."

She slumped to the edge of the unmade bed and sat quietly for a while in a graceless position of loose-jointed repose. Impaled by loneliness, she thought of calling her father but rejected the idea because of a remembered incident that caused her to fear his response. Hadn't he once stood against her and taken David's side? Hadn't he said that David Benjamin was a strong, gutsy man and that strong, gutsy men sometimes did things their wives didn't approve of? "I've done them myself," he had concluded.

She had taken the *I've done them myself* as a confession. It had caused her to think of her mother. She wondered why she felt a closeness toward her that she had never experienced before. She relived the day her mother had left, and understood how Adele's feelings had finally blossomed because Naomi believed that she too had been victimized by her choice of a husband. She fell back on the bed and, covering her face with her hands, moaned, "Oh, Mommy, I'm so sorry. Forgive me. I need you so now. I miss you so."

The need for sleep was overwhelming. She staggered into the bathroom and found the small bottle of sleeping pills.

Returning to the bedroom, she carefully and meticulously remade the bed with clean linen. After putting on a fresh nightgown, she fluffed the pillow and slipped between the cool sheets. She took the pills from the nightstand and poured two into her hand. As she studied them, a strange smile twisted her mouth.

"I'll show you," she said to the specter of David. "I'll get even with you." She gulped the pills down and with her arms folded across her chest, let her mind toy with the idea of what she was doing.

"You'll be sorry." She swallowed two more pills. "Oh, will you be sorry."

She lay quietly with a satisfied smirk on her pallid face. She fantasized, delighting in the prospect of David's torment. The bottle of pills she was gripping made her aware of what she was doing. "I'm not going to kill myself," she cautioned herself as she took two more. "I don't want to die. If I die, how will I watch you suffer because of what you did to me? The maid will find me in time." She took two more pills and felt a twinge of nausea. "You bastard . . ."

She emptied the bottle and was unaware when it fell from her hand.

The telephone ringing on the nightstand beside their bed interrupted their lovemaking.

"Don't answer it and maybe they'll go away," Sheila murmured. But it kept ringing.

Reluctantly, after looking at his watch, David reached across her and picked it up. "This is Rabbi Benjamin."

It didn't surprise her that he had gotten a call. Since his arrival in Washington the night before, he had received several calls from people who had somehow learned he was in town and staying at the Mayflower Hotel.

Sheila watched his face lose color while he listened. Then impulsively she sat up and kissed David's bare shoulder. When she became aware that whoever was talking to him had his undivided attention, she slithered out of bed.

Pulling on a robe, she seated herself on a chair against the far wall. Suddenly she shivered and whispered to herself, "The devil just walked over my grave."

David hung up, and from his grim look, she knew that he had shut her out of his mind. She sat quietly across the room, watching and waiting. He finally said in a voice laced with disbelief, "My wife is dead. The maid found her body. An overdose of sleeping pills."

He buried his face in his hands, his body racked with sobs. She didn't know whether to try to comfort him or to stay where she was and let him endure his agony. He suddenly lifted his tear-stained face and looked at her. As if ashamed, he stumbled into the bathroom and she heard him filling the sink. When he returned, though his eyes were red, the trace of tears was gone.

He went to the phone and dialed. "Senator, this is David." He couldn't make himself say the rest.

"What are you doing in town? I thought you weren't coming in until next week. Where are you staying? Maybe we can have lunch together."

"Senator, never mind that now. I've got bad news. I just got a call from Detroit." He paused and then, after a deep sigh, said, "There's been an accident. Naomi's dead." There was an immediate anguished cry of despair. "Senator, are you all right?" When there was no response, he said, "I'll be right over. We'll go back to Detroit together. I'll make all the arrangements."

He hung up and looked at Sheila. "Did she know about us?" she asked. "Is that why she committed suicide?"

"It wasn't a suicide!" The thought was intolerable. "There was no note. They're calling it an accident." He sounded relieved. "And she couldn't have possibly known about us."

"I'm glad," Sheila said. "For her sake, not for ours. I don't suppose you want me to go back to Detroit with you . . ."

David shook his head—too quickly, she thought—and began to gather his clothes. "I'll call you when I can," was all he said before going into the bathroom and turning on the shower.

Sheila sat against the wall, huddled in misery, listening to the running water. Then she looked around the nondescript room and thought, I'll never come back here again. This is the second time in this hotel that we ended before we began.

CHAPTER
21

At the autopsy, requested by Naomi's insurance company, it was discovered that her body was riddled with cancer. David, recalling her lethargy, her paleness, her low, persistent fever and weight loss, managed to half-convince himself that knowledge of her condition had caused her to take her life.

The funeral service was held, as required by Jewish law, two days later, and began exactly at eleven o'clock.

Concealed and isolated from the congregation by a translucent curtain, David, flanked by Senator Mendes and Martha and Brian McGraw, sat in the Mourners Room at the right of the bema, the large stagelike structure with the Ark at its rear. The plain, closed pine coffin, also prescribed by Jewish tradition, had been brought into the sanctuary an hour earlier and was centered on the floor directly below the lip of the bema. A delicate spray of lily of the valley decorated the casket. An array of flowers, wreaths and bouquets had been sent by the non-Jewish mourners who were accustomed to such displays at funerals.

But for the stature of Naomi, the services would have been held in the chapel of Ira Kaufman's mortuary, in Southfield, Michigan. Her role prevented that. Ushers had seated the mayor, the governor, several senators and congressmen, influential businessmen and bankers, two cabinet members and a representative from the White House in the main sanctuary of Temple Beth Sinai. Senatorial staff members, temple personnel and friends of the family filled the re-

158

maining seats. Because of the mixture of those in attendance, a Mourners Book in both English and Hebrew had been given out. Assistant Rabbi Morris Simon and Cantor Jay Sachs, both dressed in black robes, waited patiently for the mourners to quiet.

Sheila Harrington, seated at the end of the row reserved for Detroit's automotive executives, was startled when she recognized David's silhouette through the curtain. Though she ached to console him, she could not intrude on his private grief. He was burying his wife, and she felt totally out of place. She wouldn't have come if Anson Phillips hadn't been called out of town at the last moment and insisted she take his place.

She forced herself to turn away from David's silhouette and looked at the plain coffin. One thought shattered her composure: Now that she's gone, things will be easier for us. Sheila reluctantly admitted to herself that she felt no guilt. Only anticipation. As she looked at the coffin again, she wondered about David's future. And whether it included her.

In the Mourners Room, Martha reached over and gripped her brother's arm consolingly. David patted her hand and said, "I'm all right." Then he leaned forward, as if in supplication, as Morris Simon offered the opening prayer:

> What is man, that Thou
> art mindful of him?
> And the son of man,
> that Thou thinkest of him?
>
> Man is like a breath,
> His days are as unto a shadow . . .

Cantor Sachs's resonant baritone filled the sanctuary with the 121st Psalm. He sang the lament in Hebrew, and all were ensnared by the mood expressed by the cantor's mournful voice:

> I will lift up mine eyes
> unto the mountains:
> From where shall my help come?
> My help cometh from the Lord.
> Who made heaven and earth.

David stared at the closed casket through the curtain. His feelings when he had received the telephone call while making love with

Sheila Harrington in a Washington hotel room had ranged from shock to remorse to guilt. How could I not see what was happening to her? I'm there for every member of the congregation who is in pain, and yet I didn't recognize it in my own wife. What kind of a rabbi am I? But why didn't she tell me? Why did she have to endure her inner torment by herself? Were you punishing me because I didn't love you the way you needed to be loved? Maybe our life would have been different if you had told me what was wrong and why you were so miserable. I'd have taken care of you, and we would have been closer. He grimaced then because he knew that wasn't true. That even if he had known the truth, it wouldn't have changed anything between them. His acceptance of that reality brought answers to the questions that had plagued him.

They had been strangers.

Naomi had believed, as had David at first, that the widening chasm between them would be bridged by the move to Farmington Hills. A new life together. Instead, it had separated them even further. The chasm had widened, for while David, by thrusting himself into his work and into the world, had avoided the disappointments of their barren marriage, Naomi could only withdraw. Ultimately, they were so far apart, such bitter strangers, that she couldn't even tell him of her hurts and her anguish. That refusal was her final denial to him.

Rabbi Simon's reading of the 91st Psalm interrupted David's thoughts:

> O thou that dwellest in the covert
> of the Most High,
> and abidest in the shadow
> of the Almighty . . .
> His truth is
> a shield and a buckler.

Because of his acceptance of the painful reality of his marriage, and his contribution to its failure, David closed his eyes as if in respose while Cantor Sachs sang the 23rd Psalm, again in Hebrew.

> The Lord is my shepherd;
> I shall not want . . .

The mixed congregation repeated the words in English, and Morris Simon offered another prayer which set the mood for a somber moment of meditation. At the conclusion of the period of self-reflection, David pushed through the separating curtain and stood quietly while the mourners studied him.

He was ready to deliver the eulogy.

Instead of going to the lectern on the bema, as was expected, he walked directly from the Mourners Room to the head of the simple wooden casket. He stood with his head bowed and his hands folded before looking out at the hushed and expectant audience. He began the eulogy in a voice that was barely audible. As if he didn't want to be heard.

Making no reference to the manner of Naomi's death, he began quietly by saying, "We are not just burying my wife today. We are burying your rebbetzin." In hushed tones, he told them of Naomi's role in his life. Of her profound belief in his need to be a rabbi and of her struggles and self-sacrifices to help him. He reminded them of her life within the congregation and the community and, that because she had been an extension of him, their loss was as great as his. He concluded by saying, "My sentiments about Naomi are personal and private. I share them with no one. But I can share this single thought about her with all of you. In the Book of Proverbs it is written that *"though house and wealth are inherited from our fathers, a sensible wife is a gift from the Lord."* I have been blessed, for I have had such a gift from the Lord."

He returned to the Mourners Room feeling that he had failed. That the eulogy had been a flimsy piece of camouflage under which he had hidden his true feelings. He was wondering what he could say to those who had seen through his feeble effort when Senator Mendes grasped his hands and said in a choked voice, "Thank you, David. Thank you."

Mendes, along with the entire congregation, stood as Rabbi Simon intoned *El Moley Rachamim,* the memorial prayer for the departed:

> O God, full of compassion who dwellest
> on high, grant perfect rest beneath
> the sheltering wings of Thy divine
> presence among the holy and pure
> who shine as the brightest of the firmament,
> to Naomi Cynthia Benjamin,
> who has gone to her eternal home.
> Father of mercy, bring her
> under the cover of Thy wings

and let her soul be bound up
in the bond of eternal life.
Be Thou her possession and may
her repose be forever peaceful.
Amen.

After the prayer, Sam Bender, as president of the Board of Trustees, mounted the bema and announced from the pulpit, "The burial services will be concluded at Clover Hill Park Cemetery. The Benjamin family will sit in mourning from today through next Saturday evening. Services will be held at the home of Rabbi David Benjamin each morning at seven-thirty and each evening at five-thirty. If you feel that you would like to make a contribution to the memory of Naomi Benjamin, please select your own charitable organization."

David and the others waited in the Mourners Room while ushers, starting with the rear rows of the sanctuary, permitted congregants to come down the aisle to view the casket and to say, each in his or her own way, a final good-bye to Naomi. It wasn't until the last mourner had departed that David, Senator Mendes, and Martha and Brian approached the coffin.

Deep in their own thoughts, they stood in a mute semicircle. After a few moments had passed, they looked at David for guidance, as if unsure of what to do next. They left when he said quietly, "I'd like to spend a few moments alone with my wife."

He opened the top half of the coffin and looked down into her pallid, waxen face. She wore a simple white dress, the strand of pearls he had given her on their sixth wedding anniversary at her throat. He took her cold hand in his and said his eulogy.

A Talmudic saying flashed into his consciousness and brought tears to his eyes as he said the words: "*In death, two worlds meet with a kiss; the world going out and the future coming in* . . . I did love you. Maybe not the way you needed me to love you, but I did love you. It's just that we were so wrong for each other. That was our tragedy. Not your dying, but our living. Would our marriage have worked if we had been wiser and more mature? More giving and less self-centered? If we had talked more often and really listened to each other?" He paused as if waiting for Naomi to answer, then shook his head sadly and continued. "The optimist in me wants to say yes, that we could have made it work, but this is not the time to lie to you—and we both know the truth."

He stared down at her silent, composed face, and tears filled his eyes. "You gave me your support and your love for as long as you could while I struggled in my way to become the rabbi you believed I was capable of becoming. And because you did I'll always be grateful to you and there'll always be a small part of you within me."

He tenderly brushed a stray curl off her forehead and in a low voice whispered, "Good-bye, my darling. Lech B'shalom. Go in peace."

He walked out of the sanctuary, the acid rain of his tears etching the grief in his face.

BOOK
TWO

CHAPTER
22

In the month following Naomi's funeral, David immersed himself in the temple's affairs. He also maintained a full-time schedule outside the temple, filling every free hour with public meetings and personal appearances. His seven-day-a-week schedule began at six-thirty and rarely ended before midnight. Too busy to indulge in gloomy personal reflections, often physically and mentally exhausted, he was not surprised when his thoughts of Naomi became less and less frequent, then faded entirely. He struggled with his continuing thoughts of Sheila, but he forced himself to stay away from her.

The last time they had seen each other had been at the funeral. After thirty days of silence, Sheila's patience had worn thin and she had called the temple and left a message. It took David two days to call her back. When he did, he was on his way to a meeting and he told her he would call her again when he had more time. Another week passed before she heard from him. He was going out of town and would be gone for most of the week. She accepted the fact that he was avoiding her.

It was nearly one in the morning and David had just returned home after pushing himself through a brutal fourteen-hour day at the temple when the telephone rang.

"Hello, Rabbi Benjamin? My name is Sheila Harrington. Do you remember me? Rabbi, I think you've been avoiding me. No, I don't think so, I know so." Sheila's bantering tone vanished. "David, it's time we stopped pretending. You may not be able to face the reason you won't see me, but I can. I could tell you the reason, but I won't. If I did, you'd defend yourself and you'd argue and you wouldn't even hear me. But your avoiding me has nothing to do with Naomi's death or your crazy schedule."

"When I need understanding, you give me lectures," David answered angrily.

"See what I mean?"

He knew she was right. After a long silence, she said, "And in spite of what you think, I do understand. I do know what you're going through. Your wife died weeks and weeks ago. You're not sure whether it was an accident or if she killed herself because of your insensitivity to her needs. But even though you had a lousy marriage, you're lonely and your world's come apart at the seams. You probably feel some anger as well as a lot of guilt. David, I'm not trying to play amateur psychiatrist—those are natural feelings. Those feelings I can live with. It's your avoidance of me and your absurd excuses for avoiding me that I can't live with. That I won't live with."

"Is that an ultimatum?"

"No, David, it's a challenge. Maybe some women will take rainchecks indefinitely. I don't. I don't have to. And that's why I'm telling you that you've got to face the truth about yourself. Call me when you do. Even if it's to tell me you've decided that you can't ever see me again. That's the decision I'm insisting you make."

He thought he heard a muffled sob when Sheila hung up, but there was no answer when he called her back. The next day, when he called United Motors, her secretary told him she was out of the office. When, after two days, she had not returned the call, he knew what he had to do.

Self-confrontation, he told himself, remembering the many times he had forced congregants to look within for answers. It's tough and it's hard and it's painful, he always told them. It's like ripping adhesive tape off your soul. But it's the only way you're ever going to find and face the truth about yourself.

He forced himself to think back over his reactions and behavior since he had buried Naomi. When the temple service had ended, with numbing robotlike emotions, he had gone to the internment at Clover Hill Park Cemetery. During the seven-day mourning period of "sitting shiva," he had thought of Sheila, not of Naomi. No longer constrained by Naomi's presence, he had daydreamed, eagerly anticipating their future together. He felt guilty about not feeling guilty. But when his mourning period was over, although he had ached to see Sheila, he had avoided doing so. He had been evasive about when they would meet, and he didn't understand why. Though his feelings hadn't changed, he knew he felt differently about himself. Until her phone call, he had hesitated to probe any deeper. Now he had no choice and, painful as it was, he came to realize why he had been so evasive. He had been afraid of losing her.

Though disturbing, he could handle the conflict presented by being a rabbi in love with a gentile. He could separate the yin and yang of his feelings by convincing himself that one had nothing to do with the other. His loving Sheila Harrington didn't make him less of a rabbi and didn't contaminate his convictions or his purpose. He was not faced with making a choice between the two. If that ever happened, he believed he would deal with it when it occurred.

But what he had avoided facing was the effects of his being a rabbi on Sheila. While married to Naomi, there was nothing to discuss. Naomi, his wife, had stood like a silent barricade between the present and the future. But now, with Naomi gone, the barricade had been removed. But, because he was a rabbi, what could he offer her? Stolen moments when they could be alone? Apprehension at being found out? No future, only a present? A clandestine relationship that could never become more? Naomi's death had removed only one obstacle and that was personal. Now he could go to Sheila without the agonizing truth of knowing he was betraying his wife.

He had evaded the questions because he knew the answers. A woman like Sheila Harrington didn't have to accept the kind of relationship he had to offer. She had too much pride to do that. Once he voiced the questions, he knew he would lose her. But he didn't want to give her up. That was why he had been avoiding her. But because she was the kind of woman she was, she had forced him to first face those questions. Because he was the kind of man he was, he was not ready to ask them of her.

"Miss Harrington, Rabbi Benjamin is on the phone," Sheila's secretary said over the intercom. "Will you talk with him or should I take a messsage?"

Sheila had spent a miserable week waiting to hear from David, answering every phone call with anticipation. Toward the end of the week of silence she was tempted to call him, and had struggled to resist the impulse. But the self-inflicted emotional agony caused by both the temptation and her impatience to hear from him made her accept a dimension of herself that he had never even guessed existed. On one level, she was as sure of herself and where she was going as she always had been. She was still out to win and always would be. She was still an overachiever with an orderly, logical mind that had often made her appear devoid of emotional response. But now, anguishing while she waited for David's call, for the first time she was aware that the picture was only partially true. She was appalled to realize that she was now capable of losing control of her feelings.

Always the pursued and never the pursuer, Sheila had never permitted herself to suffer the sort of anxieties, the highs and lows, that she was now tormenting over because of her feelings about David Benjamin. She had never allowed her emotions that much leeway. Not even with Spencer Tolliver, whom she had almost married. Realizing how vulnerable she had become, she both resented and reveled in the feeling. It was a part of her femaleness that she had kept carefully concealed from herself, and from others. And, though she anguished, an inner voice dimly told her that the pleasure she was deriving from her dependency far outweighed the pain. Before David Benjamin, Sheila would have scorned such an attitude as evidence of weakness and immaturity, of "femininity."

Keeping her voice as even as possible, she said to her secretary, "I'll speak to the rabbi," and pushed the phone button.

"Busy?" he asked. Sheila had to fight to maintain her composure. "Yes, I'm pretty busy," she said, looking at her desk piled high with reports and trade journals to be digested before a meeting with Anson Phillips and Lawton Collins at the end of the week.

"Too busy to talk?"

"What about?"

"Harrington, don't be coy with me. The last time we talked you chewed my butt out for being evasive and you had every reason to do it. You know damn well what we have to talk about. Besides, coyness is not one of your charms."

David's sharp retort pleased her. And, from the tone of his voice, she knew his self-confidence had returned. He had not only faced but had come to a conclusion about the only obstacle that she believed stood between them. That he was a rabbi and she was not a Jew. Because of his attitude, she was convinced that he had come to a resolution that she had to hear. "Go ahead," she said firmly. "Let me have it."

She was confused by his response because it had little to do with their problem as she had conceived it.

"I didn't call you before because I didn't want to hear your answer," he began. "I was thinking only of myself and that was unfair of me."

"What are you talking about? Your being a rabbi? That being a rabbi stands in the way of your feelings? And mine?"

"No, my being a rabbi has nothing to do with my feelings. But because I am a rabbi, I've got nothing to offer you but a sordid, dirty, back-street romance. I'm talking about the fact that we have no future together. I'm talking about the fact that we've got to hide our relationship. You have to sneak around to meet me and scheme and connive to eliminate any chance of our being found out. You've told me yourself that you're too much woman to accept that. Now that I know you, I believe you. I'm talking about the fact that—"

"Wait a minute, Benjamin!" she angrily interrupted. "You've figured all that out without discussing it with me? You've made decisions for me about what I'm going or not going to do without talking to me! You've got your fucking nerve! You and that holier-than-thou attitude of yours! I'm not one of your congregants coming to you for advice. When are you going to realize that I'm capable of making my own decisions? I don't need or want you to make them for me, and if we're ever going—"

"Hold it, hold it. Calm down."

"No, I'm not going to calm down. I'm pissed that you're ready to make a decision for me without talking it over with me."

"But—"

"No buts, you've got a lot to learn about me."

He remembered Naomi's anger over his decison to take the pulpit in North Carolina. Her telling him of the senator's explanation about gutsy men making gutsy decisions without a discussion and he grinned as he thought, Not with strong gutsy broads, they don't. They'd better not.

"You get your ass over here tonight and we'll talk," she said firmly. "Then I'll make my decisions about what I want to do. I'll make you a dinner and after—"

"I didn't know you could cook," he said softly, interrupting her mood. "I'll bet you're damn good."

Her anger began to subside, and she said huffily, "There's a lot of things you don't know about me. And I'm damn good at most of them. I'll make a dinner tonight that you'll never forget."

"What time should I come over?" he asked quietly.

"Seven. No, make it about seven-thirty."

"I've missed you," David said softly. "I've thought about you often. About us."

His words caused her resistance to disappear and she whispered, "I've missed you, too, David. Come early. Seven will be fine."

Hanging up before he could respond, Sheila pushed the papers on her desk to one side. Then she began to scribble a shopping list and a timetable of things to do on the back of an envelope. She concentrated on deciding what to serve so she wouldn't have to think about anything else. Pausing over one item on the menu, she punched the intercom and said to her secretary. "I want to speak to my mother. She's at the number in Virginia."

She drummed her fingers nervously, waiting for her mother to answer. Hurrying through the pleasantries, she said, "Mother, do you remember those special Sunday afternoon dinners Grandmother used to make when we'd drive down to Charleston to see her?"

"Of course. Your grandmothe's Sunday dinners were famous. That was the only reason your father was willing to make the trip."

"You wouldn't have her recipe for candied yams, would you?"

"Not offhand. But I'll find it and send it to you."

"Mother, I need it for tonight. It's very important to me."

"I'll try to find it and I'll call you back if I do."

"Mother, I'll hold on while you look for it."

There was pleasure in her mother's voice as she asked after a second's pause, "Sheila, you're entertaining a very special man, aren't you? Tell me about him. What's he like? What does he do?"

"Mother, please," Sheila rolled her eyes and grimaced. "Not now. I've got a million things to do. I don't have the time to talk now." Besides, she told herself, after tonight there might not be any need to tell you about him. After tonight, he might not be so special.

"Okay, sweetie, hold on. I think I know where it is."

CHAPTER
23

Sheila never did serve dinner that night.

She was critically surveying the table set up in front of the picture window overlooking the beautifully wooded area behind her apartment when she heard the buzzer. With a shaking hand she struck a match to light the candles and then hurriedly made one last inspection and nervously smoothed down the skirt of her pale green taffeta hostess gown. Passing through the living room on her way to the front door, she dimmed lights, fluffed pillows and turned on the stereo to a Brahms concerto. Before opening the door, she contemplated the effect she had created and giggled like a schoolgirl.

She opened the door and David, a large bouquet of yellow roses in his arms, stood there grinning broadly at her. They looked at each other for an ill-at-ease, interminable moment before he said, "You're wearing your hair differently, aren't you?"

She patted the close-cropped red curls and asked, "Do you like it?"

David cocked his head and studied her. "No." Sheila blinked with disappointed surprise. "I liked it better longer."

"I'll let it grow." She took his hand and led him into the living room.

Conversation was stilted. They hadn't seen each other in nearly six weeks and were trying to cross an abyss carved by anticipation, fantasy and need. The afternoon's conversation had made the path back even more difficult. Realizing he was still holding the bouquet,

David clumsily thrust it at Sheila. She buried her face in the blossoms.

"I love roses," she said. "My favorite flowers. When I was a child in Virginia I used to eat the petals." She picked off a petal and began to chew it. Then, seeing the look of incredulity on his face, she added, "I thought that anything so beautiful must taste wonderful."

She plucked at a blossom and handed David a single petal. He looked at her skeptically before gingerly nibbling at it. She watched him intently, waiting until he was finished before asking, "Well, what do you think?"

"Not bad. Not great, but not bad. But I hope this isn't what you plan to serve me for dinner. I'm sorry, but a rose petal doesn't qualify you as being a damn good cook."

"Dinner! Oh, my God!"

She spun around and headed for the kitchen, David following. Arms folded across his chest, he leaned against the doorjamb and admiringly watched Sheila bustle efficiently from refrigerator to counter to stove. Seeing a side of her that he had never seen or imagined, her domestic side, his nervousness eased and he relaxed. He made no offer to help, but stood quietly absorbing the warm feeling of belonging.

"Do you want to talk while you're getting dinner ready?" he asked. "What I have to say won't take long. I'm more interested in what you have to say."

"That might take some time, so why don't we talk after dinner? That way there won't be any interruptions." She opened the oven door and said to him over her shoulder, "Now you're going to find out just how good a cook I am."

Watching her tug at a large platter in the oven, David suddenly stiffened. "Is what I smell what I think I smell?" he asked softly.

Stooped over in front of the open oven, Sheila glanced at him questioningly. Then she looked down at the platter and comprehension brought a shocked and embarrassed expression to her face. "Oh, my God, David, I'm so sorry! I just didn't think. It never dawned on me." Sobbing, she covered her face with her hands.

He took her in his arms and, as if seeking a place to hide, she buried her head deep in his chest. Though he tried to comfort her by patting her consolingly, he was laughing. "You're wonderful," he said. "You truly are. Who else but you, with all your sophistication and style, would be so innocent as to serve a Virginia baked ham to a rabbi?"

"Oh, David, what you must think of me," she mumbled. She was struggling with far more than mere embarrassment. She feared that her blunder would in some way add another stone to the wall that existed between them.

He tilted her chin and looked into her face. After kissing away two teardrops of mortification, he gently said, "You're not so tough after all, are you? And I just did tell you what I think of you. That you're wonderful. That's what I think. That you're wonderful."

His mouth engulfed hers and she shivered as his tongue roamed over her lips. When they drew apart, she was trembling. "Know something, Rabbi? You sure turn me on. Let's talk some other night."

Holding hands tightly, as if afraid to let go of each other or their mood, her head resting on his shoulder, they slowly left the kitchen. When he hesitated, she lifted her arm and pointed languidly down a hall toward a bedroom. Though a small part of her wondered if this was going to be the last time they would ever make love, she didn't care . . .

She felt almost virginal with him. A little fearful and shy but responsive. Her warm, bare flesh against his was a network of exposed nerve-endings, and every touch was a fingernail scraping across the blackboard of her consciousness. She was so absorbed in what was happening to her, in the delicious cascades of pleasure that continuously washed over her, that her entire being was focused on anticipation.

David seemed to intuit not only what she wanted him to do but when to do it. And she responded with slithering movements and little sounds. Squeaks and delighted, contented purrings of pleasure. She clung to him, nails digging hard and deep into his shoulders and arms. Wanting to prolong the quickening pulse of her pleasure, she endured the sweet sensations for as long as she could, but finally she could bear postponement no longer. She had to have him deep inside her. Now.

David lifted his face from her breasts as her fingers grabbed his penis. Their anticipation turned into dismay when nothing happened.

His head fell back to the pillow. He felt her fluttering touch as she moved her hands up and down his torso. Her mouth desperately tried to suck a response, and as she kissed him, he was more aware of her technique than of received pleasure. That awareness of what she was doing caused his oneness with her to evaporate. He was horrified when Naomi's face passed through his consciousness, then disappeared.

His eyes closed as he struggled with his failure to respond, and he tried to will an erection. He felt the delicate, almost imperceptible brush of her fingers before her mouth closed around his manhood. He opened his eyes and she looked up at him over the slight rise of his belly. He was observing her, entranced by the wantonness of her expression and by her vain efforts to arouse him. Like a movie, was his only thought. Shaking his head, he reached down and tugged her away from between his thighs. His face was a mask of torment. On it was written his shame, his embarrassment, his despair.

"I'm so sorry," he whispered.

A single finger across his lips silenced him. "No, don't be sorry. There's nothing to be sorry about. David, please don't torture yourself."

"This has never happened to me before."

"It's all right. It doesn't matter."

He looked deeply into her eyes, then began to cry almost soundlessly when he realized that her concern was solely for him. That there wasn't a single trace of anger or even disappointment. She leaned forward and kissed away his tears, then took him into the protective cave of her arms. Not once in all the years of their marriage had Naomi ever made a gesture of such understanding. Naomi's image appeared, then faded. Sheila finally felt the tension ebbing from his shoulders. Still holding him, she sensed he wanted to talk, to apologize, and she silenced him by the soft press of her lips against his and a throaty, "Shhh, there's nothing to talk about."

She continued to hold him even after he fell asleep. She studied his gradually relaxing face and, not wanting to wake him, stayed in the uncomfortable, awkward position. Her free arm seemed to move of its own volition, and her hand covered his groin, as if trying to protect him. She too fell asleep.

Sheila awoke, drawn out of her dreamless slumber by the tip of his tongue touching her ear. Her eyes blinked open and she looked up into David's smiling face.

"Good morning," he said. "It's almost six o'clock."

"Good morn—" She stopped when she became aware that she was clutching his thick erection.

He didn't have to arouse her. Their lovemaking was immediate, without subtlety, and savage. There were no nuanced caresses, and their thrusting movements were blunt and direct. She couldn't help herself; when she finally plunged into the breaking waves of passion, a deep guttural scream was torn from her throat.

Spent, David lay sprawled across her. When he lifted his face and looked at her, he said, "About last night. I want to—"

"You were fantastic," she interrupted.

". . . explain what—"

"Benjamin, I have never felt the way you make me feel."

"Harrington, will you shut up and let me explain?" David said with feigned indignation.

Playfully, she reached up and tweaked his nose before asking, "Am I complaining? Do I or don't I look like a satisfied woman?"

Her mood silenced his need to tell her of the terrible image of his dead wife, of why he had been impotent. On his knees, he moved to her side and looked down at her nakedness. She felt strangely shy as he studied her, and she wondered if David was aware of how she loved his scrutiny.

"Yeah, you do look like a pretty satisfied woman," he said. He reached down and gently traced the outline of her nipple with his index finger.

"Damn it, Benjamin, that's not fair!"

She slapped his hand away and leaped out of bed. Draping the discarded hostess gown over her body, she pointed with pretended severity at a closed door and ordered, "You, go take a shower while I hustle us up some breakfast. Then we'll talk."

"Ham and eggs?" David asked and winked at her.

She leaped across the bed, the gown dropped away, and, naked, she flailed at him. David caught her arms and held her as she beat at his chest. He wasn't sure if her anger was pretense or not.

"You bastard, you're never going to let me live that down, are you?"

"Nope. Not even after you've cooked me a thousand dinners starting with chopped liver and matzoh balls am I going to let you forget the first one."

Sheila stopped her mock resistance and stared at him, realizing the significance of what he had just said. Nothing she could reply would be adequate, and a witty comeback would be out of place.

Perhaps, at another time, in another place, they would sit down and analyze, carefully delineating the pros and cons, the possible solutions or compromises, that would enable David to deal with the ambivalence of his role as her lover and as a man of God. But now was not the time.

"I would love to cook you a thousand dinners. At least a thousand."

"God, I love you, Sheila Rogers Harrington."

"God, I love you, Rabbi David Lee Benjamin."

CHAPTER
24

They met for lunch in the romantic setting of the Clarkston Cafe. It was a very special restaurant for her. Holding hands, he told her of his love for her, and also of his doubts about their future and the demeaning effects his role would place on her.

"I'm a rabbi and I'm a man and I can't separate the two," he said. "And my being a rabbi diminishes and restricts what you and I can share."

She shook her head. "Don't you think I've thought of that? But I didn't fall in love with the rabbi. I fell in love with the man. Did you fall in love with me because I'm a hotshot automotive executive? No, you fell in love with me because of the kind of woman I am."

"But—"

"No buts. As a rabbi, you have reasons to say 'but.' As a man, those reasons don't exist. I fell in love with the man because of what he is and what he makes me feel about him and about myself. The rabbi has nothing to do with me. And with me, David Benjamin, you can separate yourself. You can just be the man I love. I don't even want to hear about *Rabbi* David Benjamin."

"But there will be times—"

"I know exactly what you're going to say. I've thought about it constantly. That you will have to fragment yourself. That there will be times, because you are a rabbi, you won't be able to see me. That you can't share that part of your life with me. That when our paths cross in public, you will have to ignore me. That we'll have to meet clandestinely, whenever our schedules permit. Let me tell you something, David Benjamin. You might not be aware of this, but the same restrictions hold true for me. Do you think I can appear with you at a United Motors function? Do you think I can openly have an affair with a rabbi? Do you think Anson Phillips would accept you as the man in my life? If he ever found out, he'd ask, no, tell me to resign. Maybe the unwritten rules of the automobile industry are archaic, and some people would even say anti-Semitic, but that's the way they are and I have to live with them. Because as important as your temple is to you, so is my being on the ninth floor to me."

He looked down at her hand in his and said softly, "And what we can share is enough for you?"

"I love you," she said simply, as though the expression of her feelings were the answer to everything.

"What about our future?" he insisted. "What about—"

"Don't, David. Please don't. I don't want to think about a future with you. Only a present. That's all that matters to me now."

"And should you change? Should you want more with me? Should I want more with you? What happens then?"

"I don't know," she said adamantly. "Maybe that will never happen. But if it does, we'll talk about it then. Just like we're talking now."

Her words rekindled a Talmudic expression in his mind: *Yesterday is your past; today is your future—because your tomorrow is unknown.*

The ground rules of their relationship had been established. Aware of his true feelings, David felt the constant pressure of her growing presence in his life. His need to talk was intensified because of the occasional eruption of Naomi's memory. If they had only been honest with each other. If they had only talked. He was determined that would never happen with Sheila again. He would lay his thoughts and his feelings on the line, expose himself, and if she rejected him because she couldn't accept what he had to say, he would understand. But at least they wouldn't be living a lie. He couldn't conceive of that ever happening between them.

They settled into a pattern that allowed them to see as much of each other as possible. They met infrequently in Detroit and its environs, but carefully arranged their travel schedules so their paths crossed whenever possible. In the bedrooms of resort hotels or convention centers, they could be as free and uninhibited in expressing their love as newlyweds. In their own world, they held nothing back. And they never talked about the future, or the intrusions in their lives because of his being a rabbi. Just when and where they would meet next.

Sheila, her arms laden with packages, came into the hotel suite and saw David sprawled acrosss the sofa, apparently asleep. Through the wide picture window of the living room, she could see Mount Rainier, a mantle of pristine snow blanketing its slopes. Looking to the north, she watched a parade of fishing boats, pleasure craft, ferries and tugs waterbeetling on the black-green surface of Puget Sound. She decided that Seattle was the prettiest city she had ever visited and made a mental note to tell David she wanted to come back when their schedules coincided again. She hoped he wouldn't be so tired during their next visit.

Kicking off her shoes, Sheila padded down the small hall in her stocking feet toward the bedroom. David opened one eye. His expression was an expectant anticipatory smile while he listened intently for her response. He grinned when he heard Sheila's joyous shriek and he quickly joined her. She stood in the doorframe, her eyes brimming and her fingers covering her open mouth as she stared in disbelief into the bedroom.

The room overflowed with yellow tea roses, long-stemmed red roses, unsoiled whites and shades of pale pink and vibrant orange hybrids. The fragrance was overpowering and the blossoms were everywhere. They covered the queen-sized bed, they carpeted the floor, they smothered the dresser and the twin night tables. They were hung over picture frames, tucked into lampshades, strung across the backs on the seats of the two chintz-covered chairs. They were even Scotch-taped to the ceiling-to-floor pleated mauve draperies.

Sheila was unable to speak. Shoeless, she walked across the carpet of leaves and flowers, oblivious to the stab of tiny thorns. Occasionally she stopped her inspection tour to finger a single stem from the spaghetti-like snarl on the dressing table; to bury her face into the long, hanging garlands that dangled like tendrils from the draperies; to carefully and meticulously rearrange the scattered bouquets on the chair. Overcome by her feelings, she had to sit down on the edge of the bed.

David looked at her with a boyish grin of pleasure and self-satisfaction lighting his face. Sheila sobbed once, then buried her face in her hands.

Unsure of what to say or do, he stepped over to the bed. She groped blindly for him when he halted in front of her. He knelt and impulsively laid his head in her lap. She gently touched his cheeks with her fingertips, and in response, his hands inched under her skirt and he grasped the flesh of her thighs.

Sensing that movement or sound would shatter the moment, they froze in a tableau of intimacy. But the thorns pricking his knees finally caused him to shift his weight and he looked up at her, his face glowing.

"Do you want to make love?" he asked softly.

"We just did."

CHAPTER
25

After his scheduled study session with Kelly Prentis, David met with a group of young people in his study. He was concerned about the sparse attendance of younger people at his services and with their limited involvement in temple affairs. The group met with him to discuss the problem. The spokesperson for the young people, a dark intense woman of twenty-two who reminded David of a younger Naomi, summed up their feelings: "Rabbi, we don't come to temple very often because what you talk about doesn't fit in the real world. It just isn't relevant because it doesn't have much meaning to us."

A silently remembered Talmudic quotation shaped David's response: *Don't limit a child to your learning. For he was born in another time.*

"How do I find out what is relevant to young people?" he asked with sincerity.

"By listening to us, Rabbi," the young woman said fervently. "Listening to the things we talk about to each other. We talk about everyday kind of things. Sex. Shacking up. Disarmament. Politics. That kind of stuff. Not the lessons in the Bible. We talk about marriage. But not the way you or our parents talk about it. You all have this image that we'll marry Jewish kids and live happily ever after. But did it ever enter your minds that we might want to marry gentiles? Or blacks?"

He felt hypocritical as he responded: "I'm a Jew and a rabbi, and my religion opposes mixed marriages," he said softly.

"We know that, Rabbi, but that's not the point. The point is that you have to admit that mixed marriages do happen these days. Even to Jewish kids. That's reality to us. That's relevant to us. Those are the kinds of issues we need to talk about. But we never hear them discussed in our homes or in your temple."

When David finished the questioning, an hour later, he had a legal pad full of notes and suggestions. After reading over what he had written, he buzzed the intercom. Florence, carrying her steno pad, came into his office. Her expression, after looking disdainfully at the group of young people, said, Rabbi, I hope you're not going to waste my time . . .

David told her he wanted a letter to go out to every congregational member between the ages of sixteen and thirty-five, inviting them to a series of discussion groups to be held on Wednesday evenings in the large auditorium. He defined them as "rap sessions" and listed the topics that would be discussed, adding, "I want you to find some guest speakers who are experts on those subjects. Florence, this discussion group is very important to me and to the future of the temple, so I want a lot of publicity put out about it. Sandy Becker owns an ad agency, maybe you can get together with him and work out a campaign. I'm sure he'll be glad to help."

Even though she left his office without comment, David knew from Florence's expression that she disapproved.

An hour later, he returned from lunch with Brian to find Harold Fedder waiting for him in his office. The board member's first angry statement was, "What the hell do you think you're doing?"

"I assume you're upset, Harold, because Florence called you about my proposed lecture series," David said calmly. "The pupose of those meetings is to bring young people back into the temple."

"How? By talking about fucking and sucking! About shacking up! Are you out of your mind! You don't discuss things like that in a synagogue. Especially with kids."

"Harold, it's time they were discussed. We can't continue to ignore them. They do happen. Even to Jewish kids. And we have to confront them. The best place to do that is right here in the temple."

Both hands anchored on the desk, Fedder leaned forward and vehemently said, "Rabbi Benjamin, I forbid you to go ahead with this crazy idea of yours."

David stood up. "Mister Fedder, I'm going to remind you that I'm also the rabbi of the young people in this congregation. And

I'm going to do what I think is necessary to satisfy their needs as well as yours."

"You're going to fight me?" Fedder asked in disbelief.

"I am on this issue."

"Do you know what you're doing!"

"Mr. Fedder, a rabbi whose congregation doesn't want to run him out of town isn't a rabbi; and a rabbi whose congregation does run him out of town isn't a man. I'm a rabbi and I'm a man, so yes, I know exactly what I'm doing. And what I have to do."

His face flushed with anger, David punched the intercom. "Florence, come in here." When she appeared, he said, "Next time I tell you to do something you go ahead and do it. I'll give you the right to discuss it with me because I value your experience and your opinions. But that's the only right I give you. There'll be no fighting with me about my decisions."

Disturbed by Harold Fedder's continuing opposition to every program he wanted to develop, David couldn't concentrate for the rest of the afternoon. He thought of Sheila, who was in San Francisco meeting with Anson Phillips, Lawton Collins and district sale managers in the Bay Area to hear her plan to revamp United's dealers in the region. She had worked on the plan for several months and was sure her proposals would be approved. David was to meet her in two days and they would then leave for the Hawaiian island of Kauai. Needing the comfort of her presence, he changed his schedule. He would surprise her by appearing a day early.

He impatiently paced the crowded sidewalk in front of the office building in downtown San Francisco where she had told him the conference was being held. He hadn't informed her he had changed his schedule and hoped to surprise her by taking her to lunch. Palms sweating with anticipation and because of his need to be with her, he anxiously watched the revolving doors.

It was a lovely warm spring day and she had chosen to wear a full-skirted, narrow-waisted, lime-green summer dress with a white, spaghetti-strapped bodice covered by a short jacket. As she pushed through the doors, blinking in the bright sunlight, men passing by turned to look at her and smiled in appreciation. David reacted as he always did when he saw her—with intense excitement and pleasure. He noticed immediately that she seemed angry.

Edging through the crowd toward her, he thought, The meeting didn't turn out the way she planned. She didn't get what she wanted. He forgot about his own needs and tried to think of something he could do to change her mood.

She was so intent on her thoughts, so involved in replaying the meeting to determine where she had made her mistakes, that initially she didn't recognize David when he stopped her with his arms spread wide.

Annoyed, she snapped at him, "What do you want? Get out of my way before I call—"

"—a cop?" He burst out laughing when recognition flooded over her face. But he continued the game. "Hey, c'mon, lady, this isn't a pass. I just want to tell you that you're a very special lady."

Sheila, a smile on her lips, played along. She studied him guardedly. "Listen, mister, there are all kinds of weirdos in San Francisco," she said, trying to make her voice stern. "Get lost." Pushing him aside, she stepped off the curb and pretended to look for a cab. David followed and heard the shriek of a shrill whistle as Sheila's two fingers dropped from her mouth. He clapped his hands in exaggerated applause and bystanders grinned as they watched. Then she abruptly motioned for David to join her. He pretended not to understand by questioningly pointing to himself. When she nodded and snapped her fingers, he stood close to her.

"Don't I know you from someplace?" she asked with a quirky little smile. "You look very familiar. Haven't we met?"

David studied her face intently and then shook his head. "I don't think so. I'm Merwyn Fink. Does the name mean anything to you?"

Smothering a giggle, Sheila shook her head. She held out her hand and said, "But I'm pleased to meet you, Merwyn. I'm Blossom Fansler." She hesitated and then asked seriously, "What did you mean when you said I was a very special lady?"

"Blossom, you have a lot more grace and a lot more charm and style, and you're a hell of a lot more feminine than most women. In my book that makes you a very special lady."

Sheila pretended to reflect on his. Finally she asked, "Merwyn, where are you going now?"

Quickly, he pointed diagonally across the street at a tall, glass building on the opposite corner and said, "I've got an appointment over there in less than an hour." Then, with a suggestive laugh, he added, "Blossom, what did you have in mind?"

"Do you have time to buy me a drink?" With a tinkling laugh, she added, "Merwyn?"

"Blossom, you're on."

Noticing the sign, he steered her by the elbow and guided her back into the building she had just left. As they walked down a wide flight of black marble stairs, men turned to stare at her and Sheila chuckled when she heard David mumble, "Eat your hearts out." He escorted her into a dimly lit, walnut-paneled cocktail lounge that was decorated as an English pub. They seated themselves at the empty bar.

"Something cool," she said to the bartender. "A Tom Collins."

"Make it two," David said. With his elbow on the bar, he leaned his face on the cup of his hand and grinned at her with appreciation. "Blossom, are you married?" he asked seriously. "A girl like you must be married."

"Oh, yes, I'm married. Very happily. For over ten years."

He mimicked a disappointed pout. "That's too bad—because I was going to romance the hell out of you."

"Well, maybe not all *that* happily," she said quickly. Then she looked at her watch, checking the time until she was to meet with Anson Phillips to discuss her mistakes at the meeting. "Why don't you go ahead and romance me for as long as our drinks last?"

David called loudly to the bartender. "Make those two Tom Collins tall. Very tall."

She slid off the barstool, saying, "I've got to make a call, but I'll be right back. Merwyn, that's a promise."

David waited until she was gone before asking the bartender, "Is there a florist in the lobby?" He took a fifty-dollar bill out of his wallet and handed it to him. "Order a bouquet to be sent down here immediately. I don't care what kind of flowers, but the card has to read: 'To Blossom Fansler from Merwyn Fink. Two very special people.' "

The bartender, caught up in the mood, chuckled as he went to the phone on the backbar and placed the order. The delivery was made a few minutes after Sheila returned, and the bartender's pleased expression matched hers as she clutched the huge bouquet to her breasts. "Romance me, Merwyn," she whispered. "I'm waiting to be romanced."

They held hands. They touched. They laughed. They talked intimately. They kissed softly. They were so deeply involved with each other and what they were feeling that they thought they were the only man and woman in the world.

Sheila finished her drink and with a final deep sigh sadly said,

"Merwyn, I don't want to, but I've got to go. Can you wait with me while I get a cab?"

On the sidewalk, David motioned to a passing taxi, which swerved to the curb with tires screeching. Reluctantly, he held the rear door open. Cradling the bouquet, Sheila started to get in. Suddenly she stopped and turned to face him. The flowers creating a fragrant barrier between them, she kissed his cheek and said, "Good-bye, Merwyn Fink. As long as I live, I'll always remember these twenty-five minutes I spent with you. I'll never forget them."

"Neither will I, Blossom Fansler. Neither will I."

"God, I love you, Rabbi David Benjamin," she mouthed from the taxi.

"God, I love you, Sheila Rogers Harrington," he mouthed back.

Twenty-four hours later, they were on the Hawaiian island of Kauai, standing silently in front of the primitive cabin perched on the edge of a high, sheer cliff that knife-dropped to the pristine, empty beach below. For a while, they watched the late afternoon sun dip toward the horizon line of the ocean. Then David took her hand and stepped off the lanai and began to walk toward the terraced steps cut into the cliff leading down to the white sand. Behind her, in the dense, junglelike underbrush, she heard the crash of a waterfall. She tugged him away from the cliff's edge and instead they followed a narrow, flower-scented trail until they came to the cascade. Side by side, they watched it thunder down into a deep pool. She stripped, poised herself, then flung her body into the darkening blue sky. She seemed to hang suspended for a moment, then knifed deeply into the crystal-clear water.

Surfacing, she grinned and motioned for David to join her. He seemed to hesitate before hurriedly shucking his pants and sneakers. He too poised naked, then arched skyward before plunging into the pool. Side by side, occasionally touching, they swam back and forth leisurely. Discovering that the fragrant pool fed into a river that flowed slowly to the sea, they let the warm current gently cushion them down to the beach. It was night when they lay close to each other on their backs on the still-warm sand. Overhead, an eternity away yet close enough to touch, an infinity of sparkling blue-white diamond chips illumined the blackness of space.

Awed and overwhelmed by the mutual feeling of being the only human beings alive in the universe, as if by instinct they felt the compulsion to make love. The only sound, other than their own responses to the exquisiteness of their aroused and then satisfied sensations, was the quiet clap-clap-clapping of wavelets breaking on the shore.

Afterward, deliciously spent, they lay as before, side by side, but this time with David's arm around her shoulders and her leg sprawled across his. When they began to talk, it was in whispers. As though they were afraid that any louder sound would shatter the solemnity of their feelings.

"David, do you feel like I feel? That we've finally found Paradise?"

"Of course. This island *is* Paradise. Here we can pretend." He thought of the continuing conflict with Harold Fedder and added, "Here the world doesn't intrude. There's just you and me. Here, we can shut everything else out. Nothing else exists."

"Can we come back here again?"

"And again and again. Whenever we can."

She rolled over onto her stomach and rested her head on his chest. He heard her whisper, "Wouldn't it be wonderful if we could find a way to spend the rest of our lives here?"

"Paradise . . . ," he said.

The recollection of his confrontation with Harold Fedder returned and caused a tightening of his muscles and a change in his mood. Aware, Sheila lifted her face and, spiking her elbows into the sand, asked, "Is anything wrong?" Though he shook his head, his expression caused her to pursue. "Benjamin, are you afraid to talk about it with me becaue you know you'll get straight answers and you don't want to hear them?"

He laughed as he sat up. "Harrington, you're about as subtle as a kid caught with his hand in the cookie jar. I can't talk about it with you because that would break the ground rules we established. Remember? Just loving. Fun and games. Romancing. Nothing else."

She stared out at the ocean for a long time and then said gravely, "I remember. Those were the rules we set up because it was the only way you could accept being with me. You could forget about being a rabbi because I was only interested in you as a man. Right?"

"Right," he nodded. "But I can't pretend any longer."

"I understand. I knew it was just a matter of time before that happened to you. Too bad it couldn't last longer, because now the teenage love affair is over and it's time to grow up. Time to let in the real world."

"Disappointed?"

"Of course. For a time I shared something with you that every woman dreams of experiencing. It was all feelings, all emotions. We built nothing, we created nothing, we made no plans, we had no future. We just shared each other. With you I reached emotional heights that I never even knew existed. Do you remember all the times I said, often with my eyes filled with tears, that I loved you more today than I did yesterday and that I'll love you more tomorrow than I did today? Do you remember my saying that to you?" After David nodded, she said, "Well, every time I said those words to you, David Benjamin, I meant them. Because every time I said them, they were true. And I'll always be grateful to you for letting me love you that way."

He was silent and she continued. "But now you can no longer separate yourself?" He nodded again. "Okay, then it's time to change the ground rules. You *are* a rabbi. I can no longer pretend that doesn't affect us."

The accepting of the reality caused their minds to play with what that meant and the images caused them to withdraw from each other. She was aware that for the first time they were no longer sharing the formerly delicious sensation of intimacy and belonging. When his fingers crawled across the sand and entwined with hers, she could tell the same realization was torturing him, that he too wanted to close the chasm that both of them saw opening before them. But he didn't know how.

"What's happening to us?" she asked barely audibly.

"The teenage love affair is over," he said. "We just stopped pretending and the real world just stepped in."

CHAPTER
26

After the weekend on Kauai, they didn't see each other for two months. The highest priority at United Motors was a new line of compacts that was to be unveiled in the early fall, and because of an emergency caused by illness among several members of a team of top management personnel, Anson Phillips had thrust Sheila into the demanding role of assistant division manager of the division that was developing the experimental line. Her seven-day-a-week, sixteen-hour work day was so consuming that, other than an occasional hurried telephone call, she had no contact with David. He related to her demanding schedule, for his was equally as exacting.

Because of the increased obligations caused by their expanding careers, negating even their clandestine meetings, they rarely thought of where the future would lead. Their future was the idyllic moment, and tomorrow was only the anticipation of being together again. Occasionally when alone and missing the other, the thought erupted. But because the catalyst was always the sweet nostalgia of tender memories, of how it was when they shared a weekend at Aspen or Palm Springs, they never talked about a change in their relationship. They weren't afraid to face it; they had no reason to face it.

In early October, the new line of compacts a success and on their way to dealer showrooms, Anson Phillips insisted that an exhausted Sheila take at least a week off to recharge herself. David, after rearranging his schedule, took his long delayed vacation at the same time. They headed east from Detroit in a rental car, driving across Ohio and into Pennsylvania. Their destination, at the end of the trip, was Richmond, Virginia, and the annual gathering of Sheila's relatives from all over the country to celebrate her mother and father's wedding anniversary. David would continue on to Washington and she would rejoin him after the reunion was over.

In no rush, savoring every moment of being together again, they drove slowly and aimlessly. The trip was a continuation of their previous relationship. Romantic and fulfilling because they were isolated from their careers and from the intrusion of outsiders. They stopped to make love whenever the mood struck them, usually in a bed-and-breakfast home in a small town. They behaved like tourists, taking lots of pictures and burying useless souvenirs wherever they went. They spent almost two full days at Gettysburg and other Civil War battlefields before, on a whim, heading on to the restored colonial settlement in Williamsburg, Virginia.

The days fled by until finally it was time for Sheila to join her family in Richmond. They drove along the James River and then north along Route 5. Closer to home, she animatedly pointed out the private academy where she had gone to school, the horse farm where she had learned to ride, the country lane, where on a hayride, she had been kissed for the first time. She wanted to share that part of her past with him and his reaction pleased her.

"I wish I had known you then. I'd have more reasons to love you."

She had never missed the yearly family reunion, but went only out of obligation and respect to her parents. Though she enjoyed seeing her cousins and aunts and uncles, she felt out of place and was always in a hurry to leave. Because she had been so absorbed in her career and had felt nothing in common with her relatives, she was usually quietly introspective and retiring during the boisterous, happy affair, behaving more like an observer than a participant. But as they approached the outskirts of Richmond, she realized that for the first time since she was a young girl, she was looking forward to the gathering of her clan. There was something new and wonderful in her life that she wanted to share with them.

Impulsively, she turned to David who was driving, and said, "Why don't you come? I'd love for you to meet my folks. Especially my mother."

He drove in silent thought for a while before responding. "Why?" he asked slowly.

"Because I love you," she answered quickly, "and I want my mother to meet the man I love."

"I understand why you want me to meet your mother and I'd like to meet her, but how would you introduce me? As your secret lover? What would you tell her about the two of us? That we can't be seen in public because I'm a rabbi? Do you know what your mother would say? 'What's my nice gentile unmarried daughter doing with a rabbi? What kind of a future is that for her?' And she'd be right. How do you think she'd react to meeting me?"

David's response to her impulsive suggestion caused her to think of the questions her mother would ask. *How serious are you about this man? Have you made any plans about the future?* How would she answer? With lies? Sighing disappointedly, she said to him, "And so the outside world intrudes again on us, doesn't it?"

"But only when we let it," he answered. "And we can't afford to do that. We have no reason to let it intrude because nothing has changed between us." He slowed and studied her face and asked, "Or has it?"

His question jolted her. Has anything changed? she asked herself. Realizing that he was right, she couldn't introduce him to her mother, not ever, she now had a reason to take a first tentative step in facing their future. Because the images were unacceptable, she wished she was back on Kauai making love rather than driving into Richmond and the family reunion. She thought of calling her mother and making an excuse for not showing up and going on to Washington with David.

When she didn't respond to his question, he squeezed her hand reassuringly and said, "Think about it. It's important to both of us that you do. In the meantime, direct me to the airport and I'll go on to Washington. I've got some things that I need to take care of anyway. You spend a few days with your folks and we'll meet in say, two days? Then we'll talk."

"Where will you be staying?"

"At the Mayflower."

She felt a sense of apprehension and wanted to say no, any place but the Mayflower. But because she felt foolish, that her anxiety was unwarranted, she said, "Okay. I'll meet you at the Mayflower in two days."

The family reunion cracked the mirror of her mind. Blurred images cleared and then focused. Until that day she had only reacted superficially to the new baby, to the cousin who was getting married in the spring, to the related incidents of the previously inconsequential small triumphs and tragedies that made up the texture of the lives that were entwined with hers. Because in times past, she had been solely motivated by her career, she had felt distant and disconnected. Now she needed to be a part of it.

The focus of the reunion, the repeating of their marriage vows by her mother and father, the role model of their union, her awareness that they completed each other, made her realize what was missing in her own life. The total sharing of that life with someone else. She had her career, she was successful, a highly respected professional. However, for the first time, she wanted more. What she shared with David no longer had dimension enough and was too limiting. What she had rejected eight years ago with Spencer Tolliver was what she wanted. Home, wife, mother. She hadn't been ready then. Now she was. She was thirty-three years old. Her biological clock was running out. She had proven herself. It was time.

She would never have been susceptible to the acceptance of her awareness if she hadn't found the man she wanted to share her life with. David Benjamin. She was overwhelmed by her need for him to be there. She wanted to be able to introduce him to her family, and to say, "This is the man I'm going to marry."

She had her reason for thinking about their future.

But she didn't pretend or fantasize. Wryly smiling, she said aloud, "But with a rabbi! How are you going to get it . . . ?"

Two days later, driving toward Washington, overwhelmed by her feelings, she told herself, I don't know how. Propelled by her image of what their life together would be like, she couldn't conceive of it not happening. If he wants what I want, we'll find a way.

David had never been so lonely. He had filled the two days with conferences and meetings, but when alone he was miserable. He thought of how he and Sheila had parted at the airport in Richmond, with reluctance and apprehension, and realized why. The idyllic moment was no longer enough. Their future could never again be an unrelated string of tomorrows, filled only with clandestine romantic trysts. He, too, wanted more.

His thoughts about her had more depth because he realized the impact she had made on his life. How she had filled his every image and every expectation. He couldn't help, for the first time, projecting a future with her.

He struggled with the smothering effects his role would have on them. But only for a moment. "Don't borrow from tomorrow's troubles," he told himself, pacing the hotel suite while he waited for Sheila. "How do you even know she wants what you want? If she does, you'll find a way."

He answered her knock and she flew into his arms. They clutched at each other, as if they hadn't been together for months. It was as if by the closeness of their embrace, they were drawing strength from the other. Or was it reassurance? After he kissed her, she said, "God, I've missed you. How long has it been? A year?"

"Seems that way, doesn't it?" Still holding her, kissing her hair, he asked, "How was the reunion? Did you have a good time?"

The memory of the birth of feelings during the family get-together caused her to close her eyes. "It was okay," she murmured. "It would have been better if you had been there." She tensed, waiting for his reaction.

"I wish I had been." He paused and then added, "Maybe next year."

She stepped back and asked, "Do you mean that? Benjamin, don't tease me. Don't play games."

"Have I ever played games with you?" he asked seriously. Then, not sure of how to continue, he was relieved to be able to momentarily change the subject. "Where's your bag?" he asked.

"I left it in the car."

"You're not planning to stay?"

"Depends on how you react to what I have to say," she said.

"Is that a threat?"

She shook her head vehemently. "Maybe it's an inducement." When he grinned again, she continued. "Benjamin, before I let you put your hands on me again, we've got to talk. When you left me in Richmond, you told me to think about us. I have. Long and hard. We're terrific in bed, but every so often we've got to get out of bed. I love our style together; the romancing and the excitement of just being with you. If we could lock ourselves away on that island, it would be enough."

"But we can't lock ourselves away on that island," he quietly interrupted.

"That's right," she agreed quickly. "And because we can't, the question we have to face is where do we go from here?"

"Harrington, where do you want to go from here?" he asked seriously. "What will you settle for?"

"My father once said to me that I never had to settle for less. I've always believed that. I still do. So I can't, I won't settle for anything less than the whole ball of wax with you."

"Which is?"

"Everything. Marriage. Home. Babies. Lots of babies."

"That's the bottom line?"

"That's the bottom line, mister."

"And your career?" he asked.

"What about my career? I can handle it all. Lots of woman do."

He thought of asking, What about my career? Can you handle that? But he refrained, because at the moment it didn't seem important. She was studying him with a near-defiant expression, waiting for his response. "Harrington," he said with a smile, "I didn't know you were the marrying kind."

"Try me, mister. Just try me."

"Is that a proposal? If it is, I accept."

Astonished, and then with a cry of delight, she flung herself at him. Clinging to him, her eyes brimming, she murmured, "Why did you change your mind?"

"Because I wanted to meet your mother. The only way I can is to make an honest woman out of you."

She burst out laughing and then began to beat at his chest with her tiny fists, saying, "You bastard. And I bet you'll never let me forget that I had to propose to you."

"I'll even tell our children," he said. Framing her face in his hands, he added, "And I hope they all have red hair, just like you."

They stood silently in the embrace, the intruding thought of what he was, a rabbi, momentarily silenced by the joy caused by the images of their future. However, as time passed the thought became more insistent. When the pressure became unbearable, she lifted her head from his chest and in a low voice, said, "But what about—"

He interrupted her by lifting her into his arms. As he carried her into the bedroom, he said, "No more questions. We've talked enough for now."

"It won't go away."

"I know that. But this isn't the time to talk about it. As it says in Ecclesiastes, *There is a time to love* . . . this is that time."

As she surrendered, she remembered the rest of the quotation: . . . *and a time to hate.* She suddenly shivered; partly in response to his touch, partly from fear . . .

They lay comfortably in each other's arms talking about a future. As if by silent agreement, they avoided facing the issue they knew they would have to confront sooner or later. They were so caught up in the joyous excitement of their future that they didn't want to contaminate it in any way.

They explored and discovered each other's everyday likes and dislikes, the conversation often punctuated by boisterous laughter. ". . . Yes, I certainly can cook other things besides ham." ". . . Don't ever ask me to fix anything, I'm a danger to society with a hammer in my hand." ". . . I'm allergic to pink and I hate kitchen wallpaper filled with ivy." Their excitement was contagious because they had moved into areas they had never explored together. There had never been a reason or a purpose before. But, because of the unspoken, they fantasized, attempting to create the same idyllic relationship but in a different setting and with a new cast of characters.

But though they had moved into the future, they had taken the past with them. It was there in the way they assiduously avoided talking about his role. In the past, there had rarely been the need to discuss it. Now, because they were playing at planning a future, they didn't want to discuss it. To talk about it was to end the richly satisfying and fulfilling game.

The phone rang and David reached across Sheila to answer. Remembering the last time they had been in this hotel and he had answered the phone, a sense of foreboding clutched at her heart.

"Senator!" he said in surprise. He looked at her and his eyes widened as if with helplessness. "How good to hear from you."

"David, where the hell have you been! I've been trying to find you for two days. There's a state dinner for Begin tonight and the Prime Minister and the President want you there to give the invocation."

"Why me? They can get any rabbi to give an invocation."

"Begin doesn't want any rabbi. He wants you. The 'Rabbi's rabbi.' Remember? 'The Rabbi for all reasons.' Besides, he wants to talk with you after dinner. He'll be leaving tomorrow and this is the only time he has."

"What does he want to talk about?"

"How the hell would I know? David, the Prime Minister of Israel doesn't tell me his business. I'm sure he doesn't want to talk to you about the weather. Whatever it is it's important, and he wouldn't want to talk to you about it if you weren't who you are."

He looked at Sheila and said apologetically into the phone, "If you had only let me know sooner, I could have made it. I'm sorry, Senator, but I have other plans. I'm busy tonight."

"What other plans? How busy? Cancel them"

Lies flicked through his mind, but none of them would justify an excuse. Sheila, unsure of what was happening, slowly got out of bed. Wrapping the counterpane around her body, she walked to the chair against the wall and sat down. Watching David, she thought, He's talking about our future. Fight for it, David, she silently prayed. Oh, fight for it . . .

"Personal plans," he finally said.

After a long silence, the senator, in a low monotone, said, "David, I don't know what's going on and I don't want to know. But, Rabbi, you don't have a personal life. Any more than I do. You made the choice just like I did. A personal life is not your priority because you're not just David Benjamin, you're *Rabbi* David Benjamin. Just like I'm *Senator* Walter Mendes. You can't separate who and what you are anymore than I can. I'm not asking you to make a choice. I'm telling you to do what you *have* to do. Because what you want to do doesn't matter. What you have to do does matter."

It wasn't the senator's threat that caused him to shiver, it was the reacceptance of the dichotomy of what he was. Caught up in the excitement of planning a future with the woman he loved, it was easy to pretend that division of self didn't exist. Looking at Sheila, clutching the counterpane around her as if in protection, and listening to the senator's voice, he faced the separation within. The man or the rabbi? His response told him he couldn't divide himself.

"I'll be there as soon as I get a cab, Senator."

"You don't need a cab. My limousine is waiting in front of your hotel."

As he slowly hung up he realized that the senator had never doubted what he would do. That he had no reason to doubt. That as a rabbi, David had no choices. He had only one path to travel.

"I've got to go out for a few hours," he said to Sheila.

"Where?"

"A state dinner at the White House."

"Take me."

"I can't."

"Why not?"

"You know the answer to that as well as I do."

"Why not?" she demanded. "Because you can't be seen with a shiksa on your arm?"

"That's unfair."

"No, it isn't. Not when just a few minutes ago you were talking about marriage and children and our life together. Which is more important, David, loving me and being loved by me or being a rabbi?"

"I can't answer that. That's like comparing oranges and apples."

"You have to answer that. You must answer that."

Because of her frustration and her anger, he sensed that to continue the conversation would only drive them further apart. He went to her and tried to take her hands in his but she yanked free. Looking at her, he said, "There is an answer for us. There's got to be. I don't know what it is, but we'll find it."

"I'm not so sure anymore that there is an answer, David," she replied thoughtfully. "There's something wrong when a religion separates a man who loves me the way you do from the woman who loves him the way I love you."

He kneeled in front of her and reached for her hands. She didn't resist. "Try to understand," he said. "That's not what's wrong. What's wrong is that I'm a rabbi who loves you the way I do. That you love a rabbi the way you do."

"I don't understand," she said wearily. "Explain it to me."

"I can't," he answered. "I'm not sure I understand it myself."

She sat quietly in the chair while he dressed quickly in a dark suit. Before he left, he came to her again and said, "I'll be back in a couple of hours. We'll talk then. We'll find a way. I promise."

He bent to kiss her. Her lips were lifeless against his. At the door, he said, "Good-bye," and she nodded. After the door closed, she added, "Rabbi."

She dressed as if in a trance. Finished, she sat on the edge of the bed with her hands folded limply in her lap. Thoughts cascaded into her mind and she felt herself being swept away by her inability to understand.

"He's a rabbi," she said aloud, "and I don't even know what that means. I don't know that part of him. I don't understand it. If he were a priest, I could understand. His commitment to his God would be greater than his commitment to me. But that isn't true. All I understand is that's the part of him that shuts me out. That I can't share." She stood up and, after straightening her skirt, asked herself, "Will I ever be able to share it?"

When David returned a little after midnight, he called her name as soon as he opened the door. There was no response and he rushed through the suite looking for her. She was gone. He saw the note propped on the pillow and read it hungrily:

David,

I know you want what I want, but can we ever have it? Will I have to settle for less? Am I willing to do that? Can I do that? I don't know. I'll let you know when I have the answer. For the time being, I need to be alone in order to find it.

I love you very dearly.
I always will.

Sheila

CHAPTER
27

David had to force himself not to call her. His anxiety about her decision prevented him from concentrating on anything but hearing from her. Trying to project her answer, he devised compromises that might satisfy both of them. Realizing that none of his proposed solutions answered the single factor that separated them, his being a rabbi, he rejected every one of them.

He struggled to resolve the predicament he had never been faced with before. His being a rabbi had always been his highest priority; everything that had happened to him had reinforced that decision. He had always accepted without question that his role was his reason for being. But because it was his life it never before had intruded on his life. Never before had his being a rabbi stood like a barrier between what he was and the fulfillment of the personal and private world he wanted. He was confronted by questions that he had never asked himself. He had never had a reason to ask them before. *Is it so important that I be a rabbi? More important to me than the woman I love? Does being a rabbi mean I have to sacrifice that woman? Is what I accomplish as a rabbi worth the sacrifice?*

Though he had no answers, for the first time, he began to have doubts.

Sheila called him on the day of Kelly Prentis's conversion. As a nervous Meyer Loeb paced his office, David tried to respond to her with terse answers.

"David, I've come to a decision."

"Tell me."

"No, not over the phone."

"I understand. Tonight?"

"No. Can you get away? Say next weekend?"

He shuffled through his calendar. "Yes. I can make it."

"Good. Meet me."

"Where?"

"On Kauai. Paradise."

"So we can shut the world out?"

"So we can try to shut the world out," she agreed before hanging up.

He was grateful for Meyer Loeb's presence. For the moment, he didn't have to think about what had just been said. Or try to interpret hidden meanings in her words.

"Meyer, for goodness' sake, stop pacing and relax," he said to the old man. "Kelly is as ready to face the Beth Din as you are. She's going to do just fine. So sit down because you're making me nervous."

"Good. That makes two of us. If I'm going to be nervous, I want company. You're sure she's ready? I know she's been preparing for almost a year, but—"

David's understanding laugh interrupted the old man, and David motioned to the chair on the other side of his desk. Reluctantly, Meyer Loeb sat down. "Meyer, she's ready because she wants this as much as you do."

Unable to contain himself, the old man got up and began to pace again. David gently led him back to the chair. "Please, Meyer, for your own good I want you to try to relax. Why can't you believe me that everything is going to be all right? Kelly is going to meet with the Beth Din in about an hour and they're going to accept her. Then she'll be converted tonight at Shabbat and the wedding will be held this Sunday afternoon. Just like we planned."

"Then where is she?" Loeb demanded. "Why isn't she here? I want to wish her luck before she goes to meet with the Beth Din."

"She's at work. Meyer, I hate to tell you this, but I told her not to come here because I knew you'd make her more nervous than she already is. It's not Kelly I'm worried about. She'll do fine. It's you."

"My son is getting married on Sunday. My future daughter-in-law is being converted tonight. How do you expect me to be?"

"Meyer, people have gotten married before, people have been converted before, and this world didn't end."

"This isn't just a wedding. This is more like a convention. We got relatives and friends coming in from everywhere. Some even all the way from Israel. And everything depends on her being converted tonight."

The old man agitatedly studied an itemized list of tasks to be done for Sunday's wedding. Mumbling to himself, he said, "Haircut, cleaners, musicians, liquor, ushers, bridesmaids . . ." He reached the final item on the list and shook a warning finger at David. "You're not going to pull a fast one on me this Sunday, are you? You're definitely going to be here to marry my son, aren't you?"

"Meyer, stop worrying. Meyer, I'll be here."

"And if Brezhnev calls and wants you to go to Moscow, you're going to tell him you're busy, aren't you? That you have a previous engagement?"

Shaking his head in amusement, David said, "This Sunday Meyer Loeb has got me. I promise."

Loeb suddenly smiled sheepishly and said, "Maybe if you had a son who was getting married, you'd understand how I feel."

"Meyer, I've imagined having a son for so long, believe me, I understand how you feel. And someday I'll probably act just the way you're acting now."

He couldn't help thinking about the son he had never known and the family he had never had. He couldn't hide the brief expression of agony that passed across his face. He thought of Sheila and couldn't conceal the depths of his need for her.

Seeing the look of pained empathy on the old man's face, David forced himself to change the mood by bantering, "And when I have that son, Meyer, I'll ask you to be his godfather."

"Rabbi, it will be my pleasure and an honor."

David, embarrassed by the open emotional display, looked at his watch and said, "We'll talk about it when I have more time. Right now I have to go pick up Kelly."

Kelly wasn't waiting for him in the hospital waiting room as they had arranged, so David went to the counter where a charge nurse was working on a pile of metal-covered medical reports.

"Nurse Kelly Prentis?" he asked hesitantly. "She was supposed to meet me here."

Without looking up, the nurse pointed down a long corridor to the left. She kept thrusting her index finger at the distant hall until David shrugged and backed away.

The closed doors lining the corridor added to his confusion. Not wanting to disturb the patients, he debated whether to go back to the charge nurse. Hesitantly, he peeked into an open door at the end of the hall.

Still in her nurse's uniform, Kelly was kneeling at the altar rail in the hospital chapel.

In front of a statue of the Madonna and Child.

Though David couldn't make out the words formed on her moving lips, he realized she was praying.

His first thought was of Meyer Loeb and he groaned loudly in despair. Startled, Kelly looked over her shoulder, saw David and stood up. After she crossed herself, with eyes brimming, she walked down the aisle to meet him. They stood silently for a moment, looking into each other's faces as if seeking an acceptable explanation.

"Why?" David asked. "Why, Kelly?" His voice was choked with anguish.

"Because I'm confused and I'm frightened."

"I can understand that," David said. "I'd expect you to be."

"I wanted help. Answers. Peace of mind." She looked over her shoulder at the Madonna before she continued. "I thought maybe if I prayed, if I talked to Her, She'd help me." Kelly turned, looked at David and added, "Please try to understand, Rabbi. Don't be angry with me."

He took both of her hands in his and said softly, "I'm not angry with you, Kelly. Disappointed, yes, but not angry. And I think I'm more disappointed with myself than I am with you. But I do understand."

She looked at him hopefully. "Then everything is still all right? I can go meet with the Beth Din?"

He shook his head. "No. I can understand how giving up your heritage and a belief for something that has to be strange and alien to you would cause your confusions and your fears. It would be a rare convert who didn't have those feelings."

"Then why can't I meet with the Beth Din?" she asked in a pleading voice. "Haven't I done everything you've asked of me for almost a year?"

"Even more than I've asked," David said with a sad sigh. "And, intellectually, you understand what it is to be a Jew. But acceptance of Judaism must come from your heart and soul and not from your mind. Embracing the faith intellectually is not enough."

"But how do you know that I haven't?" Kelly asked timidly. "How can you be so sure of how I feel when I'm not sure?"

"Because if you believed with all your heart and soul, if you had that kind of faith, you would have done your praying in a synagogue instead of a chapel. You would have come to me, your rabbi, for guidance and answers instead of talking to a statue."

She thought about his words and he wished he could take the sad expression of disappointment off her face. "You're not going to give up, are you?"

She slowly shook her head, then asked, "But will I ever feel that way, Rabbi? Will I ever have more than just an intellectual acceptance."

"I think so, Kelly."

"How will you know?"

"I won't. But you will. And you'll tell me. And that's when I'll convert you."

His words caused her to realize the consequences of David's decision, and her hands went to her face. "Oh my God, what about the wedding? What about the ceremony tonight?"

He shook his head. "There'll be no wedding. There'll be no conversion. Not in my temple. If you want, you can be married in a civil ceremony."

"I can't do that to Meyer Loeb. It would break his heart."

David tried to comfort her. "I'll talk to Meyer and try to make him understand."

"I can't let you do that, Rabbi. It's not you who failed him. And the night you accepted me as a would-be convert, you let me share that joy with him all by myself. I must also share this sorrow with him alone. I'll go see Meyer before the Shabbat service tonight."

David watched Kelly, her shoulders square and her head high, leave the chapel. He thought, Kelly Prentis, I love you for what you're doing, but Meyer Loeb will never forgive me for rejecting you. For destroying the most important day of his life.

He started to leave but stopped when he saw the Madonna. Studying the mournful expression, he addressed her softly: "I'm not in competition with you. And no matter how this turns out, neither one of us will have to worry about her soul."

Meyer Loeb was the first congregant to enter the sanctuary for the Friday night Shabbat service. He was alone, without his family or Kelly, and he marched ramrod straight down the center aisle and took his seat in the middle of the first row. David, alone on the bema, nodded at the old man, who didn't respond. Loeb's expression, which was never to change during the service, was a blend of anger and contempt cemented in place by his feeling of having been betrayed.

As other congregants filled the sanctuary, David sensed their mood of apprehensive expectation. They were waiting to see what would happen between their rabbi and an admired and revered member. The standing-room-only crowd of worshipers, many of them guests from out of town, served to hone the building tension.

Throughout the day, the news of David's rejection of Kelly Prentis and the wedding cancellation had firestormed through the congregation. They could understand the old man's seething fury and were as curious how it would be vented at their head rabbi as they were about David's justification of his acts. To many of them, talking excitedly outside before the services began, he had no justification.

At exactly eight o'clock, David stood up, and his movement caused a stir of excitement throughout the audience. He felt as if he were a combatant entering an arena, not a rabbi welcoming the Sabbath.

Though the mood softened somewhat during the service, David sensed that the fervor which was usually present during the singing and the responsive reading had been replaced by an almost belligerent impatience. Even Cantor Sachs and the accompanying choir seemed to be in a hurry to finish their songs and prayers.

When he stepped to the lectern to deliver his sermon he realized, as he looked over the tense, expectant faces, that his congregation was hoping he would apologize and make his peace with Meyer Loeb. Even the old man, who had been immobile and impassive throughout the service, leaned forward as if not wanting to miss a single word.

David delivered his sermon quietly, without ever raising his voice. He directed every word at Meyer Loeb.

"This evening's sermon will be short and I will begin with a quote from Midrash. It is written that *a carpenter without tools is no carpenter.*" He leaned across the lectern as if trying to get closer to Meyer Loeb. "And a rabbi without Torah is no rabbi. I *am* a rabbi. I am *your* rabbi. The decision I made this afternoon, I made because I *am your* rabbi. And I would resign before I change it!"

He paused and straightened and his expression as he looked around the sanctuary dared opposition. Firmly, he continued: "You all live in a world filled with doubts, because you all live in a world of grays. Of expectations. But a rabbi, because of Torah, lives in a world without doubts, because it is a world of black and whites. There are no grays and there are no expectations. Because of Torah there is only Law, only absolutes." He paused and saw that understanding had caused a crack in Meyer Loeb's expression. But there wasn't acceptance, and David shook his head with disappointment when the crack disappeared and the rigidity returned.

"Every man had three names," David continued. "One his father and mother give him; one others call him; and one he earns himself. Tonight, what you call me and what I've earned bear no resemblance." He hesitated while they digested his words and then said, "I will close with another quotation: *The Torah is truth, and the purpose of knowing it is to live by it.*"

He quickly added, "Shabbat Shalom," before stepping away from the rostrum.

In the receiving line after the service, he watched Meyer Loeb approach. The old man's expression was unreadable. David held out his hand and repeated the ritual the two of them had shared after every Shabbat service.

"Shabbat Shalom, Meyer. Well, how did I do?" he asked, referring as always to his sermon. He waited for the usual response of, "Not bad, Rabbi. Not bad. A pretty good beginning but a little too schmaltzy at the end."

But Meyer walked past David to where Morris Simon was standing in the receiving line and shook hands with the surprised assistant rabbi. "Shabbat Shalom," he said. Then, slowly and deliberately, as he looked at David he added the single word, "Rabbi."

"Shabbat Shalom, Mr. Loeb," a surprised Morris Simon responded.

Harold Fedder, across the room, watched, a smile playing at his mouth. A smile of victory.

CHAPTER

28

Sheila entered the beachhouse and, with a sigh, kicked off her shoes. Seeing David's open suitcase in the small bedroom, the tension and fatigue partially caused by the long hours of flight to Kauai began to fade. Impatient to be with him, she hurriedly undressed. Clad in a pearl-white bikini, she walked across the veranda and over to the cliff, looked down and saw David jogging along the beach. But she wasn't ready to face him until she had marshaled her thoughts, so she delayed going down the steps that had been cut into the cliff.

Like David, she too had struggled facing the decision that they couldn't avoid. She too had tried to determine how his being a rabbi affected their lives. Other than the intrusions and restrictions his role had placed on their relationship, she had no idea of what it meant. To her, the ritualistic "man of Faith" had always been a lifeless caricature comprised of hundreds of ready-made symbols and illusions. Until forced by her wanting to share her life with him, she had no reason to ever think beyond that image.

Until that night in Washington, she had been able to exorcise his role from her mind. Though she had been aware of it intellectually, emotionally she hadn't let it interfere with her image of him or of the two of them together. In spite of his many invitations, she had never seen him conduct a service. To do so would have been to admit to that part of him which she had instinctively known she could never touch or share or comprehend. Now, wanting everything with him, she had no choice.

She too had played with compromises and had been forced to reject them as being implausible. She had tantalized herself by fantasizing a return to their previous arrangement. The clandestine meetings of a back-street romance. She rejected that thought almost immediately. She knew what she wanted with him, what he wanted with her; she was ready. No matter how tempted, she knew she couldn't settle for less than marriage.

Her conclusion, painfully arrived at, was that there was only one choice. For them to marry, he would have to give up being a rabbi. It was his decision to make. If he couldn't, if he wouldn't, even though she sensed the anguish she would have to endure, she knew she had the strength to walk away from him.

Watching him jog along the water's edge, she remembered the last time they had been here and had made love and had vowed they would somehow find a way to spend the rest of their lives in splendid isolation on this beach, on this island. At that moment she would have given anything in the world to make that vow come true.

Standing unobserved at the edge of the cliff, watching David, she tried to sustain her mood and feelings by saying to herself, Once I tell him, David will find a way. Once he knows, David will know what to do. For he wants what I want. Sighing deeply as she finally went down the steps, she said aloud, "After you hear what I have to say, maybe you'll tell me we never have to leave here again. Or maybe you'll say we can never come back. The choice will be yours."

On the beach, she called to him. David, turning, saw her and waved. She waved back and they jogged toward each other, flew into an embrace. Holding each other tightly, fingers like talons digging into bare shoulders, they kissed brutally. Breathlessly, Sheila finally pulled her mouth free. She rested her head against his chest and purred with inner contentment as he gently stroked her hair.

Arms around each other's waists, they began to walk slowly down the beach. They were silent, as if afraid to hear each other's thoughts. They moved away from the shoreline and went over to a sun-bleached log. They sat side by side, not talking, looking out at the ocean. A line of pelicans filed by close to the water. A school of mackerel broke the calm surface as they panicked in their efforts to escape from predators knifing up from the depths. Sheila glanced at David's profile, and sensing his pain, she put a comforting hand on his thigh. He quickly covered it.

"Well?" he asked. "What have you decided?"

She debated how to tell him. Unable to make her demanding ultimatum because of his naked hurt, she shook her head and said with forced gaity, "You first, Benjamin. I need to hear what you have to say before I can answer your question."

To her surprise, he didn't say a word about the two of them. He sucked in a breath and then slowly let it out in a deep sigh and told her about Kelly Prentis and Meyer Loeb. As he talked, she sensed his bewilderment, but she didn't begin to comprehend it until he told her about the reactions of his congregation.

". . . those who are still talking to me want to know why I didn't look the other way when I saw Kelly at that altar rail. Why I didn't just turn around and leave. They ask me, 'What difference would it have made? Nobody but you, Rabbi, would have known. Look at the unhappiness you've caused and the lives you've wrecked. Rabbis are supposed to be compassionate, aren't they . . . ?' " He paused and shook his head and then bitterly asked her, "Do they believe I *wanted* to reject that poor girl? That I took pleasure in doing what I did to Meyer? Don't they realize I couldn't look the other way? That I had no other choice but to do what I did? What kind of a rabbi do they want me to be?"

What kind of a rabbi do they want me to be?

Because of the anguish in his voice, she realized for the first time that his role was far more than ritualistic. What she had avoided and had never understood—his sacred commitment to his people— was revealed to her with painful clarity. She was so overcome by what he was that she bent forward as though struck in the stomach, but David was too absorbed by what he was feeling to notice her reaction.

"I have a confession to make," he said, placing a hand on her shoulder. "In the back of my mind, when I went to pick that girl up and take her to the Beth Din, I was thinking that if I could convert her, I could also convert you. That was the way I was going to solve everything for us. It was such a simple way out. But when I saw her at that altar rail and knew I couldn't convert her, I also knew I could never convert you either. No matter how much we love each other. If poor little Kelly Prentis, who tried so hard and who believed so strongly, wasn't acceptable to me, how could I accept you?"

He sighed and added thoughtfully, "I did what I had to do. Can't my congregation realize that? Because I'm the kind of rabbi I am and not the kind they'd like me to be, I didn't have any choice!"

He stood and stretched. She turned to look up at his face as he added, "Not that it really matters anymore. My congregation is so incensed because of their interpretation of what I did that I don't even know if I'll have a congregation much longer. My contract comes up for renewal in less than a month and the board is scheduled to meet to decide whether to renew it. Right now I don't give a damn if they do or don't."

A small nondescript dog trotted up the beach toward them. Sheila was grateful for the pup's interruption of the turmoil caused by her thoughts. What David had just said to her had given her renewed hope and had delayed the need to issue her ultimatum.

She scratched the mutt's ears, and it wagged its stumpy tail happily. David reached behind the log and found a piece of driftwood. The dog responded by prancing in front of him, then tore down the beach toward the water as David flung the chunk of wood. It splashed some ten feet out from the water's edge. The dog skidded to a stop, looked hopefully at the bobbing piece of wood and then reproachfully at David before trotting away.

Sheila, deep in thought, unconsciously probed the sand with her foot, uncovering a large pink conch shell. She forced herself to concentrate on the meaningless task of digging a hole with her toe. David watched her silently, waiting until she looked up at him before asking, "Thanks for hearing me out. Now it's your turn. What do you have to say to me?"

"David, tell me you love me."

"I love you."

"Why? I'm a terrific lady. I know that. I'm great in bed. I know how to turn you on. But those aren't good enough answers any more. So why do you love me, David? *Why?*"

"You want the truth?"

"Only the truth."

"I could tell you a million reasons why I love you the way I do, but there's only one that really matters to me. With you, I see myself having the life I never had." He paused and squatted in front of her. He let a handful of sand slowly trickle between his fingers before continuing. "I love you the way I do because with you I can fantasize about the things I've never had. Children. A real home. Sharing a life."

Her emotions squeezed her heart and tears of joy filled her eyes. But when she didn't respond, he said, "But I guess you're going to tell me I can't have that with you, aren't you? That's why we're here, isn't it?" He took both of her hands in his and contemplatively said, "We're a tragedy, aren't we?"

"No," she said emphatically. "I don't think so. I think we're a miracle."

"But what about—"

She silenced him with a finger across his lips. "I have nothing to say until we hear how your board votes on renewing your contract. That could change everything."

"I don't understand," he said questioningly.

"Don't worry about it," she answered. "I do."

She stood up and brushed the loose sand from her thighs. Looking at him, she grinned and added, "Yes, I do have something to say: There's a time for loving, and, Benjamin, that time is right now."

Holding hands, they slowly climbed the stairs toward the beach-house.

Sheila couldn't sleep. She lay rigidly beside David and watched the dawn filter through the latticed bamboo blinds. Turning her head, she studied his face resting on the pillow. She closed her eyes and repeated the silent prayer she had been repeating through the night:

. . . Please don't let them renew his contract. Let them fire him. That's our only hope. When he's no longer a rabbi, we stand a chance . . .

CHAPTER
29

All fifteen board members were present at the meeting to decide whether to renew David's contract. The usual agenda of the scheduled monthly meetings, held in a small conference room, contained items about the nuts and bolts of the everyday operation of the temple. The meetings were usually sparsely attended by both congregants and board members. Tonight, however, because the only topic on the agenda was the debate over their rabbi's contract renewal, the meeting was being conducted in a large, multipurpose room in the temple's basement that was normally used for choir practice and as a rehearsal hall by the drama club. Two tables had been pushed together at the front of the one-step stage to seat the full complement of the Board of Trustees. Every seat was filled by somber-faced congregants. Most of them, upon entering the room, had either pointedly ignored David or had given him a perfunctory nod of greeting.

Meyer Loeb, his arms folded determinedly across his chest, sat in the middle of the first row with his wife, his son and Kelly Prentis. Though he had been the first to arrive, Loeb had yet to look at David or to acknowledge him in any way.

David could feel the sullen mood of defiant hostility from the audience as they shifted in nervous anticipation, waiting for Sam Bender to call the meeting to order. From his position at the far end of the table, David could see the board members. No one would look directly at him. Harold Fedder, seated next to Bender, smiled a secret smile while waiting for the meeting to begin.

David expertly read the mood of the room and knew the vote would go against renewal. But it didn't matter to him. He wasn't going to fight back and try to change the positions of the more easily swayed trustees—something he had always been able to do. As he sat quietly at the table, toying aimlessly with a pencil, his thoughts were not of the coming vote but of Sheila. He knew why, on Kauai, she hadn't told him of her decision but was waiting until the outcome of tonight's meeting. Because she believed that everything would change if his contract weren't renewed. He would be free to marry her then, for he would no longer be a rabbi.

But wouldn't he always be a rabbi?

The paradox failed to convince him. He didn't even know if he wanted to remain a rabbi. The price was too high. Being a rabbi was no longer the idealistic and rewarding challenge and pursuit he had imagined in his youth. Being a rabbi now meant unending inner conflicts as well as open battle with his congregation. Being a rabbi could force him to sacrifice the woman he loved.

Looking out over the audience of hostile faces, he wondered if he wasn't afflicted with "rabbi burnout." The rewarding rare moments of satisfaction no longer seemed to be worth the constant struggle. Besides, he asked himself as he thought of Sheila, how can I possibly have answers for them when I no longer have any for myself?

The increasing noise level in the room interrupted his thoughts. He saw Meyer Loeb studying him intently and wondered if the old man, who hadn't spoken to him since that memorable Shabbat service, would take pleasure in rubbing salt in David's wounds after the vote was over. He looked away only to lock eyes with Harold Fedder, wearing his all-too-familiar smirk.

I can guess what Harold's going to say after the vote is taken, David thought. I can read from that grin that he has the eight votes he needs to beat me.

But Fedder, though he didn't show it, wasn't that sure of how the final tally would go. He had stopped his politicking of board members and his open criticism of David when he realized these were self-defeating and only caused resentment. That his opposition was still being viewed as a personal vendetta and had nothing to do with David's success or failure as the congregation's spiritual leader. It had been a frustrating waiting game for Fedder, but his patience had paid off.

The impact on David of his congregation's reaction to his decision regarding Kelly Prentis had caused him to lose patience with them. He had become abrasive and demanding and had offended and angered many members of the temple. The sheen of his image had been tarnished to the extent that Fedder could count on five, maybe six, definite votes against the renewal of David's contract. He needed two, possibly three more votes. As he waited for San Bender to call the meeting to order, he mentally rehearsed the plot he had so carefully orchestrated and which he felt sure would give him the necessary majority. A plot he flattered himself on by calling it Machiavellian and subtle.

Bender's beating of the gavel silenced the audience. "We're here tonight to vote on the renewal of our contract with Rabbi Benjamin," he began. "Does anyone have anything to say before we open the discussion?"

"Perhaps the rabbi would like to make some comments?" Harold Fedder asked innocently.

"What kind of comments are you referring to, Harold?" David asked. "I'm not sure I understand what you mean?"

"Well, if you're planning to resign or to accept an offer from another congregation, then we can avoid what might turn out to be an unpleasant evening for everyone."

"Harold, is my resigning or accepting another offer a hope or a suggestion?" David asked with sham innocence. His retort brought a hard look to Fedder's face and laughter from the audience. "Let me give you one of my famous quotes, Harold: *It's good to hope but bad to depend on it.*" The laughter died, and Harold Fedder shifted nervously in his chair. "However, I have nothing to say now. If I feel the need, I'll make my comments after the general discussion."

But probably not, he thought, because I'm not sure whether I give a damn how the vote turns out.

Fedder recaptured the audience's attention by saying, "In spite of Rabbi Benjamin's flippancy, I wish I could find something amusing about this evening's agenda. This is one of the most important decisions a board of trustees is ever called on to make. The rehiring of our rabbi. I feel we should give it the seriousness it deserves. And though we could have an immediate vote, I think it only fair to Rabbi Benjamin that he hear how we feel about his conduct and his performance so he will understand our decision. No matter what it might be. If we rehire him, our comments might help make him be more spiritually attuned to our needs and our expectations." He paused, then scrutinized David for a moment. "And if we don't rehire him, I'm sure he'd want to know why."

Fedder had two reasons for not wanting an immediate vote. He wasn't sure at that moment in the proceedings how the vote would turn out. And he wanted his pound of David's flesh. After it was over, he wanted people to point at him and say, "Harold Fedder always knew the truth about Rabbi Benjamin. He's the one who got rid of him and he's the reason we have a new rabbi."

He relished the hatchet job he was about to perform—it was obvious to all in his expression and in his tone of voice.

"It's no secret how I feel about renewing Rabbi Benajmin's contract," Fedder said piously. "So there's no need for me to discuss my objections to rehiring him." He glared at each board member before continuing. "And obviously there are others who feel as I do. However, I think it is our duty as board members who may be prejudiced or influenced by other members to hear the opinions of our congregation. After all, we represent them, and therefore it is our obligation to follow their wishes. Maybe they don't feel about Rabbi Benjamin as we do."

After a murmur of assent from other board members, Fedder left his seat and stepped off the raised single step of the platform and went down into the audience. He stopped dramatically, turned to face the board and said, "And the first voice I think we should hear is that of one of our most respected and revered members. During past board deliberations, we have often called on him for guidance and direction." He looked toward the first row and said, "Mr. Loeb, what are your feelings about the rehiring of Rabbi Benjamin?"

Clever, Harold, David thought. If the board had any doubts before, there won't be any after Meyer finishes crucifying me.

With calculated deliberation, Meyer Loeb walked to the rostrum at the side of the room reserved for members of the audience to address the board. He positioned himself so that he could look directly at David. Fedder, reseating himself, observed the reactions of the board members to the old man and made no effort to conceal his satisfaction. He would move for an immediate vote after Loeb finished reciting the litany of his accusations. He hoped for a final tally of 15 to 0, and even more encouraged by David's dejected mien, he believed he would get it.

The room became tomb-quiet as Loeb began: "When Harold asked me here to address the board, I relished the invitation. This is my chance, I thought, to heal in public the wounds of anger, hurt and embarrassment inflicted on me and my family by Rabbi Benjamin. A rabbi I believed to be without compassion or understanding. And without sensitivity.

"I asked myself, How can such a rabbi be the spiritual head of this congregation?

"Because I wanted no misunderstandings about my feelings, I rehearsed exactly what I would say here. I even discussed what I was going to say with my family, and though they made no comments, I felt they had given me their silent approval. Only one person disagreed with me. The person most affected by Rabbi Benjamin's actions. Kelly Prentis."

The audience, confused, stirred uneasily. Harold Fedder studied Meyer Loeb's face and shook his head questioningly. David, more alert now, sat up straight and attentive in his chair.

Loeb smiled lovingly at Kelly Prentis, who sat with her head bowed. He continued: "You all think of me as a deeply religious man, don't you?" Several people nodded and he went on. "Well, I want you to know that sweet, feisty little Irish shiksa is a better Jew than I am. After she heard what I had planned to say here, oh, how she argued with me. And got me to admit the truth. That I was angry and upset with Rabbi Benjamin because he had hurt my pride and damaged my ego. Because he had embarrassed me in public. She also made me admit that my disappointment in my son for wanting to marry her was not because he had broken faith, but because of the reflection of his actions on me. Was I to blame for my son's decision? she asked me. Was I less of a Jew because of what Stephen had done? Of course not. My son's decision is between him and his God and has nothing to do with me. Was I any less of a Jew because of Rabbi Benjamin's decision about Kelly Prentis? Of course not. But I have been less of a Jew because of my reaction to the rabbi's decision and I've been ashamed to admit it."

My God, David thought in disbelief, he's on my side! That old man, in spite of the hurt I caused him, is on my side!

"How dare Rabbi Benjamin not do what *I* wanted, what *I* expected him to do?" Loeb continued. "And even though I knew in my heart of hearts that he was right, who was the only person in this congregation of Jews who had the courage to stand up and agree with the rabbi? Who told me he was not only right to deny her conversion because she wasn't ready, but that he had no other choice? At the time, because I was so incensed, I didn't even listen to her. But this young woman, this young Catholic, made me face the truth."

The audience sat shocked and entranced. David looked at Kelly Prentis who, as if embarrassed, looked up, bowed her head again, then stared at the floor. Fedder rose hurriedly from his seat and said anxiously, "We understand your feelings, Meyer, but I think—"

"You be quiet," Loeb interrupted, stabbing a finger at Fedder. "You yourself said it. We're here to make the most important decision a congregation can make: the renewal of our rabbi's contract. And that's exactly what I'm here to talk about."

He waited until Fedder slumped back into his chair before going on. "Just what is a rabbi?" Loeb asked the audience. "What do we want, what do we look for when we ask a man to guide us? Do we want him to be our social director? Is that the kind of rabbi this congregation is looking for? Someone who will kiss our tuchas and wipe our noses? I say no. I say we should be looking for a rock, who by the strength of his belief and the example of his acts forces us to face our Jewishness. No matter what the personal price we must pay. A rock who doesn't care if we like him or not, because he knows he's not in a popularity contest. A rock who wants nothing from us except that we never forget that we are Jews and who demands that we try to be good Jews. David Benjamin is such a rabbi. David Benjamin is such a rock."

The now-silent and chastened congregation seemed startled when Loeb turned to face them and asked, "Do you know why my son is still unmarried? Sure, there could have been a civil ceremony. I know plenty of judges who would have been honored to do it for me. You all know we could have found a rabbi who would have looked the other way and converted Kelly Prentis with no questions asked. Or we could have had one of those hippy renegade rabbis who are neither fish nor fowl perform the ceremony. But my son is not married today because this feisty stubborn child refuses to marry him until she can be married in his temple"—Loeb paused and like a prophet of old, pointed a finger at David before adding—"and by that rabbi!"

David looked at Kelly Prentis, who now sat with her hands folded demurely in her lap. She gazed back, eyes shining. He didn't know why, but he winked surreptitiously at her. With a shy grin, she automatically winked back.

He wanted to thank her in some way for having melted the frozen rigidness of his piety. He was aware that his self-doubts, his depression, his disillusionment, had vanished. At that moment David felt that if during the rest of his rabbinical career not one other person understood what it meant to be a Jew, he would still feel that he had succeeded as a rabbi. But the only gesture he could think of to make to her was to shield his hand from the view of the Board of Trustees, and, by moving his fingers, make the sign of the cross.

Kelly's reaction was one of surprise and confusion. She knew he was blessing her and she wasn't sure why. The radiance in her eyes spread over her face, because the answer didn't really matter to her. What mattered was that she touched and had been touched. They had shared an exquisite intimacy, so rare that neither one of them would ever forget the moment.

"This temple is my life," Meyer Loeb continued. "But it is not a social hall or a country club. Nor is it merely a building which mirrors the wealth and power of this congregation. No, it is my sanctuary and my haven. It is where I come to be reminded of my Jewishness. And the custodian of my Jewishness is Rabbi David Benjamin."

He looked at David before shaking his head with heavy sadness and deep disappointment. "Let us admit the truth. We didn't come here this evening to discuss the rehiring of Rabbi Benjamin, but the firing of Rabbi Benjamin. And why? Because he forces us to swallow the unpalatable and because he bruises our delicate vanities and our fragile egos. What are we, little children who don't want to take our medicine? Admit it, don't we all take pride when we see him on television or read about him in the magazines and newspapers. Don't we like having such a prestigious and influential man as our rabbi? 'If only he wouldn't be so hard on us,' we say. Well, my friends, with this rabbi we can't have it both ways."

Obviously tiring, Loeb paused, then wearily said to Harold Fedder, "You asked me here to give my recommendations. I'd get down on my knees and beg him to stay. I'd offer him a lifetime contract. And I'd apologize to him for this disgraceful exhibition of our lack of faith and for our wanting him to be something other than what he is. Our rabbi."

Slowly he left the rostrum and motioned to Kelly Prentis. They were oblivious to the babble of voices from the audience and to the rising sound of the argument among the Board of Trustees as they approached David, who had risen to his feet.

"Well, Rabbi, how did I do?" Loeb asked, a twinkle in his eyes. David answered in a choked voice, "Not bad, Meyer, not bad. A good beginning but a little too schmaltzy at the end."

"Shalom, Rabbi?"

"Shalom, Meyer."

David clasped the old man by his shoulders and tightly squeezed his arms. With eyes welling, he turned to face Kelly Prentis.

"I pushed a little harder and I think I'm ready now, Rabbi," she said.

"I think so too," David answered. "It will be my honor to perform the ceremony accepting you into our faith, for you exemplify what is written in the Midrash: *The true proselyte is dearer to God than the Israelites were at Mount Sinai; for had not the Israelites seen the thunder and the lightning, the quaking mountains and the sounding trumpets, they would not have accepted the Torah; but the true proselyte, who saw none of these things, has surrendered to the Holy One. Can anyone be dearer to God?* Yes, I will be honored to perform the ceremony of your conversion."

"And my wedding too?" she asked shyly.

He laughed. "Do you think I'd let anyone else marry you?"

"Mazel tov!" Meyer Loeb said and made no effort to wipe the tears on his cheeks.

Arm in arm, followed by a proudly smiling Stephen Loeb and his mother, the old man and the young woman walked erectly to the exit. Kelly suddenly stopped and ran back to David. Standing on her tiptoes, she kissed him on his cheek. With his hand covering the area where her lips had touched him, he watched her leave.

Harold Fedder, making no attempt to mask his rage, said, "After such an emotional outburst, I don't think tonight is the time to discuss the rabbi's contract, much less vote on it. Therefore, I move that the meeting be adjourned until a more appropriate time. Will someone second the motion?"

Ben Adelson rose from his seat. "Harold, we Jews are always too emotional. Sometimes it is our undoing and other times our salvation. But I believe we function better when we express our feelings, because then we are expressing what is in our hearts and not what is in our minds. So there'll be no seconding of your motion. As planned, we'll discuss the renewal of the rabbi's contract." Turning to David, he added, "Rabbi, this is likely to get hairy. In the heat of the moment, many things are likely to be said that maybe you shouldn't hear. Your presence will only inhibit this discussion. So we'd appreciate your leaving until we finish."

David went to his office. He sat quietly, thoughts of Sheila filling his mind. She was working late, waiting for his call. Less than thirty minutes later a sullen Harold Fedder entered and told David the news. The board had voted 14 to 1 to renew his contract for five years.

He felt no elation or vindication. He looked at Fedder, who had gone to the door, and asked, "Harold, you've always believed that I'm not the right rabbi for this congregation. Others obviously don't agree. Why do you feel this? Do you resent my becoming so important, so prestigious?"

He looked at David and shook his head. "No, Rabbi, your importance hasn't got anything to do with my feelings. This congregation is more important than you. And that you don't understand that makes me more convinced than ever that I'm right about you. But it also makes me afraid of you. Because not only are you the wrong rabbi for this congregation, but someday, if you have to make a choice, you're going to betray us."

He called Sheila the moment Fedder left his office.

She clenched her eyes closed in disappointment when he told her how the vote had turned out. In a sad voice, she said, "My prayers weren't answered. I prayed, oh, how I prayed they would vote against you."

"Why?"

"Because you'd no longer be a rabbi. Because we would be free to plan our future."

"I don't think so," he said. "If they hadn't rehired me, I'd be looking for another congregation."

Her hopes smashed, she finally accepted the inevitable. Nothing was going to change for them. Not now. Not ever. After a long silence, she said, "You bastard. You knew what you were going to do. You knew we had no future but you let me believe we did. We never had a future."

He offered the only explanation he could. "We fell in love. We didn't plan it that way. It just happened."

"No, David, it didn't just happen. Nothing just happens. Maybe at first we didn't want it to happen. But we made it happen. I could hate you for what you did to me."

"I didn't do anything to you. I just loved you. And I have no regrets about that." When she didn't respond, he said in a sad voice, "I'll see you later tonight. We'll talk."

She forced herself to ask the question: "What for?"

"To—" He couldn't finish.

"—say good-bye?" she concluded for him. "Benjamin, what the hell do you think we're doing right now?" She looked at her watch. "At eight forty-nine. We're saying good-bye."

"It's not right to end it this way. I want to see you one last time."

"Will that lessen the hurt or soothe the pain? No, it will only make it worse. Let me walk away from it now, David. Please."

"As simple as that?" She could hear the disbelief mixed with his hurt.

"As simple as that." She spoke evenly, managing to bury the pain in her voice.

"And what happens when we see each other again? It's inevitable. We're on the same committees. We'll meet often. How will you deal with it?"

"I'll resign from those committees," she said quietly. "I only volunteered because you were on them."

"Harrington, it won't be that simple. Detroit is a small town— our paths are going to occasionally cross socially. What will you do when that happens."

"Damn it, Benjamin, how the hell do I know what I'll do! Do you want me to say I'll leave the room when I see you? I'll probably shake hands with you, and on the outside I'll be polite and businesslike. But on the inside I'll be eating my guts out."

"And so will I."

She was struggling to control her tears when Anson Phillips strode into her office. He, too, had been working late and had even taken her to dinner. Preoccupied, not noticing her desolate expression, he thrust a report across her desk and said tensely, "I want to discuss this with you before you leave. It's important. It's about those damn compacts."

"Anson, I'm busy right now. Can't it wait?"

"This will only take a few minutes."

She lost control and the tears fell like acid tracks down her cheeks. She pointed at the door with a trembling finger, and said, "Will you get out of here?!"

Phillips studied her briefly. His tone of voice softened. "I'm available if you need to talk." He reached across the desk and patted her shoulder.

She waited until he left, regained her composure and said briskly to David, "I'm sorry about the interruption."

"That's all right. I had time to think. You're right, there really isn't much more to say, is there?"

"Just good-bye."

They were silent, each waiting for the other to make the final gesture, to say the last words. Finally Sheila picked up Phillips's report and said hurriedly, "Something important has just come up—I've got to go now." She dropped the phone into its cradle before he could reply.

David went into the sanctuary. Seating himself in the last row, his mind continued to flood with thoughts of Sheila. You were wrong, he told himself, we two weren't a triumph. We're a tragedy. Why should two people who love each other as we do, who are so right for each other in every way but one, be denied. As he searched for an acceptable answer, the Eternal Light above the Ark attracted his attention. As if hypnotized, he focused on the flame. He bowed his head and softly said the words: *With faith, there are no questions. Without faith, there are no answers.*

Remembering Kelly Prentis and his feelings, he looked back at the Light and said, "I have faith again. I know it. I think I can live without you now. Our paths crossed and our lives touched, and now, Sheila Rogers Harrington, we go our separate ways. Who knows? Maybe someday the roads we travel will bend and our paths will cross again."

He smiled a sudden warm secret smile, for he instinctively knew how she would have reacted if he had said the words directly to her: "Benjamin, a little hammy. Effective, but still a little hammy."

He had just taken the first step in letting go of her.

CHAPTER

30

The emotional trauma triggered by her shattered dreams caused Sheila's feelings toward David to vacillate between love and hate. As if to emphasize her frustration about his decision, she read of a rabbi in Los Angeles who had been having an affair with a gentile and had given up his congregation. Like all lovers who believe that they share the most unique of loves, she didn't understand why David couldn't have done the same.

Intellectually, she understood his dilemma: how to separate what he was as a man from what he was as a rabbi. Emotionally, she couldn't conceive of his decision not to make that separation. She didn't know that many rabbis faced that choice. After much inner torment, many succumb to their passions and to the emptiness of their personal lives. Many, like David Benjamin, are so committed that no matter how strong their desires, they cannot cleave their psyches. Though tempted, the division of self is impossible.

Her ego suffered. He had rejected what he could have shared with her, the richest of lives, for rewards she didn't understand and he couldn't define. Part of her believed that his choice had been influenced because he was snared by the trappings of power. What man could resist the role of prestige and influence? The red carpet treatment wherever he went. Because she too was driven by ambition, she could understand that compulsion. It soothed her hurts but didn't heal them.

Because she loved him and had no doubts of his love for her, she clung to the hope that somehow a miracle would happen that would cause him to reverse his decision. But aware of his determination and his strength, she knew it was but the faintest of hopes. Some cataclysmic change would have to happen for there to be any chance of its fulfillment.

She believed the change had happened, three weeks later, when she realized she was pregnant.

"There's no doubt about it," the plump elderly doctor said to Sheila as he looked up from the lab report he had been reading. "No need to kill any more rabbits. You're pregnant. A little over two months pregnant."

Two months, she thought. That was the last time David and I made love. The memory of the two of them on the beach on Kauai iced through her mind and she shivered with suppressed excitement. All the times, in all the places, we made love and nothing happened. Except on that last time. Was that an omen? Am I being punished or rewarded?

Though she was a little frightened and a little angry, Sheila was also pleased. The gynecologist interrupted her reverie as he began filling out a medical form. "Just for your records, we will need to know the father's name—"

Sheila looked up and said simply, "There is no father."

The elderly man raised his thick eyebrows and muttered, "Oh, another immaculate conception. Well, you have basically two choices: an abortion, or you can bear the child and give it up for adoption. Either way, I can make the arrangements."

Sheila stood and before leaving his office said, "No, I have a third choice. I can keep the child."

Though the change she had prayed for had occurred, she realized that nothing had changed. On the contrary, she was now faced with a new painful resolution to make. What to do about the baby? Should she have an abortion or not? As she drove back to Detroit from Lansing, she struggled with the decision.

She remembered how badly David had wanted a child, how often he had talked with such deep longing in his voice of someday becoming a father. If he knew, it would change everything, she thought. Being David, he would marry her. Though tempted to tell him, she shook her head and said aloud, "But it would be for all the wrong reasons. He would marry me because of his child, but in time we would end up hating each other. He'd think I forced him into a marriage and he'd be right." Another grim reality added to her mounting anxiety. "And if we don't marry, he'd be a rabbi with a bastard child. My God, that would ruin his career forever. I can't do that to him. I can *never* let him know."

She argued with herself almost to the edge of the Detroit suburbs. "What do I do? I can give myself a million reasons for not wanting it, for getting rid of it, and only one for wanting it. For having the baby. Because it's David's child."

She realized the enormity of the decision she was facing as she pulled into the parking stall stenciled with her name in the underground garage of the United Motors Building. "I love you, David Benjamin, and I guess I will always love you. But despite my fantasies, I know you're never going to be able to marry me. If I have your child, though, I'll always have a part of you. But if I have your child, how will I ever get you out of my heart and mind?"

Safely back in the environment in which she was in command of her emotions, in which she made decisions based only on reality, she felt a momentary quiet sense of peace as she rode the private elevator to the ninth floor. It wasn't until she walked down the carpeted corridor toward her office that a thought shattered her serenity.

The price of keeping the baby was the loss of her job.

If she kept the baby, she wondered how long she could continue working before her pregnancy became obvious. Thoughtfully, she said to herself, "When that happens, I'll have to quit. Or be fired. If they ever find out who the father is, the fall-out from the scandal would be disastrous to the United Motors' image."

As she approached her office, her little "throne room," Lawton Collins called it, she said determinedly, "But I don't want to quit. I love what I do and I'm damn good at it. Without David, it's my life!" With a flash of understanding on her face she realized perhaps that's how David felt about being a rabbi.

Sheila opened the door to the executive suite and greeted her secretary who handed her a batch of messages. She scanned through them as she crossed into her private office. Nothing that couldn't wait. She dropped the messages on her desk and looked out the large window, staring at downtown Detroit. After an hour in which she didn't move, she was no closer to making the decision. Her only realization was that she had about a month to decide. She would be three months pregnant then; an abortion beyond that point could be dangerous.

Anson Phillips came into her office and interrupted her thoughts. Seating himself alongside her desk, he said, "You don't look so hot. Is that why you weren't at this morning's staff meeting?"

She smiled ruefully as she sat down behind her desk. She nodded, saying, "I haven't been feeling well lately."

"Anything serious?" he asked with concern.

She shrugged. She thought of telling him that she was pregnant and asking his advice but didn't because she knew the decision of what she did about the baby was hers alone to make. Besides, she wasn't sure of how he'd react. Though he was her friend and her mentor, he was also the president of United Motors.

"You've heard about Lawton Collins?" he asked.

"Only rumors. And I make it a point to ignore them."

"It's no rumor. Lawton is resigning at the end of the year. That's seven months from now."

And that's when I'll be having a baby, she thought. If I decide to keep it.

"Who's going to replace him?" she asked. "Tom Beckenridge?"

He shrugged. "I could name six people in this company who want the job. All qualified." He lit a cigar and, after inspecting the glowing end, quietly asked, "How about you?" When her eyes widened, he laughed and said, "A little executive-itch, huh? Good. I'm glad to see that."

"Why?"

"Because I'm thinking about throwing your name into the hat of candidates to replace him."

"Anson!" She beamed at him and said confidently, "I can handle that job."

"I know you can. I wouldn't be thinking of you as a possible replacement for Lawton if I didn't think you could. But calm down. I'm not guaranteeing you the job. I can't. There'll be a lot of opposition and resistance. If I decide to recommend you, I'm going to face a lot of flack if only because you're a woman. And maybe I'm ten years ahead of myself, but someday there is going to be a woman Operations Manager in the car business. I figure why not now? And with my support, if I decide to give it to you, you'd stand a damn good chance of winning."

She was trembling with excitement. "Like you say, there'll be a lot of opposition. It'll be a fight."

"A fight like you've never seen before because you've never been involved in high level office politics. This one will be a dirty one. They'll probably write textbooks about it. So before we go on, I've got to know that your skirts are clean. For me to recommend you, you have to be like Caesar's wife, above reproach. Knowing what you're going to get into, before I do anything, I need to know if you want me to recommend you for Lawton's job."

She spun around in the chair so he couldn't see the disturbed expression in her face. I blow it if anyone finds out I'm pregnant, she told herself. That means having an abortion. Giving up the baby. Her face paled when she realized Anson's offer had only complicated the decision she hadn't made. Though she now had a motivation that would enable her to justify having an abortion, she still wasn't ready to make that decision.

When she turned to face him again, her expression hadn't changed. Concerned, he asked, "Are you okay?"

"I told you I wasn't feeling well." Her mind whirling, she asked thoughtfully, "Do I have to make that decision right now?"

"Of course not. We have time." He studied her face and with a warm smile added, "I know you too well, young lady. I ought to, I've taught you just about everything you know. Looking at that expression on your face, I'd have to agree with Lawton Collins that you *are* a scheming, conniving woman and that you want me to do something for you."

"You're right, Anson. This scheming, conniving woman wants you to authorize a six month sabbatical so I can go off and think about what I want to do."

"What's to think about?" he asked skeptically. "Either you want me to try to get you the job or you don't."

"It's not that simple, Anson. I wish it were."

"Does it have to do with your health?" he asked with concern. "I've got to know."

"Nothing serious. But serious enough that I need that sabbatical. Will you do it for me?"

"I've lost track of the number of times I've gone out on a limb for you Sheila. Until now, you've always justified my faith in you."

"Then I can count on your support?"

"Up to a point. When do you want to leave?"

Realizing that in her loneliness she might be tempted to call David and tell him about his baby, and because she couldn't bear to see

228

him again, she said, "Immediately. I can clean everything up by the end of the week."

"You want to talk about it?" her friend, Annie Brookes, asked. Reaching across the island counter in the center of the large farm-style kitchen, she patted Sheila's hand comfortingly. "When you called and asked if I could put you up until you decided where to have your child, I said of course, and no questions asked. But you've been here a week now, and you're ready to explode."

Annie Brookes, divorced and childless, was her best friend. They had met at Yale during their undergraduate days and the friendship had strengthened through the years. Brookes had stayed on at Yale doing graduate work, working for her Ph.D. in Urban Planning. They kept in contact through frequent phone calls and met once or twice a year when their schedules permitted.

Sheila nodded. She had made the right choice in asking Annie Brookes to take her in. After a few days with her mother in Virginia, she had rejected moving in with her parents because she knew that her presence as the unmarried pregnant daughter, if it had to come out, would cause too many questions and breed too many pressures. On the other hand, Annie Brookes, with no questions asked, had made her feel at home. She didn't even know of David Benjamin's existence, for Sheila never mentioned his name, and she didn't ask.

Annie had recently been granted a full professorship at Yale. Her future decided, planning to spend the next few years in New Haven, she had bought an old barn and had converted it into a comfortably charming rustic domicile. Isolated from prying neighbors, it was an idyllic hideway where Sheila could hibernate until she decided whether to have her baby or have an abortion. Whether she was going to tell Anson Phillips she wanted the job or not.

"Maybe it *would* help to talk," Sheila said, sipping at her coffee. "I know what you're thinking. Why don't I tell him? Why carry the child of a man I can't possibly marry? Because if I told him, I would be forcing him to make a choice. I'm almost certain he would marry me and if he did, I would be forcing him to give up everything that is his reason for being and his motive for living."

"I can relate to that," Annie responded thoughtfully. "I was once married to the same kind of man. We loved each other but we couldn't live with each other. We should never have gotten married in the first place because we came together for all the wrong reasons.

We should have just had an affair and then we could have walked away with our memories . . . and a minimum of hurt and disappointment."

"In a way that's what we've done," Sheila mused aloud. "It's better it ended this way."

"But it isn't ended. What about the job? Your career? Something you've worked for all your life. Or do you keep the child of the man you love, who not only doesn't know that you're pregnant, but you won't tell him because you're afraid it would ruin his life. What about your life, Sheila? Which do you want? The child or the career? You have less than a month to decide."

"I still want both," she said helplessly. "Even though I know I can't have both."

"You're a born romantic, Sheila Harrington, just like me," Annie said.

"And I've paid the price," she answered.

CHAPTER
31

Two months after David's contract had been renewed, Harold Fedder was elected to the presidency of the Board of Trustees. Because of the need for cooperation between the spiritual and secular leaders of the congregation, both men knew their antagonistic relationship would have to change. It was Fedder who made the effort to heal the breach. His first act of reconciliation was to come into David's office unannounced, a gesture that surprised David.

Not wanting to say anything controversial, he said, "Congratulations on your election, Harold. You'll make a good board president."

"I hope so," Fedder answered. After an awkward pause, he quickly added, "I hope I'm as good a board president as you are a rabbi." Seeing the surprised expression on David's face, he continued, "Since my election, I've spent many hours thinking about you. Maybe I've misjudged you. If I have, I want to apologize."

Thoroughly confused, David answered, "Harold, I don't know how to respond. But let's be honest with each other. I know what you think of me as a rabbi. You've told me often enough. I don't understand what caused you to change your opinion of me."

"I'm sure you don't. But because you stood up to Meyer Loeb and all the rest of us, what Meyer said is true. You've caused us all to embrace our Judaism. I don't know if you're aware of what's been happening within the congregation since that meeting, but everyone else is. Do you know how many young people have reassumed the Jewish-sounding names that their parents had Americanized? And in spite of their families' objections."

"Though I'm glad it's happening, I can't take credit," David said quietly.

"That's not the only change that's happening because of you, Rabbi. Men and women in their forties and fifties who never became Bar Mitzvah are attending classes to go through a ceremony they didn't go through when they were thirteen. For whatever their reasons, they didn't become Bar Mitzvah and it wasn't important to them at the time. But now, by example, you showed them that a passive expression of faith is not enough. Is meaningless."

"By their acts they shall be known," David quoted.

"Exactly!" Fedder responded enthusiastically. "And have you noticed how filled the sanctuary now is during every service? There isn't an empty seat. Not even during the early morning services. The Building Committee is having a meeting next week to discuss what to do about the expected overflow crowd during the High Holy Days. We'd like you to be there."

David agreed to attend with a silent nod.

"Good. And there's more, Rabbi. Lots more. Maybe you aren't aware of it, but now there isn't a cause or program that this temple is involved in that we don't have more volunteers for than we need. And I'm talking about involvement in the gentile community as well as the Jewish community. People are—"

Embarrassed, David interrupted. "Please, Harold, you're giving me too much credit." There was a tinge of humility in his voice as he said, "I can't take the laurels for something that—"

It was Fedder's turn to interrupt. "Rabbi, though it's difficult for me to say this, you had everything to do with the miracle that's happened here. What you did and the way you've been has set off a chain reaction within this congregation that will never stop. And why? Because as Meyer Loeb said, you stood up to us. But you were really standing up *for* us—even though you knew it would probably cost you your pulpit. You were fighting *for* us. That took a kind of courage we had never seen before. The courage born of belief and conviction. I realize now that you've achieved something within this congregation that my grandfather never achieved. That you've accomplished the goal of every rabbi. The goal that my grandfather, who was twice the man that you are, never reached. You've made people in this congregation actively embrace their Jewishness."

Because he had endured six lonely weeks and was still painfully grieving over his loss of Sheila, the feeling of isolation triggered his silent thoughts. *If that's true, then why don't I feel good about it? Why don't I feel a sense of accomplishment? Some kind of reward? Why am I wondering if the sacrifice I made, for that's what it was, was worth it? Do I really give a damn anymore about these people and their well-being?*

Though he was aware that Harold Fedder was waiting for him to react positively to the laudatory statements, because he was so torn by doubt, David couldn't do it. Instead, after a pause and because he couldn't hide from the thought, he then asked quietly, "What about your telling me that someday, if I have to make the choice, I'll betray this congregation? Do you still believe that?"

Fedder answered without hesitation. "I've always believed that because of my image of what a rabbi should be, a rabbi was above temptation. You didn't fit that image. But I can now accept that every rabbi is going to be tempted because he is a man as well as a rabbi. Therefore, a rabbi is flawed just like the rest of us. I suppose what I've done is to stop putting rabbis on pedestals."

In a way, because David felt a sense of validation, Fedder's words softened his pain over his denial of Sheila Harrington. He stood up, held out his hand and said, "That will make it much easier for me." They shook hands and he added, "I'll try not to disappoint you ever again. I don't promise that I won't, but I'll try." He paused and then with a wry smile continued. "Harold, I too have a confession to make. Though you fought me every chance you had and though you continually stood in my way, I never hated you. Matter of fact, I've always admired you. More so than any other member of my congregation, you were a challenge. You've kept me on my toes."

For the first time since they had met, David heard Harold Fedder laugh. "And I have a confession to make to you, Rabbi Benjamin. In spite of my opposition, begrudgingly I've always admired you. And you don't have to worry; I'll continue to be a challenge because there's something about you that I still don't feel right about. Maybe it's because you're too ambitious for a rabbi. Maybe it's because I sense that you're bigger than any congregation you've ever served. 'The Rabbi for All Reasons,' with all that prestige and influence and power. Maybe I feel that more strongly than ever because now that you have achieved the goal of every rabbi, I have to wonder where do you go from here and can you get there without betraying this congregation?"

As Harold Fedder left David's study, he turned at the door and said, "Think about it, Rabbi. What are you going to do for an encore?"

The catalyst of his response was his projection of what he might do if ever tempted again. He quietly said to the closed door, "Harold, I've already thought about it. And the answer scares me."

As always, when he wasn't occupied, his thoughts turned to Sheila. Because they caused him too much distress, he tried to hide from them by picking up the newspaper and turning to the sports pages. A headline caught his attention and he began to read the story. He was surprised to see his brother-in-law's name. When he was finished, he mused softly, "If Brian has read this, he must feel terrible about what has happened to his friend. And I think I've got problems . . ."

Brian read the headline and was terrified: SONNY THORNTON INDICTED ON DRUG CHARGES

The lurid story detailed how after a six-month undercover operation by the FBI and the Los Angeles Police Department, a raid had been conducted on Thornton's Beverly Hills home and evidence had been found linking the football player with an international drug operation.

Brian's name had appeared in the story as background material, relating to Thornton's years as his teammate during their careers at the University of Michigan. He had been called by a local reporter after the story had broken for his reaction and nervously had replied, "I haven't seen Sonny in years. We didn't keep in touch after graduation. But the Sonny Thornton I knew would never be involved in drugs. Other than that, I have nothing else to say." He had lied because of the last line in the story quoting an FBI spokesman: ". . . This was a well-financed drug operation and more arrests are expected in the near future . . ."

But his anxiety at being arrested was the least of his fears.

He had been involved in financing six drug buys and the scam had worked perfectly. Using part of the monthly monies that David had raised for the Israelis, he had made almost four hundred thousand dollars, which was secretly deposited in a numbered Swiss bank account. Not wanting to take the risk, he had deliberately limited the number of times he had bankrolled the drug buys. During each deal, he had always been judiciously careful, never investing more money than he could cover from his personal holdings if something

234

went wrong. As an added precaution, before giving Thornton the money, he made sure that there was plenty of time for the football player to return the investment along with his profit before the Mossad agents made their monthly pickup.

His greed caused him to get careless.

It was the next to the last month of the operation of the Mossad plan. The opportunity to use their money would end in sixty days. His goal had been a profit of half a million; he had convinced himself with that much money as security he would be able to free himself of Frank Terhanti. He only had one more chance to raise the balance. Because of the ease of the six past successes, when everything had always gone exactly as planned, he had given $200,000 of the Israelis' money to Sonny Thornton. The money, plus his share of the profits, was to have been returned three days ago. He was sure it would be because Thornton had called telling him when he would arrive in Detroit with the money.

He had met the plane but Thornton wasn't on it.

Frantically, over the next forty-eight hours, he had called every number in Los Angeles he could think of leaving messages, but Thornton never returned his calls. It wasn't until the story of the arrest broke that Brian understood why. When he heard the news his first concern was whether Thornton would implicate him.

That concern was momentarily forgotten because of his realization that in twenty-four hours the two Mossad agents were scheduled to make the pickup and he was $200,000 short. He knew from the first meeting with them what they would do to him. At that moment, with time running out, he was more afraid of the Israeli agents than of the possibility that Sonny Thornton had implicated him.

He had no choice in what he had to do.

Going down to the bank vault, he had taken out two safe-deposit boxes. One contained the money that belonged to the Israelis. The other contained $387,000 of Las Vegas casino skim money that Terhanti had given him to launder a week ago. He took $200,000 of it and replaced the missing Mossad money. Terhanti would never know the difference for he planned to cover the shortage with $200,000 from his numbered Swiss bank account.

Returning to his office, he felt a sense of security. It had been close and it had cost him almost half of his drug profits, but he had pulled it off. The danger was over. His security vanished after he had sent the telegram to the Swiss bank directing them to wire $200,000 to his personal account in Detroit. Telling his banker to let him know the moment the money arrived, he had been told, "Because of the time difference and the weekend, that money won't be credited to your account for four days, Mr. McGraw. But I'll let you know as soon as it comes in."

That was two days ago. He had just received the call from Frank Terhanti ordering him to deliver the $387,000 of laundered cash.

Two days, Brian thought, that's all I needed. Another two days and I would have gotten away with it. Sitting in the first row of the bleachers in the empty football stadium, he stared out across the soggy, neglected field. When Frank Terhanti had called to tell Brian when and where to meet him, he had thought of dropping out of sight for forty-eight hours until he had the cash from Switzerland. He didn't because he knew that if he didn't keep the appointment, Terhanti would immediately believe he had disappeared with the money. He knew firsthand what happened to people who had worked for Frank Terhanti and had stolen from him.

Too nervous to sit still while he waited, Brian paced the sideline. Faded line markers brought back memories, and he broke into a slow trot. He was breathing heavily when he reached the goal line. He looked toward the other end of the field and smiled. Like beckoning open arms, the goalposts waited for him. Frank Terhanti was momentarily forgotten.

Positioning himself at the center of the end line, he fielded an imaginary punt. Tucking an illusory football under his arm, he churned up the field. As he passed the twenty-yard line, sidestepping two would-be tacklers, he could hear the capacity-filled stadium screaming his name. "McGraw! McGraw! Go! Go! Go!"

He shifted the ball to his left arm and high-stepped his way to midfield. Above the stadium, the scoreboard clock ticked away the final seconds. He avoided the last tackler with a stiff straight-arm, and the roar of the crowd intensified as he ran the remaining yards into the end zone, where he spiked the ball after scoring the winning touchdown. Index fingers pointing to the sky, he raised his arms in victory to the chant of "McGraw! McGraw! McGraw!"

He was breathing so heavily now that he had to bend over and, with his hands on his knees, he struggled to catch his breath. He looked up when he heard a voice ordering, "Hey, jock, over here!" The recalled moment of triumph faded as he saw Frank Terhanti, a look of disdain on his face, motioning to him.

Embarrassed and fearful, the expensive three-piece suit now muddy and adhering to his sweaty body, Brian walked apprehensively across the field and sat down next to Terhanti on the bottom row of seats. Two bored thick bodyguards sat several tiers behind them.

"Relax, jock, I'm not laughing at you. I understand you," Terhanti said. "Those were your glory days. For four years you were a Saturday-afternnon hero. So I don't blame you for trying to relive those days. But did you ever think of why everything went downhill after that? Because you never grew up and because that's all you were ever good at. Playing a game. But even though the game ended a long time ago, you still live in that fantasy world. It's over, jock, when are you going to accept that?"

The taste of bile filled his throat as Brian wiped the perspiration from his brow with a silk handkerchief. Frank Terhanti had just torn down the wall Brian had built around himself to shut out the truth.

"Now, let's get back to the real world and talk some business." He held out his hand for his money.

Nervously, Brian took the envelope out of his inside jacket pocket and handed it to Terhanti. He casually counted it and then counted it again. "Where's the rest of my money?" he asked in a matter-of-fact statement which replaced Brian's anxiety with terror. "You're short a couple of hundred thousand."

When Brian didn't respond, Terhanti, as if talking to a son who had disappointed him, said sadly, "Oh, Brian, Brian, you used two hundred thousand dollars of my money. What did you do with it?"

Although he had spoken softly, and without apparent animosity, Brian sensed the implied threat and still couldn't bring himself to answer.

Terhanti shook his head repeatedly and said, "I knew the temptation was going to get to you sooner or later. With all that dirty money passing through your hands, you were bound to get itchy fingers. But I didn't think you had the courage to touch it. I misjudged you. You must have been pretty desperate. Brian, if you were in trouble and needed some cash, why didn't you come to me? I'd have helped you out."

Brian managed a weak smile and said, "I wasn't in any trouble."

"Then why did you take the money? To gamble? You're not playing the ponies, are you? Brian, Brian, betting on horses is for losers. For a crap game? Poker? No, you don't have the guts to be a high roller. Were you paying off the loan sharks? *Brian, what did you use my money for?*"

The words Brian wasn't brave enough to say gagged in his throat. So I could look you in the eye and tell you off. So I could get out from under you. So for once in my life I could stop being just a Saturday-afternoon hero.

After a moment's silence, Terhanti said, "You jocks are all alike. You get out of your league and when you get in trouble, you don't know how to handle it. Look what happened to your buddy, Sonny Thornton—" Realization caused him to stare at Brian. "You were in on that scam with him, weren't you? You heard about all the big money to be made in the shit business and so you decided to take a flyer. And what better way than with my bankroll. That's what happened to my two hundred thousand dollars, isn't it?"

Brian didn't have to answer. The look on his face was his confession.

"You're in over your head," Terhanti said disgustedly. "But that's your problem. My problem is getting my money back. When, Brian? When?"

"Two days," he said in a voice that made Terhanti look at him suspiciously.

"This isn't the first time, is it?" he quietly asked. "How many other times have you used my money to make a deal?" When Brian didn't answer and looked away, Terhanti dug his fingers into either side of Brian's jaw and forced his face around. "How many times, Brian?" He demanded an answer.

"Five," he said in a strained voice.

"And how much have you cleared?"

Brian's silence caused Terhanti to dig his fingers deeper into the soft flesh. Sweating because of the pain, his voice choked with fear, Brian finally said, "Almost four hundred thousand."

Terhanti whistled softly, said nothing for a few moments, then asked quietly, "Why, Brian? You know my rules. Nobody who works for me moonlights without my permission—and certainly not without cutting me in for a piece of the action. And you used my money to do it."

"I—I didn't use your money, Frank," Brian said apologetically.

"What the hell are you talking about? I know the way you live, you haven't got that kind of cash."

Haltingly, for the first time, he told him of the Mossad money-raising plan and of his part in it. He hoped the excuse would soften Terhanti's anger. Terhanti exploded. "For the past year and a half you've had your hands on a million dollars a month in clean money and you didn't tell me about it! We could have laundered almost twenty million during that time. Brian, you work for me and you double-crossed me. And what for? For a few measly bucks you picked up in a drug scam. What did you plan to do with that money? How were you going to hide it from me?"

Unable to look at his tormentor, Brian sat with his head bowed. But the repeated, painful, viselike pressure on his jaws finally made him raise his head. The look of hatred on Brian's face gave Terhanti his answer. "You thought you could buy your way out, didn't you? Look, you dumb shit, you knew the rules when you came in. I laid them all out for you. You could have said no. Remember? But you didn't say no because you were greedy and because you couldn't make it on your own. What the hell were you when I picked you up? A broken-down goddamn Saturday-afternoon hero who lived in the past because you didn't have a future. You were broke, you had no job and no chance of getting one because you have nothing to offer. You knew what you were getting into, but you didn't say no because you wanted the money. The high living. The recognition. All the perks you get. The bonuses. McGraw, nobody twisted your arm. You made a deal and you paid the price. I own you. Lock, stock and barrel. When I say jump, the only words I want to hear from you are how high. When I say shit, you squat. But you didn't live up to your part of the deal and because you know too much about me and my business, there's only one way you'll ever get out. That's in a pine box. Do we understand each other?"

Standing up and brushing his hands as if they had been soiled by touching Brian, Terhanti concluded: "Now what about my two hundred thousand? When are you going to pay me back?"

"You'll have it in two days, Frank. I promise. That's when my money comes from Switzerland."

"No, McGraw, that four hundred thousand in Switzerland is my money. I'll have someone at the bank to pick it up when it's deposited to your account. Someone I can trust. That's the price you pay for double-crossing me by not telling me about the Israeli funds you could have laundered. So you still owe me two hundred thousand dollars."

"But, Frank—" Brian started to protest.

"No ifs, ands or buts, Brian. You're getting off easy. You're lucky I don't have both your knees broken. Along with your thick skull.

You got a week to raise that money. When I get it, maybe I'll forget this ever happened—because I know you'll never try it again. You don't have the guts."

"But suppose I can't get it to you in a week?" Brian's voice shook. "I don't know if I can raise that kind of money."

"Brian, I'd make sure I raised it. Because if I don't get my money in seven days, if I were you, jock, I'd punt."

CHAPTER
32

After Terhanti left, Brian sat for two hours in the deserted stadium. Partially because of his terror and partially because he knew that what Terhanti had said about him was true, that he was out of his league, Brian was in a state of near panic. He felt abandoned. Terhanti hadn't threatened him but had told him the truth. *There's only one way you'll ever get away from me. That's in a pine box.* Not knowing what to do or where to go, even if only to unburden himself, he desperately needs a sympathetic ear. He couldn't make himself confide in a friend because he feared condemnation and rejection. Too weak to face the situation alone, he needed someone who would listen and not judge. He thought of going to a priest, but he needed solace and understanding, not absolution. He needed advice, not penance.

He thought of David.

He's a rabbi, he told himself. Helping troubled people is David's business. He'll understand. He won't judge or condemn.

Brian called from a pay phone and from David's reaction, he knew he had made the right decision. "Of course I'll see you right away. You're in trouble and you need help. It's not Martha or the kids, is it?"

"No, they're fine."

"Then come right over. I'll wait for you."

But facing David across his desk, it was difficult to say the words.

Delaying, he asked nervously, "Is it safe to talk here? Someone might walk in on us."

Patiently, David said into the intercom, "Florence, I don't want interruptions. Hold all my calls." He got up and locked the door. Returning to his desk, he sat quietly and waited for Brian to regain his composure. "Nobody will disturb us," he added reassuringly.

After running a trembling hand over his face, Brian finally spoke: "I'm in big trouble, David." Because he didn't know where to begin, it was still difficult for him to say the words.

"Maybe it'll be easier if you start at the beginning," David said with a sense of compassion.

Sucking in a deep, deep breath, Brian told his story: "I don't know how or when it all began. Maybe the first time I ever picked up a football. Who knows?" He paused and sadly shook his head.

Slowly, the words came out. Throughout the long telling, without going into the specifics of how he had laundered money or how the drug deals were set up, and though the story occasionally wandered from the point, David sat expressionless and made no comment. It wasn't until the pieces began to merge into the mosaic that he reacted. He could feel his anger begin to smoulder. Brian, unaware of David's reaction, finished and his body seemed to unravel as if exhausted by the ordeal of his confession.

David's initial response was one of inner anger. My brother-in-law is crime-connected! he told himself. He placed me and everyone around me in jeopardy. If it had ever come out, he could have ruined my career. However, seeing the hopeless, desperate expression on Brian's face, David began to calm. But nobody ever did find out, he thought. Nobody even guessed the truth. What did I expect of him, to tell me he worked for Frank Terhanti? I wonder why he did it? He must have known the consequences. Brian isn't all bad. He's a good man. A good husband. He's loved and protected my sister. Helped her to raise two lovely children whom he adores. He's always been there for me when I needed him. Helped me raise that money for Israel. Done more for my temple than some of my congregants. No, he's not all bad. None of us are. So who am I to judge him? Am I any—"

The sound of Brian crying interrupted David's thoughts.

"How can I help you, Brian? I'll do whatever I can."

Brian, wiping away his tears, looked at David strangely. A flicker of hope was born and then quickly died. "I didn't come here for your help, David. I came here because I needed to talk. Besides, how can you help me?"

"I'll go see Terhanti. I'll talk to him."

Brian snorted. "What are you going to do, David? Take a gun and shoot him? Preach to him? Quote from the Bible? He'd laugh at you. Then he'd probably give you a donation. You don't know the Frank Terhantis of this world because you don't live in the same world as they do. Better men than you have tried to take him out and have failed. Most of them are on the bottom of the Detroit River."

Seriously, David said, "I'm not afraid of him, Brian. You need help and I'm going to help you. I don't know how yet, but I'll find a way." After a moment's thoughtful silence, "Maybe through my father-in-law. The senator's a powerful man."

"With all due respect to Senator Mendes, what can he do? The FBI and the IRS and the Crime Commission have taken Terhanti on and they can't touch him. Nobody can touch him. He's too tough and he's too smart. He doesn't fight by any rules except his own. If the senator got into a fight with Frank Terhanti, he'd be destroyed. His reputation, his image, everything. He couldn't be elected dogcatcher after Terhanti was through with him. There's only one way to make Terhanti listen. By paying him back the two hundred thousand dollars I owe him before next Friday."

"Whatever I have is yours, Brian. It isn't much. I've got between eight–nine thousand in the bank. You're welcome to it. I've got a few shares of stock I could sell, worth maybe another five–six thousand. Will that help?"

Brian shook his head sadly. "Even with your help, all I can come up with is around forty thousand. That's not enough."

"Can't you borrow the rest? Maybe if you gave him what you have, you could get him off your back for a while until you raised the balance."

"Like I said, David, you don't know Frank Terhanti like I do. He'd laugh at me. And before he had someone cut my throat, he'd tell me he's not in the finance business. So much down and so much a month isn't the way he operates, David. He won't settle for less than all of his money and it has to be delivered in a week. I don't have enough time to borrow that kind of money."

Propelled by the hopelessness of his situation, Brian flung himself out of the chair and began to pace. David sought to calm him by saying, "Take it easy, Brian, there's got to be a way out. Maybe if we went to the police and—"

Brian spun angrily and shouted, "David, come into the real world! What am I going to say to the police? That I need your protection because I stole two hundred thousand dollars from Frank Terhanti and he wants it back! Besides, if I went to the cops, in less than fifteen minutes he'd know about it."

He began to pace again, slamming his fist into his palm with frustration. "Damn it, why did I ever get involved with you and those Israelis and their crazy money-raising scheme? If I had only waited another month, it would have all been over. I would never have had the opportunity to use their money."

"But you did use that money, Brian. So what are you going to do now?"

Brian shrugged and slumped back into the chair. "Run, I guess," he said. "That's my only hope of staying alive. Hide myself someplace in Europe or South America and try to figure a way out of this."

"What about Martha and the kids? Will you take them with you?"

"I can't," he said with misery in his voice. "They'll be okay. The Frank Terhantis have a strange sense of morality. They wouldn't think of harming a man's wife or his children. Oh, they don't give a second thought to making them widows and orphans, but they won't be in danger."

"But when will you be back? How will you live?"

"I'll be back when it's safe. And I'll manage. It's Martha and the kids I'm worried about. You'll watch out for them?"

"Of course I'll watch out for them. But Brian, I can't let you do this. We've got to fight back. We can't let Terhanti get away with this. There's got to be a way to stop him."

Brian shook his head. "I'm not strong like you, David. I'm a weak man. I can't fight Frank Terhanti."

"Well, I can."

"How?"

"I don't know yet. Give me a day or so to think about it. Don't do anything rash like running off to Timbuktu. I'll come up with something. I'll give you a call when I do."

Three nights later, at ten o'clock, Brian reappeared in David's study. With guarded hope, he watched his brother-in-law reach into his jacket pocket and take out an envelope which he handed across the desk. The check was made out for $200,000.

"God, David, I don't know what to say. Where did you get this money?"

"Are you sure you want to know?"

"I've got to know. Not from loan sharks, I hope."

"No, Brian, not from loan sharks. That's part of next month's donation for Israel. Ben Adelson's check."

Understanding caused Brian to lean across the desk and ask in a disbelieving conspiratorial whisper, "And you'd advance me two hundred thousand dollars of that money?" After David nodded, he said, "What would you tell the Mossad agents?"

"I'd lie," David said. "Tell them Adelson only donated fifty thousand dollars."

Brian whistled. "David, I can't let you do this. I can't let you lie for me. Steal for me." He thrust the check back at David who ignored it. It fluttered to the desk. "Why are you putting your neck out on a chopping block for me?" he asked.

"Because it's the only way I know to save your life," David said quietly.

"You'd be violating every code, every standard you live by."

"I'd be saving your life," David repeated softly.

"But you're a rabbi," Brian argued.

"But I'm also a man. And you're right, it is time I got into the real world. Living in a rabbi's world is easy. You cloak yourself in the Torah and as long as you live by those laws and rules, nobody is going to dispute what you do or say. That would be arguing with the word of God. Matter of fact, you're going to be admired and respected. But do you know how the Frank Terhantis answer when I say: *Do unto others as you would have them do unto you?* He'd laugh at me and ask *Why should I when I can take whatever I want from them?* Do you know how he'd respond if I sanctimoniously quoted: *Turn the other cheek?* He'd say, *Not when I'm bigger and stronger.* It's all a question of values. Secular or temporal. It's safe for a rabbi to live in his temporal world for he's never tempted. It's only when he tries to behave like a man that he is tempted. And Brian, this time if I stay in my own world where it's safe, if I magnanimously say to you, 'I'd like to help but I can't', you die. I won't let that happen. So yes, I'll steal for you and I'll lie for you. That's my choice. But not as a rabbi. As a man."

He took the check which lay on the desk between them and

handed it back to Brian and said with warmth, "Now you go back home to your wife and kids where you belong. Make love to Martha. Kiss the kids for me."

"And you?"

"I'm going to stay here and try to figure out a way to return that money."

"We'll need a miracle to do that, David. Maybe you'd better start praying for one."

"I already have."

CHAPTER
33

The day after he had returned the money to Frank Terhanti, Brian had gone to his office and found that he had been locked out. His personal possessions had been packed in cartons and left in the small waiting room. His name in gilt lettering had been scraped off the door. That was almost two weeks ago and because he was frightened by his interpretation of the meaning of his dismissal, except to run a few meaningless errands for Martha, he hadn't left the safety of his own home. She didn't ask any questions.

The first week he enjoyed being home. He filled his time by playing with the kids and amusing himself by puttering around the landscaped property and by tinkering in a workshop he had never had time for before. But by the beginning of the second week, the children were no longer entertaining and the do-it-yourself chores had become drudgery. Brian began to think about how he was going to earn a living that would sustain the life-style he and Martha had enjoyed for over eight years. He didn't say anything to her because he didn't want her to be concerned, but after a day of telephone calls, he realized he had been blacklisted. Whatever he did now, he would have to begin from scratch. Somehow, realizing he would have to start all over again buoyed his spirits. That night he suggested to Martha that they go to dinner and the movies. She loved the idea and rustled through the entertainment section of the paper and picked out the show she wanted to see.

They ate at a quiet, out-of-the-way restaurant in the suburbs, and arrived early at the movie theater. They got in line, and played a little game speculating on the kind of people who were waiting with them: a quiet elderly couple, some noisy teenagers, a tiny wrinkled woman in her sixties, a young man absorbed in a paperback, and then a pair of lovers holding hands. The lovely blond girl with her long hair cascading almost to her shoulders reminded Martha that Brian had always wanted her to wear her hair that way. Somehow she had resisted. Perhaps now she would. The girl's boyfriend was baby-faced, and when he laughed it was loud and cracky. Then a latecomer shuffled by, an expressionless man in a dark suit and fedora. He headed toward the front of the line, and mumbled an apology as he bumped into Brian. For a startled moment, Brian felt a stab of fear. He pushed Martha behind him protectively, but the man kept on moving ahead of him, talked to the cashier, and then burrowed his way into the head of the line, despite protests from some others. Still, Brian and Martha were grateful when the early show emptied out and they were allowed to move inside.

They settled in the aisle seats at the far end of a rear row. The man with the hard face sat in the next row in the aisle seat. The young lovers struggled past the man, politely making excuses when he snarled at them. They ended up directly behind Brian, and he wondered why because there were still some better seats available. But Martha, giggling a little, pointed out that the lovers would have more privacy in the rear of the theater. As if to prove her point, the couple immediately embraced and began kissing.

When the theater lights dimmed, because the refreshment stand was less crowded, Brian got up and headed into the lobby to buy some popcorn. He bought two separate cartons, one without butter for him and one with "the works" for Martha. Then he headed toward the darkened theater, hoping to make it back to his seat before the end of the opening credits. He wasn't that lucky. The moment the door closed behind him, he felt the stiletto slice into his back. A hand with long tapered fingers covered his mouth before he could scream, the blonde's flowing tresses brushed his face, and he could smell her perfume as she leaned over. He heard her whisper, just before she cut his throat, "Frank says to make an example of you. A warning to anyone else who might get a bright idea about double-crossing him . . ."

* * *

"Martha, I want you and the kids to move in with me and stay as long as you want," David said to his sister. "And I'm not taking no for an answer."

They had just returned from Brian's funeral, and David had made sure Martha had settled into the sofa in the living room of his house. He had taken care of the kids, made them supper and put them to bed. Then he had gone down to the kitchen and made Martha some hot tea in a glass, the way she liked it. As she sipped at the tea, her pallid face was still as lifeless as the husband she had just buried. The hot vapors of the tea put a flush in her cheeks, and in a quiet voice, she began to unburden herself.

"You didn't know Brian long enough to understand the kind of man he really was."

David nodded sympathetically.

"I know what you're thinking," she continued. "You're wondering if I knew about his Mafia connections." David looked at her stoically, not quite sure how to respond. Martha sighed and said, "Of course I heard the stories and innuendos. I didn't have to ask him if they were true. I saw the way he lived with fear and I knew it was all true. If I had asked him, it would have only made it worse for him. But it didn't matter to me. I loved him and he loved me and he showed it in every way. Everything he did, he did for me. He was devoted to me, as I was to him. Loving is as much giving as it is taking, and that's how Brian loved me."

"It's my fault Brian's dead," David confessed. "He wanted to leave the country and I talked him out of it. Made him stay. If I hadn't, he'd still be alive. Can you ever forgive me?"

She paused and sipped her tea before continuing. She shook her head and said, "There's nothing to forgive you for, David. Don't blame yourself. Sooner or later, Frank Terhanti would have found him. So don't blame yourself. Brian was a weak man. I, better than anyone else, know how weak he was. But that didn't matter to me. All that mattered was the way he loved me. He sacrificed everything because of that." She dabbed at her eyes with a small handkerchief and looked at David. "You don't have the faintest idea of what I'm talking about because you've never really loved anyone. No, not even Naomi. Especially Naomi. But I've had that kind of love. I've shared my life with someone, so I know what it means. How could you know what it means when you don't know how to give to someone, to sacrifice for them? David, maybe I'm crying for you, as well as for myself, because you've never loved anyone that way and have never been loved that way."

He bowed his head so Martha couldn't see the pain his face, and thought, Yes, I do know what you mean for I have been loved that way. And I've grieved like you because of the loss. I was a fool to give it up. I made the wrong sacrifice. And I'm going to spend the rest of my life trying to make it up to her . . .

CHAPTER
34

The conversation with his sister awakened his slumbering demons and caused David to spend a sleepless night. The next day, unable to face the demands of his congregation, he canceled all his appointments and stayed away from the temple by going for a long drive during which he confronted his confusions. He found himself stopping to eat at the Clarkston Cafe, where he had shared so many hours of closeness and intimacy with Sheila. His mind filled with memories of their trysting and how she had looked as she sat across from him. He knew he had to see her again.

As he drove back to Detroit, he thought of stopping to call, but he didn't because he feared her response. He fantasized her saying, "No, David, I don't want to see you. It's over between us. Spare me any more pain." Because of his fear of her rejection, David convinced himself that it would be better to appear unannounced at her apartment door.

He stopped only at a florist to pick up a bouquet of her favorite yellow roses. Then, bracing himself, he took the elevator to the seventh floor, where he strode down the corridor and boldly knocked on her door. He was shocked when a man answered. During the long drive, he had never once thought that she might be with another man.

He glanced at the number above the door. Maybe he was at the wrong apartment? The man's handsome chiseled face broke into a smile when, pointing at the yellow roses, he said, "If you're looking for Sheila Harrington, you're in the right place."

"B-but at the wrong time," David awkwardly stammered. He turned to go.

"Hey, don't get the wrong idea. I'm just subletting this place. The rental agent told me Miss Harrington had left town."

"Do you know where she can be reached?" David asked.

The man shrugged. "I'm sorry, I don't. Why don't you try her office?"

On the street, he gave the bouquet of yellow roses to a passing bag lady, who delightedly sniffed at the blossoms as David walked away.

Sheila's secretary wasn't any more helpful than the stranger in her apartment. "I'm sorry, Rabbi, she said she was taking a sabbatical. She didn't leave any forwarding address; just told me to send her personal mail to her mother in Virginia. But Mr. Phillips might know where she is."

"Anson Phillips, her boss?"

"Yes . . ."

When David was put through to Anson Phillips's office, he was thwarted again. "Mr. Phillips is in Africa on a hunting trip. He isn't expected back for two weeks."

Every possible reason David conjured up for Sheila's taking a sabbatical leave increased his anxiety and intensified his need to find her. But because of their clandestine back-street romance, they had always isolated themselves; they had no mutual friends he could turn to who might know where she had gone. After a few more frustrating days of getting nowhere, he mustered up enough courage to call her mother in Virginia.

". . . Yes, Mrs. Harrington, I'm a friend of Sheila's," he began nervously. "David Benajmin. Maybe she told you about me?"

He was relieved by her answer. "N-o-o-o, I don't think so, Mr. Benjamin," she said thoughtfully. "I'd have remembered a gentleman friend's name." She laughed and he shuddered because the tinkling sound duplicated the laughter he had heard so many times.

"I'm sorry to bother you, Mrs. Harrington, but it's important that I reach her. Can you please give me a phone number? An address?"

"I'm afraid not, Mr. Benjamin. May I call you David?"

"Of course."

"Well, David, Sheila just dropped some of her things off when she sublet her apartment, and said she was going away with a friend on a long, unplanned trip. I took that to mean they weren't making any specific plans. That she just wanted to get away from it all. And God knows, from the way she looked, she desperately needs that kind of a vacation."

"I understand," David agreed with false enthusiasm.

"David, forgive me for being so personal . . ." she hesitated before asking, ". . . but how well do you know my daughter?"

He didn't know how to answer. Like mother, like daughter, he thought. She's as blunt and as direct as Sheila. "We have been friends for quite a while," he finally said. He felt the need to add, "Good friends."

"Then it occurs to me, knowing my daughter as I do, that she would have given you her itinerary . . . if she wanted you to have it."

"You could be right, Mrs. Harrington. I'm sorry to have bothered you."

"Oh, no-o-o bother. When I hear from her I'll be happy to pass along your message."

David hung up slowly, more disappointed than ever. He was certain now that the strong-willed Sheila was traveling somewhere with another man. Perhaps it was a quick fling on the rebound, he tortured himself. But he curbed his jealousy by reminding himself that what had happened was his fault. He was a damn fool for not telling her the truth about the decision he had made. But at the time, he didn't know the truth . . .

David couldn't put Sheila out of his mind, not even for a day. Trying to find her became an obsession. A compulsion. If for no other reason but to tell her why he had made the decision he had, even though he was convinced by now he had lost her to another man who was probably better for her, less troubled and less encumbered.

He called every hotel they had ever been at in the hopes that, perhaps driven by nostalgia, Sheila had stayed in one of them shortly after she had left Detroit. He had reasoned that if she had, she would have to have filled out a registration form with a return address. One desk clerk's response added to his growing despondency: "Sir, according to our computers, the last time Miss Harrington was registered here was on the date you also were here. If she's stayed here since then, if would have to have been under another name."

Gradually, he ran out of even the remotest of possibilities. Periodically, he called United Motors only to be told that Anson Phillips was still in Africa. Yes, he was reassured, they would definitely let the rabbi know when he returned.

It was Sheila who had planned the party celebrating Annie's birthday.

Teetering on a high stepladder, she was stringing gaily colored streamers and bright balloons from the high beams of the large open living room in preparation for the evening. In the three weeks since she had arrived at Annie's, her demeanor had changed. Isolated most of the day, she spent the time walking in the nearby woods and relaxing on the banks of a stream. The pressures of job and circumstance faded because of the calming environment and introspection resulted in acceptance of her reality. It was over, and she could go on because that part of her life was in her past. It was time to grab hold of the present and prepare for her future. The challenge filled her with a sense of renewed optimism and vitality. But she had yet to come to a decision as to whether to keep her baby or not.

Sitting on the top step, she critically surveyed the room and was satisfied. A few more touches and she would be ready to help Annie greet the faculty friends that had been invited. "I need a few more balloons," she yelled toward the kitchen, where Annie was carefully arranging trays of canapés. While she waited, she reached up to restring a streamer that had become undone.

A sharp grab of pain caused her to double over and clutch at her stomach as Annie, holding a dozen balloons by their gathered strings, came into the room.

"Are you all right? Is anything wrong?"

Recovering, Sheila let out a breath. "Of course I'm all right," she said immediately. As if to prove her condition, rather than have Annie hand her the balloons, she defiantly came down the ladder and took them from her. Returning to her position, she began to stretch as she tied them in place.

Annie watched cautiously. Satisfied, she was about to return to the kitchen when she saw Sheila suddenly let go of the remaining balloons and grab at her stomach. She screamed as Sheila fell from the ladder.

On the highly polished floor, though apparently unhurt from the short fall, a film of sweat bathed Sheila's face. She moaned when a bubble of nausea burst within her throat.

On her knees beside Sheila, Annie asked with concern, "Sheila, something's wrong. Are you sure you're all right? You look so pale."

Shaking her head, Sheila tried to sit up. "Well, I haven't been feeling well the last couple of days. Maybe I've picked up a touch of stomach flu. It's been going around." She rose shakily to her feet and when the pain continued to stab deep into her abdomen she added, "I think I'll feel better if I lie down for a few minutes." She left the living room and somehow made it down the hall to her bedroom on trembling legs.

A concerned Annie stood in the doorway as Sheila, wincing with the effort, stretched out on the bed. As if afraid to say the words, she whispered, "I wonder if I'm having a miscarriage?"

Annie hurriedly dialed Sheila's doctor, a friend on the medical school faculty. His probing questions of Annie elicited Sheila's symptoms. The constancy of the sudden severe pain. The rapid pulse. The nausea. The fading ashen pallor.

Annie sensed the urgency in his voice. "It doesn't sound like a simple miscarriage. I'll send an ambulance from University Hospital and meet you at the emergency entrance."

Sheila went into shock as the vehicle, siren wailing, pulled into the hospital driveway. She was unaware of being trundled on to a gurney and was drifting in and out of consciousness as she was wheeled into an emergency room. A deeply worried Annie Brookes heard her moan incoherently, ". . . my rabbi . . . David . . . I want my rabbi . . ."

Annie was puzzled. Why would Sheila want a rabbi? She wasn't Jewish. She thoughtfully looked down at Sheila, who had slipped back into unconsciousness, and then disregarded the plea as being the incoherent ramblings of someone in shock.

A few moments later, Sheila, drifting upward into semi-consciousness, grasped Annie's hand tightly and again moaned, ". . . I want my David . . ." Annie strained, trying to make sense of the fragmented thoughts when suddenly, Sheila, in a loud, angry and frustrated voice, screamed, *"Benjamin, where are you? . . . Why aren't you ever here when I need you!"*

She knew it was a longshot, but Annie, piecing together segments of what Sheila had told her and intimated when she first arrived, placed a call to the Detroit operator from the hospital lobby. "Operator, would you connect me with a Jewish temple in Detroit?"

"You have to be more specific, ma'am, there are many Jewish temples in Detroit."

"Oh, God, how stupid of me," Annie murmured aloud. "Please connect me with the telephone number of the temple at the top of your list. And hurry."

There was a slight pause, before a pleasant voice said, "Temple Adat Ari-El. Shalom."

"Hello, I'm calling from New Haven, Connecticut, trying to locate a rabbi whose first name is David or Benjamin, and who may or may not be associated with your congregation. Have you heard of such a man?"

"Why, of course. He's quite a local celebrity. That's Rabbi David Benjamin of Temple Beth Sinai. I'll look up the number for you."

Two hours earlier, David had received the call that he had been waiting for from United Motors. "Rabbi Benjamin? This is Nancy from Mr. Phillips's office. I just heard from my boss. He's back in the country attending the East Coast regional sales meetings in New York. He can be reached at the Sheraton."

David immediately placed a call to the hotel. "Anson Phillips's room, please," he said to the operator and waited impatiently, drumming his fingers on his desk.

"I'm sorry, sir, Mr. Phillips is out all day at meetings. My instructions are to hold his messages. Would you care to leave your message?"

"No message, I want to speak to him directly," David said angrily. "Put me through to the meeting room."

"I can't do that, sir. My orders are not to forward any calls. But if you'll leave a message, I'm sure Mr. Phillips will get back to you as soon as he can."

David didn't answer. He was so frustrated, he slammed the phone into its cradle and began pacing. He had to speak to Phillips. A solution caused him to shout into the intercom, "Florence, get me on the first flight to New York. I'll pick up the ticket at the airport."

"Will you be staying there overnight?"

"I'm not sure."

"Well, where can I reach you if I have to?"

"You can't. But I'll be checking in with you as soon as I can." David didn't wait for an answer as he struggled into his coat and left.

As David's plane was taxiing down the runway, Annie Brookes reached Florence at Temple Beth Sinai.

". . . Yes, I understand, Miss. Someone is dying. But I don't know where the rabbi is . . ."

CHAPTER
35

David arrived in New York in a slashing rain and caught a cab to the Sheraton. In the lobby, he collared an assistant manager. "I'm looking for Mr. Anson Phillips of United Motors. Tell him that Rabbi David Benjamin has flown in from Detroit to see him."

The manager looked at David a little bewilderedly after he checked Anson Phillips's box and said, "He's been in and out of meetings all day, Rabbi. He left word he's not to be disturbed."

"Disturb him. *Now!*" David ordered. He squashed the man's reluctance by pressing a fifty dollar bill into his palm.

Twenty minutes later, the assistant manager led a perplexed Anson Phillips up to David, who was pacing in the lobby. When the man left, David introduced himself. "I'm sorry to bother you at a time like this, Mr. Phillips, but I'm looking for Sheila Harrington."

"And that's why you dragged me out of an important meeting!"

"Mr. Phillips, I'll apologize when I have the time. Right now I must find Sheila Harrington."

"How the hell do I know where she is?"

Disappointed, David said, "I thought if anyone would know where she is, you would."

"You thought wrong, Rabbi, I haven't the faintest idea where she might be." Impatiently, Phillips began to turn away.

David tugged at his sleeve, delaying him with another question. "Mr. Phillips, can you at least tell me why she took a sabbatical? That might give me a clue as to where she went."

Phillips paused. Staring into David's beseeching eyes, he wondered why he was so anxious to find out what had happened to Sheila. "Obviously, this is a matter of some importance to you, Rabbi?"

"Believe me it is, sir."

"I don't mean to pry, but how well do you know Sheila Harrington?"

"Well enough," David said uneasily, caught off guard by Phillips's remark.

"In that case, Rabbi, if Miss Harrington wanted you to know where she was, surely she would have told you."

David let go of Phillips's sleeve and his arm dropped limply to his side. "Yes, I suppose you're right, Mr. Phillips."

"Then even if I did know, it wouldn't be proper for me to disclose that kind of information to you. Now, would it?"

Too disturbed to answer, David merely nodded.

"Good day. Rabbi, I must be getting back to my meeting." He turned on his heel and disappeared down a corridor.

David sagged as all hope seeped out of him. He was so emotionally drained by the unfriendly meeting with Anson Phillips that he couldn't move. He barely made it to the nearest empty chair in the lobby and dropped into it. Not knowing what to do next, he sat there numbly for almost ten minutes before he could pull himself together and get in touch with Florence at the temple.

"Rabbi, I'm so glad you called. Do you know an Annie Brookes from New Haven in Connecticut?"

Half listening, David shook his head and said, "No."

"She's been trying to get in touch with you. She wouldn't tell me why except that it was an emergency. She can be reached at area code 203 . . ."

Two hours later, after racing through the night in a rented car, David, pale and unshaven, paced the waiting room in University Hospital, where Sheila was undergoing emergency surgery. His nerve endings were raw from fatigue. The only time he paused was when someone in a surgical gown entered the room.

He lost track of time before Sheila's doctor, the strain still showing on his face, appeared. "Bad news, Rabbi." David's heart sank. "We couldn't save the baby. It was a tubular pregnancy. She was bleeding internally because it was ruptured." The doctor sighed, his mouth parched, his voice raspy. "The jury's still out on Sheila. It's going to be touch and go for the next couple of hours." He turned to leave and paused. "There's nothing you can do here. Why don't you get some sleep. You look like hell."

Almost inaudibly, David answered, "I'll be all right. I'd rather stay here. I feel closer to her that way."

After the doctor left, David sank into a chair. Closing his eyes and with his hands clasped prayerlike between his knees, he prayed to his God. "I've lost the son I've always wanted and I didn't even know she was pregnant. Oh, dear God, please don't let Sheila die because she was carrying my son. You've taken the child, isn't that enough? Her only crime was falling in love with a rabbi and she's more than paid for that. I'm the guilty one. Surely You know that better than anyone."

It was dawn when the doctor reappeared. David had fallen asleep in the chair and had to be shaken awake. When he looked up through bleary eyes, the physician was smiling.

"We pulled her through. She's going to be okay."

"Thank God," David cried with relief.

Smiling, the doctor said, "I deserve a little credit too, Rabbi."

David stood up and impulsively hugged the physician. "I know, I know, and I'm so grateful. When can I see her?"

"Calm down, Rabbi. She's been through a lot and she's still under the anesthesia. She'd probably have a relapse if she saw you now. You go clean up and come back in the afternoon."

David quietly entered Sheila's room and stood uneasily at the foot of her bed. She was still sleeping. After a moment, he moved to the side of the bed and looked down at her. She was pale and weak, but there was also a strange sense of serenity about her. As he studied her, she turned her head on the pillow and gradually awoke. Though she felt the same tremble of excitement whenever she saw him, she frowned because of his presence.

"Wh-what are you doing here?"

"Your friend, Annie Brookes, found me," he said in explanation.

"How did she know about you?" Sheila asked, bewildered and disoriented.

His face flushing, David shrugged. "It seems you called out my name several times when you were delirious."

Sheila felt embarrassed and turned her face away.

"I'm glad you did. I wanted to feel that you needed me."

"Why are you here?"

"Because I love you." He paused and, after taking her hand, added, "And because I know you love me." She was too weak to withdraw her hand.

"Yes, I do love you," she said in a small voice.

"Then why didn't you tell me you were pregnant?"

She found the strength to yank her hand free. "If you had known, would that have changed anything? Would you have married me? *Could* you have married me?"

His silence caused her to struggle and sit up. "Benjamin, maybe if I hadn't lost the baby, you would have married me. And I would have wanted you to marry me. But because it would have been for all the wrong reasons, we'd end up hating each other. So in a way, there's a part of me that's glad I lost our child!"

"How can you say that!"

"Because, Benjamin, I finally understand you. Your being a rabbi is your whole life. It influences everything you do, everything you think, everything you say. You can't separate it from any other part. But because of some stupid rules and laws that only you seem to understand, I can't be a part of that life. No, nothing's changed. And *I* can't change it. Not even my being pregnant can change it. Only *you* can change it. And because I finally know and understand and accept what it means to you, I don't think you ever will."

"But I love you and you love me!"

"That's true," she said sadly. "And I probably always will. David Benjamin, I've loved you like I've never loved any other man. We were the right love for each other, but at the wrong time. We were both so needy."

He knew she was right. *The right love but at the wrong time.* "Will there ever be a right time for us?" he asked in a quiet voice.

"Can there be?" she asked. Then she shook her head quickly from side to side as she answered. "I don't know. I don't want to know because I'm not sure I ever want to love anyone this way again. It's too painful. So leave me alone. Please! Go back to being a rabbi. At least you have that. Let me pick up the pieces of my life and find my way back to sanity."

She turned her face to the wall and began to cry. He touched her shoulder and she flinched as if in pain.

Shattered, David walked blindly out of the hospital . . .

EPILOGUE

He made his decision at three in the morning kneeling in front of the golden doors of the open Ark.

Returning to Detroit at midnight, he had gone directly to his temple and had spent the hours trying to determine the path he would take. He felt splintered, divided by what he was; a man deeply in love who had lost that love and a rabbi deeply confused by his doubts. As he had done so many times in the past, he went into the sanctuary and sought, if not answers, strength, from his daily conversation with his God.

The custodian, Isaiah Norman, scrubbing and polishing the tiled floor in the rotunda, paused in front of the open door to the sanctuary when he heard the muted sounds of an anguished voice. Perplexed, he looked into the large auditorium and saw David on his knees in front of the Ark.

"I have broken Your commandments, O Lord," the custodian heard David confess. "Almost every one of them. I have committed adultery. I have been a thief. I have dishonored my father and my mother. I have accepted as truth what I knew to be lies and so have betrayed my wife, my sister, my friends and my congregation. Yes, I have even contributed to the killing of a man. O Lord, I am unworthy but I ask Your forgiveness. I beg Your forgiveness."

As if preparing for punishment, he was silent for a long moment. When he slowly lifted his head, the haggard and forlorn expression had changed to one of determination. He knew what he must do.

"From anyone else, O Lord, such behavior is understandable.

But not from a rabbi. As a rabbi, I don't need forgiveness, I need to atone. There is but one path to atonement."

The custodian, embarrassed by overhearing the rabbi's confession, hurried from the rotunda as David struggled wearily to his feet . . .

That night, in the small meeting room, he sat quietly facing Harold Fedder. In his hand he held a carefully worded nine-page letter which had taken him the entire day to write.

"You said it was an emergency, Rabbi," Fedder said. "I've learned that with you an emergency usually means you need money for another one of your pet projects. Every time we have one of these emergency meetings, it costs us."

David's low and solemn tone erased the smile from Fedder's face. "I'm not here for money. I am here to resign."

Suddenly there was dead silence in the room, disbelief on Harold Fedder's face.

"But why. You just signed a new contract with us a few months ago. Maybe you're overworked. Why don't you take a vacation for a month or so. Go to Israel. The temple will pay for it."

David shook his head and said, "I'm resigning, Harold, because you were right about me. I am the rabbi you thought I was. I am not the rabbi for this congregation. I have been too ambitious and have often put that ambition ahead of your needs. I have allowed my vanity to place a value on achieving prestige and influence and, at times, have sacrificed this congregation to achieve that prestige and influence. And if that was all I was guilty of that would be enough. But I am guilty of far more than that." He handed Fedder the letter he had written earlier in the day. "After you read this, you will understand why I *must* resign."

Harold Fedder, utterly confused, began to read the letter. It contained a long litany of David's misdeeds, his sins, as he described them; about his adultery, though he didn't identify that his affair was with Sheila Harrington; about Brian's murder, and of his contribution to it; about how he had stolen $200,000 of Ben Adelson's donation, monies that were to go to Israel but, because of his action, had ended up in the hands of the Mafia; of how he had planned to lie to the Mossad agents about it; he talked about his doubts and his confusions and asked how could he be a rabbi, a spiritual leader for this congregation, or any congregation, when he couldn't be a rabbi to himself?

When Fedder finished reading, his face was frozen in an ashen pallor. He listened carefully as David said, "Harold, this was my encore. I failed you and I failed this congregation. I have also failed to honor my rabbinical oaths. You can best protect yourselves and the good name of this congregation against my shameful behavior with that letter written in my own hand. My confession."

"What about the money?" Fedder asked quietly. "You embezzled that money."

"I know I did. I didn't have any other choice. I'll speak to Ben and hope that he understands. If he does and gives me the chance, I'll spend the rest of my life working to repay him."

Harold Fedder, visibly shaken, spoke in a broken voice. "As president of this board, Rabbi, at this time I will not comment on your actions or the contents of this letter. I must reluctantly believe they are true, and therefore, I have no choice but to accept your resignation."

Then he reached into his pocket, brought out a cigarette lighter and ignited the bottom of the letter. As if hypnotized, David watched it burn. When the last page had become ashen, he asked, "Harold, I don't understand. Why would you do that for me?"

"I'm not doing it for you, Rabbi. I'm doing it for this congregation. If word of this scandal ever got out, it would destroy this congregation. I can't let that happen." Looking up at David after he stirred the ashes, he added, "Rabbi, as required by the bylaws of this temple, you will have to offer a public explanation for your resignation before the entire congregation. I will arrange the meeting as quickly as possible."

"But what can I possibly say to them?"

"That's your problem, Rabbi. I'm more concerned with what I say to them."

David looked out at his congregation. The sanctuary was quiet, a subdued air of expectancy silencing any interrupting sound. He was seated on the bema in a high-backed hand-carved oak chair to the right of the Ark. Harold Fedder, seated to his left, shuffled his feet anxiously while he waited for the ushers to close the doors at the rear. The two men hadn't spoken since their confrontation three days previously, the only communication between them being a note that Florence brought from Fedder informing David of the time of the meeting.

It suddenly occurred to David that this would be the last time he would address these men and women as their rabbi. The thought was disturbing, for until that moment he had been concerned solely with their opinion of him and of what they would think after Fedder got through with him. Conscious of his self-centeredness, he shook his head in shame and bewilderment. How can I still call myself a rabbi? he thought. How can I stand up in front of these people and pretend that my concern is for them, when my feelings are focused on myself. All I care about is how to sugarcoat the truth about myself and what I did and what I am—and why I'm resigning.

He glanced from familiar face to familiar face. Nodding at Meyer Loeb, smiling at Kelly Prentis, acknowledging Ben Adelson, Sam Bender and many of the others who had been so important in his life. They wore expressions of baffled expectation, shifting their eyes from David to Harold Fedder and back again as if trying to read the two men's minds.

He wondered what they would think of him after they found out. Would they be appalled and disgusted? He wouldn't blame them if they turned their backs on him. Wouldn't I feel the same if my rabbi abandoned me? he asked himself.

The ushers, with arms folded, took positions in front of the closed rear doors. David looked questioningly at Harold Fedder, who whispered, "That's to keep out the media hounds. This is a private family affair. I want to keep it that way." At first David thought Fedder's concern was for him. Then it occurred to him what the press would say. Because of his reputation, his resignation would make national, even worldwide, headlines.

Fedder stood up. His face grim, he turned to David. "It's time."

"Yes, Harold, it's time," David agreed. "Let's get this over with."

David tried to steel his nerves as Fedder strode to the lectern centered at the edge of the bema. He wondered what cunning method the board president would choose to crucify him. Would he elaborate on every detail of culpability? Would he remind them how through the years he had never ceased to warn them that David Benjamin was not the right rabbi for Temple Beth Sinai? Would he take a cruel, voluptuous pleasure in being proven right?

He was totally unprepared for what Fedder had to say.

"Tonight, I wish I were not your board president. Then the obligation to call this meeting would not have fallen on me. But I am your board president and so I will come right to the point. To delay telling you why we are here would cause more pain than we are all shortly going to feel. For we are here tonight—" He paused dramatically before concluding in a voice so muffled that several congregants turned to each other for verification of what they believed they had heard. "—because we are going to lose our rabbi. Rabbi Benjamin has told me that he is going to resign. Now he is going to tell you the reasons for his decision."

Fedder calmly turned his back on the lectern as though unaware of the startled and dismayed reaction to his announcement. The anguish that marked his face as he went to his chair made David realize that his old enemy hadn't refrained from reciting his catalog of accusations out of mercy, in order to protect David's reputation, but because he believed it would be less damaging both to David and to the congregation to hear the words from their rabbi himself.

As Fedder seated himself, he whispered to David, "You can tell them whatever you want, Rabbi. I won't contradict you."

David approached the lectern with a heavier burden of guilt than he would have borne had Fedder openly and brutally castigated him in front of the congregation.

As the audience hushed and waited, he tried to study each puzzled face. He had no idea of what he was going to say until he looked at Meyer Loeb. *What is important is not a man's style, but his substance.* Style is a man's image, substance is his core, he told himself. Naomi loved the style of me, as I loved her. Sheila loved the substance of me. For too long I have lived only to enhance an image. Martha, Brian, Naomi—they were all victims because of it. Senator Mendes, Sheila Harrington tried to rip it away. Harold Fedder finally did.

He looked over his shoulder at Fedder who stared back, his face twisted with grief. It was the same expression he had witnessed on the face of Sheila Harrington the last time he had seen her. David's one thought as he summoned his remaining strength to face his congregation was that somehow he had to free Harold from his agony. He knew there was only one way.

By atonement.

"You are not going to hear the words you expect to hear. I am not going to tell you how much I enjoyed the time I have spent with you at Temple Beth Sinai, nor of the many personal rewards I have reaped as your rabbi. And above all, I am not going to lie to you. What you will hear will shock you, disgust you and undoubtedly

266

anger you for you will feel that I have betrayed you. But what you will hear from me will be the truth."

A murmur of voices rose, then subsided.

"I am resigning because I am not qualified to be your head rabbi. I am resigning because I am not capable of being your spiritual leader.

"I say I am not qualified, not capable, because how can I be your rabbi, your spiritual leader, when I'm not those things to myself? Cloaking myself in the Torah and the Talmud, pontifically reciting the words and the laws of God, I refused to accept behavior and attitudes that violated both those words and those laws. It was either black or white, I told you. There were no grays. But I, your rabbi, your spiritual leader, have done what I condemned you for doing. I have violated and broken the Lord's commandments. And have done so willingly."

He watched the skeptical expressions that crossed the faces of the congregants and imagined them thinking, What could he have done that is so awful? Surely nothing that could cause him to resign.

David hastened to convince them.

"I have stolen money from a member of this congregation. I have committed adultery. I have even contributed to a man's murder. By my acts, I have lied, I have dishonored my father and mother and I have taken the name of the Lord in vain. I have borne false witness, justifying my behavior by saying that even in God's world it is acceptable to sacrifice the few to do good for the many. What was I really saying? I was saying that the end justified the means and that anyone who stood in my way had to pay the price. I was saying that it was not important how I used my power and prestige but only that I possess it."

He heard the angry buzz of their shocked voices and waited for silence. Then looks of expectancy returned to their faces and David realized they were now waiting to hear explanations they could accept. He had but a single explanation to offer.

"What I have done and the price I must pay are not important. Only you, this congregation, is important. There will be a new rabbi here. Through the years there will be many new rabbis. Some will be competent, some perhaps not. Some will inevitably sin, as I have; others will remain virtuous. But it won't matter what they are, because although they may affect your lives, they cannot destroy you. You, this congregation, will go on. There will always be a congregation. It will always endure. That's why we, as Jews, have survived. Not because we are the chosen people, but because even though we are dispersed to the corners of the earth, we are one. We are one congregation—and that is our strength."

There remained but one final word. He held up his open hand, and, as though in benediction, said, "Shalom."

The reaction took him by surprise.

A sudden combustion of sound surged throughout the sanctuary. From the intensity and fervor of his congregants' voices, he expected to hear cries of outrage and condemnation, and steeled his nerves for the onslaught.

Nothing happened. He waited a moment longer, then shrugged, both perplexed and relieved, and started to walk to his seat by the Ark.

"Wait! Rabbi, wait!"

Meyer Loeb rose slowly to his feet. The old man looked at David, then around the room, commanding silence by his frown.

"Rabbi Benjamin, I cannot and will not comment on your personal reasons for wanting to resign. But I remember something you once quoted to me during those wonderful hours of discussion we shared. Maybe it will you help you now as it helped me then: *If we do not help a man in trouble, it is as if we caused the trouble.*

"What you have done to yourself does not alter in any way what you have done for me. Because of your unyielding stance, tradition and heritage still live on in the Loeb family and will continue to live on. If you had given in, they would have died."

He reached down and assisted Kelly to her feet. She blushed because she was obviously pregnant. It was the young woman who concluded for the old man. "You may be a sinner, Rabbi, but to me you are and you will always be my rabbi. I will always feel that I am a part of your congregation." As she and Meyer Loeb sat down, their eyes brimmed.

Ben Adelson stood up. "I remember your words when I angrily shook my fist and was ready to curse God because of what I was going through: *Abraham said to God; If You want the world to exist You cannot insist upon complete justice; if it is complete justice You want, the world cannot endure.* Rabbi, maybe you've forgotten those words, but I haven't and I never will. You've made mistakes in judgment. So have I. We all have. They don't matter. And though I may never see you again after you leave my temple, you will always be my rabbi." Wiping his eyes unashamedly, he sat down.

Before he was settled, a tall, bespectacled teenager stood up and hurried down the aisle toward the bema. Standing at an angle so that both David and the congregation could see him, the deaf mute boy fluttered his fingers, signing. David, with a warm smile, responded both physically and vocally.

"Yes, Billy, I can still read and talk in sign."

The delighted expression on Billy's thin, delicate face said that he never doubted it. His fingers began to talk, and David softly translated the words to himself. They were overheard by the people in the first rows, who turned and repeated them to those behind. Wavelike, the conversation flowed throughout the sanctuary:

"I am deaf to everything but what you have done for me. You are my rabbi. I will always think of you as my rabbi." Embarrassed, Billy bowed his head and went back to his seat.

One by one the congregants stood up and, often with tears, told David and the attentive audience of the influence he had had on their lives. How he had always been there for them. How he had become a part of their lives, freely sharing their joys and their sorrows, their triumphs and their failures, their pains and their pleasures. He had changed their lives. He was their rabbi, they were his congregation. No conceivable sin on his part would ever change that.

After the last testimony had ended, David noticed Harold Fedder at his side. In a choked voice, Fedder merely said, "Thank you, Rabbi Benjamin. Thank you." Then, to David's amazement, his old enemy clumsily embraced him.

David remained standing at the lectern, not knowing what to say or do next. Although the meeting was obviously over, no one moved. No one spoke. They all seemed to be concentrating their energies, watching him. They were waiting. He finally understood. They were waiting for him to leave. For the last time.

An usher held open the double doors as he walked down the center aisle. A few heads turned, but there was utter silence. After the doors closed behind him, he stopped for a moment and listened. Not a sound came from within the sanctuary. He crossed the rotunda and went into his office and dialed the University Hospital in New Haven. While he waited, he thought of what Sheila had said: *The right love at the right time.* He slowly hung up, saying, "No, not yet. This is the wrong time. Someday, I don't know when, there may be a right time."

He looked at his office for the final time and then closed the door before going out the main entrance of the temple and into the night.